PRAISE FOR
She THAT FINDETH

"Have you ever convinced yourself that taking matters into your own hands isn't such a bad idea? If you have, then you will certainly relate to the main character, Shenita Love, in *She That Findeth*. On her thirty-fifth birthday, Shenita strongly feels she's waited too long for the right man to come into her life. Award-winning author Kim Brooks's character development will draw you into *She That Findeth* and leave you breathlessly anticipating if Shenita will truly find the love she's so desperately seeking."

—Tyora Moody, author of the Victory Gospel Series

"The Spirit is willing. . . . Ohhhh, but the flesh!!! If you have been single for longer than five minutes, you have been here, at the very least in your mind! Kim Brooks uses a cast of quirky friends to address this very real issue in Christendom. Kim does again what she does best: [she] reminds us that we, as Christians, face some very real and tough issues and encourages us Not To Get It Twisted! A very fun read!"

—Evangelist Audrey Lee Watkins, author of
On The Way Here: The Path That Chose Me

"This book keeps the reader's attention from the beginning. Kim does a wonderful job of bringing the characters to life, showing their vulnerabilities and strengths, and painting the visualization to make you feel as if you are there. The storyline is so captivating that you don't want to miss what will happen next! I would love to see this in a movie version."

—Shon Hyneman, author of *It's the Woman You Gave Me*, and *Wisdom: Preventing Problems Before They Happen*

"Once again, Kim has created a real and relevant masterpiece addressing a growing issue in the church. How far are women willing to go in order to find love? *She That Findeth* deals with this question in an up-to-date way that many will be able to relate to. Both men and women will be able to learn something from Kim's latest release. I look forward to the group discussions that will be organized in order to weigh in on this topic."

—Kenny Pugh, author and relationship strategist

She
THAT
FINDETH

She THAT FINDETH

KIM BROOKS

ATRIA PAPERBACK

New York   London   Toronto   Sydney   New Delhi

ATRIA PAPERBACK

A Division of Simon & Schuster, Inc.
1230 Avenue of the Americas
New York, NY 10020

First Atria Paperback edition May 2014

ATRIA PAPERBACK and colophon are trademarks of Simon & Schuster, Inc.

For information about special discounts for bulk purchases, please contact Simon & Schuster Special Sales at 1-866-506-1949 or business@simonandschuster.com.

The Simon & Schuster Speakers Bureau can bring authors to your live event. For more information or to book an event contact the Simon & Schuster Speakers Bureau at 1-866-248-3049 or visit our website at www.simonspeakers.com.

Designed by Jill Putorti

Manufactured in the United States of America

10 9 8 7 6 5 4 3 2 1

Library of Congress Cataloging-in-Publication Data
Brooks, Kimberley.
  She that findeth / Kim Brooks.—First Atria Paperback edition.
    pages cm
  ISBN 978-1-4767-1533-9 (paperback : alk. paper)—ISBN 978-1-4767-1534-6 (ebook) 1. Psychological fiction. I. Title.
  PS3602.R6454S54 2013
  813'.6—dc23

                                                         2013015993

ISBN 978-1-4767-1533-9
ISBN 978-1-4767-1534-6 (ebook)

This novel is dedicated to my
extremely supportive and deeply loved parents,
Lawrence and Lutricia Brooks

ACKNOWLEDGMENTS

Thank You, Lord, for the opportunity to write another novel that entertains, inspires, and encourages Your people. You are so faithful and are truly my very best friend.

I would also like to thank my parents, Lawrence and Lutricia Brooks, sister Kelley Brooks, and my entire family and closest friends for being supportive of whatever I do, and always being there with an encouraging word or a listening ear.

A special "thank you" to my aunt, Henrietta Spiller, retired head librarian, for blessing me with a book every year since before I could read, which opened my eyes to the wonderful world of books and stirred up my love for the written word.

Many thanks also to the team that helped bring this book together, including my awesome editor, Todd, and countless others who worked on everything from the interior format to the cover—thanks so much! We did it!

Much love to media outlets and on-air personalities for their continued support, including radio, such as Dr. Deborah Smith Pollard, Ace Alexander, Morgan Dukes, and several others, as well as TV, magazines, online media, and periodicals.

Thanks also to my PR coach, Pam Perry, for your inspiration over the years, and Mr. Art Cartwright, for encouraging me to think BIG every day.

And last, but definitely not least, I'd like to thank my readers for their feedback and constant support. Thanks for showing up for every book signing, book-release concert or special event, and for letting others know about my books, whether through social media or word of mouth. Thanks for promoting positive media such as this, which has the ability to change the world! Muah!

She
THAT
FINDETH

CHAPTER 1

"Happy birthday to ya . . . Happy birthday to ya . . . Happy birthday!" sang and clapped my three closest girlfriends at a small table inside a quaint restaurant in downtown Detroit. Too bad it wasn't karaoke night; that was Thursday. But I was still too excited that my birthday fell on a Saturday in September this year. That made up for the fact that it's my thirty-fifth and here I am celebrating it with a bunch of females.

I love my girls and all, but sometimes a sister just wants the presence of a man. Here I am all decked out in my one-armed purple blouse, short gray skirt, silver stilettos, and matching Gucci bag—yet with no man to compliment me on how good I look. I had just gotten my hair cut and colored, with a light brown mohawk on top that faded to black in the back, and my makeup was flawless. I even wore hazel contacts, which I was hesitant to buy at first because of my brown complexion—but they actually looked kinda cute on me.

I was feeling this "new look" and new me, yet there was no man seated next to me to whisper in my ear how I was the finest thing in the room. Nope, at thirty-five, here I am with not a prospect in sight. No man, no boyfriend, not even a "special friend."

Nobody.

Lord knows I just knew I would have been married with at least two kids by now.

I've been believing God for a husband for ten years now.

I keep my list of ten things I'm believing God for in a mate tucked away in the zipper part of my Bible cover and have done so for years. I guess I never really attached a timetable to my requests—maybe I should have said something to the tune of *Before my eggs dry up and I have to believe God like Sarah and Abraham, Lord.* Maybe then my prayer may have been granted a little earlier. At the rate I'm going, I'm going to have to take in vitro and believe God for twins. Thank God for technology.

"Haaaa-peeee-birthday . . . Happy birthday . . . Happy birthday . . ."

I could tell the waiters and waitresses, all of diverse hues, were getting a kick out of my friends' rendition of the Stevie Wonder classic as they grinned from ear to ear, nodding their heads. I wondered if they had ever heard it before.

Or maybe they were laughing at my girl Danielle, also known as Dani, who swayed wildly with her Android taking pics in one hand and waving her glass of Sprite on the rocks in the other. If you didn't know Danielle was saved you would think she was drunk, and at just two years shy of forty, one would never know by the way she carried herself. Always ready for a good time, Danielle took pics of herself showing off her fresh makeover, which brought out the peach undertones in her tan complexion, and her new black-and-gold minidress, which flattered her tall, curvy frame; and she also took pics of me and the rest of the crew and uploaded them to Facebook simultaneously, half of which I hadn't even seen yet to approve. Lord, I hope she doesn't tag me in any pics where I'm looking crazy. Candid shots get on my nerves.

"Make a wish, girl!" Danielle yelled while snapping her head and swerving her long, black layered weave to the other side, almost hitting Jackie in the face.

Jackie just looked at her and rolled her eyes as she proceeded to stir her black coffee. She wiped the cheek where Danielle's hair almost smacked her, probably hoping it didn't turn her fair skin pink, as Jackie bruises easily. She had stopped singing the song a while ago and looked ready to go home. At thirty-six, Jackie appeared as if she had had enough of all the many years of singing birthday songs and probably wanted to catch a rerun of her favorite show, *Law & Order,* again. With her being a prominent, well-respected attorney in the city, she was greatly intrigued by that show. I wouldn't be surprised if my birthday festivities weren't ruining all her normal Saturday-night fun. Jackie ran her fingers through her short curly red hair, then rested her hand on her forehead.

"Yeah, Shenita," sprang Pippa while scooting her chair in closer to the table and positioning her round frame just right as she pointed her light brown manicured finger toward me, matter-of-fact. "The Word says in 3 John 1:2, *Beloved, I wish above all things that thou mayest prosper and be in health, even as thy soul prospereth,* so it's okay to make a wish and blow out the candles."

At thirty-two and the youngest of the crew, I wondered if Pippa really thought I needed her approval based on *The Word* on whether or not I should make a wish? I guess she didn't know me as well as I thought she did, otherwise she would know I've been making wishes and blowing out candles ever since I got saved fifteen years ago. I wasn't convicted about it then and I sholl ain't convicted about it now.

Man, that birthday cake had so many candles on it that it looked like if I didn't blow them out fast someone would have to call a fire truck.

Thirty-five candles—one for each year of my long, unfruitful life.

I take that back. As a public relations specialist for the Detroit chapter of a national nonprofit, One Love Initiative, from the outside looking in, I had all the makings of a success. I literally have had many approach me in tears and say how the nonprofit I work for, which provides housing options for single parents and low-income families, changed their lives. I love what I do, and thank God for the job that definitely keeps a sister's condo association fees paid and Benz car payment up to date, but even still, I feel my life is lacking in one area. Love.

So, with a big inhale and then a huge blow over the strawberry shortcake with my favorite cream cheese icing, I silently made the same wish I've been making since I was twenty-five: *"I wish to find true love and happiness."* Except this time I did something I had never done before with my wish. I added these four words, *"This year, Lord . . . please."*

"So, girl, what you wanna do now that we're done with dinner?" Danielle asked with a forkful of her second piece of cake, as we four ladies sat with full bellies and I with a nice stack of gifts and greeting cards by my side.

I really hadn't made any plans for after dinner . . . what else was there to do? I didn't feel like going to a movie; too boring. And with no guys with us it wouldn't be that much fun. No one to play practical jokes on. I guess this *is* supposed to be ladies' night out. Whoever invented that concept anyway? With all girls, who's going to open the door for us when we leave? The waiter, I guess.

"What about heading over to my place to play Parcheesi, eat snickerdoodles, and have girl talk all night!" chimed Pippa.

Jackie, Danielle, and I looked at one another, then at Pippa, and said in unison, "Um, no."

"How about we check out that new jazz joint on First Street?" Danielle suggested.

"Hmm," I said. "Not a bad idea."

Then again, I thought about the last jazz place I visited— nothing but old, bald-head, no-teeth-having sugar daddies over sixty-five wanting to "holla at ya girl" while showing me their Viagra pills. The thought of reliving that experience all over again frightened me.

"Nah," I said.

"Well, we can always go to Club Xtasy," suggested Danielle, while licking the icing off her fork.

I couldn't believe she was making reference to the very spot where she used to pole-dance before she got saved three years ago. Since then she gets her dance on for the Lord and is the first to tell me about the next Christian white party, but sometimes I still wonder about that girl.

"I'm just playing y'all, dang," she said, taking a sip of water.

"Mmm-hmmm," Jackie said.

"I know we not going there," Danielle assured us. "Ain't nothing there but a bunch of married men trying to get they sneak peek and freak on anyway."

"Nah, we can't be going there," Jackie said abruptly. The three of us looked at Jackie as if to say, "How do *you know* what's in there?"

"What?" Jackie said in defense. "I just said we can't go. We saved women of *Gahd*—for real, remember?"

We all broke out laughing.

I know I'm saved.

Sholl 'nuff saved.

I'm so saved that I hadn't been to an actual club in over six years.

I had gotten so involved in church life that my appetite for the club scene eventually wore off, but a girl still wants to get her dance on from time to time.

I've never been totally drunk, and the last time I had sex was at age twenty-five with my first. After that horrific experience of his breaking up with me only two days later, I said I would remain abstinent till marriage. Beside, if it makes God happy, I'm happy. Period.

But then again, my thirty-fifth birthday has made me realize that I spent the last decade of my life pleasing someone else. Don't get me wrong, I love the Lord with all my heart, but somewhere along the way I believe I've lost myself.

I have fun with my girls and we go out, and we even invite fellas from the church sometimes, but for some reason I feel like I still haven't really *lived*.

I love to dance, but part of me gets scared every time I start dancing somewhere for fear of who's watching me. Like Scripture says, I don't want to give the appearance of evil. It's almost like for every secret desire there is a counter-conscious that says, *No, don't do it*.

Part of me is tired of not doing it. Tired of being the "good girl" and so-called really saved one in the family. Part of me just wants to explore. I should be able to go dancing somewhere and not lose my religion in the process, right?

"What about Boogie Nights?" I suggested, as if a lightbulb came on above my head.

"Boogie Nights?" Jackie asked with disgust.

"Yeah, Boogie Nights, just outside the city. Now that I think about it, it's Old School Saturday. We can get our cabbage patch on," I said with a cabbage patch shake of the shoulders. "C'mon, y'all—live a little—it should be fun," I pleaded.

"Girl, I haven't been to Boogie Nights in a minute. Count me in, I'm game," Danielle replied as she finished off her last piece of cake.

"They don't serve alcohol there, do they?" Pippa inquired.

"Yes, they serve alcohol," I said. "But only to the patrons who are over eighteen."

"Oh, okay," Pippa said hesitantly.

"Plus, you don't have to drink. You can just drink pop or water, Pippa Wippa," I assured her with a smile.

"Okay, count me in, then," she said with a returned grin and a toast of her glass of water with mine.

The group fell silent for a moment as all eyes rested on Jackie, who had her chin in her hand.

"You hanging with us tonight, Jackie?" Danielle asked, partly already knowing what her response would be.

"Naw, you ladies go on and have a good time. I'm going to go home and chill."

I guess she wanted to catch the latest episode of *Law & Order* after all.

"Aw, Jackie, come go with us. You can always just go home— come hang out," Pippa insisted. "You need to get out the house more. It should be fun."

"Well, if my memory serves me correctly I'm presently out of the house now, here at this restaurant," Jackie said. She noticed my disappointed expression and added, "Don't look so down, Shenita. It's your birthday. Look, I'll cover everyone's meal tonight. Don't worry about it, it's all on me. I'll just have to take a rain check on the afterglow. Y'all ladies be careful out there, okay?" she said, sounding more like our mother than our close girlfriend, and arose. Little did Miss Jackie realize that her paying for my meal does not make up for the fact that she didn't want to hang with me on my thirty-fifth for the rest of the night. Don't get me wrong, I'll accept the gesture, it just doesn't make up for how I feel about her not being with us.

"Well alrighty then," I said as Jackie made her exit. "Looks like I'll be gettin' my Holy Ghost boogie on with you two, oh faithful ones," I added with a Bankhead Bounce toward Pippa and Danielle.

"I don't know about your Holy Ghost boogie on," Danielle said with a laugh. "There may be some ghosts there, all right . . . some demons dressed in pinstriped suits and brim hats or button-down silk shirts showing taco meat."

All three of us cracked up before we each took our cars and followed one another to the spot.

While driving my silver Benz SLK, I thought, *Heck, I deserve to let my hair down and have a good time. I'm thirty-five tonight, dang-it—good and grown. I've been doing things the so-called "right way" and holy way for fifteen years now. It's time to whip my hair back and forth and have some fun.*

The line outside Boogie Nights was pretty long—longer than usual, actually. It may have been because though it was mid-September the weather was unusually warm, almost springlike—then again that's nothing compared to Michigan weather, which could change at any given moment. Tonight it may be 75 degrees, tomorrow it may drop down to 20.

"Excuse me!" Danielle said while waving her hand to get the attention of the huge dark-skinned bouncer wearing a black cap and shades. "I'm here with Shenita Love, PR specialist for One Love Initiative here in the D. It's her birthday today, and we're trying to get in to help her celebrate."

The hard-core-looking bouncer suddenly flashed a charming smile and motioned for Danielle's party to come right in.

That girl.

Danielle always gets her way.

I don't think the word *no* is even in her vocabulary.

"Thanks, hon," Danielle said, thanking the bouncer with a kiss on his cheek. He motioned for her not to leave his side, as Pippa and I went in and grabbed a booth near the door so she could see us.

"That Danielle is always pulling game," I said, shaking my head and spying on the two of them. She appeared delighted as he slid her something that looked like a business card. It was probably his phone number.

"What's she doing? She's not coming to sit with us?" Pippa asked, scanning the menu as if we hadn't just eaten less than an hour ago.

I knew Dani's game.

"She's coming," I said, still keeping my eye on her. Now she had one of her hands on his broad shoulder. "Just give her some time."

"Oh, okay. I wonder what the specials are," Pippa said.

"Didn't you just eat?" I asked.

"I did. I might just want some curly fries or something, or another dessert. I don't know." Pippa shrugged her shoulders.

"Hey, y'all," Danielle said, finally joining us.

"Hey, Miss Dani. So what was that all about? You pull them digits?" I asked.

"Girl, you crazy. You know how it is. A brother wanted to holla. Only thing is I can't see a bouncer being able to afford the mortgage on my future mansion, so I had to pass."

"Girl, you know you ain't right," I said.

"What? I ain't sayin' I'm a gold-digger . . ."

Danielle and I cracked up.

"So what were you guys talking about all that time?" Pippa asked, keeping her eyes glued to the menu in front of her.

"Nothing much. He talking about how he also teaches CCW classes downtown and asked if I'd be interested."

"I'm sure that's not all he's interested in," I said under my breath.

"Girl, stop. He got us all in, didn't he?"

"Yes, he did. Hey, weren't we supposed to pay somewhere? I thought I saw a sign say twenty dollars at the door or something," Pippa said, while looking around for the sign again.

"Girl, don't worry about it," Danielle said. "I said he got us in, didn't I? So when I say he got us in, he got us *in*."

"Oh, I see now," Pippa said, enlightened. "We got in for free!"

"Girl, don't be so loud about it!" I shot at her abruptly. "Can't let everybody know."

I tell you, that Pippa. Sometimes I wonder what planet she came from and how we ended up being even remotely close friends.

"Wow, well amen, glad I saved my l'il twenty dollars, then. Thank God for favor."

"Amen to that," Danielle said with a high five to Pippa. "Thank God for favor with God and a man," Danielle said, giving her bouncer friend another wink.

"Y'all are so wrong," I said, looking around the dimly lit club. "Not a bad crowd tonight," I commented.

Pippa looked up from the menu. "No, it's not bad, except the women all look like hoochie mamas who need Jesus. Most of them all weaved up from their scalp to their behinds, and they think it's cute. No one believes in natural beauty anymore, I guess," Pippa said, then looked over at Danielle and patted her shoulder. "Oops, don't take it personal, Danielle."

Danielle snickered. "Girl, none taken. I'm happy with my weave. My weave takes me places," she said, combing through her long, layered black weave with her fingers. "Don't you know God invented weaves?" she asked Pippa, and added, "Thank God for witty inventions."

We all cracked up as Danielle and I high-fived each other. Though I was au naturel tonight with my new do, Lord knows by next week I may be weaved up again. Thank God for variety.

Just then one of my old-school jams came on: "Now That We Found Love," by Heavy D & The Boyz. The three of us jumped up out of excitement for the treasured former hit and made our way to the dance floor, which was filled with folks of different races and backgrounds, all dancing their own special way to the feel-good song. The strobe lights and fake smoke made for a festive atmosphere, and as I swayed from side to side with the music, I felt like I was on top of the world.

We three ladies danced with one another, since we didn't know any guys there, yet we still didn't seem out of place because a lot of women there either danced by themselves or with one another as well.

In between our own dance moves we cracked up at some of the neighboring dancers, who couldn't hear the beat, made up their own moves, or danced like they had two left feet.

It didn't matter, though, because we all had one thing in common: we were all dancing and having a great time—even if there were some drunk ones on the dance floor with us, they somehow managed to keep their distance, thank the Lord.

While I was dancing, feeling the beat, and getting my groove on, I suddenly noticed a tall, slender, light-skinned gentleman with a smooth shave and a goatee standing directly behind me, barely dancing at all. It was as if he was just staring at me with a sneaky smirk, his hand cupped underneath his chin.

I kept dancing and laughing with my girls, then somehow gathered up enough nerve to turn around and start dancing with the guy, even though he just stood there like his feet were frozen to the ground.

I didn't care.

I just kept dancing.

Shoot—he was cute and I was celebrating my birthday. I drowned everyone else out and danced my little heart out.

It had been so long since I danced or went to a club that I was almost afraid I didn't know how to dance anymore.

Back in the day, or shall I say BC days, Before Christ, my former bestie and I were known to hit up a club on any given weekend and be the life of the party. With her on one side, me on the other, and a guy in between us, it used to be common practice for us to coordinate our dance steps, while commanding all the attention on the dance floor.

I miss those days sometimes.

She's six years married now, with two kids, and I haven't heard from her at all in three years. Times change, I guess.

I continued to dance with the cutie, and I could tell he was enjoying my dance moves as I continued to gyrate right in front of him until the song finally ended and another one came on.

This time it was an old-school hip-hop love song, LL Cool J's "I Need Love."

I leaped with excitement, hoping my dance partner wouldn't go away. He didn't but instead grabbed me as we slow-danced to the old jam. He looked like he was in his thirties as well, so I'm sure he could appreciate the hip-hop ballad that made then-burgeoning rap music even more popular and multidimensional.

I was in a trance as we swayed from side to side.

I closed my eyes and imagined this complete stranger was my man—my knight in shining armor and everything I could ever need and secretly desired—as I held him close. He squeezed me tighter as well, and he comfortably rested his hands just above my behind. Though I didn't even know this man's first name, I felt like I knew him nonetheless. I wanted to ask him, "Where have you been all my life?"

When the song ended, my mystery man kissed my hand and then disappeared into the crowd, leaving me sad, confused, and lonely once again.

I retreated back to our booth and my two friends screeched with delight. "Hey, girl, I saw you getting yo' groove on out there on the dance floor!" Danielle chimed. "Or shall I say groove back—shall I call you Stel-la?" Danielle and Pippa laughed.

"Yeah, girl, he was cute," Pippa said, munching on curly fries.

"That he was," I said with a grim look on my face.

"What's wrong with you? What happened? Did you get his phone number?" Danielle asked.

"What church does he go to?" Pippa inquired.

"No, and I don't know."

Dani and Pippa looked at each other, confused.

"What do you mean?" Danielle asked. "You know the main

rule is to not leave an interaction like that without the number. What happened?"

"I don't know what happened," I said, frustrated. "All I know is dancing with him felt like heaven. The feel of his touch. The smell of his cologne. How he held me so close in his arms like he couldn't let go."

"Ahhh," Pippa responded, starry-eyed.

"But then he just disappeared into thin air like it wasn't nothing. I didn't even get his name!"

"Dang," Pippa said.

"That's messed up. That means you can't even google a brother, or even look up his Facebook page," Danielle reminded her.

"I know, right? Why does stuff like this keep happening to me lately? It's like I meet these guys and I think they're all interested and it just ends up being nothing."

"I don't know, girl. But that's okay," Pippa reassured me. "Keep ya head up, pretty lady. Your Boaz is out there somewhere."

"Yeah. All of ours," I agreed. "We just gotta hold on so we won't get too old to enjoy 'em."

"Right, I don't want to be all saggin' when Mr. Right finds me," Danielle said with a hearty laugh.

"I know," Pippa added. "And I don't want my teeth to fall out before he finds me. I'll be like, 'Hold on, baby, I wanna kiss you real good, but let me get my teeth first.'" We all cracked up at Pippa's poor imitation of an old woman with no teeth.

Though the man of my dreams may have slipped from my arms on my birthday, my friends always know how to make light of it all and keep me smiling. I couldn't help but laugh right along with them.

CHAPTER 2

"Attention, everyone!" proclaimed a male voice from the speakers.

The music stopped and everyone turned to the DJ booth to spot where the voice was coming from. The DJ continued into the mic, "Today is a special day for a special girl. Will you all please join me in celebrating the birthday of Detroit's very own Shenita Love!"

Everyone clapped as a spotlight appeared out of nowhere and shone on Shenita's booth. Some even gave her a standing ovation, as most were aware of her community work and reputation as a nationally recognized homegrown PR specialist for One Love Initiative.

Shenita was so embarrassed by all the attention that her brown face turned pink. She looked at her girls to see who was the cause of all this ruckus, and they both shrugged their shoulders. Next thing you know a waiter came over with a German chocolate cake topped off with a silver tiara and the waiter gave her a note that read, "A chocolate cake for a chocolate queen. Happy birthday, Ms. Shenita Love."

Shenita, confused, wondered who in the world got her this cake, her favorite kind to boot. She took the tiara off the cake, licked off the coconut-pecan icing with her fingers and a napkin, then placed it on her head while looking around the entire club trying to figure out who had made such a nice gesture.

"Oh, girl, looks like you got an admirer!" Pippa sang. "Must be nice. I never had anyone do anything like that for me. It's your day, girl. Enjoy!"

"I will. But who in the world did this? I didn't even know anybody here really knew who I was," Shenita said.

"Maybe one of your coworkers spotted you," Danielle suggested.

"Or maybe it was your future man," said a mysterious deep voice behind her. Shenita turned around and saw a familiar, smooth face. Mr. Goatee again, in the flesh, hadn't forgotten about her after all.

"But how did you know my—"

"Shhhhh," he said, cupping her hand in his and lifting her up out of her seat to lead her to the dance floor as her favorite old-school slow jam, "Let's Chill" by Guy, played over the speakers.

On their way to the dance floor, Mr. Smooth turned toward Danielle and gave her a nod and said "Thanks."

Pippa spotted the gesture, then asked, "So it was you! *You* told him?"

"Yeah, girl, you're right; you got me," Danielle confessed. "I told him Shenita's name and that it was her birthday. I'm the guilty one, as charged."

"But when did you . . ." Pippa asked in a daze, still confused.

"Aw, girl, quit thinking about it, let's get our dance on."

"Dani girl, I love you and all, but I don't do that slow-dance stuff with no female. I don't even dance with my little niece," Pippa said.

Danielle laughed. "I know, girl, follow me." Pippa obliged as Danielle walked right into her bouncer friend's arms, and a short male friend next to him reached for Pippa's hand to dance as well.

"I thought you had forgotten about me," Shenita said.

"What made you think that?" her dance partner asked, wiping a strand of hair away from her eye.

"Well, the way you just disappeared. I didn't even get your name."

"Luke. Luke McDaniels."

"Okay. Well, hello, Mr. Luke McDaniels."

"Hello, gorgeous."

Hearing him speak made Shenita's heart race as she rested her head on his broad chest.

"Why don't we leave this place so we can go somewhere and talk," he suggested.

Shenita lifted her head. "Wait a minute now. I don't get down like that. I'm not a one-night-stand kinda girl."

"Hold your horses, Miss Love. I'm not talking about that," Luke said with a slight laugh. "Let's hit up a coffee shop or something and grab some coffee so we can get to know each other better."

"Oh. Okay." Shenita rested her head on his chest again. She couldn't believe she was about to go out with a guy the same night she met him. The Shenita from ten years ago, or even five years ago, would never do that. She wouldn't even have accepted such an invitation unless she found out for sure that a brother was saved first.

"That way I can get to know you, you can get to know me, we

can get to know each other," Luke continued. Shenita glanced up and gave him a suspicious look. "In a civil, friendship-type manner," he clarified. "That is, *if* you don't mind."

"Nope," Shenita responded. "I don't mind at all." She swayed with him to the music until her favorite song was done.

CHAPTER 3

"So, birthday girl, I just want you to know I count it an honor and a privilege that you accepted my invitation to a night out on the town—at Starbucks," Luke began, at a small table for two inside the quaint coffee shop.

Shenita laughed.

"What? What's so funny?" he wondered.

Shenita couldn't help but grin and shake her head. "Nothing. It's nothing," she said. "It's just way past my bedtime, that's all."

"Past your bedtime? It's only twelve thirty. The party just started, baby."

Did this man just call me baby? Shenita thought. *He is too much.*

Shenita looked up and smiled through her bangs. She was glad that after all her dancing her new do hadn't sweated all the way out yet.

"I love that smile of yours. Hopefully I can keep it there," Luke said.

"Woo-wee." Shenita said, fanning herself. "It's getting hot in here. Are you hot?" she asked him.

"Maybe it's this caramel latte of mine," he said. "Caramel is my favorite flavor, you know," he added with a sly grin.

This man is so sexy, Shenita thought. *Jesus, help!*

"So, what do you do?" Shenita asked in an attempt to shift focus.

"I'm a chiropractor."

"Oh wow, that sounds interesting," Shenita said, hoping her response didn't sound as if she considered it interestingly boring. *At least brother man got a fairly decent job,* she thought.

"I must agree, it *is* interesting," he said. "I'm a healing specialist. I like to heal people in all manner of sickness and diseases. Kinda like Jesus."

"Like Jesus?" Shenita asked, and almost choked on her caffè mocha. *No, this man didn't just compare himself to Jesus.*

"Yeah, like Jesus. I long to see people made whole. Except I specialize in folks' backs."

Shenita laughed out loud for real and replied, "Okay."

She scooted in her seat, looked him dead in the eye, and asked him, "So tell me, Luke, what do you exactly *know* about Jesus?"

"I know a lot about him. He's my Savior."

"Oh, so you're saved?"

"Are you surprised?" Luke asked. "I believe in Jesus. I go to church."

"But is Jesus your Lord and Savior?"

"Absolutely."

"All right then," Shenita said with another sip of her drink. "Just checking."

"I believe it's Jesus who brought us together here tonight," Luke added, and her eyes widened.

He continued, "I believe everything happens for a reason and in the right season. I believe in divine connections."

"All right now, you betta preach!" Shenita said with a wave of her hand. *This brother is preaching,* she thought. *I wonder if he's a PK—preacher's kid.*

Luke continued, "It's almost as if the universe has opened its windows of heaven and is pouring out a blessing on us right now."

"Oh, okay," Shenita said with a confused look. *Is this man for real?*

"Are you seeing anyone right now?" asked Luke.

Shenita paused for a moment, initially surprised at how he just cut right to the chase.

"Seeing, like seriously dating?" she asked, knowing good and well she wasn't seriously or casually dating anybody right now.

"Is there a special man in your life?"

"Well . . . besides Jesus—no," she admitted.

"Oh, okay." Luke leaned in. "Do you want there to be?"

Shenita cleared her throat. "Maybe."

No one had ever been this blunt with her before.

"Maybe?" Luke asked. "Shenita, I know you," Luke said. "You may not think I know you, but I do. The stars are lining up perfectly tonight. You want more than anything for there to be a special man in your life to love you, hold you, protect you and keep you, and tell you everything is going to be okay."

Is this man a psychic or something? Shenita wondered.

"Well, since you put it that way," she said, "you're right. I do want there to be a special man in my life, but I'm very careful not to let just anybody in my heart."

"You're right, and you have every right to be careful. You should be," Luke agreed, and continued, "You're a very beautiful woman, and from what I can tell tonight, you're a very intelligent, well-respected individual as well."

"Thank you," Shenita said proudly.

"Do you like to read?" Luke asked.

"I love to read."

"I figured you did. Why don't you come over to my place so I can show you my library? I think I have some good books you may want to check out."

Is this man asking me to go to his place this time of night? Shenita thought.

"I appreciate the invitation but—I think I'll have to pass on that one."

"Don't worry. I live in a safe neighborhood—Rosedale Park."

"It's not that, it's just that I don't get down like that. We just met."

"I know, but even though I just met you, it seems like I've known you for years. Our spirits are in sync. You like what I like. It's like we're the same."

In a weird way, Shenita agreed with him. Though they'd just met, she, too, felt like she had known him for years.

"Tell ya what—you stop by, I'll show you my library, then you can leave. It'll be no more than thirty minutes tops. I promise," Luke said.

Shenita looked at him for a minute, contemplated, and eventually concluded, *Sure, why not. It's been a while since I been on a date with anybody; I'm a grown woman and he seems like a decent guy—what could possibly go wrong?*

"Wow, you do have a nice library," Shenita said as she stared in awe of his collection of books, which went from the floor almost to the top of the high ceiling. Shenita had always dreamed of having a library with bookshelves built into the walls, and now here it was right in front of her eyes. She loved how she could still smell the scent of fresh oak and paper all around her.

Luke stared at her from the doorway, wearing a red-and-black satin smoking jacket and black pants and holding a glass of red wine.

"Would you like a drink?"

"No thanks. I don't drink," Shenita said, wondering how in the world he'd changed clothes so fast.

"You sure?" he asked, making his way back to the bar area in the other room. "I can make anything you want. I have a great wine collection. Come check it out."

Though hesitant to leave the library, Shenita made her way over to the next room, where seemingly every liquor you could imagine hung above her head and inside a cooler near his bar. Cristal, rum, Hennessy, vodka, and more were lined up, along with two-liter bottles and glasses of lemons and cherries.

"You have a lot of drinks here. You drink a lot?" Shenita asked.

"Nah, not often," Luke said, bending over to reach for something underneath the bar. "Just every once in a while, like socially, if I'm entertaining guests. I'm not much of a drinker myself, but I do love to have a glass of wine every once in a while. So long as I don't get drunk. Even Jesus drank a little wine." Luke looked up and winked at her.

"Yes, he did," Shenita remembered. *But not this much wine,* she thought as she looked around.

"Sure you don't want anything?" he asked, prepping another glass for her.

"Nah, I'm cool. Thanks, though," Shenita said while peeking back toward the library.

"Okay, well then . . . want to finish checking out the books?" She thought he'd never ask.

"Sure," she replied, and swiftly vanished into the other room, her dream room, leaving Luke behind.

Classic books by Alex Haley, Richard Wright, W. E. B. Du Bois and more modern books, by Michael Baisden, Omar Tyree, and Michael Eric Dyson filled his collection, along with the Bible, several versions of it, including the *King James, New International Version, Amplified,* and *The Message.*

To the left of his Bible collection was *The Secret,* books by Deepak Chopra, the Dalai Lama, and several books on the study of medicine and natural healing techniques.

"This is quite a collection you have here," Shenita said, loud enough to make sure Luke heard her in the other room. She wondered where his Christian books were—most of his books were either classic or new-age and Buddhist teaching–type books. Over at the end of the bookshelf she saw stacks of cards, but they weren't playing cards. She picked them up and looked at them—large, multicolored, with weird images on them. They looked like some form of tarot cards. As she examined them more closely, she didn't realize that Luke had not only walked into the room but was standing right behind her.

"See anything you like?" he asked, startling Shenita and causing her to drop all the cards.

"Oh, I'm sorry, I didn't mean to drop all of these," Shenita said as she scrambled to pick up the cards and place them back on the shelf.

"No worries, my love. You don't have to worry about picking all those up, let me pick up the pieces for you." He picked up the remaining cards while not taking his eyes off her. Shenita couldn't stop staring at him either; it was like he had her in a trance.

Once he'd placed the rest of the cards back on the bookshelf he said, "Now let me put them back together again," and with that he kissed her.

Shenita backed against the bookshelf, and though initially stunned she eventually gave in and rubbed his hair.

Part of her wanted to escape from his grasp, yet part of her loved how he made her feel and wanted to continue to explore more forbidden territory.

She hadn't felt like this in a long time, and barely realized when he led her to his brown leather couch in front of his bookshelf.

Once he laid her on her back on the couch, Shenita opened her eyes and realized that something might be going down.

He stood up and took off his satin jacket to reveal his six-pack.

"Luke, I don't think . . ." Shenita said, attempting to rise.

"Shhh," Luke said, softly kissing her neck. "Don't fight it, baby. You know you want it. You summoned me into your life. I'm here and the time is now."

Luke stretched himself on top of her and kept kissing her neck until her commands for him to stop turned into surrendering moans.

Shenita felt like she was high—like she had just smoked five pounds of weed—yet she had never smoked a single joint in her entire life.

She couldn't believe how good this man made her feel.

Admittedly, she hadn't felt this way in a long time. Years. The last time she gave it up was ten years ago, and being with Luke right now brought back memories of how that made her feel—and she liked it.

"I've got, got the victory, I got the sweet sweet victory in Jesus." A

familiar song suddenly played loudly from the other side of the room. *"For me He died but He rose on the third day, that's why I have true victory every day."*

Shenita's cell phone played the popular Yolanda Adams tune, and Shenita popped up from the couch as if Jesus Himself had just walked in the door.

Embarrassed, Shenita sat up.

"I'm sorry, Luke, I gotta go," she said, straightening her clothes.

Luke looked disappointed.

Shenita continued, "You're a nice guy and all, but I gotta get going . . . it's getting late."

Shenita walked over and grabbed her open purse with her cell inside, grabbed her jacket from the back of a chair, and briskly walked toward the door.

A shirtless Luke followed her out. "Look, Shenita, I'm sorry if I came on a little too strong. I'm just so attracted to you, that's all."

"That's okay, Luke, and thanks. I gotta go," she said and left.

"Jesus!" Shenita screamed once inside her car.

She peeked at her phone to see the missed call. It was Danielle, making her normal routine roll call to be sure all of her girls had made it home okay after a night on the town.

Little did Danielle or Pippa know that their girl Shenita Love decided to take a detour that night.

CHAPTER 4

Tears flowed from Shenita's eyes during the praise and worship segment at her church Sunday morning at the 11:00 service as she sang along with the praise team, *"I just want to say that I love You more than anything."* She cried out of worship and adoration for her Lord, and also out of deeply felt guilt and despair. She was so disappointed in herself for behaving out of character last night with a complete stranger. She had been successfully celibate for over ten years and couldn't see how she was about to let one night of passion just mess that all up.

She couldn't see how she was about to allow some man she might never talk to ever again ruin what she had going on with her one true Lord and Savior, Jesus Christ. She felt like she'd cheated on Him, and in spite of how faithful He had been to her all her life, she felt as if somehow she'd let Him down.

During the tithes and offering portion of church she grabbed a ten-dollar bill and stuck it inside the envelope. She completed the envelope in its entirety, checking off the "Miss" title before her first name. Eyeing a couple—the husband filling out one envelope for the both of them, then his wife and he lifting up their one offering to give to the Lord together—Shenita longed for the day she would be able to do that with her husband, and check "Mrs." instead of "Miss" on the envelope.

She longed for the day she could lift up holy hands without wrath or doubting, more specifically, her left hand, which not only would praise Him in the sanctuary but also show off the bling-bling on the ring finger that she prayed would blind her neighbors.

One day, she thought with a sigh as she dropped her offering into the receptacle.

Everyone stood as Pastor Solomon made his way to the pulpit, casually dressed in khaki pants and a red polo shirt. Shenita appreciated how her fortysomething pastor kept it real and down to earth not only in his speech but also in his dress. He was the perfect blend of old school meets new school and knew how to get his Holy Ghost bounce on while taking 'em back to *chuuurch* at the same time.

"Let the church say amen," Pastor Solomon said from the pulpit.

"Amen."

"Let the church say amen again."

"Amen."

"Good morning, church!" Pastor proclaimed with his usual enthusiasm. The congregation responded, "Good morning, Pastor."

"Turn to your neighbor and say, 'Neighbor!'" he said.

"Neighbor."

"You look good."

"You look good."

"I look good."

"I look good."

"And God *is* good."

"And God is good."

"Now give your neighbor a high five, and if they really look good to you and you don't see a ring on it, then ask them out for coffee after service."

The congregation laughed.

Shenita could definitely feel where Pastor Solomon was coming from, since 70 percent of his congregation was single and most of the small number of men who attended regularly were the married ones who probably attended because their wives made them.

Shenita laughed right along with the congregation but secretly looked around to see if any potential Boaz had taken notice. She looked extra cute with her modest but still flattering tangerine silk dress—she definitely didn't want to be a stumbling block to her brothers in Christ. She had thought about topping off her outfit with her matching brim orange hat, but figured she didn't want to hurt 'em too badly.

"Now today's sermon is entitled 'God's Grace to Run Your Race,'" Pastor Solomon said, and repeated, "God's Grace to Run Your Race."

Shenita firmly placed her Bible on her lap.

"Now we thank God for grace, the kind that forgives in the midst of a storm," the pastor continued. "Whether it's a storm the devil created, our mind created, or one we created." Shenita nodded.

"No matter what we may have done regarding the situation we're now in," Pastor Solomon preached, "there is grace available for you! Grace to forgive! The grace that Jesus went to the cross and died just for you—so you could live. You see, the Word of God says that He went to that cross, despising the shame, but for the joy that was easily set before Him, He stayed on that cross—He did not complain—and that joy was you! You were the joy He endured for. If it weren't for you, and for His carrying out the instructions of His Heavenly Father, He wouldn't have done it.

"But God!"

"But God!" an older lady from the congregation shouted.

"He shed His blood for you," Pastor admonished, "so that you can have eternal access to His grace through the shed blood of Jesus Christ!"

"Hallelujah," a lady in a red dress and matching brim hat stood up and shouted.

"But God!" Pastor repeated.

"But God!" the congregation echoed.

"He ran His race," Pastor said, wiping his forehead of sweat, "ended up at that place, stayed, endured, and made it so you could make it!"

"Thank you, Jesus!" a man proclaimed.

Once the sermon was done, announcements were given and the offering was received, Shenita made her way up the aisle toward the lobby and spotted a familiar face along the way— Terrell Glover, a part of her crew and someone she'd secretly had a crush on for the last couple of years.

"Hey, Love," Terrell said as he greeted her with a great big church hug.

Terrell, who was brown-skinned with dimples and only a few inches taller than she was, had been calling Shenita by her last name for the longest.

Too bad he never tried to do anything with it by stepping up to a sista and asking her out, Shenita thought.

She couldn't understand why, after two whole years of their hanging out with mutual friends when they obviously clicked, he'd never decided to formerly ask her out on a date. Sure, they'd shared a few conversations here and there, and friends even tried to suggest to him that he ask her out, but he never did—and it wasn't like he was dating anyone, unless it was some female outside the church, because nobody around here had ever seen her, which wouldn't surprise Shenita.

"Hey, Terrell," Shenita replied in kind.

"I got something for ya, girl," he said.

"What?" Shenita asked, curious.

"Bam!" he said, and whipped out a pink greeting card envelope from the side of his black Bible cover.

"Happy birthday, Love."

"Thanks," Shenita said with a wide grin.

"Since your l'il shindig was ladies' night out last night, I figured a brother wasn't invited, but I still wanted to get you something," he said, popping the collar of his crisp white shirt that complemented his burgundy tie, matching pants, and burgundy gator shoes.

"Why, thank you, Terrell," Shenita said with a kiss on his cheek and a "Muah!"

"Aw, sookie sookie now, don't get a brother all hot and bothered in the church house. Let me borrow your napkin—a brother's gotta wipe off the lipstick evidence!"

The two of them cracked up.

Shenita was used to their flirtatious banter. If it wasn't her kissing him on the cheek this week, it was him winking at her at church next week. Shenita wished one day one of them would just see the light and say something. She had hoped he would be the one to do it, because the Word says, *He that findeth a wife findeth a good thing* . . . and Shenita didn't want to appear out of order by initiating anything.

"Pastor sure did preach a good sermon today, didn't he?" chimed Danielle, who joined Shenita and Terrell's convo once they made it to the crowded lobby, where some gathered around and chatted after service for what some considered second service, or church fellowship time.

"He sure did, girl," Shenita said. "And you did great on the praise team this morning. I love your new black dress . . . and those red pumps? Banging!" Shenita gave her friend a high five. "The Lord was all over them shoes," Shenita said, pointing at them.

"Y'all ladies are to much," Terrell said. "What's up, Danielle?" He turned his attention toward her.

"Hey, Terrell," Danielle said. "I'm loving your new suit hook-up. Looking mighty sharp, matching head to toe! Are you just now getting around to wearing your Easter outfit and here it is September?"

"Girl, be quiet," he said, and they laughed.

"Danielle . . ." Shenita interrupted, "speaking of today's sermon . . ."

"Hi, Danielle," a nasal-sounding male voice said to Danielle's right. She looked over and didn't see anyone right away and wondered who had called her name.

"It's me, Willy." Danielle looked downward and spotted Willy wearing red Coke-bottle glasses with his pants up to his chest and a small Afro, looking like Urkel's cousin.

Danielle grabbed her own head and rubbed it. "Oh, hi, Willy," she said as he failed to acknowledge anyone else in the group.

"Pastor sure did preach a good Word today, didn't he?" Willy asked about five minutes too late.

"Yes, he did," Danielle said.

"Danielle," Willy said, inching close to Danielle and zoning everyone else out. "I took some extra-good notes from service today if you ever need to copy them. You have my number," he said with a wink.

"I do, Willy, I do. I'm okay, though," Danielle said. "I plan to just download the MP3 for this one. That way I can hear the message anytime from my computer."

"You know, that's a great idea," Willy proclaimed. "Technology nowadays makes the Word so much easier to access. Praise the Lord!"

"Yes, Willy, praise the Lord," Danielle said.

"Bye," Willy said with a raised hand, then walked away.

Shenita cracked up. "What just happened here? That man didn't see me or you, Terrell. It's like we were nonexistent."

Terrell laughed. "You have a point there, Shenita. He was all up in Danielle's grille."

"And since when did you exchange numbers with Willy?" Shenita asked. "Am I missing out on something?"

"Girl, be quiet," Danielle said, embarrassed. "We did not exchange numbers. Willy joined the choir last week and new choir members are given a list of everyone's phone number. Let's just say he made sure I added his number to my revised list."

"Oh, really?" Shenita said. "You sure you don't have something you want to tell me? I'm just saying. Brother man was all in. Don't be sleeping on your Boaz."

"Girl, whatever. Besides, that little man is broke as a joke. Did you see that hole in his gym shoes? Who wears old worn-out dirty gym shoes with white dress pants in September to church?" Danielle asked.

"Oo, girl, you wrong," Shenita said.

"Look at you, scandalous!" Terrell chimed. "Gold-diggers all up in the church. Security! Security! I would like to report a gold-digger here at New Life Tabernacle Saving Grace Church. Where's a good MOD when you need one?"

Danielle punched Terrell in the side. "Boy, shut up!" she said, and went right back to Shenita. "Forget him. Now what were you saying earlier, Shenita, before we were so rudely interrupted? Something about today's message?"

Shenita thought back for a moment to remember and then said, "Oh, I was saying, speaking of today's message, um, can we meet at the House of Pancakes after service to talk more about it?"

"Uh-oh," Danielle said with a suspicious look. "Girl what you done did? Pastor's message was on grace—are you telling me you done messed up and need an extra helping of grace today? Am I going to have to have Pippa stop by your house to lay hands on you later this afternoon?"

Terrell and Danielle cracked up.

"You crazy, girl; it's all good," Shenita said. "We'll talk about it later."

"Hey y'all." Little Miss Sunshine sashayed over to the small group.

"Speak of the angel," Shenita said in reference to Pippa, who was swinging her long white floral-and-lace dress from side to side as she approached them.

"Hi, Pippa," Danielle and Shenita said in the same dry tone.

"Hey Pippa, girl, you looking good," Terrell said, causing Pippa to blush. "You must have been working out, girl, you losing weight?"

"A little," Pippa said with a third-grader sounding giggle. "Glad you noticed, man of God," she said and glided her arms up and down her plump waist. She began, "Well, you know I have been . . . wait a minute." She raised a finger, then seemingly disappeared into thin air as she made her way back inside the sanctuary. Danielle and Shenita wondered where she was headed all of a sudden, then peeked back inside the sanctuary and saw what was really going on.

Pippa had found her way to the front of the sanctuary, where Elijah served as the pastor's armor bearer. Anyone could tell that Pippa was so in love with that man that she would drink *his* bathwater. She hung on every word he said and was always at his beck and call. They'd gone out a few times, only because *she* asked *him* and he obliged only to entertain her.

Though he wasn't the finest man in the church, his broad shoulders, headful of black curly hair, and cinnamon-brown skin more than made up for what he lacked in looks, plus the fact that he genuinely loved the Lord with all his heart and was one of the few single men in his thirties who not only loved God but served faithfully in the church made him a male diamond. Many a single woman wanted to claim Elijah O'Toole as their Boaz, and before Jesus returned, Pippa definitely wanted to make sure she got her bid in.

Danielle and Shenita looked in Pippa's direction and just shook their heads.

Danielle excused herself and headed to the ladies' room.

Suddenly Terrell's attention was diverted by an olive-complexioned, slender lady with long straight black hair who just got saved last week, and whom half the brothers at the church wanted to holler at.

"Terrell? Hello, Terrell—are you there? Earth to Terrell," Shenita said, and waved her hand in front of Terrell's face to no avail; he was obviously distracted.

Terrell finally shook himself out of it and said, "Huh? Oh yeah, you see that new girl, I mean new sister in Christ, over there?" Terrell asked, "I hear her name is Lynette and baby got back!"

Shenita looked at him like he was crazy.

". . . slidden," Terrell corrected himself. "Um, she was back-slidden, until she got saved and joined our church last week during first service. Now, you know I just joined the hospitality committee here at the church, so if you will excuse me, Love," he said, and popped his collar and straightened his burgundy tie, "a brother's gotta say hello to the newest member of the fold."

That Terrell is a trip, Shenita thought. *Too bad he doesn't exert all that extra energy toward me.* She watched him introduce himself to Lynette with his same friendly gestures. *Maybe if I looked like her it'd be different,* Shenita thought. *Brothers in the church don't seem to care that you only know John 3:16 if you look like that,* Shenita concluded. *Who knows?*

Danielle came out of the ladies' room and said, "All right, girl, I'm about to head over to our spot. Meet you in a few?"

"Sure," Shenita said dryly. "Meet you in a few."

They both exited the building and drove in separate cars to the House of Pancakes.

"Okay, girl, spill it," Danielle said, drawing closer to Shenita in her seat.

Fortunately the House of Pancakes wasn't jumping as usual, since a lot of church members normally made their way there after service. Shenita figured with it being such a sunny fall day folks must have decided to head elsewhere for a change.

Shenita perused the menu and said, "Hmm, I wonder what

I'm going to order today. An omelet? Wait a minute, this *is* a pancake house."

"C'mon, Shenita, tell me what's up—what happened?"

"Girl, we'll get to that in a minute; tell me what's up with you."

Danielle sat back and rolled her eyes as she was very familiar with Shenita stall, a tactic of Shenita's that Danielle had seen in operation for the three years that she'd known her.

Danielle played along with it for the moment and replied, "Ah, nothing, girl—you know how it is. Boss still tripping. They still talking about cutting my pay; yada yada yada . . . I gotta get out of there."

"Cutting your pay? Why?"

"Girl, something about my last performance review. I told you about my boss—she a hater."

"Aw, girl, I'm sorry to hear that."

"It's all good, though. I'm looking for something else as we speak. Working in a call center is getting pretty tired—and boring. You know me, I like excitement where I work," Danielle said with a laugh, in reference to her past vocation.

"Yeah, I'm sure you never had a dull night there, but I'm also sure the price to pay was much more than what your soul could bear," Shenita said as she decided on banana pancakes.

The waitress came by and took their orders, and Danielle continued. "Yeah, you're right, girlie. I was just teasing. I'm definitely glad God delivered me out of that place. The money *was* good, though . . ."

"Dani!"

"All right, all right. I'll stop. Thank you, Jesus. Thank you, Lord," Danielle said sarcastically with an apathetic wave of the hand.

"Now, back to you, missy, you ready to fess up now?"

Shenita stared at her water for a moment, then finally began.

"Last night, after you and Pippa went home . . . I went out with Luke to Starbucks."

"Whaaat? All right now, go 'head, Miss Shenita Love. I see you weren't wasting any time getting to know him. Or shall I say he wasn't wasting any time getting to know *you*."

"Yeah, well, uh, it went a little further than that."

"What do you mean?"

"He suggested I go to his place to check out his library collection."

"Aw, girl, tell me you didn't . . ."

"You know how much I love to read!" Shenita pleaded.

"Yeah, I know how much you love to read, but going to a man's house after midnight, um, he ain't interested in opening the pages of any *War and Peace,* he's interested in opening something else."

"Yeah, well, unfortunately you're right."

"Shenita!" Danielle sat up. "Tell me you didn't give this man . . . not after ten years!"

"No, I didn't, no," Shenita said defensively.

"Whew, girl, you had me over here sweating bullets. I know if *you* wouldn't have been able to hold out then there would be no hope for me. I'm only eleven months abstinent and you're like my role model."

"For real, Danielle?" Shenita asked. She had no clue.

"For real, for real. I love you, girl, and I really look up to you. You're so strong in your walk with the Lord. It's like you give me the strength to keep going and keep saying no to some of these jokers out here."

"Wow, Dani, I didn't know."

"Mmm-hmmm. That's real talk. You're my inspiration, chica."

"Aw," Shenita said, and got up and hugged her neck. "I love you too, girlie," she replied and sat back down. "God is good and He's faithful and I thank God He didn't cause me to stumble or fall."

Shenita didn't know which felt worse, the realization that other people looked up to her and that her position to remain abstinent till marriage wasn't just about her anymore, or the fact that she went too far and almost had sex with a man she just met . . . and that part of her really wanted to.

CHAPTER 5

Once Shenita was inside her ride headed home, her cell rang. She looked at it and Luke's fine self appeared on the screen with his name. Though she was tempted to answer, as his Twitter profile pic that showed up on her Android looked mighty nice, she mustered up enough courage after the third ring to send his call to voice mail.

Her phone rang again, but this time it wasn't Luke calling back—it was her male friend and bestie, RayShawn, whom she'd known and been cool with since high school, way before she got saved.

"Ray Ray!" Shenita answered on her Bluetooth.

"Hey, girl," RayShawn responded while cooking scrambled eggs in a wife-beater and a red doo rag that covered his long brown-and-black dreads. "What's up with you, boo?" he asked.

"Ray Ray, I was just thinking about you the other day!"

"Oh, for real? No wonder my yellow nose was itching something crazy the other day, was that you talking 'bout me?"

Shenita laughed. "No, I didn't say *talking* about you, I said I was thinking about you, silly—wondering how you been. So how you been?"

"I been good, girl, you know how it is, trying to fight all these Negroes off me, you know they addicted to the sexy." RayShawn peeked in the mirror above his stove at his fair complexion, licked his finger, then wiped his light brown brow.

Shenita cracked up at her friend, whom she hadn't chatted with in a couple of months. Even though they didn't talk on the phone every single day, when they did connect it was like neither of them skipped a beat in each other's lives.

"Nothing's changed then, I see," Shenita observed.

"Nope—ain't nothing changed here but the weather, and my underwear. What about you, Miss Thang, how *you* doing?" he said like Wendy Williams.

"I'm good, Ray, just trying to behave, that's all."

"Trying to behave? I know you not talking Miss Single and Saved. What you talking 'bout, trying to behave?"

"Ray, your girl over here almost gave it up last night."

"What!" RayShawn banged the frying pan on the stove. "Stop the press! You gave it up! How was it, girl, was it good? Was it worth the wait, cuz I know you been waiting a long time."

"No, Ray Ray, I said I *almost* gave it up—I didn't, though."

"Oh, well, hallelujah, praise the Lord! God is good! I know you ain't give it up. He's a keeper! Yes He is . . ."

"RayShawn, you are too crazy."

"Girl, you know I'm just messin' with you. So who is it, is this your new man friend you haven't told me about yet?"

"No, I wish it was, though. Just some guy I met at the club last night."

"At the club? Now who am I talking to? Shenita Love, is

this really you? This ain't the Shenita Love I know. The Shenita Love I know is a faithful tithing member of New Life Tabernacle Saving Grace Church. Did some aliens abduct your body and come to live up inside of you? Am I going to have to do an exit-schism on you? Where is Shenita Love and what have you done with my friend?"

Shenita cracked up. "It's *exorcism* and no, nobody has taken over my body, or my spirit for that matter. And yes, the Shenita Love you know went to the club. I was bored, I guess—it was my birthday and I wanted to celebrate."

"Yeah, but your idea of a party used to be you and some of your church girlfriends having Bible study over tea and crumpets. You still over there at that big ole megachurch New Life Tab, right?"

"Yeah."

"Okay, just checking. Wanted to make sure you weren't back-slidden or anything."

"RayShawn, you are a mess. No, I'm not back-slidden. But the crazy thing is, last night was kinda weird. He seemed like a decent guy, had the DJ sing 'Happy Birthday' to me and everything, but when I went back to his place and checked out his books he had, like, tarot cards, and oh, he kept talking about the universe and the stars and stuff."

"Girl, that man had a demon in him! You over there messing with a demon? Do you want me to come over there and snatch you by your hair and drag your butt to the gold line at the altar at your church so they can throw some holy water on your behind?"

"I know, Ray, and I deserve that," Shenita said, stopping at a red light. "I just was caught up in the moment and not being my normal self, I guess. RayShawn, to be honest I'm just tired of being alone. I turned thirty-five yesterday. I just knew I would be married with at least two kids by now. I need a husband," Shenita said as she sat at the changed light two seconds too long and the car behind her blew its horn.

"I hear ya, sis," RayShawn empathized. "But you know what, God got a man out there for you, girl."

"I know," Shenita replied—as if she hadn't already heard that a thousand times. She couldn't remember how many times she either got prophesied over by a minister at her church or had hands laid on her to receive her husband—and now, years later, she was in the same position she was in before—still single.

"No, I'm serious. I need you to believe it," RayShawn stated. "I need you to believe God got a husband out there for you and that he'll show up. Faith is the substance of things hoped for—the evidence of things not seen! Hobohbohsheteh. Don't get me out here praying in tongues over you."

Shenita laughed. "I know you mean well and all."

"No, I'm serious, Shenita! Lift up ye heads oh ye gates, and be ye lifted up! I can feel in my spirit that God's got a man out there for you this year, so it's now up to you to go get him!" RayShawn proclaimed in his best preaching voice.

"Go get him?"

"Yeah, go get him! Go get your blessing, girl; faith without works is dead."

Shenita was now confused. "But what about the Bible when it says, *Whosoever findeth a wife,* or *He that findeth a wife findeth a a good thing, and obtaineth favor of the Lord?* That's what it says in Proverbs 18:22." Shenita had that scripture ingrained so much in her brain that she could probably recite it in her sleep.

"Right! It says, 'He that *findeth* a wife findeth a good thing,' and, Miss Love, you are a good thing, so it's time for you to be found!"

"But you just said . . ."

"Shenita, how long you been celibrate?"

"How long I been celebrate? I don't get what you're saying; I celebrated my thirty-fifth birthday yesterday."

"No, no, not celebrate like birthday, I mean celebrate, like you been holding on to the cookie for how long now?"

"Oh, Ray, you mean how long I been celibate! I been celibate over ten years now."

"Ten years? Oh, Lawd hammercy, it's been that long? And you thirty-five? Don't you want to have kids?"

"Yeah, you know I want to have kids. Having a family is one of my dreams."

"Well, I got a news flash for you, sweetheart—you ain't getting no younger. Your eggs about to be all scrambled up like these eggs I'm 'bout to burn on this stove."

Shenita paused.

"Aw, girl, I'm not saying that to discourage you. All I'm saying is it's time for you to go get it. Don't the Word say it's better to marry than to burn? It's time for you to go get your husband, girl, cuz I know you burning. Anytime you bout to give it up to some demon-possessed stranger you met at the club the same night, you *got* to be burning."

"You're right," Shenita said sheepishly.

"And you sitting up here talkin' 'bout 'he that findeth,'" RayShawn mocked. "You been 'he that findeth' for the past thirty-five years and you mean to tell me he ain't found you yet? Where has all that 'he that findeth' gotten you? Nowhere."

"Right again," Shenita said.

"So now it's time for you to flip the script on 'em," RayShawn said.

"What do you mean, Ray Ray?"

"Forget *he* that findeth; it's time for some *she* that findeth! All these chicken-head women walking around here with these good men on they arm . . . you much better than they are; you deserve to have a good man and a good husband."

"I agree," Shenita said at yet another red light, then peeked at herself in the rearview mirror. "I *am* fine," she assured herself.

"You're fine, you're smart, you can have any man you want; any man would be extremely blessed to claim you as his bride."

"Amen, RayShawn, amen!"

"You Proverbs 31, baby."

"That's right!"

"So, like I said before, lift up your heads oh ye gates and be ye lifted up! It's time for you to rise up, Shenita Love, and go get your man, girl!"

"Amen!"

"Well, love, I have got to go—these eggs 'bout to burn and I can't find the ketchup—and I am not about to feed my man no burnt eggs. I'll send you the bill in the mail for my services—you know a servant is always worthy of his hire."

"Okay, RayShawn, you so crazy. I'll talk to you later."

"Bye."

In a weird way, Shenita figured, RayShawn was right. Shenita had been in her own little box for so long, trying to do everything the right way ever since she was a little girl—*Don't speak unless spoken to, don't say "ain't," cross your legs while seated,* and *don't say anything bad about anyone else.* Then, once she got saved it became, *Don't have sex before marriage, don't rob God, don't say anything bad about the pastor,* and *don't pursue a man first.* And where had that gotten her—it may have gotten her an upwardly mobile position in her career due to the favor of God and politeness, but when it came to the man department, it had gotten her nowhere.

Not even a heart-shaped card on Valentine's Day.

Just then that thought made Shenita think about the card Terrell had given her for her birthday.

All this talk about men not stepping up to the plate could be proved wrong by the words Terrell might have chosen to express in his birthday card to her, which was truly a kind gesture that proved he was at least thinking about her.

Once home in her condo, she threw her keys on her gray marble kitchen counter, took off her stilettos, then walked barefoot on her white plush carpet to her long white couch and plopped down, put her feet up on her matching ottoman, and opened the pink birthday card.

The outside of the card was white and had written in big red letters, "I was going to get you a birthday cake for your birthday," then the inside had a cartoon drawing of a short fireman carrying a red hose and read, "but I decided not to so the fire department wouldn't have to be called because of all the candles. Happy Birthday." Underneath Terrell had written, "Happy Birthday, Sister Shenita. God bless you, my friend. Terrell."

Disappointed, Shenita closed the card and threw it on the glass coffee table in front of her, hitting the side of her clear rectangular vase filled with water and three huge calla lilies.

Shenita couldn't understand how in spite of their mutually appealing flirtatious gestures and the fact that she obviously liked Terrell and believed he knew it, he still appeared to make every effort to make it clear that they were, and would never be, more than just friends.

Sister Shenita? she thought.

Anyone who's been in the church any length of time knows calling someone sister or brother anything is a dead giveaway that they never are and never will be interested in being any-thing more than just friends.

Then to add insult to injury he says "God bless you, my friend"? He wants to make sure I know ain't nothing going on, Shenita thought.

Though he probably didn't mean any harm with the come-dic card, it couldn't have been read at a worse time for Shenita.

She stared off into space in her quiet twenty-eight-hundred-square-foot empty condo. It was so quiet she could almost hear herself breathe.

She now understood why some single women bought dogs, at least that would be *some* other companion in the home who would be happy to see them.

While thinking back over last night and now today, and how she'd never been more miserable in her entire life than at this very moment, Shenita began to cry.

She felt bad for crying, but she couldn't help herself.

RayShawn's words rang in her ears: *"Go get your man, girl."*

She was tired of being single Shenita, the one the ushers at her church automatically knew to direct to a single seat.

The one who was always complimented but never chosen.

She was ready to be dating Shenita, and then married Shenita.

She was ready to go get her man.

She was ready to *find* love.

CHAPTER 6

Pippa parked her used white Ford Taurus in front of the quaint brown brick house on Detroit's east side and pulled down the car visor and stared at the reflection in the mirror.

"Okay, girl," she said, digging in her purse, then added Vaseline to her lips and wiped the excess moisture off her face with a napkin. She patted her short light brown mushroom style into place and said, "You look good the way God made you; now it's time to be the blessing God called you to be."

She grabbed the warm plate of fried chicken, collard greens, macaroni and cheese, and yams wrapped in aluminum foil, which was food she had cooked last night, from the passenger seat. She grabbed the extra saucer of homemade 7-Up pound cake with cream cheese icing along with it and made it up the oh-so-familiar walkway of the home of her favorite man of God, Elijah.

Ding-dong.

Dressed down in light blue jeans and a gray T-shirt that read, *Jesus Paid It All* in red print and showed off Elijah's broad shoulders, he peeked out then opened the door.

"Hey!" Pippa gave her signature warm smile that could brighten anyone's darkened day.

"Hey yourself, girl, what you got there?" Elijah asked, eyeing the wrapped-up treats in her hands.

"Well, aren't you going to invite me in?" Pippa asked, still talking with a smile.

"Of course," Elijah said, then opened the door. Pippa made her way toward the kitchen, placed the food on the white counter, and opened the refrigerator door.

"Why don't you just make yourself at home," Elijah said with a laugh, as he plopped back in his previous position on the brown couch to watch the rest of the game.

Pippa laughed in return. "Now you know I know where everything is. I figured I'd get you something to drink to bring out with the rest of the dinner I made you."

"Sweet, well praise God," Elijah said. "Aren't you just a blessing."

"I know, and I'm definitely glad you appreciate it, King—I mean *Mr.* Elijah." Pippa peeked to see if he caught her hidden compliment. He didn't respond but remained glued to the TV.

"You know," Pippa said while washing her hands with dish soap, "I come over so much, sometimes I feel like I practically live here."

"What was that?" Elijah asked, still not facing her.

Pippa uncovered the main plate, then heated it up in the microwave. "I said, I come over so much I feel like I live here sometimes."

"Oh, yeah. Well, the Word talks about the saints being hospitable toward one another, so, um, *mi casa es su casa,*" Elijah said.

Pippa took the tray table out of the hall closet, set it in front of Elijah, then placed his plate in front of him, just the way he liked it.

"Yeah, well, any woman of God would be honored to call

this place her home," Pippa said softly as she set his fruit punch drink and fork and knife wrapped in a napkin in a perfect position next to his plate.

"Yeah, yeah," Elijah replied. "Mmm, girl, now you know you can cook! This food smells good!"

Pippa grinned. "I know, and it tastes good, too."

Elijah set his remote down and dug in.

"Pippa, can you hand me that salt on the counter?" he asked.

"Sure thing," Pippa said, and as she headed his way this time she looked inside the room behind her and noticed a pile of clothes on his bed.

"What are you doing with all those clothes on your bed?" Pippa asked with the sweetest concocted Southern accent.

Elijah did a double take from his bedroom back to the TV.

"Ah, girl, those are clothes I need to wash. As a matter of fact, I better wash them tonight, because half of them I need to wear next week!"

"Now, I know your momma trained you better than to have all those clothes piled up like that," Pippa said while shaking a small amount of salt on his food, then allowing him to taste it.

"Just a little more," Elijah said, then resumed their conversation about his clothes. "I know! My mom would definitely not be proud of me—at least, not of my room. It's just that I haven't had any time lately to take care of what I need to take care of around the house. Pastor got me serving like crazy at the church, and now he has me teaching a special class to train upcoming armor bearers, which I now lead Monday nights, I'm in school, and then, to top it all off, my job has me working almost sixty hours a week; I can barely get personal Bible-reading time in."

As Elijah continued, Pippa made her way to his room and grabbed the pile of clothes, separated the whites from the colors, and placed them in laundry baskets. She returned to the laundry room with one basket and asked, "Where's the laundry detergent?"

Shocked, Elijah asked, "What?"

"Where's the laundry detergent? I want to wash these clothes for you."

"Aw, girl, you don't have to do that. I'll get to 'em eventually."

"No, I insist. I want to help you take a load off so you can focus on other things like the ministry, man of God—like they did for the disciples in Acts 6."

"But—"

"No buts. Trust me, it's an honor. Let me do this for you. Now where's the laundry detergent?"

Elijah finally gave in and said, "It's underneath the sink in the bathroom."

Once the clothes were in the washer, Pippa took it upon herself to clean Elijah's entire kitchen on hands and knees, scrubbing the floor in her church clothes before mopping it.

She wiped off all the cabinets, Windexed the black stove and the refrigerator handles, then cleaned out the entire refrigerator, ridding it of molded food that looked like it had been sitting inside Elijah's refrigerator for months. Luckily, Pippa found a pair of gloves to assist her in her cleaning efforts. She wiped sweat off her forehead and proclaimed, after getting out the last piece of moldy food from the fridge, "Boy, I don't think you've cleaned this refrigerator out in months! You need a maid!"

"I know, right?" Elijah replied, looking at Pippa then back at the game.

Once both loads of clothes were washed and dried, Pippa

went inside Elijah's room and found where he kept his ironing board and iron and proceeded to iron his clothes, starting with his white shirts.

With satisfaction she lifted up a pair of his boxers, white ones with blue stripes, and prided herself on how nice and clean they were, as she pictured how cute he and sexy must look in them. She abruptly shook that lustful thought out of her mind and proceeded to iron them with the same tender loving care she used to wash them.

"All done!" Pippa rang as she entered the living room and plopped down on the couch next to Elijah.

"Girl, you are amazing," Elijah said, then placed his arm around her and kissed her forehead. "Muah!" he said. "What would I do without you? Woo-wee! Virtuous woman— Proverbs 31 in action!"

"That's ri–ight," Pippa said with a flirty glance.

Just then Elijah's cell rang. "Hold up, I gotta take this call."

"Hey!" he said. "Nothing's going on much, just watching the game."

Pippa looked at her hands in her lap, then back at Elijah, and smiled.

"Did I? You know, I caught that touchdown!" Elijah beamed. "Pizza? And my favorite? Okay, well, count me in. I'm there! I'll see you in a few."

Elijah hung up and told Pippa, "Aw, girl, it's halftime and I gotta make it somewhere before halftime is over."

"That's okay, Elijah, I understand," Pippa said.

Elijah shot up and grabbed his brown leather jacket from the back of his kitchen chair. "I knew you'd understand, Pippa; thanks again for everything, okay—are these your keys here?" Elijah asked while picking up a set of keys with a small light blue Bible and a Hello Kitty keychain along with a half-dozen keys.

"Yeah, those are mine," Pippa said, grabbing them, heading toward the front door in front of Elijah.

Suddenly she turned around to face him and belted with pride, "Just so you know, I ironed and hung up all your newly washed clothes for you, and your kitchen is now sparkly clean—you can eat off the floor if you want to!"

"I know, and I appreciate it, woman of God. Thank you so much. Words cannot describe how truly thankful I am to you," Elijah said as he opened the front door.

"You showed out tonight, girl, you really stood out from the crowd," he said when the two of them were outside on his front porch.

"You mean that?" Pippa asked, bright-eyed.

"I do," Elijah assured her. "You're the best, girl." He gave her a nice big church hug and made his way to his truck as Pippa walked to her car.

Elijah backed out his charcoal Pathfinder, then zoomed down the street to his next destination.

Inside her car Pippa pulled down her visor again, looked at her reflection, then said, "You did good, girl. Keep it up and in no time you'll become *Mrs.* Elijah O'Toole. God's going to open up his eyes according to Ephesians 1:18 and he'll see that you, Pippa Chamberlain, are his missing rib. It's only a matter of time now. Hang in there, girl. You got this," she said with a wink to herself, then looked around to make sure no one saw her as she pulled off and drove back home to her apartment complex on the other side of town.

CHAPTER 7

"Enough is enough," Shenita said and walked into her home office, grabbed her Mac from the desk, then plopped down with it on her burgundy leather couch.

She figured if anyone could help her find a man, her best friend and one true companion, Google, could.

"Okay, baby, don't let me down," she said as she googled *How to find a man.*

What popped up were mainly blogs by single women and so-called relationship experts who seemed more interested in pushing their products and coaching CDs than in actually telling her how to find a man.

She did stumble across an interesting article by a man that listed three ways to find the man of your dreams: 1. Look good. 2. Go where men are. 3. Repeat steps 1 and 2.

Hmmm, Shenita thought as she pondered the young man's advice, which seemed so simplistic yet so profound, especially since she hadn't done anything like that before with regard to number 2.

She had been so conditioned to believe that it was the man's

God-ordained, divine assignment to find *her* and not the other way around, since she was the prize. Then again, what this guy said kinda made sense to Shenita, because how else would a man know what kind of a rare find she is if she didn't position herself in a way so that he spotted her so she could be found by him in the first place?

Shenita peeked over at her trusty black book outlined in white lace with the words *Rule Book* embroidered in white on the cover. A little black book of sorts filled with dating rules she'd compiled over the years, it almost convicted her to think about it. She placed her Mac aside, then picked up her trusty ole book and opened it to her own set of personal dating rules in descending order as she believed God for a mate:

Rule #7 Never Kiss on the First Date

Rule #6 Never Be the First to Give Out Your Phone Number

Rule #5 Never Date More than One Man at One Time

Rule #4 Never Dress Too Sexy on a First Date

Rule #3 Never Ask a Man Out First

Rule #2 Never Date a Man Who's Not Saved

Rule #1 Never Chase

Remaining pages listed, for each rule, why she believed they were sound truths that she should never break. They were created ten years ago, right after she made a vow of abstinence till marriage, and she hadn't altered them since.

Though they proved to be effective in keeping her safe from harm's way, one thing she didn't anticipate in making these rules was that ten years later she would be in the same predicament today—manless.

She thought back to the men she liked but was too afraid

to say something for fear that they might "take it the wrong way," or shy away because she would have been out of order or maybe even be perceived as a potential loose woman or Jezebel. Lord knows she didn't want that label, nor did she want to come off as an easy catch. She wanted the man to be the hunter and hunt her down to win her love; she wanted the man to do all the work. *Isn't that how it should be?* she thought. *Shouldn't the man be the one so awestruck and enamored of me that he hears a voice from heaven saying, "Shenita Love. Shenita Love. She's the one for you," which would then cause him to know after our third date that I was the one for him, so then we'd marry seven months later, have a couple kids—a boy for him and a girl for me—and live happily ever after?*

Sure sounded nice. Especially back then.

But, unfortunately, that reality never came.

So now here Shenita was, stuck seeking love advice from a computer screen.

There's a saying that it's insanity to do the same thing expecting to get different results, Shenita thought. *I've been living by this Rule Book for a decade of my life and my man of God hasn't shown up yet. So now it's time for me to create my own rules. I play the game, and in order to play to win, I first gotta get in it.*

Shenita turned past some blank pages of her Rule Book and wrote the words *New Rules* across the top of one page. She then wrote in big letters, *Forget the Old Rules* and circled it. She decided her new rules would start with breaking all the old rules to somehow get her closer to her goal of finding a man.

She thought a moment and crossed out the first rule she had already broken, which was *Rule #7 Never Kiss on the First Date;* she broke that rule with Mr. Luke McDaniels during their brief rendezvous on her birthday. Even though that proved wack,

Shenita figured the more rules she could break from her trusty old Rule Book, which apparently hadn't worked up until this point, the closer she'd get to finding her dream husband and her dream life.

Shenita next pondered the words of that male blogger, *Go where men are,* then she thought about places men frequent. She created a list entitled *Where Men Are,* then wrote *#1 Sporting Events.*

She paused for a moment and thought about how she hated sports. She figured hating sports hadn't gotten her anywhere so it must be time for her to learn. Touchdown! *#2 Bars.* She thought about that one, then figured maybe her list shouldn't be so general. She wasn't interested in meeting just *any* man looking for some action while sitting at a bar. She pictured herself sitting next to some old married man who sized her up like a piece of meat while asking to buy her a rum and Coke. Nah. She added to her title heading the word *Christian,* in between the words *Where to Find* and *Men.* She crossed out the word *Bars* from her list, thought a minute, then wrote *Men's Conferences at Church.* She then added *#3 Male Bible Studies* and *#4 Church Picnics.* She figured there would always be some single men there—anywhere there's free food.

She caught a case of writer's block, then grabbed her Mac again.

A pop-up window showed up on her screen that initially irritated her because she thought she had enabled a pop-up blocker on her laptop. The pop-up banner caught her eye, though, with a photo of an extremely handsome man and the heading read, *Meet single, saved men in your area. They're waiting to hear from you now.* Shenita clicked on the banner, which led her to a Christian dating website.

"Hmm," she said; she had never thought about using a Christian dating website before. Something about it seemed a little creepy and un-Christian—like it meant you didn't have enough faith for a mate or something.

Create your own profile and start searching for free, it stated. *Free?* Shenita thought. *Well, I guess it wouldn't hurt just to create a profile.* Little did she know her profile creation would take over thirty minutes to complete. Some of the questions seemed redundant yet worded slightly differently, but this particular online dating site claimed to be more focused on compatibility than just dating based on an eye-catching profile picture and witty catchphrase underneath the name.

The questions were pretty specific, such as, *Do you have or want kids?* or, *Would you mind dating someone with children?* Though Shenita didn't mind dating a man with kids, as long as they weren't under, say, three years old, because she didn't want to have to deal with fresh baby mama drama, ideally she would prefer a man without kids, because she realized she could be selfish sometimes when it came to time spent with her man, and she would never want to have him in a position where he would have to choose between her and his kids. She knew she would lose every time, and rightfully so, so she stated, *No,* she wouldn't want to date someone with kids.

She figured if this so-called matchmaking site was truly heaven-sent then she should be able to put her order in and get exactly what she desired. As she answered the rest of the questions, she almost felt like she was literally creating her own dream man—kinda like Build-A-Bear.

Age. She selected *35–45.* She wasn't interested in dating a man younger than she was; she wanted a mature man. Which wasn't to say some young men aren't mature, and many had told her she had an "old soul," so somehow an old soul and a young, tender soul might not mix well. Besides, she didn't want to be labeled as a cougar; then again, the young ones do know how to have a good time. Nah. She didn't want to go too old either. She didn't mind a man in his forties as long as he didn't look or act like it. She stuck with her initial age choice: *35–45*.

As far as religious preference, because it was a Christian dating website, it defaulted to the Christian faith, however it did ask if she had a denominational preference. Shenita's church was nondenominational, so she really didn't mind. Plus, the Bible only mentions that two people yoked together should be equally yoked as Christians; it makes no mention of any particular denomination, which are mainly man-made sects. So any particular denominational preference? *No.*

Shenita paused when she got to the section that asked her to upload her profile picture. She wondered if she should upload a full-body pic that flattered her frame or just a nice, angelic pic showing off her heavenly smile. She then remembered how her momma always told her how you get what you attract, and she didn't want to attract any "player player" –type men to her profile; then again, men *are* extremely visual . . . Unsure of herself, she finally decided to crop and upload a pic from her birthday dinner showing off her latest hairstyle. That way, he could see her without the weave and if he loved that, then he could love her with the weave as well.

Once her profile picture uploaded, the site prompted her to upload even more pictures and stated that those who upload more pics have a better chance of being selected. That sounded good to Shenita, so she went ahead and uploaded a few more, tasteful ones, of course. Two full-body shots and three more head shots showing off her many hairstyles and hair lengths.

Once she was done with that, Shenita wondered what she should do next. Should she go through other profile pics and read about them and pick one to reach out to through the internal e-mail system?

What am I doing? Shenita suddenly thought. She couldn't believe her life had come to this—Miss Woman of Faith and Power.

She couldn't believe that she had resorted to putting herself in a position to let man do what only God can, which is hook a sister up. *God is the one in the connection business, not man,* she thought.

Then again, she thought how God uses man to bring about witty inventions and things, such as doctors to help heal the sick and lawyers to help fight for justice for the poor—why can't this website be a vessel that God can use to bring two good, God-fearing people together?

Shenita hit *Submit,* to submit her profile page and activate her account, so that any and all prospects could now view her page.

Let the fun begin, she said to herself, sat back, folded her arms, and smiled.

CHAPTER 8

"Excuse me, Danielle, can I see you in my office, please?" Danielle's boss, Mrs. Reid, asked Monday morning in her red power suit, while sashaying her thin frame to a small glass office nearby.

Danielle left her cubicle and walked inside the office, wondering what it was Mrs. Reid needed to see her about this time. Danielle had been written up so many times before at this particular call center, whether for performance issues or attendance, she wondered what in the would it could be this go-round, or maybe Mrs. Reid finally had it up to here and wanted to give her the pink slip.

Danielle didn't care either way; part of her wanted to leave and collect unemployment for a time while she started her own business teaching dance classes to young girls in the neighborhood. Dancing was the only thing that freed Danielle and made her feel alive; working at Credit Collaborations Collections Company, or C4, made her feel like dying every time she came to work.

"Danielle," Mrs. Reid began, pulling out a notepad and pen and slinging her silky long black hair. "It has been brought to my attention that you have been sexually harassing one of your fellow employees."

"What?" Danielle asked in shock. "Sexually harassing? You have got to be kidding me. What are you talking about?" She wondered who would make such an outlandish claim. She pretty much kept to herself on the job, with occasional jests from a male employee, Clive Jenkins, who was on an adjacent team. Every day he stopped by her desk dressed in the same tan khakis and different-colored polo shirt and they would chat about whether or not they'd made their monthly goal, or about his latest "girlfriend" he'd met in an online chat room. Surely Mrs. Reid couldn't be talking about him; if anything, he would be the one accused of sexually harassing her, especially the way he tried to look down her shirt as he stood by her desk talking to her and the way he reacted disappointedly after she turned him down for a date.

Hmm, Danielle thought. Surely this couldn't be his way of getting back at her for rejecting him. She then thought about the gold bracelet he gave her when she first started working at C4 three months ago. He asked her out a week later, and though Danielle said no, she figured it was his gift to her and his way of welcoming her on board with the company—at least that's what he told her.

"Clive Jenkins mentions you've patted him on his rear end on more than one occasion even after he asked you to stop," Mrs. Reid stated.

"Excuse me?" Danielle belted and stood up.

"Now calm down, Miss Peterson. The good thing is he brought this to my attention before going to HR. This way, we can nip it in the bud right here and now."

"Mrs. Reid," Danielle said while sitting back down and trying to remain calm while speaking. "I assure you, I never hit that man's flat butt. You know me, Mrs. Reid, I would never do anything like that."

"Really, Miss Peterson, I would prefer we leave my personal feelings toward you out of this."

Oh, so this female don't like me anyway, huh? Maybe she's the one who came up with this crap, to come up with a different way to fire me so that I won't qualify for unemployment. Maybe she and Clive are in on this together. I wouldn't be surprised if her married butt wasn't sleeping with him on the side, Danielle thought.

"Okay, then, well what do you want me to do? I told you I didn't do it; now what?" Danielle said, and threw up her hands.

"Miss Peterson, I really don't appreciate your attitude or your tone."

Danielle rose again. "Well, I don't appreciate you accusing me!"

"I suggest you have a seat right now before I call security," Mrs. Reid said, then placed her hand underneath her desk to search for the security button.

"Call security, then. Security! Security!" Danielle said, flailing her arms and looking outside the glass office while others peeked inside wondering what was going on.

"Danielle, you're making a scene," Mrs. Reid said, embarrassed.

"I'm making a scene? *I'm* making a scene? You call me out of my cubicle accusing me of some crap I didn't do while all the while telling me how you don't like me, yet you accuse *me* of making a scene? Forget not going to HR; I think I'm going to be going to HR myself, on you!"

Danielle then stormed out of the office and headed downstairs.

CHAPTER 9

"So can we agree on the following?" Jackie began while checking the clock in the conference room. She eyed her client's soon-to-be-ex-husband's attorney, a Caucasian male in a navy blue suit, white shirt, and red tie, and then focused her attention on the mediator, a Caucasian male in a black suit, white shirt, and blue tie next to him, and said, "Property and assets earned during marriage divided in half, along with a lump-sum alimony payment in the amount of one-point-five million dollars to my client, Mary?"

Jackie awaited the response of the other attorney representing his client, a white male obstetrician who had had his fair share of unscrupulous behavior with his patients at home while his wife volunteered at a soup kitchen with her church on Saturday mornings.

Jackie's client, Mary, a lady in her late forties with blond hair that you could tell had been bleached one too many times, looked over at Jackie, stunned at what she considered an enormous proposition.

Jackie gave Mary a stone-faced, assuring nod.

The other attorney whispered something to his client that Jackie, though she tried, couldn't quite make out.

She peeked at the clock on the wall again; she was hungry and ready to get this over with so she could grab some lunch.

"Look, Michael," Jackie said, addressing her colleague. "Accept the offer I gave you, which could be considered quite low compared to his projected earning potential, and yes, we do know about the Swiss bank accounts that weren't included in the documents. Take the deal so my client here can get on with her life and so this thing doesn't go to trial. If it does, trust me, your client won't come off nearly half as good."

The mediator folded his hands together and faced Michael, awaiting a response.

"Agreed?" Jackie asked.

Michael's client rubbed his hand through his salt-and-pepper hair, then finally nodded to his attorney.

"Agreed," Michael solemnly stated.

"Thank you," Jackie said while holding back the excitement she so wanted to display.

Jackie's client screeched with delight, then gave Jackie the biggest hug she had ever received, which almost crushed the pinstripes on Jackie's gray suit and stained the collar on her white shirt underneath it with lipstick.

Once Michael, his client, and the mediator had left the conference room, Mary told Jackie, "Thank you so much! Is there anything I can do for you, because you've been such a blessing in helping me through all of this—praise the Lord!"

"No, no, you're fine," Jackie said, knowing her anticipated attorney's fees were cause enough for her to have her own celebration as well. "Just keep on loving Jesus and be free from that creep, that's all," she said.

"Well, thank you again—may God bless you one-hundred-fold!" Mary proclaimed.

"Thank you," Jackie said, shutting her laptop and gathering her files. "I so appreciate it."

As Mary gleefully left, Jermaine Stroud, another attorney at the law firm, couldn't help but notice Mary's excitement and poked his head inside the office, then knocked on the already open door.

Jackie, stunned at first, peeked over and immediately noticed Jermaine's tall six-foot-four frame, dashing smile, and boylike demeanor as he said, "I see you got another happy client on your hands . . . so what does that make you, seven for zero this month alone?"

Jackie smiled at him and said, "I do all right."

"Heading out for lunch? Can I join you?" he asked. "My treat."

"No, Jermaine. Thanks for asking, though. I brought something this time. Trying to save money; you know how it is."

"Okay, suit yourself," Jermaine said, heading back out. Then he turned back around and said, "One of these days I'll be able to convince you to go out with me."

"So you got your client her settlement, girl, I'm so happy for you!" Shenita belted, biting into a turkey wrap as the two of them sat at an umbrellaed table outside a quaint restaurant in Birmingham, Michigan, just twenty minutes away from Jackie's job and the office where Shenita worked as a PR specialist.

After receiving the exciting news via text from Jackie, Shenita offered to meet with her centrally for lunch to hear further details of her winning testimony.

"Yes, girl, I was so thrilled. I knew that I was asking for

much, but, girl, with the Lord on my side a boldness came over me where I just gave him some jabs, like 'take that,' and they couldn't help but settle on my terms," Jackie said, eating a forkful of her Middle Eastern carrot salad.

"All right, now. Favor ain't fair and you are living proof!"

"That's right. He was a jerk anyway," Jackie said.

"Who?"

"Mary's ex. This man slept with twelve other women during the course of their eleven-year marriage while she volunteered at a soup kitchen with her church every Saturday morning. That's more than a different woman a year during the course of their marriage!"

"Wow," Shenita said. "I guess while she was serving at church he was serving it up on somebody else."

Jackie gave a mean glare. "Girl, that's not even funny—you know you ain't right. Plus this man had Swiss bank accounts in other countries. He was horrible!"

"Sounds like it. Well, I'm glad you were able to give Mary some type of vindication—and closure."

"Yes, indeed," Jackie said. "You know, these men can be so trifling sometimes—don't even know how to cover their tracks; it's almost like they want to get caught, sorry jokers."

"Calm down, Jackie, not all men are like that." Shenita tried to reassure her friend, knowing that Jackie had suffered her own bitter divorce experience with her ex seven years ago.

"Oh, really, tell me what man you know who doesn't cheat?" Jackie asked.

"What about Sister Maxine and her husband Richard, Betty and Brian, Lisa and Samuel, who just had their fourth child—they're all happily married and are great examples at our church, and they've all been married at least five years."

"Five years? Hmph. Give it some time." Jackie spoke while chewing. "Just watch."

"C'mon, Jackie, you've got to be kidding. You can't go around here wishing divorce on everybody. That's the worst that could happen to anybody."

Shenita paused, not realizing what she had just said to her divorced friend until it was too late.

"I'm sorry, Jackie, I didn't mean to—"

"That's okay." Jackie wiped the side of her mouth with her white cloth napkin. "I know you didn't mean it. And by the way, I'm not scarred. That sorry ex of mine got what he deserved. When I married him at twenty-six I just knew I was getting a mighty man of valor. My *Boaz*. He was Pastor's favorite usher and led the men's Bible study. He wooed me and wined and dined me with virgin daiquiris all day long—made me feel like he was my Isaac and I was his Rebekah—but then soon as the ink got dry on the marriage license that's when all hell broke loose. It was like he became another person! I felt like I married the devil himself; he lied so much even he started to believe them, and he screwed around with so many women at the church I could have started a Bible study just with the women he cheated on me with. We could've had our own little 'Kumbaya' sessions," Jackie said while aggressively chomping on another forkful of salad.

Shenita felt bad for striking up a deep nerve by bringing up Jackie's ex. She forced herself to listen through Jackie's rant as she went on and on about how he was such a dog.

"And he was so stupid!" Jackie proclaimed. "Had the nerve to try and sue me for alimony, not realizing I had him on tape with at least three of the women in compromising positions. Who did he think he was trying to fool? Not me! Not Jackie

Downing. I'm so glad I got my maiden name back. I wouldn't dare carry his last name to the grave."

"Jackie." Shenita tried to get a word in but was ignored. Jackie kept going.

"Jackie," Shenita said again in the same tone but stronger.

"What?"

"Let's talk about something else, please. Oh yeah, I almost had sex Saturday night."

"You almost did what?"

"I almost had sex Saturday night," Shenita repeated. "It's crazy, girl, I know. After you went home the girls and I went to that old-school club Boogie Nights, and I met this guy and we went to Starbucks afterward and I went back to his place to see his library collection and . . ."

"Whoa, wait a minute now. Did I just hear you say you met some guy at a club then went back to his place?"

"Yeah, after we went to Starbucks."

"Did he put a shot of vodka in your frappé or what?"

"No, he didn't. I was just stupid that night, just dumb."

"Uh, yeah," Jackie said matter-of-factly.

"Why you gotta say it like that?"

"Shenita, are you crazy? You could've been raped at some strange man's house. Just because you turn thirty-five doesn't give you a license to dang near lose your ever-loving mind— for goodness' sake."

"I know. I made a mistake, man. God forgave me, now can you?"

"I don't know, Shenita. Behavior like that worries me. It's not like you're running around here with a big *D* on your forehead for *desperate*. Then again . . . I don't know . . ."

"What are you trying to say? I'm not desperate. I been celibate for ten years, that should count for something!"

"I know but . . . I don't know . . . that's some shady stuff. What If something happened and you tried to get away and couldn't reach your cell phone to call the police . . . I know!" Jackie said as she had an "aha" moment. "Here," she said, dishing out hundred-dollar bills to her friend. "Take this money and get an aftermarket GPS system built into your car. Make sure you get the kind that allows you to tell a few people where you are at all times. It looks like I'm going to have to keep a leash on you, Miss Hot Tamale."

"No, thank you, Jackie I don't want any of your money." Shenita placed the cash back in front of Jackie's plate. "I'll be all right. I was just having a moment, that's all." Shenita took a sip of her strawberry lemonade and innocently peeked at her friend.

"Yeah, well, your 'moment' could've led to a lifetime of headaches. He could've had an STD or something—you know you don't have to go all the way to get herpes."

"Jackie! I know this. You sound more like an infomercial than my good friend and accountability partner."

"But I *am* your good friend and accountability partner. Only a good friend would be bold enough to tell you the truth— even when your little fast tail don't want to hear it."

"Quit judging, God!" Shenita pleaded.

"Don't bring God into this—He obviously wasn't involved when you were getting your freak on with some random stranger."

"Jackie, stop it. You are getting me highly upset right now," Shenita said in the calmest voice she could muster, though she was boiling inside.

"Oh, shoot, hide me," Jackie said, then used her dessert menu to cover her face, reached in her Gucci bag, and plopped on her Versace shades.

"What?" Shenita said, and looked around.

Just then she saw a tall, handsome light-skinned man who looked Latino, in a suit, getting carryout at the very same restaurant where they were eating.

He looked through the glass door that separated the outside from the inside, then saw Shenita looking at him, did a double take, and headed their way.

"Jackie Downing?" the gentleman asked once he'd made it to their table.

Jackie slowly lowered her menu, gave a huge grin, and said, "Hi, Jermaine! How are you? Funny I would run into you here."

"Yeah, well, this is my spot," he said. "I get carryout here quite often . . . actually, this is where I would have taken you for lunch had you accepted my offer. If my memory serves me correctly, you said you were dining in for lunch because you brought it in order to save money."

"Oh, really?" Shenita said loudly with folded arms. "Oh, I'm sorry, my name is Shenita, Jackie's friend—please pardon my rude friend, who failed to properly introduce us. So you're saying Jackie here told you she brought her lunch today?"

"Yes, she did, in order to save money," Jermaine said.

"Hmm. That's odd—Jackie here hardly ever brings her lunch to work. She calls it one of life's indulgences, the ability to have a lifestyle that affords such luxuries as dining out pretty much daily."

"Odd indeed. Nonetheless—I just stopped by to say hello. I'll catch you back at the office, Miss Downing," Jermaine said, then left.

Jackie whacked Shenita on top of the head with her dessert menu.

"What? What'd I do?" Shenita asked sweetly.

"You know what you did—how you gon' call me out like that? I thought you were my girl."

"Oh no, now don't even try that—this coming from the same person who called me out for being Miss Freak of the Week. You ain't so holy as you thought, Miss Liar Liar Pants on Fire. And how you gon' turn that fine man down? You must be on some serious drugs."

"Now, I know you're not comparing your situation to mine. That is not apples to apples—that's totally different!"

"Oh, really? Well, it's all apples to apples in the sight of God. No sin is bigger than the next, you sinner—or shall I call you Beelzebub?" Shenita said, crossing her eyes.

"Girl, shut up," Jackie said. "I'll have you know, Jermaine is another attorney at the law firm where I work, and he's been asking me out all year. I keep turning him down, though."

"Why?"

"Why? Because all men are dogs, that's why!" Jackie said, like "Duh."

"Oh, get over yourself, Jackie."

"Get over myself?"

"Yes. Please. All men can't be dogs, and he seems nice enough."

"Nice? That man isn't nice; he just called me Miss Downing."

"So?" Shenita asked.

"So? So he was publicly acknowledging my marital status. It was a power move—he was trying to prove he was in control by pointing out the fact that I'm still single. But no worries, I'm onto his game," Jackie said with a smirk and a sip of her club soda.

"Girl, are you so smart that you've become stupid? What you just said makes absolutely no sense," Shenita said, shaking her head, amazed.

"You know I'm right. Besides, they appear to be nice in the

beginning, but just give it a little time. The real dog will come out soon enough. Soon enough he, too, will be caught with his tail between his legs."

"Girl, you got some serious issues."

Jackie continued, "Then as soon as they put that ring on your finger and get you to say, 'I do,' in front of some rented preacher and a roomful of family and folk you barely know—bam! They got you!"

"Girl, I'ma pray for you," Shenita said.

"No, you the one who need the praying, Miss Loosey-Goosey."

"Will you stop with the name-calling?"

"Okay, I'll stop. And I know I've been pretty mean to you. Let me make it up by throwing a party in your honor."

"In my honor?"

"Yeah, when do you turn eleven years celibate?"

"Next Friday," Shenita said sheepishly.

"Why you sound so gloomy about it?"

"Because I had no idea I'd have to go this long without getting some," Shenita said with a pout.

"Girl, don't feel bad. Sex is overrated anyway," Jackie advised.

"Yeah, you say that—don't forget I ain't always been celibate. Ten years is too long."

"You'll make it—as a matter of fact, let's celebrate your eleventh year of abstinence at a white party on my private yacht . . . we can call it a celebration-of-abstinence white party!"

"Woo-hoo," Shenita said unenthusiastically while twirling her index finger in the air.

"It'll be fun . . . and a positive event for the community. Get ready to send out the press release, girl, because we're about to have a party for a cause! Don't be tardy for the party, now."

"Whatever," Shenita said.

CHAPTER 10

Tuesday morning during a roundtable brainstorming and event-planning session, Shenita listened attentively as her boss, Vivian Washington, detailed plans for their next community fund-raising event for the organization.

"Okay, so who has some great ideas they'd like to bring to the table?" Mrs. Washington asked.

"I have one," stated Krissy, One Love Initiative's newest and most eager PR generalist. "How about we have a fund-raising event for singles? Kinda like speed dating or something?"

"That sounds interesting," Mrs. Washington replied. "Now, who here would be interested in researching and facilitating that event?"

Krissy raised her hand again.

"Krissy," said Mrs. Washington, acknowledging her.

"I'd like to nominate Shenita," Krissy said.

Shenita almost choked on her Sprite.

"I mean, you're great at what you do, and you're single, right? Maybe you'll get lucky," Krissy said with a wink.

Krissy herself was unmarried as well, but don't tell her

that—her man had her locked up for life in a four-year engagement and a half-carat engagement ring that had her not even thinking about going out anywhere the opposite sex would be.

"Thanks for thinking of me, Krissy, but speed dating? I don't see how that would promote what our organization stands for. We've never had a singles event and I, personally, don't think that would do anything for the community we serve, or the brand," Shenita stated.

Mrs. Washington added, "You've got a point there, Shenita."

"But don't you want to get married?" Krissy asked, and everyone in the room turned to note Shenita's response.

Shenita did her best to maintain her composure and said, "Yes, I do desire marriage and in due season it will happen for me. Let me ask you this, Krissy, are you married yet, or are you a part of the lifelong engagement club?"

"I don't believe it!" Krissy retorted. "You just insulted me! I was just looking out for you, girlfriend."

"That's okay, Krissy, and I'm sure you mean well, but what we do here at One Love Initiative should have nothing to do with my personal life or my familial ambitions."

Krissy then got up to exit the room when Mrs. Washington added, "Excuse me, I did not dismiss this meeting."

Krissy replied, "Well, I'm leaving anyway. I'm not feeling well; I think I've come down with something and will have to take a half day off today. Wouldn't want to spread any virus," Krissy said with a mean look to Shenita.

Once Krissy had left, everyone else in the room faced Mrs. Washington.

"Okay, with that said, I do believe it's best to table this staff meeting until another day. When we return I'd like everyone to have at least one fund-raising idea to help further the mission of One Love Initiative. Enjoy the rest of your day," she said as everyone gathered their things and exited the room.

"Oh, and Shenita, can you stay here with me for a moment?"

Just as Shenita was about to rise to leave, she sat back down. *Oh boy, what did I do? I really stuck my foot in my mouth this time.*

"Shenita, what just happened here?" Mrs. Washington asked.

"I apologize for what I said to Krissy," Shenita said. "I just felt like her comments to me were out of line and that—"

"But were they really *that* out of line?"

"I don't know, Mrs. Washington, I just feel like sometimes people place pressure on singles like we're running around here sad, mad, and disgusted because we don't have a man on our arm. There is life for those who don't have a significant other. I just get sick of people judging, that's all."

"So you felt like she was judging you?"

Though Shenita and her boss had a warm working relationship, she had never experienced this personal, probing side of her before.

"I don't know, boss. Maybe."

"Or did she hit a nerve?"

"Mmmm." Shenita said.

"Maybe she did and I snapped back. I shouldn't have," Shenita said, "and I apologize, and I promise before the week is out I will personally apologize to Krissy as well."

"Very well, Shenita. I knew you would do the right thing. You always do."

Shenita lowered her eyes. "Yes, ma'am."

"But back to this man thing, are you open to meeting someone new?"

"Mrs. Washington!" Shenita said, slightly embarrassed. Now she was really crossing the line.

"Well, I've observed you for a few years now, Miss Love, and you're a very well-put-together young lady. You're beautiful, intelligent, and quite witty, if I might add."

Shenita laughed at Mrs. Washington's inadvertent reference to her recent office jab.

"Any woman of stature would be delighted to have you as her daughter-in-law, speaking of which . . . would you be interested in meeting my son?"

"Your son!" Shenita said, not realizing how loud she had gotten.

"Yes, my son. He's a pediatrician at Open Door Hospital. Here he is," Mrs. Washington said, and showed a picture of him from her phone. "His name is Christian. He's six foot two, thirty-seven, never been married, no kids, and he is very much ready to start a family."

Shenita stared at the picture of the extremely handsome well-dressed, dark-skinned, lightly mustached, clean-cut man in awe. "He's fine, Mrs. Washington! That's your son?"

"I know." She blushed. "I always tease Stanley and tell him Christian got all his good looks from me," she said in reference to her bald husband with a beer belly, whom Shenita remembered meeting at an office Christmas party a couple of years ago.

"I told Stanley since we've been married thirty-two years at least one of us has to keep looking good," she said with a laugh.

"You and your husband have been married thirty-two years? That's a blessing."

"Yes, it is. We got married the day after my twenty-first birthday. I guess I'm telling on myself now regarding my age. It was the happiest day of my life," she said, reminiscing, "and to this day he still works hard to make me smile."

"Wow," Shenita said. She felt almost honored to be having such a personal conversation with her boss. Now the fact that her boss always remained calm, cool, and collected and was a very well-put-together, classy, mocha-complexioned lady all made sense. She could tell just by the look on her face that her husband was the rock in her life and her love song.

"Amen, Mrs. Washington," Shenita said. "Now that's what I'm talking about. True love in its true essence."

"Surely," she replied, as she focused her attention back on Shenita. "And my husband and I made it our top priority in life to raise our son the right way to prepare him for his future family and lifelong marriage."

The phrase *lifelong marriage* was music to Shenita's ears. Listening to her boss's story reminded her that true love does still exist, and the fact that they raised what sounded like a great son was even better.

"So, would you like to meet him? I can give him your number and he can call you and maybe you two can do lunch or something?" Mrs. Washington asked.

"I'm not sure." Shenita couldn't believe the words that just rolled out of her mouth. Was she crazy? However, she just had to have the answer to one more question. "Is he saved?"

"Is he saved? Saved from what?" Mrs. Washington asked, clueless.

"Is he a Christian?"

"Oh, I see. Now, that is a good question. He's been living on his own for over fifteen years now, and, to be honest, I'm not sure if he's actually made it to a church. Stanley and I are saved. We keep our religious affiliation private, for the most part, but

I believe Christian is, too. I'm just not quite sure. I can ask, though. I'll text him," she said, and began to type on her phone.

"Oh, no, that's okay—you don't have to do that, Mrs. Washington," Shenita said.

How could your own mother not know if you're saved or not? Shenita wondered. *If she doesn't know, and if it's not even evident enough in his life that his own mother would know, then he must not be. Fine looks and a great job are all good, but if he doesn't have Jesus as Lord in his life then the answer is No, thank you,* Shenita concluded.

"Are you sure?" Mrs. Washington asked.

"Yes, ma'am. I'm sure," Shenita said. "But thanks for looking out for me, and thanks for caring. I appreciate the gesture."

"Anytime. I believe you're a wonderful person, Shenita, with a great heart. I know what's best for my son. Maybe one day you'll come around," she added with a pleasant look.

Shenita arose. "Thanks again, but no, I don't think so. It wouldn't work." Shenita left the office and closed the door behind her, paused for a moment, and wondered, *Now where did that come from?* She then retreated back to her own office to finish her work for the day.

CHAPTER 11

The next day, after Danielle decided against going to Human Resources yesterday but instead retreated to her desk to make more collection calls, she resolved to make this day a lot better than yesterday.

Besides, Monday was over and Tuesday is a sign of new beginnings and a fresh start.

Once logged in on the computer, she did her normal routine and retreated to the kitchen to get herself a nice hot cup of coffee with a teaspoon of cream and sugar. She was blowing and sipping it to make sure it was just right when she noticed a familiar face walk inside the kitchen.

"Good morning, beautiful," said her coworker Clive Jenkins, wearing his same old tan khaki pants with a blue-and-white vertically striped polo shirt.

Danielle looked at him and frowned. "Hey," she said.

"What's wrong, sweetie?" he asked with his hands opened wide in a *what did I do?* stance.

"Don't play dumb with me, Clive. Mrs. Reid told me that

you accused me of sexually harassing your sorry behind," Danielle said, taking another sip of coffee.

"Sexually harassing? Is that what she said? I just told her how you just couldn't seem to be able to control yourself in my presence and how your hands would sometimes get to roaming all over my body and rest on my behind, that's all. I wasn't 'pressing charges' or anything, geesh. It's not your fault you can't control yourself; I don't blame you; I'm your blessing from heaven, baby," he said, then picked his teeth with a toothpick and leaned against the sink opposite Danielle, facing her.

"Clive," Danielle began, setting her cup down on the cabinet next to the office microwave. "First of all, I would never, ever, put my hands on you or your nonexistent butt. I didn't even know you had one until she pointed it out. Second of all, I'm not your baby, I'm not your sweetie, and I sholl ain't your blessing from heaven, so stop 'claiming me' when I don't want you in the first place. Leave me alone!"

Clive then got so close in Danielle's face that she could hear him breathing and said, "You don't mean that."

Danielle maintained her bulldog expression and matched his tenacity while remaining silent.

Clive grabbed her left wrist forcefully and said, "And where's that bracelet I bought you? Oh, I'm claiming you all right. You mine now. You're my investment. I put a stake in my territory." Danielle's wrist turned red from his grip and he pinned her to the counter and said, "And by the way, my butt is not flat," then munched on his toothpick some more while staring into her eyes.

"Oh, yeah?" Danielle said.

"Yeah," he said.

"Okay, well, if your butt is not flat," Danielle said slowly and softly, "then your face . . . is not BURNED!" and she splashed her hot cup of coffee on the side of his face then ran out of the kitchen and back to her cubicle.

Coworkers in neighboring cubicles snuck glances at Danielle.

Danielle stood at her desk, shaken, unable to sit down. Clive then came out of the kitchen headed her way while cursing her out for the entire office to hear. He pointed at her and was ten feet away from her when nearby security snatched him back.

Mrs. Reid stepped out of her office to see all the commotion, eyed Danielle, then saw security with Clive and headed straight to Clive's side.

Mrs. Reid gently rubbed his scalded face as he held the side with wet towels, and asked, "Clive, what happened?"

He swore even more at Danielle, who was still standing and shaking at her desk when he said, "She threw coffee on my face! I wouldn't give in to her sexually harassing me; I asked her to stop and she threw coffee on me!"

Mrs. Reid turned around and gave Danielle an accusing glare. She rubbed Clive's arm one last time, then left him with security and headed toward Danielle.

"Is this true? You were sexually harassing Mr. Jenkins again after I asked you to stop?"

Danielle could barely speak. She kept shaking her head "no."

She couldn't believe this man had lied on her and, more important than that, that her boss had believed him.

"Danielle, I'm sorry," Mrs. Reid stated. "I'm going to have to report this. We can't have our employees getting assaulted and harassed; I may have to call the police."

"But I didn't do it!" Danielle yelled with a runny nose and

frowning face. "He assaulted me! He grabbed my arm and had me pinned up against the counter. I couldn't get away!"

Mrs. Reid dialed downstairs from Danielle's desk phone. "I'm sorry, Danielle, but this has got to stop today. We can't have you causing all this ruckus here at C4. It was a great place to work until you started here three months ago. Something's gotta give, and you've got to go."

With that, a security guard from downstairs came upstairs with a brown box and filled it with Danielle's things.

Confused, Danielle looked around at her coworkers sneaking looks at her then looking back at their computers. Still in shock, Danielle softly asked Mrs. Reid, "You're firing me?"

Mrs. Reid took a few steps back, folded her arms, then said, "Yes, Miss Peterson, I'm afraid so."

"You can't do that! I just got this job!" Danielle belted. "I need this job! You can't fire me!"

"Oh, yes, I can, Miss Peterson. And I believe it's long overdue. We can no longer tolerate your unwarranted emotional outbursts here in this office, Miss Peterson. I suggest you take some anger-management courses before you go look for your next job."

Danielle gave her boss the meanest look and raised her finger to say something else, but decided not to. She then snatched her filled box, threw her work badge on the desk, then stomped down to the main lobby and exited with the security guard.

Once at her apartment complex, after crying all the way there with reddened eyes hidden underneath her black shades, Danielle felt relieved as she unlocked the main building and began walking down the hallway to her apartment.

She sighed as she looked forward to just going inside, plopping on her couch, and clutching her teddy bear, Mr. Cuddles, while catching the latest reality show—anything to escape her own present reality.

However, instead of just going inside, she stopped short upon seeing a notice taped outside her door. She snatched it, then read across the top in bold, black letters, "Eviction Notice." As she continued reading, it stated, "You have 10 days from said notice to come up with unpaid rent in the amount $1,800. If payment is not received in full by this date you will be summoned to court."

Danielle snatched the note off the door, then defeatedly walked inside her apartment, plopped on her black couch, threw the note on her wooden coffee table, and cried some more.

"What am I going to do?" she asked, looking up in the sky and hearing no response.

She grabbed Mr. Cuddles and sobbed until her head hurt. She had no clue what her next move would be.

After losing her job, and having no savings, there was no way she could come up with that kind of money in that short amount of time. On top of being behind on her rent, she was also two months behind on her car payments and had grown tired of having to park her car behind the apartment building to keep it from being repoed.

She rubbed her temple and could barely think straight.

She dared not tell her parents, because she didn't want to worry them all the way in California. She had always given them the impression that everything was fine in her life. They were retired, living off their pensions, and she dared not cause them to go into their lifelong savings just to bail her out.

Besides, Danielle was used to always being everyone else's rock. Now she needed a rock of her own, yet for some reason, at this critical time in her life, that rock was seemingly nowhere to be found.

CHAPTER 12

Shenita stopped inside the restroom before leaving One Love Initiative for the day. She tucked her silk red blouse inside her fitted gray pencil skirt, took off her stockings and stuffed them in her work bag to show off her flawless, muscle-toned chocolate legs, then swapped shoes. She took off her plain black pumps and put on her black patent-leather stilettos with shoestring-like ties up her calf. She tied both shoes, then freshened up her burgundy matte lipstick and put a coat of clear lip gloss on top to give her lips extra pop. She also added burgundy and gray eye shadow, then fluffed up her hairdo to make it come alive as she spritzed it with holding spray.

She added a new coat of black mascara, kissed at herself in the mirror, stuffed her pink makeup bag back in her black work bag, put on her brown shades, then walked out of the restroom.

The security guard at the front desk did a double take at the woman he didn't recognize as she sashayed out of the building to her silver Benz.

Shenita drove, then pulled up to her desired destination with her mission in mind.

At her local hardware store, she was on a mission to find not only some paint to paint her bathroom but a man to go along with the décor.

She stepped out of her ride and heard car horns from SUVs stopped at a red light and men hollering "My GOD!" as she went inside.

She grabbed her cart and inconspicuously observed her surroundings through her shaded glasses and headed toward the aisles. She trailed aisle to aisle and was delighted to see all kinds of men: tall men, short men, big men, small men, white men, black men . . . She felt like singing, "It's raining men!" She felt like she had died and gone to heaven as she sashayed down each aisle, pretending like she was actually looking for something to improve her home when, really, she was trying to improve her love life.

She eventually found her way to the paint counter and the salesman asked if he could help.

She noticed he was kinda cute but resolved not to flirt with him, because he made nowhere near what she did. While she'd never considered herself much of a gold-digger, she did want to date someone who at least made more than half of what she made—she figured that was only fair.

"Yes, I'm looking for a light blue color for my bathroom. Something a little lighter than sky blue—a really pale blue." The salesman handed her a book to look at different color palettes.

While she was thumbing through the pages, a tall, muscular brown-skinned male in a long beige trench coat and matching fedora pushing an empty cart came up to the counter, stood over her shoulder then pointed to an off-white yellow and said, "That color would look nice."

Shenita looked up at the extremely handsome man with a neat mustache and goatee and saw him give her a flirty smirk.

"Think so?" she asked, and he agreed.

Shenita went back to her book and thumbed toward the blues and said, "I don't know, I'm looking for more of a blue color to paint my bathroom. What about this color?" she said, and pointed to a light blue.

"Mmmm." he said and gave a "maybe" gesture with his hand.

Shenita scooted next to the fine, kind stranger and went back to the yellow he'd initially picked out. "You know, you may be right, I may consider this yellow. I never painted a wall yellow before . . . as a matter of fact, I never painted any wall before. I guess I'm in a season of trying out new things," she said, then gave him a flirty glance.

The mystery man then pulled out his wallet and handed her his card.

"What's this?" she asked, as if she didn't know.

The man hesitated, then said, "It's my business card. Name's Wallace. Call me sometime, shawty."

Shenita was taken aback as she noticed something about this man that she hadn't noticed before during their brief exchange—his grille!

This man had at least four gold teeth in the top of his mouth and half of his bottom teeth were missing, and the rest were all yellow, about as yellow as the color he'd picked out. *Ew. Can somebody get this man a dental plan?* Shenita thought.

"I might can hook you up on that paint job," he said assuringly.

"Okay, thanks," Shenita said as she hesitatingly took his card.

"Now, call me at night, because my old lady might answer the phone during the day. But that's okay though, you can be my shawty on the side and I can come over and get that work done for you, if you know what I mean," he said.

"O-kay," Shenita said as she watched him stroll away with his empty cart.

As soon as he turned the corner down the next aisle she tore his card in half, smiling at the salesman, who witnessed her gesture, shook his head, and smiled at her in return. Shenita went back to perusing the book, then looked up and asked the salesman, "Um, do you work anywhere else besides here?"

CHAPTER 13

Danielle paced the floor in the front room of her apartment trying to figure out what to do.

She had never been in this tight of a bind and needed a solution—fast.

She suddenly thought of a brilliant idea, one that could give her some quick cash. Though it might not garner her the full $1,800, it might be just enough to appease her landlord until she could figure out a way to come up with the rest.

Danielle parked her used navy blue drop-top Sebring in the back of the store parking lot, then headed inside. After waiting in the single-file line for a good twenty minutes, she took out a small velvet bag and dumped the goods in front of the glass window that came between her and the pawnshop clerk.

"How much can I get for this?" Danielle asked.

She figured she should at least get $500 for the bracelet that jerk Clive gave her; at least something good could come out of that horrific experience at her old job.

The pawnstore clerk grabbed her merchandise, weighed it, then examined it more closely with a small magnifying glass.

Any day now, Danielle thought as the female clerk moved a little slower than she had wanted and popped gum so loudly that Danielle could hear it through the glass. *Just give me the money so I can go.* Danielle looked around and saw young kids sitting on their mothers' laps as they waited to get approved for loans at the local cash-for-gold location that also gave out high-interest loans in exchange for goods.

Danielle placed her hand on her chin as she kept waiting. *How long does this take?* She had gotten cash for gold a couple of years ago when she decided to cash in on some old sack-chasing earrings, but she didn't remember it taking this long.

Danielle sighed out loud.

The store clerk stuffed her bracelet back underneath the glass window.

"What's wrong?" Danielle asked.

"I'm sorry, this is not twenty-four-karat gold. It's fake."

"What?" Danielle asked. "What do you mean it's fake?" she demanded.

"Sorry, ma'am. It ain't real. Next!" the clerk shouted, and the person behind Danielle stepped up to the window, leaving Danielle dumbfounded on the side.

Danielle approached the window again. "Now wait a minute, I need to see a manager! I'm not done, ma'am," Danielle said to the lady who had stepped up to the window from behind her.

"I can get you a manager but you have to wait," the store clerk said in a harsh tone. "Have a seat and someone will be out for you shortly."

Danielle sat down on the hard black chair with arms folded and mouth pouting.

This can't be happening, Danielle thought, *It can't be fake. After all I went through to keep this stupid bracelet—it's gotta be real.*

After Danielle waited another twenty minutes and almost fell asleep in the chair, a tall woman wearing a gray pantsuit with her hair in a black bun finally greeted her.

"I understand you need to see a manager?"

Danielle popped up out of her seat.

"Yes. I have this bracelet here, and it was given to me as a gift, and I was told I couldn't pawn it because it isn't real. But it has the twenty-four-karat-gold stamp right there, see?"

"Let me see it," the manager said, then retrieved it from Danielle and examined it closely. She reached into her pocket, took out a small magnifying glass, and inspected the bracelet. She then reached into her pocket again and pulled out what looked like a small rectangular metal object, placed it next to the gold, and the gold clung to it like a magnet.

The manager then detached the gold from the small magnet and handed it back to Danielle.

"I'm sorry. It's not real. Somebody gave you a fake gift. Hope it wasn't your boyfriend," she said, and walked back inside the back office, leaving Danielle speechless.

Embarrassed, Danielle looked around, grabbed her shades from her purse, plopped them on her face to hide her watering eyes, then waltzed back outside to her car and drove home.

CHAPTER 14

Knock knock.

Jackie looked up from her pile of papers and spotted Jermaine knocking on her door with his normal gleeful expression. "A little birdie told me you like to indulge in eating out every day. Mind if I join you?"

"No thanks, Jermaine," Jackie said. "I'm working through lunch today. I've got an important case I'm working on."

Jermaine helped himself into her office anyway while hiding something behind his back. He said, "Well, I figured you'd say that, so I actually brought us carryout from our spot," and revealed two lunch bags.

Jackie smiled in disbelief.

"Ah, now I get to see that beautiful smile."

"I can't believe you—"

"Believe it, Attorney Downing. Even the best of us have to make time for lunch." He grabbed the extra chair by the door and sat in front of her at her desk and unloaded the lunch bags, which contained a chicken-breast salad with a side of avocado and a club soda for her.

"A salad and a club soda; how did you know?" Jackie said, impressed.

"Don't worry about that," he said. Jackie still wanted to know. Jermaine continued, "I know the owner, and he helped me out when I told him who I was getting lunch for. I tipped him real good for helping a brother out," he said and winked.

"Ah," Jackie said, "touché."

As she cut her salad meticulously, she couldn't help but notice Jermaine staring at her French-manicured hands.

"Do you know you have the most beautiful hands?" he asked.

"Excuse me?" Jackie asked, confused.

"Your hands. You have the most beautiful hands. They're so well manicured and well-kempt. I love that. Unlike my ex-wife's."

"Your ex-wife?" Jackie asked.

"Yes. I'm sorry— I never told you I was divorced? Then again, this is the first time you ever let me say more than two words to you in one sitting."

Jackie smiled. "No, I didn't know that you were divorced. I'm divorced, too," she said, then there was a brief silence.

"Well, I guess that means I'm in good company, then." He lifted up his iced tea and held it in the air. "To freedom."

Jackie followed suit and held her club soda high and repeated the sentiment. "To freedom."

Just then one of the interning executive secretaries, who resembled a freshman in college, stopped at the open door and walked into Jackie's office uninvited.

Jackie looked her up and down and wondered where the rest of her skirt was and why she chose not to button the top three buttons of her pearl-colored silk blouse.

"Excuse me, Attorney Stroud, there is a call for you. Your secretary had to run and asked that I take calls for you. I didn't know you were here having lunch with your mother. I can have Mr. Landow call back."

Jackie grew hot. *Who did this little Pop-Tart think she was, coming in my office unannounced interrupting my meal to insult me?* she thought.

"Thanks for letting me know, Antoinette, but can you take a message for me? I'm in the middle of something right now," Jermaine said, and remained seated.

"Okay, I'll let him know you're busy right now." She then looked Jackie up and down. "Oh, and I'll take you up on your offer and leave my number by your desk phone. Call me sometime, when you're not babysitting your grandmother," she said, and rolled her eyes at Jackie then sashayed out of Jackie's office.

Jackie was so offended that she couldn't even think straight.

"Excuse her, she's new here," Jermaine said. "I believe she's the owner's great-niece, and she has some work to do in the manners department."

Jackie played with her salad for a minute and then asked, "So you asked her for her number?"

Jermaine replied, "Me? No," with a laugh.

Jackie looked at him with a raised brow. She knew how office romances usually began, which was another reason she'd resolved not to get involved in one.

Jermaine shifted in his seat, then pointed to the door. "You don't believe her, do you? That intern? She's lying. I never asked her for her number."

"Get out," Jackie said.

"I would never—"

"Get out!" Jackie yelled, loud enough for people outside her office to hear.

With that, Jermaine arose, gathered his lunch, and left.

Jackie placed her hand on her head, ashamed that she'd ever accepted his offer for lunch . . . ashamed that she ever let him in.

CHAPTER 15

"I'm sorry, what did you say?" the salesman at the hardware store asked Shenita.

"Never mind. Hey"—she leaned into the counter—"I think you're kinda cute. Gotta girlfriend?"

Just then Shenita's cell rang. She peeked and saw it was Danielle.

"Hold on, I gotta get this," she said.

"Hey, girl, what's up?" she asked. An older man passed by in a cart and blew Shenita a kiss, and she waved at him with a fake smile.

Danielle didn't reply on the other end.

Shenita shifted ears. "Hello, Danielle . . . are you there? Can you hear me?"

"I'm here," Danielle finally said.

"What's wrong?" Shenita asked. She could tell by the way Danielle sounded that she was crying.

"I lost my job today."

"Oh, girl, I'm sorry. What happened?"

"And I'm about to lose my place."

"What? Girl, hang tight, I'm about to come over there."

Shenita hung up the phone and told the cute salesman, "I'm going to have to come back another day." She walked away a few feet, returned to him, dug out a business card from her purse, and said, "Here's my number." The salesman retrieved it and just looked at it. Shenita looked him up and down and told him in the best Marilyn Monroe voice she could muster, "Call me sometime," with a wink and then did an about-face with a sashay back to the aisle that got faster as she got closer to the glass doors, and she slipped on her heel on her way out.

Once inside her car, she pulled out her old black book and crossed out *Rule #6 Never Be the First to Give Out Your Phone Number* and said, "Yes!" with a fist pump.

Shenita couldn't believe her ears as she sat on Danielle's black couch listening to her pour her heart out about how she got fired.

"He sexually assaulted you at work?" Shenita asked in shock.

"Almost. Had that pot of coffee not been there, no telling what he would have done to me in that kitchen. Then again, I may have kicked him where the sun don't shine and thrown some of my karate moves on him," Danielle said.

"Girl, what moves?" Shenita asked.

"I've been watching YouTube videos on self-defense. Move over, Jackie Chan," Danielle said, and gave a halfhearted karate chop in the air and lightly laughed.

"Seriously, though, Shenita, the timing couldn't have been any worse. I just got a notice from my landlord; they're about to kick me out of here. I have no idea what I'm going to do." Danielle looked down at her hands folded in her lap.

Shenita placed her hand on Danielle's shoulder and said, "I know it looks rough right now, but everything is going to be all right."

Danielle peeked up at her with watery eyes. "I hear you, Shenita, and I understand what you're saying, but I just don't see *how* it can be done."

"I know. But that's what faith is, Dani. You may not see it right away, but God is going to make a way for you; He's always right on time."

"Yeah, well, I need Him right now," Danielle said. "Did I tell you I was two payments behind on my car note, too? They could repossess it any minute now. The only reason they probably haven't already is because I hide it in the back. If I left it out, it would probably be gone by now."

"I know, Danielle."

"No, you don't know!" Danielle screamed and stood up. "You don't know what it's like to struggle! You don't know what it's like to go through this! You got a great job—you get paid." Danielle sat back down and said in a normal tone, "I used to get paid, before, but now it seems like after I quit so I could be totally sold out to God, all I been doing is struggling. Kinda makes me want to get back on that pole. At least then my bills were paid. God'll just have to understand."

Shenita grabbed Danielle's hand. "You don't mean that, Danielle. This ain't nothing but a test from the enemy. As soon as you give up something from this world in order to truly live for God, the enemy comes to try and steal the Word you received in your heart. You're good ground, Danielle; don't let the Word you received be fallen on stony ground where you receive it but then the cares of this world and lust of other things take it away. You've been doing fine for three years, Dani. The

Lord's been taking care of you for three years. Surely there's something you can do right now, job-wise, that doesn't have you compromising what you believe by selling your soul on that pole."

"But I don't have any skills," Danielle said. "I'm not like you and Jackie. I don't have my degree, barely got my GED, and most non-degreed jobs these days barely pay over minimum wage and that's not enough to cover my car payment and rent. I don't understand, Shenita—I pay my tithes and everything. Why is God not taking care of me? Why am I struggling?"

Knock knock knock.

Danielle looked at the door, wondering who in the world that could be. She hadn't invited anyone else over. Hopefully it wasn't her landlord.

Shenita arose and opened the door.

"Hey, Jackie!" Shenita said. "Dani, I hope it's okay I invited Jackie over, too. You had me worried on the phone, so I figured with the three of us we can really put the devil in his place."

Jackie walked toward Danielle seated on the couch. "Hey, Danielle!"

"Hi, Jackie," Danielle said in a dry tone. She really didn't want Jackie to know all of her personal business, and secretly wished Shenita hadn't called her.

Jackie sat on the matching chair next to the couch, set her white leather Prada bag on the wooden coffee table in front of her, then asked, "So what's up, girl? I heard it was some type of emergency."

Shenita sat on the couch next to Danielle and said, "Well, it *is* an emergency. A spiritual emergency. And I'm glad you came, Jackie, because now we can join forces to put the enemy to shame."

"Well, alrighty then. So what are we praying about?" Jackie asked.

"Nothing!" Danielle said, and folded her arms.

Shenita gave a surprised look. "Well, Danielle is, um, experiencing financial hardship and we're just going to come together and pray that God supplies her needs before it's too late."

"Before it's too late?" Jackie looked over at Danielle.

Shenita paused, then continued, "Yes, before she, uh, loses her place."

"Okay, but don't you have a job?" Jackie asked, perplexed.

"I lost my job today!" Danielle snapped.

"Oh, well, I'm sorry." Jackie cleared her throat. "Sure, we can pray, but may I have some water first? My throat is a little parched."

"Sure, Jackie." Shenita went to the kitchen to prepare Jackie a glass of ice water.

Jackie examined the glass for stains, and when she didn't see any, she drank, while Danielle shot her a disgusted look.

"All right now, let's all stand and pray in agreement," Shenita said.

Jackie and Danielle joined Shenita standing up and they all joined hands.

Shenita began, "Father God, we come to You now in the name of Jesus, giving You all the praise, honor, and glory. We thank You that You are a God of a breakthrough and that You already supply every one of our needs. We join together on behalf of Your daughter Danielle, that she will hold fast to her profession of faith knowing You are faithful Who promised. She will not be weary in well-doing but will remain steadfast in Your Word. You said where two or three are gathered together in Your name that there You are in the midst, so we know that, right now, You are in the midst of this situation. We pray for favor with Danielle's landlord, favor with her future employer, favor with her car's finance company, and we release ministering angels to cause the return for the many years she has sown to come to her suddenly. We join our faith together so she may receive a hundred-fold return blessing right now. In Jesus' name we pray, amen!"

"Amen!" Danielle and Jackie repeated, and Danielle gave Shenita a big hug for her heartfelt prayer.

Jackie sat back on the couch and said, "Danielle," and Danielle turned around. Jackie said, "Come sit," and patted the seat next to her on the couch.

"Now, I know we just prayed and that God hears and answers our prayers when we pray," Jackie said, and Danielle agreed and suspiciously listened to what Jackie had to say. She continued, "He also uses people to be a blessing in our lives and He uses men to give to our bosom."

"Uh-huh," Danielle said, wondering where this was going.

Jackie grabbed her purse from the coffee table and pulled out her checkbook and said, "But first, let me ask you this . . ."

Danielle looked at Jackie as if to say, "What?"

"Do you still tithe regularly? You know there is such a thing as operating under the curse if you don't tithe. That could stop the flow of financial blessings as well."

"Yes, I tithe!" Danielle retorted. "I've been tithing faithfully for the last three years—every single paycheck off the gross! It's not my fault I lost my job!"

"You're right, Danielle," Jackie said. "But it's not God's fault either." Danielle cocked her head to the side as Jackie continued, "Now that I've been made privy to your situation . . . I realize we all, at some point in our lives, could use a handout every now and then."

"Excuse me?" Danielle asked, appalled.

"Well, I shouldn't call it a handout . . . maybe more like a hand up. Just like the automotive industry received their bailout, you can consider this my bailout to you," Jackie said, handing Danielle a check for $2,000.

"Except you don't have to pay me back," Jackie added. "Now, it's not much; I was going to use it to buy a new pair of Christian Louboutins, but the Lord dealt with my heart and I decided to give it to you instead," Jackie explained with a smile.

"Oh, thanks, Jackie," Danielle said, amused as she received the check. Jackie maintained her grin.

"But no, thank you." Danielle ripped the check into small pieces right in front of Jackie's face—"I don't need your bailout"—and threw the shredded check on her lap.

Jackie couldn't believe it. "Here I am being a friend and this is how you repay me?" she asked.

"You weren't being a friend, Jackie Downing, you were being a bank. Once I met your little 'holier than thou' criteria, I was able to qualify for a loan from you. Oh, wait, not a loan— a gift. Not a handout, a hand up."

Jackie was dumbfounded. "No, you didn't," she said.

"Oh yes, I did," Danielle said. "I'd rather have to live in a box than receive anything from you. Unlike everybody else." Danielle looked at Shenita standing near the door with her hand covering her eyes from the whole ordeal. "Unlike *some* people," Danielle said, "my friendship *can't* be bought."

"Danielle, I wasn't trying to buy your friendship," Jackie said in defense. "Lord knows I didn't mean to offend you. I was just trying to help."

"I know you were just trying to help, Jackie, but why don't you help where your services are more needed—like at the local soup kitchen. Oh, but maybe not, because you may get your nails dirty. You wouldn't want to ruin your French manicure, now, would you?"

"Danielle, you got me all wrong." Jackie put her hand on her hip.

"That's okay, Jackie," Shenita chimed in, "I think it may be best that we leave at this point. Danielle's going through a lot right now and our sticking around may not help the situation."

"That's the best thing you've said all day, Shenita Love." Danielle walked them both to the door.

Once she closed the door behind them, Danielle leaned back on it and cried in her hands.

CHAPTER 16

"Knock knock!" Pippa sang at Elijah's doorstep.

She'd decided to stop by there after choir rehearsal. She wondered why she didn't see Elijah that night, since it was the same night as his armor-bearer meeting with the pastor, so she decided to stop by afterward to make sure everything was okay, and just happened to bring a homemade sweet potato pie in case he needed something sweet to brighten up his day.

"Knock knock!" Pippa sang again, this time her voice accompanying a few actual knocks on his door.

Elijah answered the door in a black T-shirt with a picture of Jesus on the cross after He arose and, *He Reigns* in red letters.

"Hey, Pippa, what's up?" Elijah said.

"What's up? What's up is where were you at your armor-bearer meeting today, Mr. O'Toole?"

Elijah looked at her, confused, then replied, "Oh, yeah, I had to miss it today because I'm working on my thesis for my bachelor's degree in education."

"Your bachelor's degree? Praise the Lord!" Pippa said. "Mind if I come in and set this sweet potato pie I made for you on the counter?"

"Sweet potato pie? You made for me? Girl, yeah, come on in—you right on time!" Elijah said. "Pardon my manners," he begged. "I should have let your pretty little self in way before now."

Pippa blushed at the compliment. "Oh, no worries. You'll get used to having me around one day."

"What was that?" Elijah asked, not hearing exactly what she said.

"Oh, nothing," Pippa said, and sashayed in her purple floral dress as she made her way to the kitchen and plopped the pie on the white counter.

"Mind if I warm it up in your oven?" Pippa asked.

"Sure, Pippa, that'd be great. I'm sorry I don't have anything to really offer you, like a drink or anything. I was just here trying to knock out this thesis." He sat on the couch with his laptop on his lap.

"Oh, that's okay. You didn't know to expect me. How's it going?" Pippa asked.

"What was that?" Elijah said, still staring at his laptop.

"I said how's it going? Your thesis . . ."

"Oh, that, it's going okay . . . I guess. Writing was never one of my favorite subjects. Or shall I say, English. I'm more of a math and science kinda guy, so this is a little struggle for me. But God is good and He'll help me through it."

"Let me see it." Pippa wiped her hands with a towel after placing the pie in the oven, sat next to Elijah on the couch, and grabbed his laptop.

She noticed tons of typos on what appeared to already be forty-three typed pages. She corrected the typos and grammatical errors immediately.

"Pippa, you don't have to do that," Elijah said.

"No, I insist, Elijah. I want to." She corrected a few more sentences.

She then got up and retrieved the warmed pie from the oven, cut him a slice, and topped it off with whipped cream she had in her purse.

Elijah grabbed his laptop again and worked on his thesis once more with a puzzled look on his face.

"I told you, I'll take care of it," Pippa said as she brought over his slice of pie and set it on the coffee table next to the couch. She took a forkful then fed it to him. "Mmmm," Elijah said. "This is good; you made that?" he asked with his mouth full.

"I sure did," Pippa said proudly. "My uncle is the head chef at a soul food restaurant in Mississippi, so he taught his youngest niece how to cook."

"Well, like they say in the South, girl, you put your foot in that!" Elijah and Pippa laughed.

"Now why don't you relax, eat the rest of your pie, and let Mama take care of this thesis for you," Pippa said as she grabbed the laptop once again.

"You'd do that for me, Pippa?"

"Definitely. If this is what God has called you to do and if you feel this is your purpose, then of course I want to help. That's what I'm here for," Pippa explained.

"Aw, you know you my girl, right?" Elijah said, and gave her a high five.

"That's right," Pippa sang, "the one and only." They laughed. After a brief pause Pippa asked for clarity, "You mean that?"

"Do I mean what?"

"What you just said . . . that I'm your girl."

"Sure, I mean it," Elijah assured her. "You my girl! You da-bomb-dot-com, lady!"

Pippa cheesed from ear to ear and looked at him, then looked back at his laptop and said quietly to herself, "Yeah, I'm your girl."

She then looked up to heaven and mouthed the words "Thank you, Jesus!" then went back to working on his paper.

Elijah turned on the TV and played video games in between eating pie while Pippa happily worked on the rest of his thesis until she had proofread and edited it in its entirety.

CHAPTER 17

Back home, Shenita dropped her car keys on her gray marble kitchen counter then headed straight to her office.

She logged on to her laptop to check her e-mail, scrolled through the countless Facebook updates from group pages and gospel "spam" letting her know seemingly every upcoming gospel event happening in the next thirty days in the city, until she finally found what she was looking for—a notification from equallyyokedup.com, her Christian dating site, letting her know she'd received an internal e-mail from a possible suitor.

She logged on to her account and immediately checked her e-mail, where the subject line read: *I saw your profile online.* She opened it and read the e-mail: *Hi, Shenita. How are you? I saw your profile online. Nice legs. Maybe we can get together sometime.*

Nice legs? Shenita thought. A couple of the photos she uploaded were full-body shots, one of her in a long skirt, sitting with her legs crossed, and one where she wore black cotton pants, leaning against the wall. She didn't think either picture highlighted her legs at all. *What kind of first e-mail is this? He sounds more like a creep than somebody I would be interested in get-*

ting to know better. Ugh. She clicked on his profile and saw the picture of a shirtless guy wearing shades. *So that explains it. This guy ain't nothing but a bag of flesh himself. How was he even able to be allowed on a so-called Christian dating website looking like that? They may need to redo their screening process,* she concluded.

Shenita checked again for any other e-mails from, Lord knows, someone else. Unfortunately, there were no other communication attempts from anyone.

"Sigh," Shenita said, then put her laptop to sleep and got dressed for bed.

The next day during her first break at One Love Initiative, Shenita, in a cotton gray dress with a thick red leather belt, headed to the kitchen to get a granola bar out of the vending machine. She thought she heard the sound of someone crying and looked in the corner in between the refrigerator and the vending machine and saw Krissy curled up in a chair with tears streaming down her face.

"Krissy?" Shenita asked. "What's wrong?"

"Go away!" she barked.

"Krissy, I'm glad I found you in here." Shenita grabbed a chair from the table, then sat directly in front of her. "I wanted to sincerely apologize for the other day. I shouldn't have acted that way in the meeting. I know in your heart you were only trying to help."

Krissy looked up at her through reddened eyes and didn't respond.

"Will you please forgive me?" Shenita asked.

Krissy nodded while staring at the kitchen floor, then she looked up at Shenita and said, "He called it off."

"He called what off? And who are we talking about?" Shenita asked.

"Richard. My fiancé. He called off the wedding Monday night, and I haven't stopped crying since."

"Oh, Krissy, I'm sorry to hear that." Shenita reached her hand toward Krissy's palm.

Krissy snatched her palm away and retorted, "No, you're not! You're not sorry! You're the reason all this happened in the first place!"

"Excuse me?" Shenita said, confused.

"After our little spat in the office on Monday, I got curious about what you said. You know, about 'lifelong engagement,' so I asked Richard about it. I asked him exactly when did he plan on marrying me. Then we started arguing, and next thing you know he got a call and I looked on his phone and it was his ex from college, and he answered it right in front of me and started talking to her like I wasn't even there, about how he's single now and wanted to hook up. So I got mad and threw his phone out the window and he slapped me and we started fighting and I called the cops and moved out."

Shenita definitely was not expecting all that.

"Oh, Krissy, I'm sorry," she said, and went to hug her.

"Get away from me!" Krissy yelled before Shenita's arms could even reach her.

"Krissy . . . I understand you're upset. But you can't honestly blame me for what happened. There was nothing wrong with your asking about when he planned to solidify your future together, especially if you wanted to know. You had a right to know."

"Yeah, but had I not said anything about it, he wouldn't have gotten mad at me and called everything off."

"But, Krissy, from what you just told me, he was still in communication with his ex. For all you know, he may have already been in a relationship with you and his ex at the same time before now; he could have just been using the argument as an excuse to carry on the relationship with his ex that he already had rekindled."

"But Richard wouldn't do that!" Krissy insisted.

Shenita didn't buy it. "You mean to tell me that until now you didn't suspect he was seeing somebody else? I remember you used to tell me here at work how he would come home late, or be out of town on weekends a lot. Last time I checked, nobody loves their job that much that they're pulling in overtime on weekends. C'mon now, Krissy—don't be naive. He already had plans to end the relationship, and it's better that it ended now than later, because you already had too much invested in it already. You're worth more than that, Krissy."

Never-ending tears flowed down Krissy's face.

"Look, I'm sorry if I came off a bit harsh. I'm not good at this stuff." Shenita arose to leave.

"Don't go," Krissy said. Shenita looked at Krissy and sat back down.

"I don't know how you do it, Shenita."

"Do what?"

"I mean, you're smart. You're beautiful. You can have any man you want, yet you choose to be single."

"Well, I don't know about *choosing*," Shenita said with a slight laugh. "You know what, I take that back, Krissy—you're right. I do choose to be single. I choose to have standards, and I choose not to settle—so I guess that is my choosing to be single. I never looked at it that way."

"I don't like being single. I don't see how you do it," Krissy confessed. "I have to have a man in my life. Someone to live for. I lived for Richard. And it hurts to know that all this time he wasn't even thinking about me," Krissy said and cried again.

Shenita grabbed Krissy and rocked her in her arms. "Shhh, no more of that. No more tears. You're too special to be crying over someone like him." Shenita looked her straight in her ocean-blue eyes. "I'm sure it hurts your heart, but, Krissy, you've got to move on. Trust me, I hear ya, it's not easy being single, but I choose to love myself more than anyone who would not receive and appreciate all the love I have to give."

Krissy held her head down and Shenita lifted her chin and said, "I'm waiting for the right one God has for me and until that day comes that he appears, I'm just going to have to wait." Shenita couldn't believe what she just said, especially after she thought about her incident with the guy at the home-improvement store. *Forgive me, Lord,* Shenita thought.

"You mean God is giving out men?" Krissy asked. Shenita laughed. "Yes, He is, actually, but you know what, the greatest thing is that God is giving out Himself, first, as the one Man Who will love you no matter what and will be there for you no matter what. He's ever faithful, ever loving, and wants more than anything for you to be happy."

"You mean God cares about whether or not I'm happy?" Krissy asked.

"Yes. He does." Shenita said and wiped Krissy's tears, "He cares about everything about you, Krissy, and He knows everything about you. He knows and made every little blond hair on your head. He just wants you to love and trust Him and depend on Him for happiness, instead of some man. And that's how I'm able to be content while single. Instead of giving a man my entire life and then getting upset when that man disappoints, I decided to give my entire life over to God—the one Man Who will never disappoint."

Krissy's tears stopped as she contemplated what she'd just heard.

"Are you gay?" Krissy asked.

"No, I'm not gay." Shenita laughed. "You can trust me on that one."

Shenita dug in her purse and pulled out an invitation card to her church. "Here. If you want to hear more about God's love for you, come to my church. As a matter of fact, meet me there this Sunday and I'll have a seat waiting for you. Will you do that, Krissy?"

Krissy shifted in her seat and finally said, "Sure, that shouldn't be a problem; I'll be there." She glanced at the card, then faced Shenita and said, "Thank you."

"No problem, my sister, no problem."

CHAPTER 18

After waking up on her black couch after a long, hard night, Danielle's back ached, as it wasn't used to not reclining on her regular bed. She had cried herself to sleep the night before and forgot to change into her pajamas or wrap her hair. Her body felt like a hot mess and she also looked like one.

After a huge yawn and stretch, Danielle scratched her eyes and looked around at her surroundings. Everything was the same way she'd left it yesterday, including Jackie's half-empty glass of water on the coffee table.

It was weird for Danielle to wake up on a Wednesday morning and not have a job to report to. While she enjoyed the freedom, her head hurt just thinking about how she was going to pay all her bills.

"C'mon, girl, you can do this," Danielle said out loud to herself as she sat up and dragged herself to the bathroom, showered, and found an old pair of ripped blue jeans and a black T-shirt to wear. She brushed her long jet-black weave in her bathroom mirror until it was straightened out and she even applied pink lip gloss and black eyeliner to hide how she really felt. She figured just because she felt like crap didn't mean she had to look like it, too.

She made her way to the stove and put on a pot of grits for breakfast. As she washed dishes from the night before, she noticed something folded on her counter. She unfolded what looked like money and revealed a one-hundred-dollar bill. Delighted, Danielle figured Shenita must have left it there for her. Even though it couldn't pay half of her bills, it might be enough to cover a light bill. Danielle picked up the one-hundred-dollar bill and kissed it.

Just then her phone rang; it was the finance company calling about her missing car payments. Danielle had to remember where she'd even parked her car last night, as she'd been hiding it for the last two months. She then remembered she'd parked it in the back alley this time, where only residents with an entry card could get inside. She threw the call in voice mail. She didn't want to have to deal with them right now.

She made scrambled eggs, toast, and bacon to go with her grits, then plopped in front of the TV on her couch, about to dig in, when she got another call. No name showed up on her caller ID, so she answered this time.

"Hello."

"Hello, is this Danielle Peterson?"

"Yes."

"Hi, Danielle. This is Regina. I work in the office with Alexis."

Shoot, Danielle thought, as Alexis was her landlord.

"She wanted me to give you a courtesy-call reminder in regard to the notice she delivered to you yesterday. Did you receive it?"

"Yes, I received it," Danielle said gloomily.

"Well, good. She also wanted me to tell you as new management we are definitely enforcing the expectation the notice states, as we currently have a waiting list of prospective tenants. So if you're unable to come up with the full balance of $1,800 by the date stated on the notice, then you will definitely be evicted that day. Do you understand?"

Danielle couldn't believe what she heard on the other end of the phone. *What were they, landlord bullies?* "Yes, ma'am, I mean, Regina," who sounded not a day over eighteen on the phone. "I understand." Next, Danielle heard a click and then a dial tone.

Danielle thought about how Jackie's two-thousand-dollar check sure would have come in handy in this situation. It definitely would have saved the day. But then again, Danielle didn't want Jackie to think that she was her savior and not God, and Danielle was tired of her judging her anyway. God was going to have to help her find a way to come up with this money herself so she didn't end up on the street. He had to make a way. Somehow.

Leaving her breakfast on the table in front of her, Danielle got up and paced the floor. She thought of ideas to make quick cash. *What if I sold stuff on eBay? Nah, I really don't have anything much to sell, not enough to get me $1,800 in nine days.*

Danielle worried even more, then did what she always did when she was worried or nervous—clean. She cleaned off the kitchen counter, then headed to her office and sorted through and trashed old papers that should have been thrown out months ago. She chuckled as she found old songs she had written down, which were supposed to catapult her budding songwriting career that never quite took off. As she went deeper through the stack, she ran into some R & B songs she had written before she got saved three years ago and laughed at some of the lyrics: "Ooh, I want you, baby. I need you now. Come to me, hold me, release me I'm free." She laughed as she remembered that, back then, she thought only a man could free her.

She next thought about the person she had written that song for, an ex named Trey. Though he looked good and kept her satisfied physically, the closer she got to God, the further and further away she drew away from him until he got fed up with her sudden decision to hold out till marriage. He ended up dumping her and cut her off from all the financial benefits she'd received from being his lady, and she was left to fend for herself. She remembered, though, that day she made the commitment to God—she told God that as long as He took care of her needs, she would not look to a man to take care of them for her. She smiled at the thought of old Trey and the times they used to share—the VIP nights of popped champagne every weekend—and look where she was now. Struggling. Unable to pay her bills. *There has got to be another way,* Danielle thought.

Just then a postcard fell out of the stack of papers and onto the floor. It was a photo of Danielle in a black leather Catwoman suit, with her right leg extended and her other leg tightly wrapped around a long silver pole. She had a fierce expression and looked like she meant business. The card had her former stage name on it, Diva D, and was an invitation to join her at Club Xtasy for a "night you will never forget."

Danielle thought about the good old days three years ago.

When she was on that pole, money was never an issue.

Men threw money at her like it was water coming out of a faucet.

There was no recession then; men paid her just to move on that stage and work the pole, and she would get extra tips if she ever came down to rub on a few bald heads of lonely married men looking for some added spice and attention in their lives. She couldn't quite understand how so many men got a kick out of her pole routine each night so much that some of them would hand over half their paychecks while she was fully clothed in costume, doing what some consider an aerial aerobic exercise.

Danielle thought about going back to Xtasy, if not to work there permanently, just for a month—which would be just enough to catch up on all her bills, get her car paid up, and definitely pay her new, unmerciful landlord. She could easily make $300 a night, at a minimum, so working a month would have her set and give her just enough time to find a different, better job. She would work at night, so no one from church would ever know, and it wasn't like she'd be fully exposed or anything, as it wasn't exactly a strip club. She figured she could still maintain her standards onstage and at the same time provide the fantasy for the male patrons.

Danielle picked up the flyer and looked again at the reflection of her former life.

The girl in that picture was so confident, so self-assured; she didn't have a care in the world. Danielle then looked in the small oval mirror on the wall next to her office desk. The girl looking back at her now was so tired, so sad, so broke and beaten-down. She wanted her joy back, her swag back, and if it meant taking this short amount of time to do what she needed to do to take care of what she needed to take care of, then so be it.

God knew her situation, and He definitely would have to understand.

CHAPTER 19

"Shenita, what was that all about?" Jackie asked as they had lunch at their usual spot. Shenita knew Jackie was making reference to their friend Danielle, and her recent outburst when Jackie tried to give her money to pay some of her bills.

"I don't know, girl. She went off on you, but it was probably just pride. She probably just didn't want to feel like a charity case, that's all," Shenita assumed.

"Charity case? I've known that girl two years now and I've known her to be a beautiful, strong, independent woman who can stand on her own two feet, now why would she think I looked at her like a charity case? She was in need and I was just trying to help. Can't a sister help another sister out without getting backlash, goodness."

"I hear ya, and I understand what you're saying, but maybe she didn't know how you felt about it. Your offer to help didn't quite come off the way you just explained it to me now. It sounded more like you were helping the needy when you were talking to her."

"Well, you know what," Jackie said while playing with her tortellini salad, "that's what's wrong with us black women today.

We're so focused on our emotions and other people's perception of us, and our need to want to always *feel* like we're in control, that we don't recognize when someone is just trying to be a blessing. It's like we think people have ulterior motives or something. We act all weird and don't give people a chance and end up missing out!" Jackie vented.

Shenita looked up after taking a bite of her salmon burger and added, "Kinda like how you're doing Jermaine now?"

Jackie shot Shenita a surprised look. "Jermaine? What does anything I just said have to do with Jermaine?"

"You just said it yourself, Jackie—folk don't trust anybody, they think people are up to something. Isn't that why you won't take Jermaine up on his offer and go out with him? I mean, if you're gonna dish it you gotta be able to take it, too—I'm just saying." Shenita sat back and folded her arms.

"Shenita Anita Love . . ."

"Oh, here we go." Shenita knew she was about to hear it anytime Jackie called her by her whole name.

"You are not fair and you know it," Jackie said, pointing her fork at Shenita. "Comparing my situation with Jermaine to a girlfriend not accepting a monetary donation is not a fair comparison. That's like comparing the OJ Simpson case to Jeffrey Dahmer's—it just doesn't make sense."

"Ugh, why'd you have to bring him up?" Shenita said in reference to Dahmer. "I just lost my appetite." Shenita set her burger down.

"Well, I lost mine five minutes ago. The nerve of you, comparing my situation with Jermaine to Danielle!"

"Calm down, chica—it's not that serious. I just think you're being a little hard on him, that's all. You're not even giving him a chance, and you're assuming some things about him that you have no clue whether or not they're correct. Just like you claim Danielle was judging you by saying you were judging her, you're judging him!"

"Well, I never looked at it like that," Jackie said, pondering. "I guess that's a lot of judging going on." The two of them laughed.

"Enough about me, what about you, missy—how's your love life?" Jackie asked.

"Ha! What love life? Hmm, let's see, after nearly making a complete fool of myself at the home-improvement store and then getting approached by some creepy-looking dude online, I'm zero for two at this point in the love department."

"What?" Jackie asked. "Home-improvement store? Since when do you shop there? I thought your idea of home-improvement shopping was a trip to Target."

"I was just trying something different, that's all," Shenita rationalized.

"And online?" Jackie asked. "What are you doing looking for a man online?"

"What's wrong with that? They hang out there, too. I ain't getting any younger. A sister's gotta do what she gotta do . . ."

". . . to get raped," Jackie finished her sentence.

"Aw, Jackie, don't go there. Don't judge me. People meet and marry online all the time."

"Uh, yeah, desperate people!"

"No, no—now that's where you're wrong, my friend. Stats show that over eighty percent of singles tried online dating, and you and I both know with social media more people are initially meeting in cyberspace."

"Well, social media is one thing, because you may actually know the person through mutual friends or something, but an online dating website? Too risky. You're liable to get anything. Folk lie about who they really are and all kinds of crazy stuff."

"Folk lie about who they are on Facebook, too! They got pictures of homes and cars they never lived in or driven before—just trying to impress somebody," Shenita added.

"You're right. Either way it's all bad, folks airing all their personal business online for the world to see. That's why I don't go online much and deactivated my Facebook account."

"Jackie, the reason you deactivated your Facebook account is because you are a social misfit who doesn't have any friends," Shenita assured her.

"I beg your pardon? So I'm being chastised because I believe there are more important things to do than see what somebody ate for dinner or a new picture of someone's child literally growing up in front of my eyes every single day? So little Jimmy started his first day of school, great, but do you have to show me pictures of him with every one of his teachers, all his report cards, what he ate for breakfast, lunch, and dinner? Some people are just so self-absorbed that they feel like everybody wants to look at that stuff every single day. Sheesh."

"You're a mess," Shenita concluded. "If you had kids you would do the same thing."

"Um, no. That's one of the reasons I have no desire to have children at all. Everybody thinks their child is the most beautiful thing on earth. Whatever."

"Girl, I'ma pray for you."

"Please do. And what do you mean, I don't have any friends? You're my friend! Last time I checked you claimed me."

"I . . . don't . . . know about that."

Jackie smacked Shenita on top of her head with a clean napkin.

"Yeah, yeah, I guess," Shenita confessed and laughed. "Oh, and did I tell you my boss is trying to hook me up with her son?"

"Your boss? No, you didn't tell me that."

"Yes, girl, Mrs. Washington is trying to set me up with her son, Christian."

"Well, what's he like and what does he do? Is he cute?" Jackie inquired with a sneaky grin.

"Whoa, Nelly. So far all I know is he's a pediatrician at Open Door Hospital, and I saw his picture, and yes, girl, the man is fine!"

"A fine doctor? This is getting good. Is he saved?"

"Now, that I don't know."

"Aw, c'mon, Shenita!"

"I know, I know; it's the most important thing to find out. The crazy thing is I asked his mom and *she* couldn't tell me. She was saying something about she thinks he may have gotten saved but she's not sure."

"Not sure?" Jackie asked, "Then my next question is . . . is *she* saved? How you gon' bring a child in the world and now they're good and grown and you not even know if he's saved yet? Did she even know what you meant when you said the word?"

"Yeah, well she said she and her husband were saved. Who knows, and you're right, Jackie—she must not be too saved herself if she doesn't know if her son is. Or maybe she missed that part in the Bible where it says, *Train up a child in the way he should go.* But my question is, how you gon' name your child Christian and you not make sure he becomes one? Was he ever christened as a baby?"

"Was he ever baptized?" Jackie added.

They cracked up laughing.

"Shenita, girl, I needed this laugh today. Thanks for agreeing to join me for lunch," Jackie said.

"No problem, sis. I needed the laugh, too."

"All jokes aside, and this is me speaking to you heart-to-heart now, I think you should go out with Christian," Jackie said.

"What?"

"I'm serious. Look at the last couple guys you been out with."

"How long ago was that?" Shenita shot at her.

"A while ago, but still . . . they were supposedly saved men and still tried to get in your pants. Maybe this guy's a gentleman. You never know until you give it a try."

"I don't know, Jackie."

"One date won't hurt, Shenita, goodness, you make things so difficult sometimes!"

"Look who's talking! All right, then, here's the deal. I'll agree to go on a date with Christian, but only if you agree to go out with Jermaine."

"But, Shenita . . ."

"No buts! You say I'm not giving this man a chance, and you're not giving Jermaine a chance, so now we both need to get off our stubborn hineys and go out with these good-looking, seemingly decent men and find out for ourselves if they're really crazy or not."

Jackie and Shenita laughed.

"Okay, girl, you got yourself a deal," Jackie said, and they pinky-swore on it.

As Shenita retreated to her car, she pulled her little black book out of her black leather duffel bag and crossed out *Rule #2 Never Date a Man Who's Not Saved,* in reference to her upcoming date with Christian.

CHAPTER 20

The men dispersed from the men's Bible study at New Life Tabernacle Saving Grace Church, which took place once a month on Wednesday night in the smaller chapel, while the women normally met for Bible study with the First Lady in the main sanctuary.

Ten minutes before service let out for the women, Shenita snuck out and swung her ride around to the chapel side, got out of the car still in her gray dress from earlier and retied the black string tie on her four-inch stiletto heels, stepped out of the car, took off her dark brown Paris Hilton–type shades, and walked toward the chapel entrance as the men emerged.

"Okay, Lord, the men just got out of service—I thank you for favor with God and a man," Shenita whispered to herself.

At first she couldn't get a good glimpse of the men exiting until she got close . . . then she zeroed in on a handsome, dark-chocolate-complexioned man in a gray suit who looked her age and had high cheekbones that were out of this world. She had never seen cheekbones so chiseled in her life! He almost looked like he belonged on TV—on a soap opera, not a reality show.

After zeroing in on her subject, she held her opened silver clutch purse close to her chest and then walked as if she was headed inside, but as she got closer to her target she bumped him "accidentally" and all the contents fell out of her purse.

"Oh, I am so sorry!" Shenita said apologetically as she kneeled to pick up her cell, wallet, and small red lipstick case, while keeping her eyes on the handsome church brother.

The kind stranger returned her glance and smiled in her eyes. "Oh, that's okay. I didn't see you; however, I don't know how that was possible."

The two locked eyes, and Shenita felt like she had died and gone to heaven.

"Name's Gerard, Gerard Braxton." He extended his hand.

"I'm Shenita, Shenita Love," Shenita said, shaking his hand as he flirted with her hazel eyes, compliments of Lenscrafters.

"Gerard! Honey, are you ready to go?" a lady yelled from a black Jimmy that pulled up directly in front of the chapel. "I have the turkey in the oven and don't want it to burn, baby," she said sweetly.

Shenita looked and saw a light-skinned woman with dyed blond hair and bright red lipstick lovingly eye her husband and then give Shenita a menacing glare.

Shenita picked up all that had fallen out of her purse, then glanced at Gerard's left hand and spotted the gold wedding band—five minutes too late.

Shoot, she said to herself. She couldn't believe she had broken the number-one rule in her man search—always check the ring finger!

Gerard rushed, stumbling to his honey's car, and didn't look back. "Coming, dear!" he said.

Shenita arose, straightened her dress, plopped on her shades, and returned to her car, feeling just like the turkey the Braxtons were having for dinner.

CHAPTER 21

House music blared inside the club and blue neon strobe lights perused the hungry crowd, comprised mostly of men, in the midst of darkness. Drinks were served by attractive women in red miniskirts, four-inch stilettos, black fishnet stockings, and white low-cut tees that read *Xtasy* across the chest. Men from all walks of life sat on the edge of their seats at small square tables. Some heads were turned toward one of four poles in each corner, where scantily clad women of different shades danced, swinging their long hair incessantly, while others zeroed in on the dancer on the large center stage, the main attraction, who was decked out in a solid-gold blinged-out costume as she worked her magic on the crowd with the pole as her playground.

It was unusually crowded for a Wednesday night, partly because the owner had decided to do two-for-one drink specials upon hearing the news that his club was Detroit's #1 entertainment spot for the third year in a row. Sparks, the owner—seated at a reserved corner booth with a woman on each arm, both of whom snuggled against his large frame and almost hid underneath his full-length brown sable coat—was feeling good that night and felt the need to celebrate.

"Another round on me!" he said in his husky voice, chewing on the unlit Montecristo cigar that rested on the side of his mouth. His lips were as dark as black licorice and his wide grin was as bright as the moon. "For e'rybody!" he added with a hearty laugh.

Folks nearby cheered as they prepared to receive their complimentary round of drinks—the third time that night. Sparks's two female guests laughed; the one to his right licked his cheek.

In the midst of his own personal entertainment, Sparks got distracted by an angelic sight that suddenly appeared in front of him wearing a white, off-the-shoulder silk blouse, tan suede pants, which complimented her thick curves, and matching fringe cowboy boots. Her hair was long in black layers, her makeup was flawless, her earrings were long and silver, touching the top of her shoulders, and her facial expression was that of an innocent, scared child.

"Well, well, well!" Sparks said, looking Danielle up and down. "Look what the cat dragged in!"

"It's nice to see you too, Sparks," Danielle said.

Sparks shooed his women from his side and rose to give Danielle a hug.

"Welcome, welcome, welcome!" he said, his breath reeking with alcohol.

"I see you insist on talking in threes," Danielle said, barely returning his embrace.

"And I see you haven't lost that little attitude of yours, Danielle. You mean to tell me all that shouting over there at that church didn't do you any good?" Sparks said. He remembered that part of the reason she, one of his highest-grossing pole professionals, left him after working at Xtasy for over two years was because she said she'd found the Lord.

"So what brings you here?" Sparks removed his cigar. "You come to pass out some tracts? Now, I don't allow any Holy Rollers inside my establishment to harass my good-paying customers with tracts and *Watchtowers*. What are you, Jehovah's Witness?"

"No, I'm not Jehovah's Witness," Danielle said dryly, "I'm a Christian."

"Oh yeah, you're Christian now. Well, uh, next time you see him tell Chris I said hello," he said with a boisterous laugh, and the two women seated at the booth he'd abandoned laughed out loud at his poor attempt at a joke.

"Very funny, Sparks," Danielle replied, then decided to cut right to the chase. "Sparks, I need a job."

"You need a what?"

"I need a job," Danielle pleaded.

"You mean you got the nerve to come back to me for a job after you left me cold talking about you done found God. What happened, did you lose Him again?"

"No, I just need a job here temporarily—to get me back on my feet."

Sparks folded his arms and stared at Danielle. He then snickered, looked over at his two female companions, took two steps toward Danielle, and asked, while blowing hot breath, "Why?"

Danielle shifted her face to the side then took two steps back, and said, "I need the money. I need it now or I'm gonna get kicked out of my apartment. By the way, I need a two-thousand-dollar signing bonus to start," she said with her hand out.

"Signing bonus? Girl, now have you lost your ever-loving mind? What do I look like, a bank?"

"No," Danielle said sweetly, then took two steps toward him and caressed his right ear with her hand. "You look like my Sparky Sugar Bear."

Sparks chuckled as he reminisced on how Danielle used to call him her Sparky Sugar Bear, especially during their alone time, when she would pole-dance for him privately in the VIP room.

"Girl, you are something else." Sparks said. "How soon can you start?"

"As soon as you need me, Sparky."

"All right, then—the crowd is heavy tonight because of the celebration, but I'm gonna need it to be bumping again real soon to keep up the momentum, so can you start tomorrow night?"

"You got it, Sugar Bear," Danielle said, smiling at him.

Sparks reached into his pocket and pulled out a wad of cash in a solid-gold money clip and peeled off two grand.

"Here, take this under the table, but under one condition."

Danielle swallowed hard for fear that she'd played up her feminine wiles a little too much and might be invited to the VIP room to "earn" her pay another way.

"Yes?" Danielle asked.

"A kiss . . . on the cheek." He pointed to his left cheek.

Danielle exhaled and planted a soft kiss on his left cheek, and he then stuffed the cash in her back pocket.

She hugged him and said, "Thanks, Sparky, I won't let you down. I'll be here tomorrow night. I still have my costumes and I remember my routines; Diva D is back!"

CHAPTER 22

Knock knock.

Shenita knocked on her boss's open door on Thursday morning, hoping she hadn't interrupted her. Mrs. Washington appeared to be in deep thought while staring at her computer. Shenita knew her boss wouldn't mind the brief disruption, though, especially since their company kindly adhered to an open-door policy, except this time it wasn't all about company business.

"Mrs. Washington."

Vivian Washington appeared startled as she snapped back into reality and peeked at the door.

"Yes? Oh, hi, Shenita. How are you this morning?" she asked in a chipper tone.

"I'm fine," Shenita said, then walked toward Mrs. Washington's desk, coffee and newspaper in hand. "I made you some coffee this morning, straight black—just like you like it, and oh, here's today's *Wall Street Journal*." Shenita neatly placed the cup of coffee and newspaper right next to each other. "I finished it and figured you may want to read it as well."

"Why, thank you, Shenita—aren't you heaven-sent this morning."

Pleased, Shenita folded her hands in front of her black-and-white tweed skirt and said, "Thank you. By the way, I'm still working on that proposal for you regarding the new community center. I'm on pace to have it for you next week instead of three weeks from now, to give you enough time to peruse it and suggest any changes so that the finished proposal for your boss will be done early."

"Well, haven't you been just the busy bee lately. Thank you so much, Shenita, I'm going to put your bid in with my boss for that raise," Mrs. Washington said with eyes piercing through her prescription glasses as she prepared to jot down her agenda for the day.

Shenita helped herself to a seat across from her boss and said, "Well, actually, it'd be nice if you could put my bid in somewhere else as well."

Mrs. Washington removed her glasses and sat back.

"With your son," Shenita clarified.

"Oh, why yes! Yes! Definitely. So I see you finally came around. I told you he was a looker, and when you meet him you'll see exactly how charming he is. He reminds me so much of his father."

"I'm sure he's very charming," Shenita said. "Oh, and I would greatly appreciate it if you gave him this." Shenita handed her boss her phone number.

"I'll take that," Mrs. Washington said, and took the folded piece of paper. "And I'll one-up ya." She hit a button on the office phone and next thing Shenita knew, a male voice was on speaker.

"Hello."

"Hello, my son," Mrs. Washington said excitedly.

"Hi, Mom. What's going on, is everything okay?"

"Everything's fine. Look, I know I don't usually call during working hours, but I have someone I'd like you to meet. Her name is Shenita Love and she is my favorite employee. Say hi!"

Shenita was so embarrassed. She couldn't believe her boss had put her on Front Street like this. *I'm gonna get that Jackie*, Shenita thought.

"Uh, hello," a confused male voice said.

Shenita remained seated and didn't say anything. Mrs. Washington urged her to reply. Shenita leaned in toward the speaker and said, "Hi," then quickly sat back in her seat.

"Mom, I don't have much time to speak right now. I'm about to prep for surgery. I have to go," replied Christian.

"Okay, son. I'm sorry, I didn't know you were working right now. Shenita gave me her number to give to you, so I'll text it to you, okay?"

Can someone just bury me now, please, Shenita thought. She wanted to go hide her face in the sand.

"That's fine, Mom; thanks." He hung up the line.

"And there you have it. Now, wasn't that easy as pie?" Mrs. Washington said. "He'll call you and you two kids can go out. I'm so excited; I've got to call Stanley."

"I have to get back to work." Shenita rose and slowly backed her way to the door. "Gotta get back to finishing up that proposal," she said with a concocted grin.

"Oh, okay. That's my Shenita—always a hard worker. That's what I love about you, and I'm sure my son will love that about you as well. You made my day, girl! Thanks so much for stopping in. I finally can look forward to having some good-looking grandkids—smart ones, too," Mrs. Washington said with a wink.

Oh, God, what have I done? Shenita thought as she left Mrs. Washington's office. She headed back to her own office, shut the door, and rested her head facedown on her computer keyboard.

CHAPTER 23

"So, based on my presentation and my preceding projections," Jackie stated, in her black two-piece pantsuit, "our law firm is on pace to become Southeast Michigan's largest-grossing family-law firm, and in most cases that is mainly due to my fellow hardworking attorneys, team members, and support staff, who make it possible for us to do our jobs and focus on pleasing our clients—which is our top priority. We all know, when the client is pleased, we all are pleased," Jackie said, concluding her PowerPoint presentation.

"And our pockets are pleased," Jermaine added, and his fellow suited male and female colleagues laughed.

Everyone clapped at the conclusion of Jackie's presentation. She was on top of the world, and she knew it. Her boss, an older white gentleman, approached her, tapped her on her shoulder, and said, "Wonderful job, Jacqueline. Excellent!"

"Thank you so much," Jackie replied, stuffing her presentation into her black leather briefcase.

Everyone left the room except Jermaine, who slowly made his way to the exit until Jackie stopped him.

"Jermaine, can you hold back a second?" Jackie asked.

Jermaine backed up, turned around, and headed her way. "Why, certainly," he said with a sly grin.

"You know, I've about had it up to here with your wise-cracks during my presentations, mister," Jackie said sternly.

"What did I do? I was just trying to break the ice. Your meetings are always so stiff; I was just trying to spice it up a bit."

"Yeah, well, you're going to have to work on that because the only thing I like spicy is my food. Dinner at my place tomorrow night?"

Jermaine did a double take. "What did you just ask me?"

Just then Antoinette, the intern, walked inside the conference room with a note.

As she bounced her way inside, Jackie couldn't help but notice, once again, her miniskirt, which was way too short for an office setting, and her extremely low V-neck blouse.

"Oh, there you are," Antoinette said, stopping right in front of Jermaine, whose eyes immediately zoomed in on Antoinette's chest.

"I've been looking all over this office for you," Antoinette said, out of breath. "Mr. Landow called again—he said it's very important. He said it's about money and that it's about time you returned his call."

Antoinette threw her long auburn hair back and said, "Remember him? He called the other day when you were having lunch with her." She looked over at Jackie, who stood eyeing her with folded arms. Jermaine remained silent and kept staring.

"Jermaine, I'm up here," Antoinette said, and smiled while pointing to her eyes. "Can you hear me? Is this mic on?"

"What? Oh, yeah, girl, I hear you. Call Mr. Landow back. Right away; pronto—sure thing," He grabbed the note from Antoinette.

"Okay, great. It's good to see you." She batted her fake eyelashes. "I'm still waiting for you to call me. I don't have any plans for tomorrow night. Bye." Antoinette blew him a kiss, then sashayed out of the conference room with Jermaine's eyes following her out the door. After a few seconds Jermaine snapped back to reality, then said to Jackie, "I'm sorry, what were you saying, Antoinette? I mean, Jackie?"

"Nothing," Jackie said. She gathered the rest of her things and stormed out of the conference room, leaving Jermaine behind, clueless.

CHAPTER 24

After positioning Mrs. Eagleman's head comfortably in her twin bed at the nursing home as she was already snoring, Pippa fluffed her pillow and said, "There ya go, Mrs. Eagleman, nice and comfy," then made her way to her car to eat her bagged lunch and picked up her cell to call her new boo during her half-hour lunch break.

After four rings a familiar male voice answered, "Hello."

"Hi, Elijah, how are you today?" Pippa asked.

"May I ask who I'm speaking with?"

"It's me, Pippa, your *girl*."

"Oh, hey, Pippa. How are you, girl? I have to add your number to my phone. Sorry about that," he said.

"Oh, that's okay, honey. I'm fine, how are you?"

"I'm doing real good. Hey, can I call you back a little later? They're calling me in for a meeting here at the job."

"Oh, I'm sorry, Elijah, I thought I synchronized our lunches." Pippa checked her watch.

"No, you're fine. I had to take a late lunch today. But I'll talk to you later, okay?"

"Okay. Bye," Pippa said cheerily.

"Bye." He hung up.

Pippa thought of a brilliant idea—she pulled down her car visor to reveal the mirror and said, "He just works so hard sometimes; this should brighten his day," and she put on a fresh coat of Vaseline with her finger, smoothed some on her teeth, held her cell phone up, and snapped a photo of herself smiling. She was excited that she had just gotten her hair done last night, and that her press-and-curl mushroom style was still intact. She figured sharing a photo of herself would be the perfect remedy for Elijah's hectic workday.

After taking seven shots, she decided on the best one and texted it to him with the message *Sending a smile your way.* She took a few bites of her double-decker BLT sandwich and scarfed down a set of Twinkies. After still not receiving a text response, Pippa decided to give him a quick call just to make sure he'd received it okay.

After one ring she got his voice mail.

"Hi, Elijah. It's Pippa—your girl. Just wanted to make sure you received my picture okay. I'm smiling real big in it just for you, because you make me happy, man of God. Thank you! Have a great day!" She hung up, held her cell to her chest, and sighed.

"Thank you, Lord, for sending me my Boaz," she said as she logged on to her Facebook account. She looked for Elijah's page but for some reason couldn't find it. "It must be this stupid phone; I have to get another one," Pippa said as she remembered logging on to his page just last week to check on him and write a nice note on his wall. But now for some reason his name wouldn't even come up as she searched for him. "Oh well, that's okay," Pippa said out loud to herself, "I can still do this," and with that she changed her Facebook relationship status from "Single" to "In a relationship."

Within minutes of changing her status, Pippa received countless likes and "Hooray," "God is good," "You go girl," "Congrats!" and "Be sure and invite me to the wedding!" from all kinds of female friends and associates. Pippa leaned back in the gray cloth seat of her white Taurus, closed her eyes for a quick ten-minute nap, and slept like a baby.

CHAPTER 25

Not feeling up to lunch outside the office today, Shenita stayed inside and ate at her desk in between checking e-mails from colleagues and making sure she was on task for current and future projects. While she was deleting old e-mails her cell rang. She saw it was Danielle and answered.

"Hey, girl, so glad to hear from you, how are you doing?"

"Girl, I am wonderful!" Danielle replied.

"Wonderful? Well, praise God," Shenita said, confused at first, because she remembered the last time she talked to her friend she was behind on her bills, about to get thrown out of her place, and copped an attitude with Jackie for trying to help.

"Yes, girl, I just paid up my rent and got a new job—God is good!"

"Wow! Well, amen, God indeed *is* good—He moves suddenly, I see. Where ya working?"

Danielle paused and said, "Oh, in the service industry."

"Cool. You're a waitress?"

"Kind of. You could call it that. I definitely have to deliver every night and will have to be on my feet the entire time."

"Sweet. That's awesome, Dani, I'm happy for you!"

"I'm happy too, girlie. God is so faithful, and He never lets me down. More than anything, He knows my heart and He always makes a way out of no way."

"That's right; you preaching, girl. Pass the offering plate, I need to sow some seed into your mi-neh-stry." They laughed.

"I don't know about all that," Danielle said. "So how are you?"

"Well, you know how it is around here. Nothing's changed. I may be up for another raise soon," Shenita said.

"That's great!"

"Thanks, but as far as the love department, I feel like I've been demoted."

"What happened?"

"Well, I can't explain too much in detail here at work, just pray for ya girl, that's all—I'll tell you the rest later."

"Okay, well, that I will do, chica. Remember, our God is a big God—He can do everything but fail, and the man out there He has for you is for you, you better believe it."

"I know, I know," Shenita said.

After work Shenita went straight home this time.

She had been so embarrassed earlier today by Mrs. Washington and was so disheartened by the lack of fuel in her love search that she decided to just go straight home and turn in earlier than usual.

Once home, Shenita plopped her keys on the marble counter, slipped off her black patent-leather heels, grabbed her Mac from the coffee table, and sank onto the couch. She figured before she went to bed she might as well check equallyyokedup.com first to see if she had any potential suitors.

Maybe she could get *some* good news to brighten her gloomy, embarrassing day.

When she first logged on she saw that the creepy dude with the leg obsession had sent her a brief questionnaire wanting to get to know her better. *Didn't he get the hint when I didn't respond to his e-mail?* Shenita x-ed out his request and deleted his profile from her page.

She next looked in the upper-left corner and saw she had two new matches. One was from a man who was forty-four years old but looked sixty-seven. He looked like he had spent his entire life on drugs or smoking weed based on his black lips and tired, worn-out, wrinkled face. His profile picture didn't even look happy; he actually looked kinda mean. Underneath his profile she saw he'd sent her a quick note that read, "Your profile made me smile. Let's go out." *Um, no,* Shenita thought. He looked more like he could be her grandfather rather than some man trying to take her out on a date. *This man must be lying about his age,* Shenita concluded and hit Delete.

The next supposed match was from a man named Kyle, who actually looked kinda cute. He wore a yellow polo, was light-skinned, and had a baby face with chubby cheeks and a wide smile showing off his single dimple.

His profile said he was thirty-six and that he worked as a veterinarian. *Decent job,* Shenita thought. As she scrolled through his pictures she saw that they were mainly taken outdoors on a camping trip, or while at work. There was one picture taken from what looked like his room, and he had a birdcage next to him with a little brown-and-gray bird inside and appeared to be happily feeding it. *Aw, how cute, he has a pet bird,* Shenita thought. She concluded he must be passionate about animals, since he was a veterinarian and had a pet. She also concluded that he must be very loving, with a soft heart, as he looked so attentive toward his little bird.

As she read his profile he revealed that some of his favorite activities included going to church, spending time with family, spending time outdoors, and going to the movies. *Kinda boring,* Shenita thought, but decided to keep reading. He also noted on his profile that he was looking for a woman who was fun, loyal, and loving.

That's easy enough, Shenita thought with interest. Shenita was big on loyalty, so she knew she fit the bill for that. His profile almost made her want to send him a message or a quick note, but then she quickly thought that gesture might give the appearance of her pursuing him first. She didn't want to appear out of order. *Then again, isn't that what online dating is supposed to be all about,* her "other self" rationalized, *meeting and interacting with new people to ultimately find your soul mate?* Surely she couldn't allow her own reservations and shyness to once again keep her from the love she deserved.

Shenita peeked at Kyle's profile picture again and saw that there was a blinking signal above it, indicating that he was online now and available to chat.

I can IM him! Shenita figured that would be painless and an ideal way to break the ice.

Hi, Shenita IM'd.

After what felt like eternity but was actually only two minutes, Shenita received a response.

Hello. How are you?

Great, he's initiating continued conversation, Shenita thought. *This is good.*

I'm fine. How are you, handsome? Shenita typed, then wondered if she was being too forward with her compliment.

She didn't want to come off as easy. *Oh, what the hey,* Shenita thought, and sent the message.

Thank you. That made my day, he replied. *I'm doing very well. Here just feeding my bird. I have Bible study tonight and may attend a little later this evening. Do you read the Bible?*

Huh? Shenita thought, then felt she might as well just go with the flow . . .

Yes, I read the Bible—every day.

Great. Me too. What is your favorite scripture?

After thinking for a bit, Shenita typed, *Romans 5:8.*

That's a great scripture, and a great reminder of God's love for us.

Great. Shenita replied, though she was really irritated that he used the word *great* so much.

She was also confused as to whether or not their online interaction was a way for them to get to know each other better to possibly one day date each other, or if it was a precursor to his Bible-study lesson tonight and he wanted to get a head start on some good notes and good scriptures for class. She wasn't sure. For the record, Shenita had had her fair share of Bible-study lessons from male friends that led nowhere other than to a "God bless you, Sister Shenita" type of relationship—she was ready for a little something more this time.

Hey. I see that we live in the same city, Kyle typed. *Do you have any plans for tomorrow night? Maybe we can catch a movie. I'd love to get to know you better in person. I'm not good with online chat.*

Now you're talking, Shenita thought.

Then again, she wondered if he was moving a little too fast. The disclosure on the dating site suggested talking on the phone first before accepting an in-person date invitation.

There I go, listening to rules again, Shenita thought, then concluded that life was too short and that she'd already wasted thirty-five years of her life only to end up with no husband and no kids yet, so she might as well take a risk to see if something good came out of it.

If you don't mind, he typed while awaiting her reply.

Aw, he must be a little shy, Shenita thought, then purposely waited thirty more seconds before responding.

Sure! Let's catch a movie. However, would you mind if I meet you there instead of your coming to pick me up? Shenita figured it was best to be safe.

That would be fine, Kyle typed, then added, *How about this— we have dinner first and watch the movie afterward. That way we can dialogue over a meal and I can get to know you better before we partake of the theatrical entertainment.*

Theatrical entertainment? Was this guy a nerd or just trying to be funny? Shenita wondered, based on his sentence structure in what was supposed to be an informal chat. Even if he was a nerd, she didn't mind. They say nerds make the best husbands: they make good money, have decent jobs, and won't leave you for another woman, because they'll be too busy reading their latest comic book collection instead of trying to figure how to dip out on you, or too busy handpicking the best mutual fund instead of coming up with creative ways to hide the latest lipstick stain on their collar.

Shenita had had her fair share of players, both in and out of the church; maybe it was time for her to slow down a little bit—even if it meant going out with a nerd. Besides, she just might like him.

Sounds good, Kyle.

They chose a restaurant and decided to meet there at 7 p.m. tomorrow evening, which gave her at least a couple of hours after work to get all dressed and dolled up for her date.

"Sweet!" Shenita said, and had grabbed her cell to call her bestie, RayShawn, when it rang before she could even dial.

"Oh, Lord, it's Pippa," Shenita said after checking caller ID and seeing her cheese grin on the screen.

"Hello," she answered.

"Hi, Shenita!" Pippa said like a country bumpkin.

"Hi, Pippa; how are you?" Shenita said, imitating her jubilance.

"I'm fantastic! Have you heard the news?"

"What news? You got picked to lead a song in the choir?"

"No, but that would be nice," Pippa replied, briefly contemplating. "But that's not it. You haven't checked your Facebook page lately?"

Shenita thought about it and remembered that she hadn't checked her page yet today. What had become an obsessive daily ritual was quickly being replaced with a certain matchmaking site that gave her hope in finding lifelong love. She had no more time for "frivolous banter," as Jackie called it, with the local commoners. Besides, for Shenita, having a Facebook account had never amounted to anything but the ability to find out who got married and just had a baby, stay connected with out-of-town relatives, secretly spy on her fast teenage cousin to make sure her latest bathroom photo was fairly decent, and catching up with friends from ten years ago, half of whom were left in the past for a reason. Equallyyokedup.com was slowly but surely beginning to take up most of her time now.

"No, girl, I haven't checked Facebook today. Not yet," Shenita said, then logged in to her account as Pippa spoke.

Once on her page, Shenita clicked on to Pippa's page, and you would think Pippa was a celebrity with how many likes and comments flooded her page. Upon a second look, Shenita noticed that all the buzz was about Pippa's relationship status change, which had gone from "Single" to "In a relationship." So far there were over 102 likes; Pippa only had 225 friends. *Goodness!* Shenita thought.

"In a relationship? Good for you, Pippa. When did this happen?" Shenita asked as she added the 103rd like to her page. "And who's the lucky gentleman?"

"You know him," Pippa said, on the other end of the phone line, setting her hair in pink sponge rollers as she prepared for bed.

"I do?" Shenita asked, as she tried to figure out who in the world Pippa could be speaking of. It had been almost a week since she last met up with Pippa for her birthday dinner and Shenita didn't remember her saying anything about even thinking about dating anyone there. Maybe she met someone at the old-school dance club that she hadn't told her about. Then again, not Pippa. He would have to be good and saved for her to even consider him. Shenita had no clue who she could be talking about.

"You do—he's handsome, and sweet, and loves the Lord with all his heart, mind, soul, and strength!"

"Does he go to our church?" Shenita asked.

"He sure does; he serves very close with Pastor, actually."

Shenita was stumped. Then she had a passing thought. *It couldn't be—*

"Elijah O'Toole!" Pippa squealed.

"Elijah?" Shenita asked in shock, hoping Pippa didn't catch on that her tone revealed disbelief rather than sheer excitement for her.

"Yes, Elijah. God has blessed me with my Boaz after all these years. God is faithful!"

"When did this happen?" Shenita asked. The last thing Shenita remembered was Elijah running away from Pippa after service on Sunday, claiming his mother was calling him.

Pippa thought for a minute. "This week! He claimed me this week, a couple days ago, actually."

"So you two are dating now?" Shenita asked. She still couldn't believe it.

"Yes, ma'am. After being just friends for seven years at church, God opened his eyes of understanding this past Wednesday and Elijah claimed me as his good thing! You know seven is the number of completion, right? So in this seventh year the friendship phase is complete and now we're dating!" Pippa said.

"Really?" Shenita asked, still puzzled. "So he told you, after seven years of knowing you from church, that you're the one?"

"Well, to be exact, he told me that I was his girl," Pippa said reassuringly.

"Did he tell you that you were his girl, or that he wanted you to *be* his girl—or his woman? Did he come out and say he thought you two should date?"

"Yes, Shenita. He said I was his girl and that there is none other. We're dating! I'm so excited! Can you come with me to go pick out a dress?"

"A dress? For what? You going out with him this weekend?"

"No, for the wedding, silly! It's only a matter of time now before the next practical step. We've already known each other for seven years, so I figure we date now and after a few more weeks he should propose. I may have to tell him I need at least six months to plan the wedding, though. Or maybe I can pull it off in four? Oh, I'm going to be so cute in my wedding dress! I'm so excited; I'm about to have the life I've always dreamed of! I'm getting married!" Pippa squealed.

Shenita held her cell away from her ear and just looked at it. *This girl got some screws loose,* she thought.

"Well . . . I don't know what to say, Pippa. I'm happy for you, I guess," Shenita said, massaging her temples.

"Thank you, honey boo boo!" Pippa sang. "See what happens when you're faithful to God? When you're faithful to God, He'll be faithful to you!"

"Right," Shenita said. "Look, Pippa, I've gotta go. I've gotta check something online. There's this dating website I'm exploring right now. Who knows, if I get hooked up maybe I can come to your wedding with a date," Shenita said sarcastically.

"Dating website? Oh, no, Shenita—that's not God. Dating websites are the devil."

"Well, it's supposed to be a Christian dating website." Shenita reasoned.

"Either way, it's still the devil. Satan is in charge of those things. God is the author of faith, while Satan is the author of fear, and only people who are afraid God won't answer their prayers use dating websites. You don't need to do that," Pippa assured her. "You're too pretty and too anointed for that. Look at me; I didn't have to use a dating website and God brought my Boaz to me. And Elijah loves me naturally, too. I don't need all that Jezebel makeup and hair weave; he loves me just the way I am. That's how it'll be for you, too, Shenita—you just wait and see."

Shenita couldn't believe what she'd just heard—this woman and her made-up boyfriend. Elijah probably didn't even know Pippa had claimed him as her Boaz to the entire world. Shenita pulled up Elijah's Facebook page and saw barely any activity. He hadn't changed his relationship status at all and there were no pictures of the two of them on either of their pages.

"Are you sure you and Elijah are dating now?" Shenita asked. She'd hate to be the one to burst Pippa's little overly inflated bubble.

"Yes, girl, I'm as sure as Sampson is strong," Pippa declared.

"Oh, okay. Well, if you're happy, then I'm happy for you," Shenita said, taking the safe route.

"Thanks, Shenita. And stay off of those dating websites. God did it for me and He'll do the same thing for you. Hallelujah!"

"Amen, praise the Lord," Shenita said dryly. "Bye, girl."

Shenita hadn't heard Pippa that excited in a long time—and that girl could get pretty excited. *Maybe she's right,* Shenita thought. *Maybe my messing with this Christian dating website is indeed a waste of time.*

Shenita then called RayShawn, the person she'd meant to call in the first place.

"Speak to me," RayShawn answered while placing fresh cinnamon cider roses on the center of his white-clothed dining room table.

"Hey, Ray Ray," Shenita said.

"Why, hello, Queen. How are you today?" RayShawn asked with his cell stuck to his shoulder as he set the table with new china.

"I'm okay," Shenita said sullenly.

"What's wrong, Love?"

"Nothing, I guess. Well, maybe there is something wrong. Since I last talked to you I took your advice and went online on a Christian dating website to get hooked up."

"Excellent! Go get 'em, tigress!" RayShawn said with a growl.

"Yeah, well, I haven't really had any cool matches, except this one guy who seems pretty nice; we're supposed to meet for dinner and a movie tomorrow night."

"Checkmate! You go, girl!"

"Yeah, well . . ."

"Well what?"

"I don't know, Ray Ray. I'm starting to have doubts. I've been putting myself out there this week and ended up flat on my face. And now with this website thing. Pippa said going on a dating website is the devil and that it means you don't have any faith."

"Pippa? Since when did you start listening to that little pip-squeak? Do she got a man?"

"Kinda," Shenita said, not sure if Pippa's made-up relationship counted.

"Kinda? Either she got a man or she don't, now do she got a man?" RayShawn asked again with his hand on his hip.

"Well, she thinks she does."

"She *thinks* she does? I rest my case. Take it from me, baby; somebody who got a man." RayShawn pointed a fork to himself before setting it down in its proper place next to the plate. "As a matter of fact, I have men barking up my tree all the time."

"I think your situation is a little different, Ray Ray," Shenita said with a laugh.

"Oh no, honey, it ain't. A man is a man, and she ain't got one and I do. Now, who you gon' listen to?"

"I guess you do have a point there," Shenita admitted.

"Don't let Pippa 'pip' you!" RayShawn retorted. "You know that girl is just shy of one who flew over the cuckoo's nest. You keep listening to her, you'll end up an old maid rocking in your old rocking chair singing 'Kumbaya' with somebody else's grandkids."

"I hear ya, Ray Ray," Shenita said. "I just don't want it to end up with yet another disappointment."

RayShawn stopped what he was doing and stood up straight. "Look, honey, life is too short, and these days you gotta go for what you know. It may not come overnight, but you at least gotta get in the game! And out here in these streets you gotta take what you can, take no prisoners, and go for yours! Like my baby daddy, 2Pac, used to say, *I gotta get mine, you gotta get yours*—now get yours!"

Shenita cracked up. "I guess, Ray Ray."

"Look, you better take your little tail to that dinner and movie tomorrow night and have yourself a good time. You deserve it. If nothing else, you just got yourself a free meal and a movie. Hello! Is he paid? Does this guy you going out with have some cheddar?"

"He's a veterinarian, so I'm sure he does."

"Cha-ching! Girl, get your groove, I mean your fun—on. For the Lawd, of course," RayShawn added with a wave. "This man could be your soul mate; you wouldn't want to miss out on that now, would you?"

Shenita sighed. "You're right. Thanks, Ray Ray; you always know exactly what to say."

"And you know this, woman. Now let Uncle Ray go, because I've got a special guest tonight. I'm cooking dinner for my beh-beh."

"RayShawn, you are a mess," Shenita said with a laugh.

"When love calls, honey, all I say is you better answer. Now I have got to go, because love is calling my name right about now. Coming, Dante!"

Shenita shook her head as she hung up the phone.

She concluded Ray was right; you do only have one shot at life and maybe even one shot at love, so you may as well take your chances. Life is about risk, right? And Lord knows Shenita didn't want to end up like Pippa, somebody who should be the lead character in Heather Headley's video for her song "In My Mind," because Lord knows Pippa's dating Elijah was all in her head. Nah, Shenita figured she'd rather take the risk.

It might be worth it in the end.

Now if she could just figure out what she should wear for her date with Kyle tomorrow night.

CHAPTER 26

"Sorry I couldn't meet with you for lunch today. I've got to get this proposal done for boss lady, so I scarfed down a little bag lunch earlier, but I still wanted to give you a call," Shenita said as she sat with her legs crossed in her office on Friday afternoon munching on a green apple. She was in a dress-up mood this morning, so she wore a cream-and-black vertically striped convertible dress to work, with cream pumps that had a blackened toe. She checked her nails and decided she was in desperate need of another manicure soon.

"That's fine," Jackie said on the other end of the phone as she sat at lunch alone at her favorite outdoor lunch spot, playing with her salad for the day, an Asian chicken cabbage salad, which was a raw vegetable salad topped with grilled chicken thighs. "You know I'm still here, right?" Jackie said. "I'm not one of those chicks who needs to have someone with them in order to enjoy a good meal. And, girl, this Asian salad is delish!" Jackie didn't mind that eating it caused her bright red lipstick that perfectly matched her skirt and her red pumps to wear off. She was careful not to get any salad on her cream-colored silk blouse, placing her hand underneath every time she ate a forkful.

"I'm sure it is," Shenita said, ready to cut right to the chase. "So how'd it go?"

"With what?" Jackie asked with a mouthful of salad.

"How'd it go with Jermaine? Didn't you ask him out?" Shenita wiped the side of her mouth.

"Oh, Jermaine!" Jackie said. "Him."

"Yeah, him," Shenita said, as if Jackie didn't know who she was talking about in the first place.

"Um, no, I didn't ask him out," Jackie admitted.

"Why not?" Shenita begged.

"Well, technically," Jackie explained, "I did ask him out at first, then I retracted my offer."

"Retracted your offer? You're not at the negotiation table. Jacqueline, what did you do?" Shenita asked, shifting in her seat.

"What did *I* do? No, it wasn't what did *I* do; it was what did *he* do—which was nothing but be a man—which was more than enough for me to change my mind."

"Girl, what are you talking about? Layman's terms, please? I am not one of your client cases," Shenita reminded her.

Jackie looked around to make sure no neighboring customers were butting in on her conversation.

In a soft voice she spoke into her cell, "Well, I asked him out at first and was real bold about it, too, then little Miss Antoinette came bouncing inside, interrupting us, and next thing you know he got all distracted and started salivating as he undressed her with his eyes, so I told myself I didn't have time for these games, so he asked me to repeat what I said from earlier, when I asked him out and I told his forty-going-on-sixteen-year-old self never mind. End of story. Girl, did I tell you this salad is good? You should try it." Jackie said, "Maybe I'll get one for you as a carryout."

Shenita sat on the other end of the line dumbfounded.

"No thanks," she said. "Now help me out here, because I'm confused. You didn't ask him out because why?"

"And did I tell you he had the nerve to call me that little tramp's, forgive me, Lord, I mean, that little girl's name, by mistake? Whatever. That's the last time that'll ever happen. I can bet you that one, and I'm not even a betting woman."

Shenita rubbed her temples. "Jackie. You didn't ask him out because he called you Antoinette's name by mistake? Didn't you say she had just left the office?"

"Yeah, and?"

"And? So he made a mistake!"

"I know, but some mistakes cost more than others."

"Jackie, you're being unfair here. So he looked at a woman— he's a man! You betta be glad he *did* look at her, cuz at least now you know he's not gay."

"I guess, but for him to look at her like he looked at her when he was supposedly trying to go out with me was just flat-out rude. No telling how many other women he's asked out besides me. Maybe I should ask a few of the ladies in the office if he's asked them out. He would probably ask out Lady Eloise if she worked here."

"Jackie! Listen to yourself. You're making stuff up! You've just tried this man and found him guilty, and he hasn't even done anything wrong. It's not like the two of you are dating and he blatantly disrespected you in front of another woman. He's single! He's a man! An alive, living, breathing *man!*"

"Yeah, well, that's his problem," Jackie muttered.

"Girl, you got some issues."

"No, I don't. I'm just a realist, that's all. That's another reason why I don't do office romances. Too much drama. Also, realistically, Jermaine is just too immature for me. He's like a walking, talking bag of testosterone that I don't want to be bothered with."

"But you pinky-swore!" Shenita cried.

"I know, but—"

Just then Jackie spotted a fine man wearing black Dolce & Gabbana shades, a tilted gray fedora and charcoal Giorgio Armani suit, and a pink shirt and matching satin pink striped tie head her way. She had never seen a man wear pink and still look every bit masculine at the same time. His broad shoulders caught her attention as he grabbed the chair across from hers and boldly helped himself to a seat in her space.

"Shenita, I gotta go. We'll talk later." Jackie abruptly ended the call.

Shenita looked at her phone and wondered what happened that Jackie had to end the call so quickly. She thought about calling right back but decided against it and cut her lunch short to get back to work. She had pulled up her PowerPoint presentation on her desktop and was filling in bullet points when her cell rang.

Not checking the caller ID and assuming it was Jackie calling back, Shenita answered, "Girl, I thought you got abducted; don't you ever hang up on me so fast like that again!"

"Hello?" A male voice answered. "Is this Shenita?"

"Who is this?" Shenita asked.

"This is Christian."

Christian? Mrs. Washington's son?

"Um, no, boo boo, you got the wrong number," Shenita said in the most ghetto accent she could muster. "Try again; you musta dialed a digit wrong or something," she added with an extra pop of her gum.

"Oh, okay," the gentleman said on the other end.

"Lord, please forgive me," Shenita whispered above, praying Christian would call her right back. He did.

"Hello," Shenita answered, sounding more like a pleasant telephone operator this time.

"Hello. Is this Shenita?"

"This is. May I ask who I'm speaking with?"

"This is Christian. Vivian Washington's son."

"Christian, yes! Oh, hi! It's so good to hear your voice. How are you?"

"I'm fine. I'm calling to see if you'd like to join me for dinner tomorrow night?"

"Tomorrow night?" Shenita asked in the same professional tone.

"Yes. I apologize for the last-minute request," he said. "It's just that Mom spoke so highly of you and I normally travel out of the country most weekends, but I found a spot I had free tomorrow night and was wondering if you would join me for a few drinks."

A few drinks? Shenita thought. *Yellow light.*

"A few drinks sounds nice, Christian, except I'm not much of a drinker."

"That's okay. I'm not much of a drinker either. I was just testing you," he said with a light laugh.

Yeah, right, Shenita thought. "No worries, though," she responded, "I'll still get my drink on. I'm always up for a virgin piña colada with extra pineapple on the side."

Christian chuckled. "All right, then, that sounds perfect. Meet me at the bar at Fishbone's downtown at eight o'clock tomorrow night? Meal following, how about that?

"That," Shenita said, now pleased, "would be wonderful."

"Great. I'll call you tomorrow around then, and I look forward to meeting you in person, Shenita."

"Me . . . too," Shenita said, shocked that she was managing to pull off two dates with two different men in one weekend—her online match, Kyle, tonight and now Christian tomorrow.

Shenita stood up, did a little jig, and squealed in sheer delight. She then grabbed her *Rule Book* from her top desk drawer and crossed out *Rule #5 Never Date More Than One Man at a Time.*

Ray Ray is right, Shenita thought. *Life is short and there's more than enough of Shenita Love to go around.*

"Is this seat taken?" the handsome gentleman asked after already having taken a seat directly across from Jackie at the restaurant.

"No, it's not . . . Jermaine, is that you?" Jackie asked as she tried to search inside the handsome stranger's shades.

"Ah, did I give myself away?" Jermaine asked, removing his sunglasses and revealing his usual boyish grin. For some reason, today Jermaine's smile was brighter to Jackie than it had ever been before.

"I should have known I couldn't fool you, beautiful." Jermaine straightened his cuffs, revealing his gold, diamond-encrusted Rolex watch.

Jackie folded her arms and grinned. "You clean up nice there, Mr. Stroud. Why are you so sharp today, meeting a special client back at the office?"

"Actually, I'm not even working today. Just between you and me"—Jermaine leaned forward and spoke in a softer tone—"I met with the one and only Mr. Greg Turner at Turner & Jackson Law Firm for an interview; they're considering making me partner."

"Well, good for you," Jackie said, still shocked at how good Jermaine looked, and with a pending offer at a more prominent law firm, he was beginning to look more like her dream man.

"Thank you, Jackie. I wanted to personally apologize again for my outburst yesterday, for interrupting your meeting and all. And I wanted to let you know, also, that you did a great job, as always."

"Thanks," Jackie said, perplexed. "You told me that yesterday."

"I know, but we kinda got, um, interrupted, and I just wanted to make myself clear."

"Yeah, we got interrupted all right, and you got distracted," Jackie said as she mistakenly recited her thought out loud.

Jermaine shifted in his seat. "Jackie, I know I've been asking you out for a while now, and if you ever tire of my attempts please let me know, but I just see something in you that I've never seen in any other woman I've dated, or married. I see that drive, that hunger for success in your eyes, and I get to witness that same passion working alongside you every day. But then sometimes I wonder if beneath all that desire there is a desire for something more. Something lasting. Something real."

Jackie sat looking at Jermaine with her head cocked to the side, and for the first time in a while she was at a loss for words.

"You don't have to respond right away," Jermaine continued.

"You can take it back to the office and think about it if you want, or you can even take two weeks or two months to think about it, but I just wanted to ask you one more time, Jacqueline Downing."

Jackie could barely comprehend anything else Jermaine said, as she was still stuck on "something real."

She snapped herself back to reality and put her game face back on. "Look, Jermaine, your rhetoric is really sweet," she began.

"Hold up," Jermaine said, then reached into his suit jacket pocket. "I got something for you."

He pulled out a small white box wrapped with gold ribbon and revealed it to Jackie.

Jackie looked at the box, then up at Jermaine, wondering where in the world this was headed.

"A gift. For you." Jermaine handed her the box.

"Jermaine, thank you, but you don't have to—"

"Just take it!" Jermaine demanded. "Please," he begged with puppy-dog eyes.

"Okay, but it better not be—"

Jackie's eyes widened as she grew elated at the valuable gift in such a tiny box. She felt like it was Christmas, though that was still a few months away. She peeked inside the box's contents to make sure it was still there, then looked up at Jermaine and said, "Oh, thank you, Jermaine!" as she rose and hugged his neck and gave him a big kiss on his cheek.

"Is that all it takes?" Jermaine commented. "Well, shoot, if that's all it takes, then there'll be plenty more where that came from," he said, surprised by the wonderful response to his gift.

Jackie pulled out the contents from the box and held it in her hands, lifting it high in the sky, allowing it to glow in the sunlight. She couldn't believe anyone would be thoughtful enough to bless her with a Salad Gift Card worth $250 that entitled her to her salad of choice at over twenty participating restaurants.

"Jermaine, you're an angel. What can I do for you? Would you like a gift in return? I can get you an early Christmas gift," she said excitedly.

"Nah, I'm good," Jermaine said. "Thanks, though. Seeing you smile is good enough for me."

Jackie sighed in delight. "Are you serious?" she asked.

"About what?" Jermaine asked.

"About what you just said, are you serious?"

"As 9/11," Jermaine said.

"Okay, then, to answer your question, the answer is yes, I'll go out with you."

"Go out with me? I didn't ask you out," he said with an attitude.

Jackie eyed him suspiciously, and he laughed. He then grabbed her hand, kissed it, and said, "Well, I'm glad."

CHAPTER 27

Shenita stepped up to the maître d's podium while adjusting the cherry-red short sleeves of her dipped V-neck fitted convertible dress. She hoped she wasn't showing too much cleavage, which was why she'd decided to discreetly insert a safety pin to completely cover up.

With gold clutch in hand, she politely said to the suited, slick-haired maître d, "Excuse me, I'm looking for a Kyle."

"Kyle Pepperidge? Right this way, madam, he is expecting you."

Shenita looked around at the fancy five-star steakhouse restaurant's gold décor and huge crystal chandelier and figured dining here must cost a pretty penny. She had never dined at this particular restaurant before and figured this Kyle must have more class than she had imagined. *The vet business must be treating him very well. He must have his own private practice,* Shenita thought while eyeing the dining guests, who were mainly of a lighter persuasion. Shenita concluded that she and Kyle might very well be the only couple of color in the entire building.

"Sir," the maître d said as Kyle arose at their two-seater table.

Shenita initially thought he hadn't stood up all the way, as he appeared not much taller than she was, and she was only five feet tall. He also wore a navy blue suit jacket over a blue-and-yellow V-neck sweater that made him look even younger than his profile picture. His build looked more tubby than stocky, as his long shirt appeared to have been hiding several nights of pizza binges.

"Shenita!" Kyle said, and extended his arms to give her a hug like she were his long-lost relative. "So good to see you, or shall I say meet you in person," Kyle said.

Shenita returned his gesture and said sheepishly, "Good to meet you, too," and was about to pull out her chair to sit down when Kyle rushed behind and pulled her seat out for her. "No, please, allow me," he said.

"Thank you." Shenita adjusted her sleeves again, making sure they didn't slide down to reveal too much shoulder. "I appreciate it," she said. *Well, at least he's a gentleman,* she thought, and decided to continue with high hopes throughout the date. *Height isn't everything.*

"So how are you?" Kyle asked.

"I'm fine, thanks for asking," Shenita said. "How are you? You seem to be doing pretty well," Shenita said, observing her surroundings. "You fancy, huh?"

"Pardon me?" Kyle asked.

"Never mind," Shenita said. "So how was Bible study last night?"

"It was good. It was great, actually; thanks for asking. Remember when I asked you what was your favorite scripture?"

"Yeah."

"Well, you want to know mine?" he asked.

"Sure; I'm itching to find out," she said sarcastically.

"My favorite passage of Scripture is Matthew 6:26: *Behold the fowls of the air: for they sow not, neither do they reap, nor gather into barns;*

yet our heavenly Father feedeth them. Are ye not much better than they?

"That's a good one," Shenita said. "That's the one just before *Seek ye first the kingdom of God,* right, found in Matthew 6:33?"

"Yes! I see you know the Bible. That's great!" Kyle said.

"Yes, great," Shenita replied, and wondered just how long she was going to have to sit through this. *You can make it, Shenita, just stick it out,* she thought.

"So what are you having tonight?" Kyle asked, pulling out his menu.

"I'm not sure," Shenita said as she lifted hers. "What's good here?"

"Their rack of lamb is good, along with their veal and filet mignon. I may try something different this time, though. I may go for their porterhouse steak."

"Sounds good," Shenita said, eyeing the menu. "I think I'll have the filet mignon."

"And what are you having?" Kyle asked again, looking downward toward the side of his suit jacket. Shenita looked up from her menu and wondered who he was talking to. She figured he must not have heard her the first time and repeated, "I think I'm going to order their filet mignon."

The waiter came and took their orders.

"Oh, and can you bring my usual—an extra-small plate?" Kyle asked the waiter.

"Sure, Mr. Pepperidge, anything for you, sir."

Shenita scooted in her chair. "Wow, I'm impressed. You must come here often."

"I do, actually. We come here every week."

"Who, you and your mom?" Shenita asked. *He looks like a momma's boy,* she thought.

"No, me and Suzie," Kyle said.

"Suzie?" Shenita said, not meaning to say it with an attitude.

"Yeah, Suzie, my sweet pea."

"Your sweet pea?" Shenita asked. *Is this man bringing up some other chick while on a date with me?*

"She's the love of my life, my everything. Next to Jesus, of course."

"Wow; that sounds beautiful. Great," Shenita said and took a big gulp of her water, not believing this man had just successfully accomplished playing her for a fool.

"You must really love her," she said. "Um, can I cancel my order?" Shenita said with a raised finger in search of a waiter—any waiter.

"I do love her. God is good, and I'm so glad he brought her in my life," Kyle said, ignoring her plea while being caught up in his own world envisioning his Suzie.

"How sweet, Kyle," Shenita said tenderly, wondering how much more of this torture she was going to have to endure.

"For sure. You want to meet her?" Kyle asked.

Meet her? Shenita thought. *Is this man some type of freak?*

"I'm sorry but, um, I don't get down like that," Shenita said.

Kyle then reached inside his suit jacket pocket and pulled out a small bird. It was a brown-and-gray bird that resembled a sparrow, except it couldn't fly.

He held it in his hands, reached it out to Shenita, and said, "Shenita, meet Suzie, the love of my life."

You have got to be kidding me.

"She's still pretty young," Kyle added. "I've been raising her ever since I saved her after she fell out of a tree as a fledgling. She never quite learned how to fly, but that's okay because I take good care of her. She's my own little house sparrow," Kyle explained while tending to his pet.

Shenita could not believe this man had a bird at the dinner table at a restaurant, and was totally okay with it.

She held her head in her hand and looked at him in shock through her fingers.

"Scripture tells us in the book of Luke how God forgets not one sparrow, and how he loves and values us even more than these beautiful little creatures," Kyle said, petting his little bird with one of his thick fingers. The poor bird's little head seemed to sink lower and lower with each pat.

"Yes, it does," Shenita said, lifting her finger for the waiter again, higher this time, as she tried to figure out the best way to the nearest exit.

"His eye is on the sparrow," Kyle sang, off-key.

The waiter eventually returned—not to Shenita's rescue but instead to give Kyle the small plate that he had requested earlier.

"Thank you so much." Kyle looked up as the waiter set the small plate next to his larger one.

"You know," Kyle said to Shenita, "God's love is so amazing. He cares for us, feeds us, and loves us just like he loves the little sparrows."

Shenita prayed God would create a way of escape for her out of this foolishness.

Kyle then reached into his pocket and pulled out dead mealworms mixed with dead tiny insects and spread them in the small plate. "Ready to eat, little buddy?" He then set the bird on the edge of the plate, and the bird ate her dinner before they did.

"Oh no," Shenita said, then held her mouth and rushed to the restroom.

After upchucking, Shenita exited the restroom, made sure Kyle's back faced her and that he was still engrossed in his bird, then dashed out of that restaurant, rushed to her car, and skidded out of the parking lot.

CHAPTER 28

"He did what?" RayShawn asked on the other end of the call. He was braiding Dante's thick black hair in cornrows as Dante sat in between his legs on the floor and RayShawn sat on his old yellow couch.

"He took a bird out of his suit pocket, then started to feed it bugs in the middle of our date in the restaurant," Shenita said, driving home in the rain. So much for the movie; she really didn't want to see it anyway.

"Are you serious? Aw, girl, you shoulda called the peoples on him to have that man taken away in a white jacket."

"I know. And he was, like, fifty pounds heavier than any of his profile pictures. I almost didn't recognize that he was the same person."

"Girl, well, you know how that is. People lie. Misrepresent. Trying to get ahead, that's all. He wasn't it; wasn't the one— next!"

"Ray Ray, after that I don't know if there's going to be any next."

"Shenita Bita Fofita, I know you ain't allowing one bad

apple to spoil it for the rest of the funky bunch. Don't the Word say to throw stuff into the sea of forgetfulness? Just throw that seahorse back into the sea and forget about it. Everybody on that religious dating website can't be crazy. You're on it, so there must be some other decent, God-fearing human beings who are just looking for love. As a matter of fact, do they allow men to . . . Ow! Dante, why you pop me with that comb? I was just kidding, dang."

Shenita laughed on the other end.

"Anyway. Folks hatin' over here," RayShawn continued as he parted Dante's hair. "All I gotta say is, keep trying, girl, don't give up after the first time. You may trip on your stilettos and fall down the first time, but at some point you gotta get back up again. You can do it."

"Yeah, but the question is do I *want* to do it," Shenita wondered.

"Okay, well, let me help you out. You could either, A. Keep doing what you been doing and keep getting the same thang, which is no ringie and no dingie, or B. Do something different for a change and snag you a husband in the process. If you ask me, B sounds way better. Oh, and make sure he got some ends, too, cuz me and Dante want to be invited to the destination wedding so we can get us a free vacay in the process. We work so hard out here in these streets; we both need some R & R, right, baby?" RayShawn asked his honey, who nodded.

"RayShawn, you are a mess. Thanks." Shenita hung up her cell.

Well, at least I still have the date with Christian tomorrow, Shenita thought. *We'll see how that goes. Anything would have to be better than what happened tonight.*

CHAPTER 29

Blue and white strobe lights flashed and theatrical smoke appeared as the music, Destiny's Child's classic song, "Say My Name," blazed through the entire club and drew the crowd of all-male patrons in anticipation of what was about to go down center stage. Word had it one of Xtasy's signature acts was back after a three-year hiatus, and the start of her theme song before she hit the stage was confirmation that their dream had come true.

Diva D stepped one of her six-inch-heeled thigh-high patent-leather red boots onto the stage, with the other following, wearing a black patent-leather leotard. After a few minutes of mesmerizing the crowd with a floor routine in which she somehow managed to make eye contact with every man in the first three rows, she slowly inched her way to the pole. It was imperative that she catch the attention of the men in the front, because she was well aware that it was those patrons who got there early enough, waited for her the longest, and more than likely cashed out their paychecks and clocked the most dollars, which was sure to command even more of her attention.

Diva D eyed the pole like an object that needed to be conquered. She looked it up and down as she cougar-walked around it counterclockwise, then leaned her back against it and slid down like it was a comforting friend. She then popped up, gave a few hip dips, reached high and grabbed it with her strong arm, then climbed to the very top. The audience cheered her on as they knew they were in for a real performance.

She next flipped upside down with one leg wrapped around the pole and the other leg extended with pointed toes, and concluded with a reverse grab spin, then a leg hook, as she spiraled downward.

The crowd went wild, blowing whistles and flashing dollars. She then crawled back up to the top and completed most of the routine doing the Peter Pan and other spins, ending her routine with her signature diva spin.

The crowd went crazy.

Diva D arose and danced more on the floor while collecting tips from eager patrons who made her feel like a superstar. Not only that, on that stage she felt accepted, she felt appreciated, she felt loved. She felt like she could conquer anything and everything. She felt like she could conquer the world.

Diva D was back indeed.

CHAPTER 30

Pippa added the final layer of vanilla wafers, sliced bananas, and instant pudding mix and topped it off with whipped cream and cookie crumbles, and even added a cherry atop her banana pudding surprise. She dubbed it banana pudding surprise because not only did she add the traditional wafers, bananas, and pudding; she also snuck in a hint of vanilla extract along with a cream cheese and condensed milk mixture folded inside the pudding mix for added flavor.

She purposefully dropped a vanilla wafer for Teacup, her white Yorkshire terrier, who eagerly eyed the banana pudding as if it were a special treat created just for her. To Teacup's dismay, Pippa stuffed the clear glass bowl of pudding inside the fridge and retreated to her couch along with Teacup, who returned to her previously reclined position in her dog bed.

Pippa painted her toes pale pink and then eyed her cell on the coffee table. In between polishing, she picked up her cell in case she had a missed call and didn't hear it. She hadn't. She checked to make sure it was turned on along with the sound and it was. She found it strange that, aside from their brief conversation earlier today, Pippa hadn't heard from her man, Elijah, all day. She knew he was hard at work, but she wondered if he'd even received the cute picture of her that she sent him earlier today on her lunch break.

Pippa finished painting and blew on her toes from where she was seated, and then grabbed her cell to call Elijah. Her call went straight to voice mail.

"Hi, Elijah, this is Pippa, your girl. I was just calling to see how you were doing and how your day went today. I know you were pretty busy earlier and I totally understand. Did you get that picture I texted you? Did you like it? Let me know, okay? Thanks. Bye."

Pippa then got dressed in a pale pink-and-blue floral dress, combed her mushroom style, washed her face, and added a fresh coat of Vaseline and small pearl earrings, then headed back to the fridge to grab her banana pudding.

"Come to mamma," Pippa said to it. "I got exactly what my man needs to take all that stress off from a hard day's work. He's got work, school, and the privilege of serving Pastor at church—I can only imagine all the stress he must be under right now. But that's all right, because I got just the thing that'll make it all better for him. You, my friend, will save the day for me and my bae. I'm sure he'll appreciate it and won't want to spend another minute without me as a result," Pippa proclaimed.

Pippa parked her Taurus in front of Elijah's house and was relieved once she spotted his black truck in the driveway. She pulled down her car visor and said to herself in the mirror, "Okay, girl, time to ease your man's stress and show him how you can be the perfect comforter for him in his time of need. You got this, girl. He needs you, and after he gets one taste of mama's homemade banana pudding surprise, there will be no doubt in his mind. That man'll be head over heels in love with you."

Ding-dong.

Pippa rang the doorbell, touched up her hair with her fingers, and made sure all the buttons on her dress were still buttoned properly to the top.

After no initial reply, Pippa rang the doorbell again.

Ding-dong.

Elijah answered wearing a white tee that stated, *Work Hard Pray Harder,* in red. His curly hair was ruffled and he looked like he just woke up from taking a nap.

"Oh, hey, Pippa," he said in a gruff voice.

"Hi, Elijah, look what I brought you," Pippa said while happily lifting her treat.

"What you got there?" he asked, suddenly awakening.

"Banana pudding surprise! It's my own special recipe and I made it just for you."

"Aw, wow, thanks but—"

"No need to thank me." Pippa brushed him aside and walked right into his house, to her usual spot in his kitchen, where she set down the food she brought him, except this time was different. She stopped in her tracks when she spotted a beautiful slender woman with long silky black hair and olive skin, wearing a spandex black tank top and gray skinny jeans, seated on Elijah's couch, the same couch Pippa used to feed Elijah on after bringing him his Sunday meal.

"Oh, I'm sorry, I didn't know you had company," Pippa said to Elijah, who eventually made it back inside his home and closed his front door.

"Yeah . . . that's what I was trying to tell you. Pippa, you know Lynette from church, right? I believe you two have met before?"

Pippa had to think for a moment, then she remembered that Lynette was the one who just got saved and joined the church last week.

"Oh, yeah. Hi, forgive me; pardon my manners," Pippa said and retreated from the kitchen to the living room to shake Lynette's hand.

"Hi," Lynette said sheepishly.

"Uh, Lynette and I were just going over church business, right, Lynette?" Elijah asked.

"Sure," Lynette said.

"Pastor told me to keep an eye on her to help her get acclimated with the church so we can see which department she would be best fit to serve in ministry," Elijah explained.

"Oh, I get it. You definitely want to obey Pastor; he's such an awesome man of God. I truly understand," Pippa said, relieved once she discovered Lynette's visit was strictly platonic church business.

"Well, certainly, I can help you with that as well," Pippa added. "But first, let me get us all nice big servings of banana pudding and then I'll mosey on back over here so we can go over the helps departments listed in the church bulletin to see where which would be a best fit for you, my sister."

"Okay," Lynette said then looked at Elijah and then back at Pippa.

Pippa brought out three tray tables and set a bowl of banana pudding on each one.

Elijah immediately grabbed his bowl and dug in. "This is good, girl. This banana pudding tastes better than my momma's. Pippa, you know you sure can throw down in the kitchen, girl, you're about to make a brother get big."

"Well, you know I like to keep my man happy, and they say

the way to a man's heart is through his stomach, isn't that right, Lynette?" Pippa asked.

"That's right," Lynette replied with a nervous laugh.

Pippa reached into her bag and brought out the helps-department directory. "Now, which do you like more, helping kids, serving in the kitchen, or would you say you have a more administrative gift? Where do your strengths lie, Sister Lynette?"

Lynette looked up at Elijah, back at Pippa, ate a spoonful of banana pudding, and said, "I don't know. Maybe you can help me find out."

CHAPTER 31

Papers flooded Jackie's long red oak dining room table as she worked tirelessly on her latest client case, trying to work the numbers and also gather all the information she needed in order to prove her latest client's ex-husband's indiscretions. A monetary value had to be attached to each transgression, and alimony alone—especially for this particular case, involving her client's ex-husband's usage of marital funds in order to set his mistress up in an apartment five miles away—simply was not enough.

Jackie scrubbed her way through the paperwork, flustered because she was still not finding all she needed to prove her case. She had on her journalistic as well as her legalistic hat, and all the whos, whats, whens, wheres, and whys simply weren't adding up.

Like most Friday nights, Jackie had brought her work home with her and hadn't stopped working on it, not even to make time to cook dinner. For now, her No. 2 pencil was the main course.

Jackie took a sip of orange juice while perusing the documents, missed her mouth, and accidentally spilled OJ all over her new beige suit jacket.

"Oh, shoot." Jackie jumped in her seat once she realized the damage. She sprang up, removed her jacket and revealed its gold shell, then retreated to her walk-in bedroom closet to look for another jacket.

As she peeled through her wardrobe, she thought she might have found another beige jacket of choice when something caught her eye. Though it'd been there all along, for some reason tonight its peach color shone as if to stand out, as it was placed on a stand behind her clothes.

Jackie took hold of the peach photo album and wiped the dust off it. Instead of retreating to the dining room with her new suit jacket, she retreated to her living room couch holding on to her new relic, which she hadn't opened in seven years.

She took a deep breath then opened it to the first page, which revealed an image that at the time signified one of the happiest days of her life, but was now a painful reminder of what was or what could have been—her wedding picture.

It was the one taken just after the two of them said "I do," kissed, and were standing on the church's porch headed out to the limo while being greeted by onlookers and well-wishers who thought it appropriate to throw rice their way.

Tall, dark, and extremely handsome, especially in his black suit and teal-colored silk tie and handkerchief that matched Jackie's three bridesmaids, the photo showed her new husband's strength and charm as Jackie remembered how he clutched her right hand so tightly that day, as if to say he would never leave her side, and how his gleaming smile made everyone he glanced at feel that they were special.

Jackie sure felt special—especially that day. She remembered the day Dexter stole her heart away and promised her a lifetime of sheer love and happiness in front of God, the pastor, family, friends and even a few strangers, and she believed him.

She also believed God when He told her that everything was going to be all right—that even though she grew up without having a father in her life, He was all the man she ever needed and that Dexter, too, would take care of her.

She felt betrayed and lied to by not one but two men, whose word she grew to trust, and whose love she had started to believe in more than her own—her husband's and God's.

Not making it beyond the photo album's first page, Jackie wept.

She laid the album on the coffee table, lay on her side, and eventually fell asleep.

CHAPTER 32

Backstage, Danielle was flooded with congrats from her peers, and even former haters came up to her and gave her a huge hug after her dynamic pole performance. Danielle prided herself on being one of the few pole dancers who was not an amateur simply using the pole as a prop while performing sexy dance moves around it but instead considered herself a true pole professional who worked hard at her aerial dynamic craft. It'd been so long since she worked the pole that her body was starting to feel the pain already, but all the congrats and what she received in tips made it all worth it as she vowed to tithe off it as soon as she made it to church on Sunday morning.

"Diva D, you done did it again!" Sparks congratulated her backstage, with his Montecristo in tow. He placed his arm around her shoulder. "I don't know how this club survived these last three years without you, girl," he said, and Danielle smiled. He looked her up and down and said, "Woo-wee, somebody get me another drank! You fine *and* fabulous, and that routine was out of this world! Those men were wearing my waitresses out ordering drinks left and right. Your performance added to Sparks's bottom line tonight, baby girl, you want me to peel you off some more?"

"Sure, Sparky," Danielle said with her hand out as Sparks peeled off and handed her another grand.

He then whispered in her ear, "You stick around here and there's plenty more where that came from."

"Yeah, buddy!" Sparks shouted, signifying his exit.

Danielle stood in awe, eyeing her extra grand, which was a bonus on top of her other bonus. That, with her tips and her regular wages, allowed her to have way more than enough to cover her bills and someone else's. She stuffed her bonus money into her bra and then noticed three young fans staring at her from the left stage entrance.

"Hello," Danielle said to three girls, who all looked to be young teenagers. Danielle had hoped they weren't underage, as the club was supposed to prohibit dancers under eighteen from working.

Two of the shyer girls eyed Danielle in awe and the other, taller and older-looking lean girl approached her and said, "Diva D, you were sick!" and offered her a fist bump.

Danielle returned the gesture and replied, "Thank you."

"No, really, how did you learn all those spins? I've never seen anyone work the pole like you do. And all that money those men gave you, and that bonus Sparks just gave you? You're a beast!" she said, and the two girls behind her agreed.

"Yeah, a true goddess," one of the younger girls, wearing a pink wig, said.

"Well, I don't know about all that," Danielle said humbly.

"No, I'm serious; we're serious; we want to be like you," the oldest said. "What's your secret?"

Danielle thought about it a moment and replied, "The secret is, no matter what you do, when you're on that stage that pole is yours. So conquer it and stay focused." All three girls nodded and Danielle continued, "And no matter what you do when you're up in the air, don't look down. Become one with the pole, and the pole will become one with you."

Her three fans stared at her in awe of the wonderful insight they'd just received.

Danielle suddenly thought about something and asked, "Wait a minute now, how old are you girls anyway? Should you even be working here?"

The girls in the background lowered their heads.

Their leader said, "Yeah, we're of age. We got proper ID. Besides, I'm saving up for college," she added proudly.

"College? How many more years do you have to go before you can even apply for college?" Danielle asked.

"Never mind that," she said. "Those are my two little twin sisters back there."

Danielle eyed them again, as one was brown-skinned and one was light and their facial features didn't look alike.

"They're fraternal twins," the older sister clarified. "Anyway, the three of us made a vow that we were all gonna make it in life no matter what it took."

Danielle gave them all strange looks. "Where are your parents? Isn't it kinda late?"

"We don't got no parents," one of the younger sisters said. She was wearing a jet-black bob wig.

"Be quiet, Chiquita. We got parents," the oldest sister said, then faced Danielle. "I'm their parent. I'm their mom for now."

"Little girl, do you want me to call child services on you?" Danielle asked sternly. "Now, where are your parents?"

"No, don't do that," their leader insisted. "I'm their mom in the sense that I take care of them right now. Our real mom is at home. She knows where we are. She knows we're fine. Hey, one day can you show me that Peter Pan spin you did? That was sweet. I've been trying to get that for ages. Maybe if you show me then I can show Chiquita and Bonita then we can get a little more in tips, you know what I mean?" she said.

"What's your name?" Danielle asked.

"Princess Dream."

"Not your stage name, your real name."

"That *is* my real name!"

"Okay, well, *Princess Dream,* I suggest you wake up from your dream and take your little self home before it gets too late. Don't you have a high school exam to study for or something?"

Princess Dream laughed in her face. "Yeah, right, I got something to study all right, and it starts with a 'Ben' and ends with 'Jamins' and it's headed my way."

Danielle looked to see what Princess Dream was referring to, and she saw a baldheaded older white male headed their way with what looked like his tongue hanging out of his mouth. Princess Dream rubbed his bald head as her way of saying hello.

"Excuse me, sir, aren't you a little too old to be messing with this young lady?" Danielle asked.

"Too old?" he replied, initially offended, then he sweetened up his tone. "I'm sorry but no, this is my niece. Didn't she tell you?"

Princess Dream nodded and her twin sisters giggled in the background.

"That's right, Uncle Otis, you tell her," she said, and kept rubbing his head.

"Old man, you are not her uncle. Now go back out front

and wait for the rest of the show!" Danielle demanded. "Who let you backstage, anyway? Security!"

"All right, all right, I'll leave," he said then headed back.

Danielle spotted Princess Dream handing him a small note, and he winked at her as he walked away.

"Look, I don't know who y'all kids think you are but this is no place for you to be, you hear me!" Danielle shouted.

"But Diva D, we want to be like you!" the younger-looking twin wailed in the background.

"Yeah, Diva D, we want your ends, and your man friends," Princess Dream said, eyeing a tall, slender man wearing a gray trench coat and a black fedora and smoking a cigarette, who had initially eyed Danielle.

"And you, Miss Hot to Trot, you better be careful out here before you get burned," Danielle said.

"Too late," Princess Dream said, "Besides, I got meds for that," she said and cracked up with her sisters.

Danielle didn't think that was funny.

"Just kidding, Diva D, dang," Princess Dream said, then lightly punched Danielle on her shoulder. "Well, I'm about to go on now." She grabbed hold of the gold cross pendant on the necklace around Danielle's neck and said, "Pray for me, okay?" then released it.

Princess Dream left for the stage and Danielle caught her performance.

Just like Danielle expected, she was a young amateur, all she knew to do was lift her legs on the pole and slide up and down doing the beginner's fireman spin. No skill at all, yet the older men still drooled over her as she took their tips and danced more on the floor than on the pole while shaking her nearly nonexistent yet half-exposed behind near their faces.

Danielle clutched her cross pendant as she watched Princess Dream dance and said, "God, please keep your babies."

Once Princess Dream's performance was done, Danielle gathered her things to leave, and before she walked out of the building she spotted Princess Dream leading the old man she'd been talking to earlier to the VIP room.

CHAPTER 33

Once home on Friday night, Shenita couldn't wait to change into her PJs and go to bed after her horrible date. Just as she turned on the light inside her bedroom, she heard her cell go off in the front room, signaling a text message. Wondering who in the world would be texting her this late, she checked her phone and saw it was a text from Christian, which read, *Sorry so late. Gotta cancel tomorrow. Something came up. Reschedule?*

Reschedule? Shenita thought. *No, this man isn't canceling our date for tomorrow night at the last minute. And why is he texting so late, as if that's supposed to make up for it—it's still last-minute, and hadn't he ever heard of a phone call? Who cancels a first date with a text message? Nah, brother man, you just messed up big-time. Like RayShawn says, next!*

Shenita thought about not responding at all, then eventually texted back: *Schedule's full; sorry can't reschedule. Thanks for letting me know, though. Bye.*

After no response, she grabbed her Mac and let her fingers do the talking on her keyboard. She figured it was on now; she was tired of all the games men play. One minute they want to go out with you, the next minute they don't.

Like RayShawn said, all these men on this so-called Christian dating website can't be nuts, so it's time I find out what it's really about.

Shenita was on a mission, and Christian's dis just kicked it into overdrive. She signed on and saw she'd been provided with twelve more matches since she last signed in.

"Forget the shy approach," Shenita said. "It's time I send little quick notes to whoever I like, and if they take the bait, then it's on like popcorn."

Shenita then sent icebreaker-type notes that the site suggested, such as, *Your profile brought a smile to my face,* or, *I think you're cute,* or, *Nice smile,* or, *Would love to get to know you better,* and even, *Let's go out,* to all of her suggested matches. To the ones who weren't necessarily matches but she still thought were cute and had potential, she sent a wink, which was the same as sending a poke on Facebook.

She checked her internal e-mail on the site and saw that at least two other men had sent messages asking her out, all from this area. She got to typing and inviting, accepting invitations while at the same time thinking about what outfits she was going to wear on all these upcoming dates.

She eyed a slinky black dress in her closet that she used to wear at the club before she was saved. She figured if she wore that, then no man would be able to resist her or back out on her at the last minute. As far as her love life, Shenita Love had declared that the drought was over.

She crossed out *Rule #4 Never Dress Too Sexy on a First Date* from her rule book and looked back at the profile picture of her next date, set for tomorrow night to replace Christian— a cute thirty-one-year-old caramel-complexioned young man wearing a Detroit Tigers cap, with no facial hair, smooth skin, and a schoolboy grin.

She also crossed out *Rule #3 Never Ask a Man Out First,* as she now saw nothing wrong with being the initiator and going for what you know.

Shenita sat back in her chair, folded her arms, grinned from ear to ear, and said, "Game on."

Danielle rushed back toward the VIP room to get inside and save Princess Dream, but the bouncer near the door stopped her with his hand. Danielle quickly turned on her charm and said, "C'mon now, let me in; I got a customer in there waiting for me." The bouncer eyed her strangely, because he didn't remember seeing her go in there earlier with anyone, nor did he recall anyone entering alone saying they were meeting her inside.

Just then Sparks passed by her and said, "You still here, girl? Shouldn't you be in bed by now? Don't you got church in the morning?"

Danielle rushed over to Sparks and said, desperately, "Sparky, I gotta favor to ask you."

"What is it, my queen?" he responded.

"Can I pick my own music for tomorrow night's center-stage performance?"

Sparks removed his drenched, unlit Montecristo from the corner of his mouth and said, "Your own music? You sure about that?"

"Yes, I'm sure. It would mean the world to me." Danielle laid her head on Sparks's shoulder and batted her eyelashes.

Sparks thought a moment and said, "Girl, if you bring it

tomorrow night like you brought it tonight I don't care what music you have on in the background! You can have on country music, for all I care." He then pointed with his cigar and said, "When you on that pole it's all about you, that pole, and them patrons, and if you can make all them happy, then go for it!"

"Thanks, Sparky!" She kissed him on his cheek.

"Watch out there now," he said, delighted.

CHAPTER 34

For Saturday-morning breakfast after feeding Teacup her gourmet dog food in her personalized pink bowl, Pippa loaded her omelet with green peppers, mushrooms, Swiss and American cheese, and onions on the frying pan while stirring her pot of grits at the same time. She retrieved two slices of toast from the toaster and spread on thick coats of butter along with grape jelly. Within a few moments she fixed a full plate, poured herself a cup of instant coffee with three teaspoons of sugar and a tablespoon of half-and-half, blew on it to cool it down, added everything to a breakfast tray, and topped it off with a vase holding a big sunflower.

She hummed as she headed to her couch, still in her pink-and-white floral onesie pajamas, and was about to turn on the television when she thought of calling Elijah to brighten his morning and see what he had going on for the day.

He answered on the third ring.

"Good morning, man of God!"

"Good morning, Pippa how are you today?"

"I'm good. Just wanted to check on one of my favorite men. How are you?"

"I'm excellent."

"Great! What ya got up for later on? Want to hang out?"

"I would love to but I have to study later on today. You know I'm still finishing up classes for my bachelor's."

"That's right, and I know you have school, work, and serving Pastor at church. You do so much at one time. I really admire you for that, Elijah; you care about so many people and so many things. I understand."

"Thank you," Elijah said.

Pippa got a great idea. "Hey, why don't I come over later on. I have some reading to do as well. I promise not to bother you, unless you want me to help you out with something. How about that?"

"Thanks, though, and I really appreciate all your help. But to be honest, I really want to get this done on my own. No offense, though. It's just that my dad, who, as you know, passed away when I was twelve, used to always tell me, 'Son, make your own way in life, create your own path, and depend on no one but yourself.' Now, I don't even know if that was the best advice, but it always stuck with me and still has to this day. I feel like once I get my degree on my own it'll be my way of proving to my dad I can do something myself. It'll be my way of making him proud from the grave."

Pippa swooned. "Oh, Elijah, that's so sweet. No worries, I truly understand, and I know you'll do fine in your studies. You can do it!"

"Thanks, Pippa, you're always so encouraging; I've always liked that about you."

Pippa grinned on the other end.

"Hey, now that I have you on the phone I do have a question for you," Elijah said.

"Really? What?"

"I'd like to get your opinion on something."

"Sure, what is it?"

"Well, it's kind of important. Kind of really important."

"Elijah, you're scaring me—what is it?" Pippa probed.

"I have this thing I want to get for someone special."

Pippa perked up on the other end.

"A ring, actually."

Pippa gasped in delight.

"Now I know you're a young lady who likes nice things, so, in your opinion, what would be the best engagement ring to get? Because I believe I've found the one."

"Really? I mean, you know already you found her?" Pippa asked.

"Beyond a shadow of a doubt."

Pippa's hands sweated as her cell almost slipped out of her hands. "How do you know? Don't you think you're moving a little too fast?"

"Nope. I'm as sure as the day is long. Unlike all the other women I've dated, God spoke to me clearly on this one."

Pippa cried tears of joy. "Well, amen."

Elijah continued, "Now I know there is the round cut and the emerald cut, do you know of any more?"

"Well . . ." Pippa wiped her nose with Kleenex and patted her eyes. She cleared her throat and said, "There's the cushion cut, the Asscher cut, the pear cut, the princess cut, the bezel, and the marquise . . ."

"Wow; that's a lot," Elijah said.

"Yeah," Pippa said and blew her nose.

"Now, out of all those, which would you prefer?"

"Me, personally, I like the princess cut. My daddy always

used to call me his little princess, so ever since then I always said I wanted one of those when I got engaged."

"So you really like that one, huh?" Elijah asked.

"Yup. That's the one," Pippa said as tears flowed again.

"Thanks! I'll definitely keep that in mind," Elijah said. "Hey, I gotta get back to what I was doing, you have a great day, okay?"

"Okay," Pippa said, "I will," and hung up, dropped her cell on the floor, popped up from the couch, and screamed, "AAAAHHHHHHH!"

Teacup perked up in her dog bed.

"I can't believe I'm getting MARRIED!" she shouted at Teacup and did the Holy Ghost dance all around her apartment, not caring if the neighbors on either side of her heard her or if her neighbors below felt her jumping up and down.

Pippa shouted, cried, and praised God five minutes straight, and yelled, "God, You are worthy, You are worthy! You are faithful! There is none like You! Heaven and earth shall proclaim Your glory, Your glory! Thank You for moving on my behalf. Thank You for watching over me, for keeping me and for favoring me, your daughter! I promise, Lord," Pippa said and clutched her hands together, "to be the best wife for your son Elijah O'Toole. I promise to do him good and not evil all the days of his life. I promise to serve and please him just like I serve and please You, because I know in serving and pleasing him You will be pleased. Thank you, Lord God, THANK You, Lord God, THANK YOU, JESUS!"

Pippa turned on her CD and blasted Donald Lawrence's "Back to Eden," and did a Holy Ghost jig in her onesie. She grabbed her broom and swept the kitchen floor while singing the chorus, with her broom handle as her microphone.

Once the song was done she fell on the side of the couch and worshipped God, thanking Him for His goodness and for giving her the desires of her heart.

She prayed and cried and used this private moment to tell God how much she truly loved Him and how she was so grateful for what He had done.

After paying homage to God, Pippa picked up her cell and called one of her best friends.

After five rings Shenita's phone went to voice mail, as Shenita was out on a breakfast date.

Online Date #2: The Gospel Rapper

Shenita sat in agony across the table from her second online date. He ate so fast in front of her you would think he hadn't eaten a thing in weeks. He had barely said two sentences, and the two sentences he chose to utter were filled with broken grammar and street lingo from the eighties.

On a more positive note, he did look exactly like his profile picture. He even wore his same Detroit Tigers baseball cap. The only thing is, though, Shenita never thought he'd wear that same cap while dining at a family-style restaurant. *Does he ever come up for air?* Shenita thought as he ate like there was no tomorrow.

"You know, shawty," Saved Young Jeezy Wanna Beezy said while chomping on a slice of bacon like it was a piece of celery. "God got a lot of plans for me, you know what I'm saying?"

Shenita nodded.

"You see, my plans are not His plans, and His ways are not my ways."

Shenita held her head as this brother just messed that Scripture all up.

"I'ma hit it big, Ma," he insisted. "Bigger than MC Hammer. Shoot, bigger than LeCrae. Actually, I gotta rap I just put on wax and I'm 'bout to send it to LeCrae and his boys. I'm 'bout to be the next biggest thing on Reach Records. Forget that, I'm 'bout to *be* Reach Records. Want to hear it?"

"Um, no," Shenita said.

He rapped anyway: "Mary had a little lamb and Jesus was a little Lamb who died on the cross, because He was the boss, not boss like a slave they put Him in a grave but yo' He didn't last cuz after three days He raised. He rose! With all power, He rose!"

"Check, please!" Shenita said.

CHAPTER 35

After several unsuccessful probes for details, Jackie finally allowed Jermaine to surprise her regarding the location of their first date. After an hourlong drive, once Jermaine exited the freeway in his black BMW and was five minutes from the destination, he asked Jackie to wear a black silk blindfold so she still wouldn't know where they were going until their arrival.

"Are you kidding me?" Jackie asked as he handed her the blindfold.

"C'mon, Jackie, put it on. I want to surprise you," he urged.

"You want me to put *that* over my eyes?" she asked, and he nodded. "Oh no," Jackie said defiantly, "You got me pegged all wrong. I will not succumb to total control just so you can exercise your right to—"

"Will you just wear the daggone blindfold?" Jermaine barked.

Jackie snatched it and tied it around her head and said, "Forget it, then, I'll wear the stupid blindfold, but wherever we're going it better be worth it, I mean, you got me out here in the middle of nowhere, no telling who could be here. KKK could even—"

"Zip it!" Jermaine ordered as he parked the car.

Jackie folded her arms and remained silent as she heard his car door close and hers open. He grabbed her hand and helped her outside and walked her over to the front building of their final destination.

After taking a deep breath he removed the blindfold and Jackie looked up and gasped in awe. He had taken her to one of Michigan's finest apple orchard cider mills.

"This is beautiful!" Jackie belted as she looked at the front porch of the apple orchard's barn, filled with baskets of red, green, and yellow apples, rows of pumpkins, and seemingly unending rows of yellow, purple, and white flowers and flowering trees. She looked all around and beheld the beautiful fall colors of the leaves on the trees, the brilliant red oranges and browns, as she soaked up the fresh Michigan air and even caught a whiff of what smelled like fresh homemade apple pie.

Jackie left Jermaine behind and skidded over to the main store to follow the pie scent, and there were caramel apples, fresh cider, strawberries, raspberries, cherries—even a small winery in the corner.

She was greeted by an older gentleman with straight, silver hair. "How do you do there, ma'am. My name's Gene, and welcome to Michigan's finest cider mill and apple orchard," he said with extended hands.

"Thank you," Jackie said, shaking both his hands, "for the warm welcome. This is a nice place you have here," she observed. Jackie had always seen commercials of apple orchards growing up and secretly wanted to visit one but knew her mother, who raised her and her older brother alone, couldn't afford it. Today's visit was like a dream come true for her.

"Why, thank you, my dear," he said as Jermaine followed behind and stood next to Jackie. "Been here thirty-eight years," Gene, the owner, added.

"Thirty-eight years? That's a long time," Jackie said.

"You darn right it is, and just like a fine glass of wine," he said, pointing toward his small winery then looking back at Jackie, "it only gets better with time. Ain't that right, young man?" he asked Jermaine.

"Yes, sir," Jermaine said.

Just then a blond woman wearing a black-and-blue plaid shirt and dark blue skinny jeans stepped out from the back and stood next to Gene.

"Hello there, Roxanne. I'm glad you came out of hibernation back there," Gene said.

Roxanne glanced at their new visitors.

"Say hello to the nice people, dear daughter," Gene said.

"I'm Jermaine," Jermaine said, and extended his arm.

Roxanne grabbed it and said, "Hello."

"I'm Jackie." She extended her hand for a handshake as well.

"Hi," Roxanne said to Jackie.

"Mr. Jermaine, I got your call from earlier today and I've made my daughter Roxanne here privy to it as well. She's going to be your 'go to' person for the day in case you need any assistance," Gene said.

Roxanne peeked at Jermaine through her long blond bangs, and Jackie caught Jermaine returning Roxanne's extended glance.

He quickly looked back at Jackie and placed his arm around her shoulder.

Gene continued, "You kids are surely going to enjoy yourselves here at Gene's Cider Mill. You can count on that," he said reassuringly.

"Okay," Jermaine said, then clapped his hands. "Well, let's get started."

CHAPTER 36

After escaping her second online date with wannabe rapper dude, Shenita checked her cell once she was inside her ride and saw she had a missed call from Pippa.

Wanting to leave the date scene as soon as possible, she drove down the highway, headed home to prepare for her next date later tonight, and decided to return Pippa's call from her voice-activated car phone.

She pressed the appropriate button and said, "Call Pippa," loud enough for the automated system to hear.

The phone rang once and Pippa answered, "Hello?"

"Hey, girl, it's Shenita."

"Oh, hey, girl, I didn't recognize the number," Pippa said as she set down her Bible and concluded she would finish her personal home Bible-study lesson on her couch at another time.

"I know, right? I'm calling from my car."

"Oh, okay. How cool," Pippa said.

"Yeah, girl, it's a blessing. Very convenient. So what's up?"

"What's up is," Pippa said while purposely pausing a few

moments before breaking the exciting news to her good friend. "I'm about to get engaged!"

"Engaged?" Shenita asked and almost ran through a red light. She stopped herself in the middle of the intersection and backed up as people in neighboring cars eyed her like she had lost her mind.

"Yes! Engaged! I talked to Elijah this morning and he asked me about engagement rings! He asked me for my favorite cut. I still can't believe this is happening, Shenita, I'm about to get engaged! I'm about to get married!"

"Whoa now, hold your horses, Tonto, are you sure that's what he said?" Shenita asked.

"Yes!"

"Are you sure he said he's about to propose to you?"

"Yes!"

"Well, I'll be darned," Shenita said under her breath.

"What?" Pippa asked. "What'd you say, Shenita?"

"Oh, nothing, uh, I said, you go, girl! I'm happy for you. Y'all set a date yet?"

"No, not yet. Actually, he hasn't proposed just yet, he just wanted to make sure he got the right ring I wanted. I bet he's going to propose this weekend, maybe even tomorrow night!"

"Just give it some time, Pippa, don't rush into anything," Shenita warned. "I just don't want you 'running with the vision' and brother man hasn't even put a ring on it yet."

"Oh, I won't. Trust me, I won't, Shenita. God's got my back on this one. He's the one who's been sustaining me and keeping me all this time, so Lord knows He can continue to keep me for at least a few more days."

"Well, okay, then. As long as you remember that, then you're good," Shenita said.

"But can you believe it?" Pippa asked excitedly.

"Well . . . there's been a lot of strange things happening around here lately. So at this point nothing surprises me," Shenita said.

"I'm so excited!" Pippa proclaimed. "Glory to God!"

"Amen. That's right. Glory to God. He's good. His timing is perfect."

"That's right, Shenita," Pippa agreed. "His timing is perfect for me! I love the Lord, for He heard my cry!"

"Amen, Pippa."

"Well, I gotta go, just wanted to share the good news. I'm about to update my Facebook status to engaged."

"Wait a minute now, Pippa," Shenita said. "Remember, he hasn't proposed just quite yet. He just asked about the ring."

"Oh yeah, you're right," Pippa said. "You have a point there. Well, you know what, that Mark Zuckerberg needs to add another relationship status in between *in a relationship* and *engaged,* like *soon to be engaged* or something like that."

"You know, that sounds like a good idea, Pippa, maybe you should e-mail him your suggestion," Shenita said, entertaining her.

"I think I will," Pippa said. "As a matter of fact, I'm going to e-mail him right now. Do you know his e-mail address?"

"No, I don't, but you can probably google it," Shenita said.

"Okay. I'll google it, then. I'll talk to you later, okay?"

"Okay. Bye, Pippa."

"Bye." She hung up.

That girl, Shenita thought.

CHAPTER 37

A set of twin brown horses with blond hair galloped along the corn-maze trail with their male driver carrying Jackie and Jermaine in a red open wagon filled with hay. Jackie sat with her legs stretched out together and her arms folded, as she felt every bump in the trail and every twist and turn.

She unfolded her arms and observed her surroundings, soaking in the brisk Michigan air on this beautiful fall day.

"Nothing like it, huh?" Jermaine asked, seated right next to Jackie with their shoulders touching.

"No, not at all. This is my first hayride and it's wonderful," Jackie admitted.

"Really? Your first one?" Jermaine asked.

"Yep," Jackie reassured him. She looked over at him and gave a flirty grin.

"Well, I'm glad I could add something special to your life." He grabbed her waist to hold her.

Still smiling, Jackie asked, "Excuse me, Mr. Stroud, what do you think you're doing?"

"What?" he asked innocently. "I'm enjoying the hayride. See

that scarecrow over there?" He pointed to a miniature scare-crow in the middle of the cornfield. "I never knew those things were real. Kinda makes you think of Michael Jackson from *The Wiz,* huh?" he asked.

"Right," Jackie said, then removed his hand from around her waist and scooted over a few inches from him.

"What did I do?" he asked.

"Jermaine, you know exactly what you did. I appreciate your taking me out and all, but don't you think our being all 'hugged up' is moving a little too fast?"

"Huh? No! I was just getting cozy with a friend, that's all," he said.

"Yeah, right," Jackie said.

"Look, don't be *scurred.* You look about as scary as that scare-crow over there right now. I won't bite, unless you want me to," Jermaine said, then growled.

"Jermaine, I'm serious! This is not funny. I want to date you to get to know you, not to get close to you romantically on the first date. I'm just guarding my heart, that's all."

"Look, Jackie, it's not that deep. You sound like my ex, just worrying a whole lot over nothing," Jermaine said. Jackie gave a mean glare, then folded her arms again.

"I understand you want to take it slow, and I think we are. Too slow, if you ask me!" Jermaine said. "I haven't even held your hand yet, and here you are getting all spooky and deep on me. Relax. I can tell you haven't been out in a while." He looked outside the wagon and at the trees.

Jackie then threw a bundle of hay on him and some straws landed in his mouth. She cracked up so hard after witnessing his shocked expression that even the horses turned around to see what was going on.

Jermaine then said, "No, you didn't!" and threw a handful of hay at her, then next thing, the hay fight was on! They cracked up the entire time, as hay went flying everywhere and almost hit the driver. By the time the hayride was over, more hay had ended up on the ground and in Jackie's hair than was left inside the wagon.

"You're gonna get it!" Jackie said as Jermaine escorted her out of the wagon and back onto solid ground.

"Me? You the one," he said, picking as much hay as he could from her short curly red tresses.

Jackie grabbed a mirror compact out of her purse, saw all the hay in her hair, and screamed.

She screamed so loud Roxanne, who was nearby, came over to check on them.

"Is everything okay?" she asked.

"Everything's fine. Jackie just had a little accident in the hayride wagon, that's all. She slipped and fell into a mountain of hay and got it all in her hair." Jermaine laughed, and Jackie punched him in his side.

"Oh, well, I have a blow dryer you can use if you want to blow-dry some of that hay out of your hair," Roxanne suggested.

"Sure, I'd love to do that," Jackie said, and followed her inside the main store and waited as Roxanne went to the back room to retrieve the blow dryer. Then Roxanne led her to the women's restroom.

As Jackie blow-dried and combed the hay out of her hair, she asked, "So how long you been here at the orchard with your dad, Roxanne?"

"Oh, about seven years," she replied with her back leaned against the bathroom wall. "I came back here after I got my degree. I got my degree in architecture, but then felt it necessary to help Dad out for at least a little while, and that little while turned into seven years."

"Do you like it?" Jackie asked.

"I love it. I love Michigan weather, especially the fall, which of course is our busiest time of year. I love how it's kinda far off and tucked away from all the hustle and bustle as well. It keeps life simple; I enjoy that."

Jackie turned off the blow dryer, satisfied that the hay was now gone, and combed her hair back into somewhat of a style. "This place is pretty far away from the city. Does your boyfriend ever come up to visit you?" Jackie probed.

"Nah," Roxanne said, "I don't have a boyfriend. Not anymore; I was engaged before but it didn't last. He loved his beer more than me, so I knew that wouldn't work."

"Yeah, you definitely don't want to get caught up in that," Jackie said.

"But I keep my options open. I'm open to trying new things," Roxanne said, and eyed Jackie. "I'm working on it."

I bet you are, Jackie thought. She added a fresh coat of powder to her face and an extra coat of pink lip gloss, puckered her lips together, and said, "Well, good for you, Roxanne," and patted her shoulder. "I pray it all works out for ya," and left her standing there as she exited.

ONLINE DATE #3: REVEREND BROWN

As Shenita sat at a two-seater white-clothed table inside a five-star restaurant in downtown Detroit, she struggled with whether or not she should wear the off-the-shoulder sleeves of her black fitted dress completely off her shoulders, directly on her shoulders, somewhere in the middle, or just up, not showing any shoulders at all, since she was about to be on a date with a pastor.

Okay, now, I don't want to show too much shoulder; gotta look like I'm "first lady" material. Shenita placed her sleeves back on her shoulders. *Then again, at the end of the day he is still a man.* She pulled her sleeves back down to reveal her shoulders.

Five minutes later, a six-foot-four man with a stocky build in a brown-and-black pinstriped suit entered with the waiter by his side and said in a loud, authoritative voice, "Shenita Love, is that you?"

Shenita stood and extended her hand to a man who definitely looked and made her feel she was talking to a pastor, maybe not *her* pastor but definitely the pastor of a local church.

"Yes, sir," Shenita said, noticing that his gray hair blended in with the black, which aged him about ten years. She hadn't noticed it in his profile picture. *Maybe he dyed his hair since his profile picture,* Shenita thought, *or maybe his profile picture was taken ten years ago.*

"Please, don't call me sir, Miss Love. Look down!" he said, and Shenita looked at the floor near him and didn't see anything. He then pointed to his pant leg, and there on his brown-and-black pinstriped pant leg was his name embroidered on the outside cuff. "The name's Reverend Brown. Don't forget it now," he said with a wide grin.

Shenita laughed so hard inside that she almost choked. She took her seat while Reverend Brown remained standing and whispered to his waiter and comrade, "Now, I want you to take care of my Ledisi for me. She's the newest addition to the family and I wouldn't want any dents or dings on her, so here's an extra little something for you to check on her every ten minutes for me, okay?" He slipped the waiter a one-hundred-dollar bill.

"You got it, sir, I mean, Reverend Brown," the waiter obliged.

"My man!" he said, and patted the waiter so hard on his shoulder that he leaned forward.

Reverend Brown finally took his seat and said, "Mm, mm, mm. Girl, heaven must be missing an angel tonight, because you over there looking just like you sholl did drop right out of the sky."

Flattered, Shenita said, "Thank you," and then asked, "Who's Ledisi?"

"Ledisi? Oh, she's my Lambo, my baby, my Lamborghini. I just got her off the lot three days ago, had her custom-made just for Reverend Brown."

Shenita laughed. "So do you have 'Reverend Brown' embedded on the tires?"

"Now that, sweet thang, is not a bad idea." He grabbed two rolls, put them on his plate, and buttered one.

He eyed Shenita and said, "Beauty and brains, what a wonderful combination. Looks like God's got a double portion of blessings in store for me. Amen." Then he consumed half a roll with one bite.

At that moment Shenita decided to let Reverend Brown do most of the talking for the rest of the night—anything to speed up the date with a man who reminded her of her great-uncle from Pittsburgh.

"So, you're a pastor. Do you enjoy it?" Shenita asked.

"I love being a pastor," Reverend Brown said. "But sometimes, to be honest, sweet thang, church folk get on my nerves! Check this out, we're smack-dab in the middle of a building fund at the church, right?"

"Mm-hmm." Shenita buttered her roll, then tore off a piece.

"Right now we have a leaky faucet, a roof that's about to

cave in, an air conditioner that doesn't work, a nursery that needs new carpet, and a bank around the corner that won't even give us a loan after we begged for it. If I could just get the congregation to dig deep into they pockets, we can get this building fund on the road. Plus my three kids need new shoes and my baby mommas stay all in my ear bugging me about child support. That's one of them calling now," he said as he checked his vibrating cell and sent the caller to voice mail.

"Now, where was I?" he asked.

"The building fund," Shenita said.

"Oh yes, the building fund. Now, I know times is hard right now, but these folk at my church just gon' have to give it up! Folk need to learn how to sacrifice these days. Take myself, for example—I wanted a drop-top fully loaded Maybach and settled for a Lamborghini. But that's okay, because I know where my help comes from, my help comes from God, and I get blessed because I tithe to myself and serve His people. But you know what?"

"What?" Shenita asked, irritated at this point.

"Half my congregation robbing God expecting God to bless them when they operating under the curse. Miss Love, you look like a tithing woman, so I know you feel me, right?" he asked, flashing a row of 24-karat-gold-nugget rings.

"Yes, Reverend Brown, I tithe."

"That's my girl." Reverend Brown sat back.

"Check, please!" Shenita said with a raised finger.

Jackie returned to Jermaine all dolled up and ready for their next activity at the cider mill and apple orchard.

"Hello, beautiful, you look great," he said, acknowledging her tireless efforts in the restroom.

"Do you come here often? Can I get them digits?" he asked jokingly.

"Shut up," Jackie said and grabbed his hand and led them to the field so they could pick apples together.

She gave him a basket and retreated to picking her own apples like she was a pro. She examined and squeezed each one before making her final decision as to whether or not it was worthy enough to put into her basket to go home with her.

"Mm, that one's bad," she told Jermaine as he added an apple to his basket.

"Huh?"

"It's bad." She took the apple out of his basket and showed him the dime-size brown spot on the corner that he'd over-looked.

"See?" she said. "I got a good eye."

"Oh, wow, I didn't even see that, thanks," he said. "Good looking out," He patted her butt.

"Will you stop?" Jackie said. "You already got blasted with hay, would you like me to make my own special apple pie with your head?"

"Is that a threat?" he asked with a laugh.

They continued on their journey, picking more fruit. Jack-ie's basket was half full, while Jermaine's basket so far only had two apples in it. He picked off another apple and examined it thoroughly. He was about to place it in the basket when Jackie said, "Nah, you don't want to do that."

"What now?" Jermaine asked.

"The apple, it's not hollow enough, see." Jackie held it to her ear, tapped it with one finger, then gave it a shake.

"How can you tell if an apple isn't hollow by just looking at it?" Jermaine asked, perplexed.

"I just know by instinct," Jackie said. "Here, have one of mine." She grabbed an apple out of her basket and put it in his.

"So are you telling me I don't know how to pick apples now? You think I need help picking apples?" Jermaine asked defensively.

"I didn't say that, Jermaine, I just wanted to give you a little help because you're a little slow on your apple picking, that's all."

"A little slow? So you think I'm a little slow? Incompetent? Don't know how to do a simple thing like pick some daggone apples?" He took the apple Jackie gave him out of his basket and threw it clear across the field.

"Look, Jacqueline, I'm tired of you correcting me. I'm not some machine that needs to be fixed. I'm not some client case that needs to be worked on," Jermaine said as Jackie stood there shocked.

"You know what?" he said. "You sound just like my ex. She was always trying to fix me. Always correcting me. She was a school-teacher, and after listening to her all day you would think I was another one of her third-grade students and not her husband!"

Jackie didn't know what to say.

"Just forget it, Jackie, you don't understand," he said, "and you probably never will." He added, "Now you stay over there and let me pick my own daggone apples!"

Jackie didn't know how to respond. She felt anything she said at this point would only hurt and not help the situation, so she remained silent.

Jermaine went to the opposite end of the field to finish picking apples. Roxanne was a few feet from where he was picking and decided now would be a good time to pick more apples for added inventory in the store.

She glanced at Jermaine, who returned her gaze, and she bit into one of the apples and kept staring at him.

CHAPTER 38

Danielle strapped her gold six-inch stilettos, adjusted her fitted purple one-piece suede pantsuit, and tied its straps crisscross up the front.

"Fellas!" the MC said to the crowd from center stage. "And ladies," in reference to a booth of women in the back corner. "We got a special treat for you tonight. In only her second performance after being on a three-year hiatus, she is back and better than ever. Let's give it up for the one, the only . . . Divaaaaa D!"

The lights went down and purple and gold strobe lights glared as the music came on.

Piano chords sounded as Lauryn Hill's voice was heard rapping from the speakers all over Club Xtasy. Horns from the track went off as Diva D made her way to the main stage, and the entire crowd whistled and stood as she cougar-walked to the pole and did a few Hula-Hoop spins around it.

Diva D next stepped away from the pole and began her high-spirited routine with hand gestures, encouraging more applause as she proceeded to do a floor routine full of old-school dances to Lauryn Hill's "Doo Wop (That Thing)."

Diva D did a kicking dance back and forth, with her final kick ending up on the pole, and then she grabbed the pole up high with her strong arm, crawled all the way to the top, did a standing fireman spin and whipped her hair back and forth, did a pretzel spin and a reverse hook spin all the way down, bent all the way back, popped back up, and did a reverse pinwheel spin and ballerina pose that ended up in a handstand.

Everyone clapped as she continued spinning on the pole like a pro, and she topped it all off with a cartwheel onto the pole, then hooked one leg up into a butterfly and extended her neck, looked out, and gave the audience a wide grin.

The crowd erupted in applause as Diva D maintained her smile. She looked near the backstage entrance to see if her three fans had seen her performance. They had.

The twins were excitedly pleased, but the older girl kept a stone face.

Diva D arose from the floor and bowed to her audience. She grabbed a few dollars from some men and made her way backstage. Though she didn't collect as much in tips as the previous night, inside she felt as rich as ever.

Once backstage, before she made it to her dressing room she was stopped by the twins.

"That was awesome, Diva D, you rock!" one of them said.

"Yeah, that was great, you did, like, ten spins in one routine!" the other girl said, in awe.

"Thanks," Diva D said in return, hugging them. "Did you like the song I danced to?" she asked.

The two of them nodded their heads wildly as Princess Dream stood by the backstage entrance with her arms folded. She faced them for a moment, then turned her attention back to the stage.

"Good," Diva D said to the twins, "because that's important. More than my dance moves is the message in the music. It talks about how some men are about only one thing, or 'that thing,' and how you as beautiful young princesses have to look out for that, okay?" Danielle said, stroking both girls' hair.

"But I thought you gotta use what you got to get what you want? That's what Princess Dream always says," one twin said, peeking over at her sister and staring at the stage.

"That's partly true," Danielle said. "You do have to use what you got"—she pointed to the young girl's brain—"to get what you want. God gave you that brain of yours for a reason. He wants you to use it. Promise me you will, okay?" Danielle begged. "Promise me you'll rely on your God-given gifts and talents and skills more than your body, okay?" The twin teens nodded.

"Now, where are you girls' mom? I wanna get you out of—"

"Danielle!" Sparks yelled as he entered backstage, swearing at her. "What was that?" Danielle looked confused.

"Danielle Peterson, this is not *Gymnastics with the Stars*. This is a club. A pole-dancing club! We get paid when our men feel like they just got laid, not when they feel like they just had front-row seats to the Olympics!"

Danielle didn't understand. She thought her routine went great. "What do you mean, Sparky?"

"Oh no, you not gon' 'Sparky' me this time. You were supposed to *bring it*—like you did last night. I don't know what you just did out there tonight but now is not the time to get all 'religified' on me in your routines. People barely ordered any drinks, and by the looks of those five singles in your hand, you didn't pull in much bank either. Oh no! We can't have that! Not up in here!"

"But, Sparks, this was just one night," she reasoned.

"One night? Every night should be a night where you clock much bank. Plus, it's Saturday night! This supposed to be the night I collect more dollars than any other day of the week. Oh no, we can't have you showing up and slowing up the payroll. Folks are not gon' be lined up to see what you just did; maybe you ought to take that act to the circus, but not here!"

The twins looked down at the ground and felt sorry for Danielle.

"I'm sorry," Danielle said in a soft tone. "It won't happen again. I'll be more . . . sexy next time."

"You got that right! I'll make sure of that! From now on, *I* pick the song. You dancing tomorrow night to one of your old classics—the song and routine where you pulled in five thousand dollars at the door in one hour!"

Danielle thought back and couldn't remember what song he was speaking of. She then remembered and thought, *He can't expect me to dance to—*

"'Pony' by Ginuwine! Yeah, buddy, you gon' really ride off of that song," Sparks said with a hearty laugh.

"Not that song, Sparks!" Danielle begged.

"Yeah, buddy," he said, counting dollars.

Danielle pleaded, "I'm saved now, and I don't wanna . . ."

"Saved now?" Sparks said, and stopped counting his money. "Saved now?" He got right in her face and blew his warm breath all over her.

"Don't you be coming up in here talking about you saved now. Yeah, you saved all right, you saved from not having to walk over to the unemployment line. Saved? Who saved you? *I* saved you, remember? I saved your butt from being out on the street! If you want to play in my playground, sweetheart, you gotta play by *my* rules. You gotta pay to play, baby. Talking 'bout you saved. Give me a break. Ladies!" Sparks yelled, and his two companions in matching short, tight red dresses and silver stilettos appeared by his side. "My coat," he said as the one on his left enveloped him in his mink coat.

He whispered in Danielle's ear, "Welcome to my world, Danielle. Remember, I own you, and there ain't no turning back." Then he added in a regular tone as he stepped away from her ear, "You can believe that. Let's go!" He said as his mini-entourage left backstage and headed out front.

Danielle stood shocked.

She looked back at her two young fans, who didn't say a word. Danielle felt as if her little pep talk with her fans was worthless now, and that her so-called positively motivating pole-dance routine was all done in vain.

Maybe Princess Dream is right, Danielle thought. *Maybe in order to get ahead in this world you gotta shake what ya momma gave ya or get thrown out in the street.*

Danielle was just as confused as her young fans, though *she* was supposed to be the one setting the example.

Princess Dream finally retreated from standing at the backstage entrance, clapped her hands slowly and loudly as she approached Danielle, and placed one hand on her shoulder. "You know what, Sparks is right. Your routine tonight was whack. It looks like his favorite girl is losing her flavor," she said with a grimacing laugh. "But that's okay, it just leaves more room for Princess Dream to take your place, and more tips for me to bank tonight." She removed her tan trench coat to reveal an orange glittering two-piece that looked more like a bikini than a dance costume. She looked like her tall, lanky self weighed no more than a buck-o-five, but she was determined to make use of the little she had in order to get what she wanted.

CHAPTER 39

Sitting on the couch watching *Martin* reruns with Teacup lying on her lap, Pippa licked the back of her tablespoon, then dug it deep into the corner of the last of the pint of cookie dough ice cream. She laughed at Martin's antics and picked up her cell to check it in case she'd missed a call. She hadn't.

She knew Elijah told her he would be studying this Saturday night, but she figured maybe he wouldn't mind a quick study break in the form of a "hello" call from his favorite girl.

She dialed his number and after the first ring it went straight to voice mail.

"My baby must be studying hard tonight," Pippa said. "Maybe I can send him a little something something to put a smile on his face."

Pippa then took a picture of herself with puckered lips, holding the empty carton of ice cream and showing the back of her spoon. She checked the photo, thought it was supercute, and texted, *I have a sweet tooth for you, boo,* and sent it along with the image.

After not receiving an immediate response, Pippa got ready for

another episode of *Martin* to come on, then headed to the fridge
to bring out another pint of ice cream, chocolate mint this time.

As stars filled the night sky at the cider mill, Jackie spotted Jermaine seated by the outdoor fireplace adjacent to its main store.
He shivered and rubbed his hands together, allowing the fire to
warm his hands and body.

Although initially Jackie just wanted to be through with the
whole date, she felt a sort of compassion for the man before her;
he shook not only like he was cold but like he was someone
who'd had a broken, hard, disappointed life.

Jackie crawled atop the cedarwood and rocks and sat beside
him to warm her hands as well. He looked at her then looked
back at the fireplace. She gave him a nudge and said, "Hey."

"What?" Jermaine asked dryly.

"You mad at me?"

Jermaine let out a sigh and kept staring at the fireplace. He
finally said, "No."

"Okay," Jackie said. "Just checking."

Jermaine grabbed a stick and put a marshmallow on it,
heated it, then ate it.

Jackie looked at what he just did with disgust.

"Here, you should try it," he said and grabbed another stick,
heated another marshmallow, and placed it in front of Jackie's
face to take a bite.

"C'mon," he said.

"No," Jackie said matter-of-factly. "No, thank you. No telling where that stick has been."

"C'mon, Jackie, these are sterilized sticks. They came from
the store," he said.

Jackie wasn't sure whether or not to believe him, but because he insisted and because she'd grown tired of staring at a huge brown-and-white marshmallow in front of her face, she took a bite.

"See, that wasn't so bad," he said. Jackie immediately grabbed a napkin to wipe marshmallow that had dripped underneath her chin.

She chuckled. "You're right," she said, still chewing. "That wasn't bad at all."

"See there," Jermaine said. "See what happens when you trust me?"

Jackie smiled at him and said, "Gimme that stick." She placed another marshmallow on it and they roasted their marshmallows together.

"I see you kids have settled in now," Roxanne said as she made her way over to the two of them.

Kids? Jackie thought, wondering why this lady often felt the need to interrupt their flow during this trip.

"Oh, hi, Roxanne," Jermaine said.

"Yep, we're pretty much settled in," Jermaine said then put his arm around Jackie's shoulder. This time Jackie didn't budge.

"Nice night, eh?" Roxanne said, and looked up at the stars and caught a glimpse of the moon. "You two are in luck," she said.

"Why's that?" Jermaine asked.

"Looks like there's a full moon tonight," she clarified.

"Sweet," Jermaine said, looking up and spotting it in the sky. "Wait a minute. Is that a good thing or a bad thing?" he asked, not quite remembering what a full moon meant.

Roxanne walked over and grabbed a marshmallow from the bag near him and ate it. "It can be whatever you want it to be, Jermaine," she said then giggled.

Jermaine got lost looking at Roxanne, until Jackie said, "Well, alrighty then, thanks so much, Roxanne, for your soliloquy. If you don't mind, Jermaine and I have a date we'd like to finish up . . . alone, I might add, that's *if* you don't mind, of course."

"Oh, I'm sorry, was I interrupting your date?" Roxanne asked sweetly while twisting her hair. "I surely didn't mean to." She added, "Bye y'all," with a wink to Jermaine. As she headed back to the store, Jermaine's eyes followed her.

Once Roxanne was completely inside, Jermaine turned to his date and said, "Now that was rather rude."

"Rather rude?" Jackie asked. "You were the one all caught up in Goldilocks, forgetting about the fact that you were on a date with me!"

"So is that what this is all about?" Jermaine asked. "The fact that she's white? You know what, you sound just like my ex. She was insecure around white women, too."

"Excuse me?" Jackie said, and snapped her neck his way. "No, you didn't just go *there,*" she said. "And if you say one more thing to me about your ex I will scream! You talk about her so much, it's like I know the woman! As a matter of fact, what's her number?" Jackie pulled her cell out of her jacket pocket. "I'm gonna call her, because it sounds like we both have a lot in common"—she turned directly to Jermaine—"like the fact that we both choose not to have to put up with some wandering-eye, easily distracted, dense-acting no-good man!"

"Did you just call me stupid?" Jermaine asked.

"I didn't say it. You did," Jackie said and folded her arms.

"Get in the car," Jermaine said.

"What?" Jackie asked.

"Get in the car!" he yelled, pointing toward his BMW.

"Fine!" Jackie said, and got up. "Fine!" she yelled once she was closer to the car. "I wanted to leave anyway!"

Jermaine opened the door for her on the passenger side then slammed it once she got inside.

He made his way to the other side, closed the car door, and remained silent as he sped off onto the dusty road.

Neither of them said a word to each other during the entire hourlong trip back home to Detroit, which felt like an eternity.

Danielle closed her full-length baby-blue trench coat, stepped out of the club, and was headed to her ride, parked directly across the street, when she saw a couple she recognized leave the restaurant next door and head down the sidewalk in her direction.

She thought her eyes were playing tricks on her and did a double take as she spotted her former boss, Mrs. Reid, and Clive, her former coworker whom she doused with hot coffee that fateful day, arm in arm. Danielle rushed to avoid them by jay-walking, except the cars zooming by wouldn't let her. Her attempt to dodge them was foiled as she heard the familiar voice she loved to hate yell out, "Miss Peterson?"

Danielle gave a startled grin, waved, and said, "Oh hi, Mrs. Reid. It's still Mrs., right?" Danielle asked, then looked Clive up and down.

"Well, if it isn't Danielle Peterson," Clive said, wearing that same old pair of tan khaki pants underneath his coat. "It looks like the Lord has been good to me, because at this very moment I am honored," he said, popping his coat, "and privileged to be standing amongst Classy"—pointing to Mrs. Reid—"and Trashy." He pointed to Danielle.

Danielle grimmed him and looked to see when the road would clear so she could make her escape from these two vultures.

"Were you just coming out of the pole-dancing club?" Mrs. Reid asked, pointing at the neon Xtasy sign behind her. She sized Danielle up and down and said, "Oh, I get it. So you found yourself another job after all. Gotta pay the bills somehow, huh, sister girlfriend?" She extended her fist for a fist bump, but Danielle just looked at it.

"Oops, my bad, isn't that what you street women say? My mistake."

"Mrs. Reid, would you like me to give your *husband* a call and let him know you're going to be late coming home again tonight, or are you going home at all this time?"

Mrs. Reid lifted her nose. "C'mon, Clive, let's go," she said, then swung around. "We don't have to be bothered with this low-life trash." She turned around to face Danielle once more and said, "Hope everything works out with your new *job*," then turned and walked away.

Danielle stood with her hands stuffed into her pockets, cold from the chilly night air, which slowly crept up her legs. She looked back at Clive and Mrs. Reid, prayed the cars would stop zooming so fast so she could cross, and felt a cold tear escape one of her eyes and take a dive in the brisk air.

ONLINE DATE #4: THE POLICEMAN

"Ten years is a long time," said the policeman, who'd forgotten to change out of his uniform for his dinner date with Shenita. He wiped barbecue sauce from his hands after eating a full slab of ribs.

"What do you do until then?" he asked, picking his teeth with a toothpick. "Keep a whole lot of batteries in your kitchen drawer?"

Shenita couldn't believe this man just asked her this question.

"Um, no," she replied.

"Well, you must do something." He leaned over the table, looked deep into her eyes, and said, "I'ma have a whole lot of fun handcuffing you."

"Check, please!"

CHAPTER 40

On Sunday morning, members of New Life Tabernacle Saving Grace Church's sanctuary choir all shouted and praised God back in the choir room a half hour before the second service began, which was their usual routine in preparation for their upcoming ministry performance just before Pastor Solomon stepped up to the pulpit to preach.

They had just gone over today's A selection, "Jesus Can Work It Out," and it was so anointed that afterward the whole choir erupted in praise.

Pippa leaned over in her gold robe, stomped her feet, threw off her black two-inch pumps, and twirled around like a pinwheel while lifting her hands, giving all praise and glory to God.

Danielle, too, was keeled over, holding her stomach, with tears streaming down her face, in worship to her Heavenly Father.

After another ten minutes of praise, the choir director got everyone's attention and asked them to form a huge circle so they could announce any more praise reports just before service.

Sister Shirley lifted her hand. "I have one."

"Go ahead, Sister Shirley," said Brother Earl, the tall, lanky choir director.

"I was in the bathroom all night long because I have a weak stomach; I think it was something I ate. Well, I was afraid that I wasn't going to make it to church this morning, let alone serve in the choir, but God woke me up at four forty-five this morning and told me that I shall live and not die, and declare the works of the Lord! So since four forty-five a.m. this morning I been praying and praising God and my stomachache has been gone away ever since! Glo-reh!" Sister Shirley said.

"Hallelujah!" some others replied.

"Anyone else?" Brother Earl asked and looked around.

"I have one!" Pippa raised her hand.

"Well, go ahead, Sister Pippa. It's always a joy to hear from you!" Brother Earl said.

"Amen, Brother Earl, thank you," Pippa said. "My testimony is, God has blessed me with my Boaz and I'm about to get married soon!"

Everyone looked at Pippa and at one another and said, "Wow, that's wonderful!"

"God is good!" Pippa said. Danielle looked over at her, wondering what in the world she was talking about.

"Awesome news, Sister Pippa!" Brother Earl said. "Take it from me, a man that's been married over twenty years, marriage is a blessing, but it can be a curse if you're married to the wrong one. So we thank God that, as you have waited patiently and faithfully, God has blessed you with the right one, Sister Pippa."

"Amen!" she said with a huge grin. Danielle still had no clue. She peeked over at Pippa's left hand but didn't see a ring.

"Any more?" Brother Earl asked. "I believe we have room for one more testimony before we go into service."

"I have one," a male, nasally voice said.

Everyone looked around to see who was talking.

"Over here, Brother Earl, it's me. Willy. I have a testimony I'd like to share," Willy said.

"Well, if it isn't our newest member of the choir. So glad to hear from you! Brother Willy, what's your testimony you'd like to share?"

Willy rubbed his ashy hands together. "The Lord has blessed me suddenly with a fifty-thousand-dollar check. I have it right here," he said, and pulled out a check from his pants pocket underneath his choir robe.

"Whoa, now, we don't need to *see* the check. You put that away, and get it to the bank right away," Brother Earl said as everyone else agreed.

"Okay," Willy said. "Well, that's my testimony. I'm out of debt now. I'm rich!"

"Well, that's wonderful, Brother Willy! Praise God! Yes, He is Jehovah Jireh and He does move suddenly, so we praise God for the sudden blessing that just occurred in your finances. Hallelujah!" Brother Earl said.

"Hallelujah!" everyone repeated except Danielle. She just looked over at Willy and thought, *Now how did he get $50,000? It must be something in the water, because these testimonies today are out of this world.*

"Sister Danielle," Brother Earl called.

"Yes, sir," Danielle said, startled.

"I'm going to need you to lead praise and worship in the sanctuary today. Sister Anissa called in sick at the last minute early this morning. Can you handle it?" he asked.

"Don't worry, Brother Earl. I got it."

"Good. I knew you could. Thanks, Danielle, you're a gem."

"No problem," she said.

Just then Willy came over to Danielle as she adjusted her choir robe while getting ready for the service that would start in a few minutes. Since she was leading the praise team today, she had to be onstage before everyone else.

"Congratulations on leading praise and worship today, Danielle," Willy said.

"Thanks, Willy." She looked toward the sanctuary stage.

"Did you hear my testimony?" he asked.

"I sure did, Willy. Fifty grand. That's nice. That's God right there."

"Yup; fifty grand." He pulled his check out again and looked at it. "That should be enough to cover the two of us on a date, don't ya think?" he asked.

"It probably could, Willy, but I'm sorry; I'm not interested," Danielle admitted.

"Not interested? How could you not be interested in this?" he said, flashing his check in her face.

"I'm sorry, Willy, they're calling me to go out front. Now you take your little check and you run on somewhere. Go buy yourself some new shoes or something." She then headed to the stage, grabbed the mic, and began leading the praise team and the congregation with Israel Houghton's "We Worship You."

Shenita stood in the front church lobby waiting for Krissy. As she waited, she checked the top button of her tan dress to make sure it hadn't come loose, and she adjusted her wide patent-leather brown belt to make sure it was still nice and snug around her waist. She checked her phone to make sure Krissy hadn't texted her again; the last text she received from her was the one saying she would still meet her at church in the lobby when church began. Shenita hoped Krissy didn't think to meet her in the back lobby. Just to be sure, Shenita dialed Krissy and had placed her cell on her ear when a vibrant, petite woman with a short blond bob haircut made her way into the front lobby.

"Hi, Shenita, sorry I'm late," she said. "My cat gave me a hard time this morning. They're like humans, you know, it's like she didn't want to see me go and kept whining."

"Oh, don't worry about it," Shenita said and hung up her cell. "Glad you could make it," she said, and gave Krissy a hug.

"Am I dressed okay? I wasn't sure if I could wear pants or not; I know some churches don't allow it," she said, looked around at other congregants in the lobby.

"Oh, no, you're fine, Krissy," Shenita said, eyeing her gray pants and pink cashmere sweater. "We're casual around here."

"Oh, good," Krissy said, relieved.

"The Word says come as you are, and that's just what we're all about around here," Shenita assured her, then led her inside.

Shenita led Krissy to the seat she had already saved for them in the front of the center section.

"Is this okay for you?" Shenita asked, and removed her coat from the saved seat.

"Oh, this is fine, thanks," Krissy said.

Shenita remained standing and clapped her hands as Danielle led "We Worship You," and Krissy followed suit.

During the worship song, Shenita lifted her hands and closed her eyes as she worshipped the Lord, while Krissy stood with her head facing downward and her eyes closed.

After two praise songs, Krissy thought it'd be safe to sit down now but didn't, as she noticed Shenita kept standing.

Pastor Solomon entered the pulpit, and the entire congregation rose and everyone gave God praise and honor.

"Good morning, church!" said Pastor Solomon, who was wearing a corporate blue shirt, black pants, and black Kenneth Cole shoes.

"Good morning," the congregation responded.

"I said good morning, church," he repeated with the same jubilance.

"Good morning!" everyone said, louder this time, including Krissy.

"Last time I checked, this was the body of Christ. Which should mean we are an alive body, and not a dead body, because a dead body should be buried, amen?"

"Amen!" everyone said.

"Amen." He positioned his Bible on the pulpit. "I don't know about you," he continued, "but the God I serve is not dead, He's alive!"

"Amen, Pastor!" a lady in a yellow hat in the front row said.

"Cuz if he was dead then that means they would have lied to us when they said they put Him in that grave."

"Well," a deacon said from the right.

"But in three days He rose!"

"Yes, sir!" an older gentleman said from the left.

"With all power," Pastor continued, "in His hands."

"Yeah yeah yeah," the keyboardist said.

"At this time I'd like to bring your attention to the stage and ask you to join me in welcoming the New Life Tabernacle Saving Grace Church's sanctuary choir as they render us a selection."

Choir members looked at one another, knowing that Pastor's

request of a selection meant that they would be singing only one song and not their normal two. They looked to Brother Earl for direction and he signaled the female soloist for "Jesus Can Work It Out" to come up front.

Everyone in the congregation sat down, and Krissy followed. The soloist grabbed the mic with authority, the pianist geared up and played the intro, and the choir swayed side to side as they proclaimed, *"Jesus will work it out. Jesus will work it out."*

At the start of the song Shenita leaped to her feet and clapped her hands along with everyone else. Krissy looked around and saw everyone fully engaged. Midway through the song she, too, got up and clapped.

Shenita got happy and did a Holy Ghost dance in the middle aisle, since their seat was in the first row of the cleared aisleway. Krissy smiled and clapped. At the end of the song Shenita returned to her seat, and everyone clapped, including Krissy, until Pastor Solomon returned to the stage.

Once he returned he and the congregation read the main text for today's sermon, found in *Jeremiah 31:3* which states, *The Lord hath appeared of old unto me, saying, Yea, I have loved thee with an everlasting love: therefore with lovingkindness have I drawn thee.*

Pastor asked everyone to take their seats as he began his lesson.

"Now the prophet Jeremiah, in this passage of Scripture, had a revelation from God. God appeared to him and manifested His lovingkindness and explains how it was God's lovingkindness that drew Him even closer to God."

"Amen!" a lady from the third row said.

"I believe His revelation is a Word for the church today."

"Yes, sir!"

"I believe, in the midst of division, corruption, and utter confusion, what we need is a manifestation of God's love in our lives today."

"Yeah yeah yeah."

"You see, God's love is not like man's love."

"Say it, Pastor!" a lady in the second row said.

"Man's love is fickle," Pastor explained. "It'll change on you. One minute they love you, and the next minute they don't. Just look at how they did Jesus. One minute they praised Him, saying 'Hosanna, Hosanna,' and the next minute they yelled, 'Crucify Him!' Man's love can change like the weather."

"Preach!"

"But not God's love," Pastor said, shaking his head. "God's love is constant and steady. You see, God is not a man that He should lie, neither is He the son of man that He should repent. The word *repent* means to change. God will never change His mind about His love for you. It was because of His love that He sent His very best in the form of his Son, Jesus, in order to die for you. Why? So you can spend your life with Him in eternity in heaven, and also enjoy a life of pure bliss and unconditional love from God here on earth."

"You betta preach, Pastor!" a lady said, then waved her handkerchief.

Pastor Solomon continued to preach on God's love for mankind.

The message was so heartfelt and real that it pricked Krissy's heart and got her to thinking about her ex-fiancé and other men in her life who had come and gone, while seemingly taking a piece of her soul with them. She found it hard to believe that there could ever be a man to love her as much as God, Who would love her unconditionally while expecting nothing in return and Who just loved her simply because He is love.

She wanted to know more about this man, about this man who died for her when she didn't even know Him—about this man who paid the price for all of her sins. She'd felt unworthy and unloved her entire life and felt she needed a man to complete her, yet here this preacher in these casual clothes was telling her that the only man she needed to complete her life was Jesus, and that He would never leave her nor forsake her.

At the end of the message, Pastor Solomon asked everyone to stand as he extended an invitation to anyone who would like to come forward and receive God's love in their lives in the form of receiving salvation.

"Is there anybody here?" Pastor asked with a raised hand.

Shenita kept her head lowered and prayed quietly to herself, and then peeked over at Krissy to see if she had raised her hand. She hadn't.

"Won't you come?" Pastor asked.

Krissy kept her head lowered, and Shenita tried peeking at her to see if she was crying. She wasn't sure. Shenita then leaned over and asked Krissy, "Would you like me to go down with you?" Krissy nodded her head, gathered her things, and went down the aisle with Shenita holding her hand. Shenita's initial suspicion was correct, Krissy was hiding a faceful of tears, which showed by the time she stood in front of the pastor, who had everyone repeat the salvation prayer according to Romans 10:8–10.

Pastor then singled Krissy out in the line of people who came down front and said to her, "Sister, God's got a special plan for you. His hand is on your life. You've been running from Him for a long time, but He wanted me to tell you that He got you now, and that He will never let you go." Krissy then wailed into her hands, and Shenita lightly hugged her and held her hand. Everyone in the congregation cheered at the new converts and clapped as they exited stage left to head to a small room in the back, where they were ministered to further and given more information about the church in case they needed a church home. Shenita followed Krissy all the way to the back room while continuing to hold her right hand and never letting it go.

"Krissy, I'd like to introduce you to a couple friends of mine, Pippa and Danielle. They're both in the choir," Shenita said as she introduced Krissy to them. They were now all in the front lobby for fellowship time after church.

"Oh, hi. I remember your face. You were the one leading the songs, right?" Krissy asked Danielle while shaking her hand.

"Yeah, that was me. Guilty," Danielle said with a raised hand and a smile.

"Oh, wow. You were great. You have an awesome voice," Krissy commented.

"Thanks," Danielle said.

"Welcome to the family!" Pippa chimed and gave Krissy a big hug. "I'm so excited for you. God is good and you have a wonderful life in store ahead of you. Praise the Lord!"

"Why, yes, thanks," Krissy said, overwhelmed, and then turned to Shenita. "Shenita, I gotta run," she said. "I have lunch plans with my mom. I'll see you at work on Monday, okay?"

"Sure thing," Shenita said as she gave Krissy a quick hug. "I'll be there with bells on."

"That was such a blessing that you led Miss Krissy down

that aisle to receive Jesus," Pippa said. "I started crying. God is so good and loves all of us the same. We all make up the perfect rainbow here on earth, an earthly family of His children coming in all different colors and different shapes and sizes."

"That's right, Pippa," Shenita said. "Hey, ya'll wanna all do lunch after service at Koney Island?"

"Ooh, girl, I'm not feeling Koney Island today," Danielle said. "Let's do House of Pancakes instead."

"Yeah, let's do House of Pancakes." Pippa concurred, "I love a good, fresh batch of homemade pancakes," she said and rubbed her belly.

"That's cool then," Shenita said. "Let's head over—"

"Oh, wait a minute," Pippa said, remembering something.

"What?" Shenita asked.

"I haven't spoken to my man yet," Pippa said, and peeked inside the sanctuary to check if Elijah was in his usual spot up front next to Pastor Solomon. He was.

"I've gotta go down and say hello, before I go anywhere," she said and fluffed her hair and went back inside the sanctuary.

Danielle peeked inside and saw Pastor Solomon praying with the next church member who stood in line for prayer. She also spotted Elijah, who stood next to Pastor with a watchful eye, and Lynette standing on the opposite side of Elijah.

"You have *got* to be kidding me," Danielle said.

"What?" Shenita asked and peeked inside.

"What is *she* doing here?" Danielle asked, pointing to Lynette.

"Her? She's supposed to be some new girl that all the men at the church seem to be fawning over."

"New girl?" Danielle said, "Well, she definitely ain't new to me, and by her age she sholl ain't no longer a girl."

"What are you talking about, Dani?" Shenita probed.

"That's my ex-boss!" Danielle belted.

"Your ex-boss?" Shenita asked.

"Yeah, the witch that fired me!" Danielle said. "That's Mrs. Lynette Reid!"

"Mrs.?" Shenita asked, not knowing she was married. She didn't remember seeing her walk around her new church home with her husband by her side. The word in the church was that Lynette was one of New Life Tabernacle Saving Grace Church's most beautiful and most eligible bachelorettes.

"As a matter of fact, I saw her and Clive next door to Xtasy last night!" Danielle said, forgetting for a moment she was still inside the church house.

"Xtasy? What were you doing back over there?" Shenita asked. Danielle brushed it off and said, "Never mind, girl. Yeah, we definitely gotta talk about this. Let's do brunch after service—I'm headed that way now."

"Hi, ladies," Jackie interjected as she approached Danielle and Shenita.

"Hey, Jackie!" Shenita said gleefully.

"Hi, Jackie," Danielle said dryly.

"Hey, we're doing House of Pancakes after service, want to meet us over there?" Shenita asked, and Danielle gave her a desperate look.

"Sure, I can meet you ladies over there; I have to take care of something first, though, and then I can stop by," Jackie replied.

"Sounds good," Shenita said. "Danielle and I are headed that way now, see ya when you get there."

"Okay, bye," Jackie said, then left.

• • •

Pippa slowly made her way down the aisle at church until she was a few feet in front of Elijah. She didn't want to interrupt the flow of the Spirit moving as Pastor Solomon prayed with the church member, so Pippa stopped and then waved wildly toward Elijah while grinning profusely.

She peeked over and saw Lynette standing on the opposite side of Elijah in a long purple dress. Pippa waved at her as well.

Pippa waited until the last person in the prayer line received prayer and had hands laid on them for healing. Once the last person retreated back up the aisleway, Pippa continued toward Elijah.

"Hi, man of God!" Pippa said and gave Elijah a hug. He returned her hug and said, "Hi, Pippa, how are you?"

"I'm good," she said. "Hi, Lynette." Pippa gave her a hug as well.

"Hi," Lynette said.

"Have you decided yet where you're going to serve in the ministry?" Pippa asked Lynette.

"Not yet," Lynette responded, and looked at Elijah. "I'm still praying about it."

"Well, if you have any more questions about any of the departments, I've served in all of them at least two months, so feel free to give me a call," Pippa said reassuringly.

"Thanks, Pippa, that's good to know," Lynette said.

"Elijah, the girls and I are headed to brunch, would you like to join us? You can come too, Lynette," Pippa said.

"Oh, no, I'm going to have to pass. You know, after serving with Pastor Solomon, that can wear you out, so I'm headed home to take a nice nap."

"I understand," Pippa said. "What about you, Lynette? Care to join us? It'd be a great way for you to meet some more of your sisters in Christ," Pippa probed.

"Nah, I'm going to pass as well. I already have some plans after church," she said, then looked over at Elijah.

"Okay, suit yourself," Pippa said. "But know that you're always welcome to join us. I'm about to head that way after I speak to Sister Shirley over there. Y'all take care now, okay?" she said. Elijah nodded as they both watched Pippa head back up the aisleway.

CHAPTER 41

"Okay, girl, now what were you saying at church? Lynette is your ex-boss?" Shenita asked once they were seated at a table for four inside House of Pancakes.

"Yes, girl, that Lynette Reid is my ex-boss, and she's a freak! First of all, she's married, yet she still sees that creep Clive, who I had to throw coffee at to get him off me at work. Just nasty."

"Well, she sure doesn't act like she's married at church," Shenita said. "Every time I look up some new dude is all up in her face. Does she even wear her ring?"

"I don't think so, girl. And to think she had to find her little way to *my* church? Of all places! Lord help me, I think this must be a test," Danielle said, and rubbed her forehead.

"You got that right," Shenita said and laughed.

"God must be trying to test my love walk and my patience all at the same time or something," Danielle said.

"Well, if He is, how do you think you're doing on it?" Shenita asked.

"F!" Danielle said with a raised voice. "Girl, F!"

The two of them laughed.

Shenita remembered something. "Wait a minute, though. What were you talking about you saw her and that Clive outside Xtasy last night—you back at that club?"

Danielle shrugged in her seat. "Well . . ."

"Danielle!" Shenita said.

"I needed the money! Besides, it's kinda cool getting back into aerial fitness. Pole dancing is not all about sex, you know. It's an art form. It's a form of fitness. They should make it an Olympics category, if you ask me," Danielle said, and received her plateful of silver-dollar pancakes with gladness.

"Olympics category? Girl, you have lost your ever-loving mind!" Shenita said, as she received her apple crepe and omelet. "I'm sure those men dishing out those dollars are not thinking about any Olympics."

"I'm serious!" Danielle pleaded. "See, folk on the outside looking in like you don't know; pole dancing requires a lot of stretching and working out. You gotta know how to balance. It's not something everybody can do. It requires skill!"

"Skill, huh? How much skill does it take to climb up a pole and swing around it?" Shenita asked, and cocked her head to the side.

"See, that's where you're wrong, Miss Shenita," Danielle said, pointing at her with her fork. "It's so much more than that." And she ate a forkful of food.

Shenita looked at her suspiciously and folded her arms and said, "Yeah, right."

"Forget it," Danielle said. "I don't have time to address closed minds today. Enough about me, what about you? How's your manhunt going, Matlock?"

Shenita sighed. "It's not going at all. Girl, I done been out with every Tom, Dick, and Scary in Detroit from that so-called

Christian dating website I told you about. I think I need to stand on the street and hold a cardboard sign that reads, 'Will work for the ring'; maybe that'll get me some attention."

"Yeah, it'll get you some attention all right," Danielle said, pouring more maple syrup on her pancakes. "The wrong kind of attention. You'll get all kinds of men taking you up on *that* offer."

"I guess."

"You don't want just *any* man, Shenita, you want the right one. You want the one God has for you," Danielle reminded her.

"Yeah, well, where he at?" Shenita flailed her arms. "He need to go ahead and show up now before a sister have to draw Social Security."

"Girl, it is not that deep," Danielle said, "and you are not that old. You're not even forty! Look at me, forty is right around the corner for me in a couple years. It's only by the grace of God that He maintained my sexy." Danielle puckered her lips and slid her fingers through her weave.

"Girl, you are a mess," Shenita said, and took another bite of her crepe.

"What about Terrell?" Danielle asked.

"What about Terrell?" Shenita said. "Girl, Terrell has known and been flirting with me for years. He texts me every year on Christmas and Valentine's Day, but not once has he ever asked me out on a date. Not even to catch a movie."

"Have you ever thought about asking *him* out?" Danielle asked.

"Girl, naw!" Shenita said. "Terrell been sitting up in that church almost fifteen years. He knows better than anybody that 'the man pursues the woman.'" She gave the quote-un-quote sign with her fingers. "He's even told me once before that a woman who approaches him first is a major turnoff. Nope, I'm not gon' be able to do it. They would probably call the church police on me."

"Well, you out here asking these strangers out and showing up in their faces, why don't you just casually ask out somebody you already know?"

"Nope," Shenita said, then licked the back of her fork. "Uh-uh."

"What about you?" Shenita asked in an effort to turn the tables.

"What do you mean, what about me?" Danielle asked.

"Why don't you ask your number-one fan out, your number-one admirer . . . Brother Willy."

"Little Willy? Aw hex, naw!" Danielle said.

"Why not?" Shenita asked.

"Why not? He's not my type. No attraction. He just don't do it for me; sorry."

"You wrong," Shenita said.

"No, I'm not; I'm right. I'm just being honest. If I can't see myself with somebody, I mean *really* with somebody like Marvin Gaye, with somebody after the wedding bells have rung and the lights are down, then um, next!"

"Girl, you're a trip," Shenita said. "And here you are two minutes out of church, after leading praise and worship, and now you over here talking crazy."

"I'm just keeping it real," Danielle reminded her. "God knows what I'm talking about. He know I gotta be sexually attracted to whoever I end up with. I keep it real with God, and He keeps it real with me," Danielle said, eating another forkful of pancake.

Shenita thought a moment, then added, "You do have a point, though. I think you're onto something."

"I know," Danielle said.

Shenita added, "I think that may be *my* problem. I've passed up many a nice guy in these last ten years because I didn't think they were cute enough. Instead of getting to know them better and becoming friends first and focusing on what's really important, I was all caught up in the physical. I probably would be married now had I not passed on the brothers I overlooked back then."

"Girl, whatever. God's not going to allow you to settle—in any area. At least that's what I'm claiming. He won't have you get married to somebody you wake up screaming at because you thought you just saw a monster," Danielle said.

"I guess. But some of them didn't look *that* bad," Shenita said. "I know. I'm wrong. I'll admit I'm a sucker for a cute face and charisma—and add Jesus on top of that, girl, I'm ready to sign them papers . . . in the form of a marriage license, not those *other* papers."

The two of them cracked up.

Shenita pondered and continued, "They say men are visual, and if that's true then I must be a man, because I'm very visual. If I can't see myself getting it on with you and liking it, I probably won't date you either."

"Okay, well uh, *Mr.* Shenita, I hope you're not talking about me, because this girl right here"—Danielle slid her hands up and down her curvy sides—"is all woman. Sorry, boo boo."

"Girl, shut up," Shenita said and threw her clean napkin at her. "I'm not talking about yo' silly butt."

"Hi, ladies!" Pippa said as she made her way to the table and took a seat. "Sister Shirley had me stuck at the church giving me more details about her testimony. Did you hear it?" Pippa asked.

"Yes, we heard it," Danielle said, remembering Sister Shirley's gruesome testimony in the choir room before service began.

"Oh, okay. I see y'all already ordered; is the waitress still around?" Pippa asked. "I'm starving. Ooh, Danielle, those pancakes look good," she said.

"They are good," Danielle said.

"Y'all, isn't God amazing?" Pippa asked as she waited for the waitress to arrive. She faced Shenita. "I was so happy when I saw you lead Miss Krissy down the altar to get saved. One more win for the kingdom! Hallelujah!"

"Amen, that's right, Pippa. God *is* amazing," Shenita cosigned.

Just then Jackie entered and sat in the fourth and final available seat at the table.

"Hello, everyone," Jackie said.

"Hey, Jackie," everyone except Danielle said.

"Hi, Danielle," Jackie said to Danielle.

"Hi," Danielle said.

"Danielle," Jackie said and lightly tapped Danielle's hand, "I just want to apologize for the way I acted last week. I surely didn't mean to—"

"That's okay." Danielle cut her off. "Forget about it; it's all right."

"No, it was not all right," Jackie said then pulled a pink envelope out of her purse.

"I was insensitive about the whole situation. If it's any consolation, I want you to know I thought about you and wanted you to have this card, and I ask that you please accept my sincere apology." She waved the card in Danielle's direction.

Danielle looked at the card, then at Jackie and over at Shenita, who was smiling. Danielle finally said, "Oh, okay," and took the card, and Jackie reached over and gave her a hug and Danielle returned the gesture. Pippa and Shenita faced each other and said, "Aw."

"Isn't that special," Shenita added.

"Whatever, girl, be quiet," Danielle said, wiping away a tear.

"Okay, well, now that we're all here," Pippa said with a raised voice, "I have an important announcement to make."

"Oh yeah, your testimony," Danielle said.

"Oh yes, I forgot, Dani, you were in the choir room, and actually I already told Shenita, too, so I guess this is for you, Jackie, because everybody else already knows."

"Okay, well then I feel honored, Pippa, what's up?" Jackie asked.

"What's up is . . . I'm getting married!"

"Really? To who?" Jackie asked in shock. "Not to say it like that, I just didn't know you were dating anyone. When did you get engaged?"

"I think we all want to know the answer to that question," Danielle said under her breath, and Shenita kicked her shin underneath the table.

"Well," Pippa began, "we haven't set a date yet, and I haven't seen the ring yet, but the other day on the phone Elijah O'Toole asked me about my ring size and—"

"Wait a minute? Elijah? Armor bearer Elijah?" Jackie asked.

"Yes, Elijah. Of all people. And to think I've known that man for seven years and God finally opened his eyes to see that *I'm* his good thing! Praise the Lord!" Pippa shouted.

"Yes, well, um, praise the Lord," Jackie said. "This is definitely news to me." She took a sip of water and cut her eyes over at Shenita.

"Now for the part none of you know about," Pippa said, straightening up in her chair. "I want all of you ladies to be my bridesmaids!" she finished with a squeal and a clap.

"Bridesmaids?" all three of them said in unison.

"Yes, bridesmaids! I consider all of you my besties and I figure now, with all four of us together, is the perfect opportunity for me to ask if you would all stand in my wedding," Pippa said with a big cheese.

There was a brief pause at the table as the three ladies glanced at one another to see who would be the first one to break the news to their eager friend.

Danielle signaled to Shenita. Shenita gave a desperate look that communicated, *I already tried.*

Shenita finally began, "Pippa, sweetheart, I would love to be your bridesmaid."

"Great!" Pippa said.

"Only thing is," Shenita continued, "we're not sure if there is going to be any wedding."

Pippa looked confused. "What do you mean?" She looked at her three friends. "There is going to be a wedding!" Pippa barked in defense.

"Girl, you ain't got no ring!" Danielle chimed in. "If you ain't got no bling-bling, then there ain't gon' be no such thing thing!"

"Oh, is that what you all are worried about?" Pippa asked, calming down.

"Uh, yeah," Danielle said.

"That's nothing to worry about, the ring is just a minor technicality," Pippa assured them. "What I have now is more important than any piece of metal—what I have now is my man's word, his honor. And I am so blessed to know that real soon he is going to honor me enough to be his beautiful blushing bride." Pippa held her palm against her heart.

Jackie held her head, Danielle gave Pippa a pitiful look, and Shenita just shook her head.

Shenita figured she might as well continue to go on with this girl's fantasy, otherwise she might beat up all three of them in the restaurant for attacking her faith.

"Okay, fine, Pippa. That's fine. You go ahead and believe that," Shenita said, giving in. "Just let me know what dress you pick out, and when you want me to go pick it up, when you get the date."

"There is no date!" Danielle said, and Shenita kicked her underneath the table again. "Ow!" Danielle said this time.

"Oh, I get it," Pippa said, eyeing all three ladies suspiciously. "You all are just jealous of me, that's all. There's no need to be jealous. I know you all had your eye on Mr. Elijah O'Toole at one point. Who didn't?"

"Whatever," Danielle said. "That man is *not* all that."

"I can see how you would want the same for yourselves," Pippa reasoned, "but God has been so good that He has favored *me* for His worthy cause. He takes pleasure in my prosperity and has blessed me to be Elijah's one and only true helpmeet and missing rib. I was designed just for him and God created him just for me before the foundation of the world!"

"You better go ahead and preach then, girl!" Jackie said, egging her on.

"Yeah, go ahead and claim your man. You can have his little square-head self anyway. Head look like SpongeBob SquarePants," Danielle said, and Shenita kicked her again. "Look, woman, if you kick me one more time . . ." Danielle said, and Shenita laughed.

Pippa didn't hear Danielle's comment and continued ranting and raving about her Elijah. "He's such a gentleman, too. Just the other day he was being a blessing to that new girl, Lynette, showing her the church website and helping her pick out an auxiliary to serve in."

"Lynette Reid?" Danielle asked.

"I guess . . . I think that's her last name," Pippa said.

"He was showing her the church website? Where, inside Pastor's office at the church?" Danielle asked, since she knew Elijah had the key and that was the only office in the church with a computer.

"No," Pippa said. "He was showing her at his house."

"At his house? Aw, that freak is trying to push up on Elijah. First Clive and now him? No wonder she used to miss so many days at work; she too busy working on all the men in Detroit!"

"What do you mean, Danielle?" Jackie asked.

"Yes, Danielle, what do you mean?" Pippa asked.

"What I mean is, that freak is—"

"Trying," Shenita cut her off, "really hard, to live saved, and get right with God. Thank God she has sisters like us to help her out and pray with her if she ever needs it," she said and grabbed Danielle's and Pippa's hands.

"I know that's right, Shenita," Pippa said. "I invited her to our brunch outing today, but she said she already had other plans."

"Yeah, I bet," Danielle said, and Shenita shushed her.

"So I told her if she ever needed a prayer partner or anything, the sisters are here for her," Pippa said.

"Well, amen, that was very noble and Christ-like of you, Miss Pippa," Shenita said.

"Yes, Pippa, real sweet," Jackie said.

Pippa faced Danielle and said, "Maybe we can get her to join the choir with us, Danielle."

"Oh no, we don't need her in the choir," Danielle said. "I think I remember her telling me before that she couldn't sing that well or something like that," she lied.

"Well, you know what Pastor says. 'Make a joyful noise unto the Lord! What may sound horrible to you may sound heavenly to God, as long as it's coming from the heart,'" Pippa said.

"You have a point there, Pippa, but nah, I don't think it'd be a good idea for Lynette to join the choir. It's just not sitting well in my spirit," Danielle said, and rubbed her belly.

"Oh, well, I understand that, then," Pippa said, then got the waiter's attention and placed her order for a plateful of blueberry pancakes, ham, sausage, and scrambled eggs. Jackie passed on ordering and said she would have to leave soon and was fine with just water.

"What, you fasting now or something, or are you trying to stay skinny for that new man friend of yours?" Shenita asked.

Pippa and Danielle perked up in their seats.

Jackie looked around, shocked that others were now all in her business. "To answer your questions, no and no. I have lunch waiting for me at home. I'm making my own salad, thank you very much."

"Salad? Now, this woman is the salad queen if I ever met one! I'm surprised you don't have lettuce growing out of your ears by now," Danielle said, and everyone laughed.

"No wonder you stay so little," Danielle continued. "I'm about to start calling you Twiggy, because all you seem to eat is sticks and grass."

"Forget the salad, I want to hear more about this new man friend!" Pippa said eagerly.

"Sorry, Pippa, there's not much to tell with that one," Jackie said.

"Didn't you and Jermaine go out?" Shenita asked.

"We went out all right, and it was a total bomb," Jackie said.

At that moment Jackie's cell rang. It was Jermaine. She sent his call to voice mail on the first ring.

"Who was that?" Shenita asked.

"That was Jermaine," Jackie said. "We must have talked him up."

"Well, if he's calling you then certainly *he* must not have thought the date was a total bomb" was Shenita's rationale. "Are you over there being bad again, Jackie? You not giving him a hard time again, are you?"

"No! I'm not," Jackie defended herself.

They all gave her an accusing glare.

"Trust me, it wasn't me this time," Jackie proclaimed. "He was a complete jerk on the date, and I don't ever want to go out with him again. I hate the fact that I still have to see his face Monday morning. See, that's why I don't do office romances. I should have never listened to you, Shenita—Miss Pinky Swear Lady."

"Well, it's better to have loved and lost . . ." Pippa began.

"Loved? Nah, we didn't go that far, Miss Pippa," Jackie corrected her. "I didn't even get a chance to really be in *like* with the man, let alone in love. I'm just glad it didn't get that far. Gotta keep my heart guarded, you know, especially after Dexter."

"So is that man going to keep you from enjoying any man you date after him?" Shenita asked. "True, Dexter was definitely a horrible husband, but do all your dates after him have to suffer because of what *he* did?"

"Preach, Preacha!" Danielle chimed.

"Don't judge me," Jackie said to Shenita. "You don't even know the half of it." She got up. "I'm headed out. Shenita, I'll fill you in later; it was nice chatting with you all," Jackie said, waved, then exited the restaurant.

Pippa's and Danielle's orders arrived and Shenita chatted with them while they ate. As they finished up, Shenita checked her watch and said, "Oh, shoot, y'all, I didn't realize how late it was getting. I gotta go."

"Where you going?" Danielle asked.

"I'm going where you should be going, somewhere to mind my own business," Shenita said.

"Mmm-hmm," Danielle said to Pippa. "She must have a hot date—otherwise she would tell us."

"Uh-huh," Pippa said, smiling while eating her second-to-last forkful of blueberry pancakes.

"Well, if you two little investigators must know, I am going out," Shenita admitted.

"With who, Leroy? Or is it Pee Wee this time?" Danielle asked.

Pippa laughed.

"I see you got jokes," Shenita said. "And, Pippa, what are you laughing at?" Pippa lowered her head while still giggling.

"If you two must know, his name is Montez," Shenita fessed up.

"Montez?" Danielle asked.

"Yes, Montez."

"What does he do for a living?" Danielle asked.

"Well, he's part owner of a car shop with his father."

"Broke," Danielle said.

"He's not broke," Shenita assured her. "He's a mechanic and part owner."

"Broke," Danielle said again, then laughed. "Living off his daddy's paycheck, broke."

"Danielle, there are more important things than money," Shenita said. "Like whether or not a man is warm, kind, loves the Lord, cute . . ."

"Cute and broke," Danielle said, and Pippa cracked up.

"Well, y'all just leave me alone, and enjoy the rest of your food. Peace. I'll see y'all later, peanut gallery."

"Peace," Danielle said.

"Hey, I'm following right after you, I have to stop by Elijah's before I head home. Today just might be the day!" Pippa said eagerly.

"Well, all right now," Danielle said. "Be sure and give me a call to let me know how many karats he plops on that juicy ring finger of yours."

"I sure will," Pippa said, and all three of them paid their bill at the register then parted ways for the rest of the day.

CHAPTER 42

Pippa figured Elijah should be done with his Sunday-afternoon nap by now as she headed over his way.

She parked her car in front of his house as was customary, patted the two grocery bags that were on the floor next to her, and said, "You, my little surprise bundles of joy, are going to make my man's day today."

She then pulled down her car visor, added an extra coat of Vaseline, fluffed up her mushroom hairstyle, then said to herself, "Pippa, you're about to outdo yourself this time. No worries, though. Breathe in. Breathe out. You can do this. Besides," she said to herself, "he's your soon-to-be husband and he is definitely well worth it."

Pippa exited the car and grabbed her two bags and walked onto Elijah's porch.

Ding-dong.

After no response, Pippa rang the doorbell again.

Ding-dong.

Elijah came to the door wearing a black T-shirt with large

white letters that read *Forgiven.* He was barely awake when he opened the door, rubbing his eyes and his curly hair.

"Hi, Elijah!" Pippa said with a wide grin.

"Oh, hey, Pippa," he said then opened the door for her and she helped herself inside. "I didn't know you were coming over today."

"Really?" Pippa asked as she set her bags on top of the kitchen counter. "I thought I mentioned after church that I would be stopping by. Sorry about that if I didn't."

"What'd you bring me this time?" Elijah asked eagerly. "Another 7-Up pound cake? More banana pudding?" He rubbed his belly and then headed to the couch in the front room, plopped down, and turned on the game.

"No, not quite," Pippa said as she pulled a pink lace apron out of one of her bags and put it on.

"Oh, what, you're gonna bless me by doing my laundry again? I do have a pile of clothes on my bed that is getting kind of out of control," Elijah said while staring intently at the television.

"No," Pippa said as she pulled a turquoise towel and a white towel from the same bag and set it beside the other bag.

She then pulled a purple-and-white foot basin out of the second bag and filled it with warm water.

"Now, I want you to close your eyes . . ." Pippa said.

"What?" Elijah said while sneaking a peek in her direction.

"Close your eyes," she repeated with her back to him so he couldn't see what she was doing at the sink.

"It's a surprise," she insisted.

"Oh, okay," Elijah said with his eyes closed and his hand gripping the remote.

Pippa made her way to him and set the basin on a white towel directly in front of him, then set the turquoise towel to the right of the basin. She then got on her knees before him.

She gently took off his right gym shoe and sock, rolled up his pant leg, then did the same with his left gym shoe and sock and rolled up that pant leg.

"Keep your eyes closed," she said softly.

"Girl, what are you doing?" he asked, lightly laughing.

"Shhhhh," she said. "I got this."

She then sprinkled raspberry-scented foot soak in the basin and grabbed his right foot and immersed it in the warm water.

"Ahhh," Elijah said.

She next took his left foot and did the same, then she spread raspberry-scented foot scrub on both of his feet and proceeded to wash them.

"Girl!" he said.

"Shhhhh. I want you to sit back and relax," she said softly as she washed his feet and took special care to massage foot scrub between each toe.

"Let me take care of you," Pippa said. "You work hard all day, serving the Lord, serving Pastor, serving other people; let Momma take care of you now."

Elijah sat back, his eyes closed and a wide grin on his face.

Pippa proceeded to scrub his feet with her hands, around his ankle, heel, and inner arches. "Let me show you how much I honor you by washing your feet, my lord," Pippa said. "You deserve it. It's the least I can do."

She smiled as she noticed him smiling; she was pleased that her man was pleased. She wanted nothing more than to make him happy, and she was excited because she could tell by the look on his face that she was accomplishing her goal.

Ding-dong.

Elijah sat up, startled, and Pippa wondered who in the world that could be.

"Oh, shoot, I almost forgot!" Elijah said, and vigorously took his feet out of the basin, dried them quickly with the white towel, then put on his socks and headed to the door as the doorbell rang again.

Ding-dong.

"In a minute!" Elijah said.

Pippa remained in a kneeling position on the turquoise towel when Elijah opened the door, and in walked Lynette.

"Oh, hi, Lynette." Pippa stood up. She wiped her wet hands on her apron, walked toward the door, and gave Lynette a big hug.

Lynette, confused, said, "Hi, Pippa. I'm surprised to see you here."

"I'm surprised to see you, too," Pippa said. "But that's okay," she assured her. "The more the merrier."

"Lynette," Elijah said, grabbing Lynette's hand and leading her to the front room. "I'm glad you came over like I asked. There's something I want to ask you. I didn't know I was going to have extra company, though," he said, and looked over at Pippa. "But that's okay, because Sister Pippa actually has been extremely instrumental in helping make all this happen and getting to this point."

"I have?" Pippa asked eagerly. Pippa's heart started pounding something crazy. *It's happening!* she thought.

"Yes, you have," Elijah continued. "Now, if you two ladies will excuse me, I have to get something out of my room. Pippa, you can have a seat." Pippa gladly sat on the couch, and Lynette followed her.

"Lynette, no, you keep standing," Elijah said.

"Oh, okay," Lynette said.

Pippa twiddled her thumbs, excited about what was about to take place. Her hands sweated profusely as she glanced at her left ring finger, praying it hadn't swelled up too much so that her engagement ring could still fit on it.

Sure enough, Elijah came out of his room with a small black box in his hand.

"Ooooooo!" Pippa squealed and almost peed her pants.

He stood in the center of his front room and spoke looking downward. "I know it hasn't been too long since we started dating, but I really feel in my heart that God has shown me my wife," he said. He opened the box to reveal a 2.5-karat silver princess-cut engagement ring.

Pippa's mouth opened wide with delight.

Elijah kept facing the floor while speaking. "It's not every day you meet a woman like you, so fine, and caring, and loving, and loves the Lord with all her heart." Pippa embraced her man's kind words.

"So as we got to know each other more lately, I feel I have such peace hanging around you, and I have so much joy added to my life now that I found you. I never want to let that go," Elijah said. "I never want to let you go." He turned around, dropped down to one knee, and faced Lynette. "Lynette Reid, will you marry me?"

Lynette grabbed her heart and squealed in delight, while Pippa's heart sank to her toes.

Pippa sat there in a daze and couldn't make out anything else that was said after that moment.

The last thing she remembered was Elijah O'Toole, the love of her life, whom she had known and loved for seven years now, asking Lynette Reid, a woman he'd barely known for two weeks, to marry him.

"I—I don't know what to say," Lynette said.

Pippa couldn't take any more.

She grabbed her coat and stormed out of the house.

She drove off and never looked back.

She ran straight through three red lights and four stop signs on her way home, but she didn't care. The one true love of her life had actually succeeded in breaking her heart into a million pieces and shattering all her dreams forever.

ONLINE DATE #5: THE METROSEXUAL

Shenita sat outside at the table in the quaint restaurant after having ordered cheesecake with strawberry topping, since she had already eaten earlier at the House of Pancakes with her girlfriends.

She sat directly across from her date, Montez, and couldn't help but notice how meticulous he was. His satin powder-blue bow tie was so neat and perfectly straight, his white shirt was so crisp, and his yellow V-neck sweater vest was so clean. It smelled like fabric softener. His nails were so immaculate, too; she didn't remember her nail technician ever doing her own nails that neatly. There was not a hangnail in sight, and his clear polish shone so bright she wondered if he ever used his nails as a mirror.

Shenita peeked at her own nails, determined her French manicure needed a touch-up, and then hid her hands in her lap. She figured he wouldn't notice anyway, since he hadn't stopped talking ever since he sat down and introduced himself.

"I'm really into fashion and wanted to be a fashion designer, but in the meantime I'm working at my dad's car shop," Montez said. "I really hate it, though, because it makes me all greasy and nasty and every day after I work I have to soak my hands in peroxide. Dad says I should enjoy it, said it will make me more of a man, but I told him I'm already a man. I just don't like to be dirty and nasty and greasy-grimy and need to have a mani-pedi every week because of it. I told my dad he's going to have to start paying for some of my mani-pedi bills, or at least give me a raise, because all this stress and wear and tear on my body is really taking a toll."

Shenita wondered if this man ever stopped talking.

The waiter came to their table to check on them. "Is everything okay?" he asked.

"Yes, sir, everything is fine," Montez said. "I love that watch you have on, is that Movado or Ferragamo?" he asked him and continued before the waiter could respond, "I was about to get a watch but I wasn't sure which one I should get and your cuff links are sharp, where'd you get those? I'm not much into cuff links but my mom says I should be since it'll attract the ladies. Shenita, are you attracted to cuff links? I don't know, maybe Mom's right, what you do think Mr. Waiter Man?"

"I think it's going to be okay," the waiter said and patted his hand. "And as for you, Miss Love?" the waiter asked.

"I think I'll have my cheesecake to go, and I think I'll have the check, please, thanks," Shenita said.

CHAPTER 43

As the evening sun set, Jackie knelt down and tapped at the logs she'd prepared for the fireplace in order to get a bigger blaze. She figured on this brisk Sunday evening having the fire going would be the perfect way to wind down and relax after a seemingly long day of church, hanging out with the girls, and working from home.

She grabbed her prepared cup of hot chocolate from her stainless-steel counter, added a few more jumbo marshmallows, grabbed a coaster, then took a seat on her long beige leather couch while praying she wouldn't spill any on it.

She curled herself on the couch and was taking a sip in the quiet, empty room when her cell, which was in front of her on the glass coffee table, rang.

She sighed at the sudden disruption of peace, set her hot chocolate on the coaster, and peeked at the phone before answering it. It was Jermaine, calling yet again. Jackie groaned, then threw the call into voice mail, set her phone back down on the table, and took another sip of hot chocolate.

Her cell chimed to let her know he left a voice mail this time.

Jackie was hesitant at first, but her curiosity got the best of her as she picked up her cell and dialed to check her voice mail. Sure enough, the one and only message was Jermaine's.

"Hello, Jacqueline? This is Jermaine. I'm sorry to bother you like this. I'm sure you're busy," he said, then paused. "Or maybe you're just avoiding me. If so, I completely understand. You have every reason to. Well, I was just calling to see how you were doing, and to let you know I was thinking about you. Hope to talk to you later. Bye."

Jackie ended the call and just looked at the phone. *Was that his idea of an apology?* she wondered. *If so, it didn't work,* she concluded, and set the phone back on the glass table.

She sat back and thought of some of the high moments from her first date with Jermaine—his surprising her with the blindfold, their hay fight in the wagon, his boyish laugh, and the way he held her by the fireplace.

She then snapped out of it and maintained her firm stance. "Nope, he messed up and I'm through with him!" she said.

She looked over to the other end of the coffee table and saw that her wedding photo album was still there. She had never taken it back to her closet after staring at the first picture the other day.

Initially figuring she probably shouldn't, she reached for it and turned again to that infamous first page of her wedding day. This time, though, she pressed past the first page and made it to the second, where she and Dexter waved at people from inside their rented black limo; the third page, where she and Dexter entered the private reception hall to greet more than three hundred guests; the fourth page, where she and Dexter danced their first dance.

She laughed as she remembered that Dexter, back then, had

two left feet, but he still made an effort to learn and attended ballroom classes with her two months before the wedding. On their wedding night, though, he seemed to have forgotten the basic steps, so instead of him leading her, Jackie ended up leading him—which made Jackie think about their entire marriage and how it transpired.

From that very first wedding night and throughout the marriage, it seemed like Jackie had to lead everything. From where they were going to purchase their first house, which job he was going to take, or where they were going to put the nursery for their first child, whom Jackie never quite conceived—she always had to lead the way and take charge in order to get anything accomplished. Now, sitting on that long beige leather couch she'd dreamed of having ever since she was a little girl who often perused home-improvement magazines, she wondered if it was her own sense of control and displaced drive and eagerness that might have caused her to drive her own husband into the arms of other women.

Sure, Jackie now lived in her dream home, with her dream furniture, dream car, and dream wardrobe, but in order to get what she wanted, did that mean she had to give up her dream husband? Sure, Dexter was a dream come true for her, in the beginning, but somewhere along the way in their marriage they grew detached from each other. She found herself not only fixing his lunch for work, or fixing his clothes for the next day, but also fixing his speeches and presentations, fixing his schedule, and even fixing his grammar.

Jackie sighed as she flipped through the remaining pages of her wedding photo album until she got to the very last page, the one that was a picture of his dark brown and her cream-colored hand showing off both their wedding bands. Jackie was once told that a wedding band is a circle because it's supposed to symbolize forever. It's supposed to symbolize a lifetime with the one you love, for better or for worse, in sickness and in health, till death do you part. Jackie figured maybe she did live out the expectation of the wedding vows after all. They did stay together till death, as she realized that somewhere in the course of her marriage, the man she met and fell in love with enough to marry somehow lost himself within the marriage and died.

Jackie slammed the photo album shut, then broke down and cried.

She wept until her head hurt. She wanted it all to go away—the pain, the hurt, the guilt, the wondering where she went wrong, the failure she felt when she realized that even though she was Miss "Fix It," the one thing she tried to fix that meant the world to her, she couldn't, which was her marriage.

She grabbed her wedding album, then knelt before the fire, placing the album in her lap.

She grabbed the metal fire poker and poked the logs until the blaze was nice and high.

She set the poker back in its tray, grabbed her wedding album, said, "Goodbye, Dexter," then tossed it into the fire and watched the album burn.

CHAPTER 44

All the house lights shut off inside Xtasy as the crowd of male and female patrons sat restlessly at their tables and booths in anticipation of what was about to go down center stage this Sunday night. Seemingly out of the blue, red strobe lights beamed onstage and the beginning of Ginuwine's "Pony" was heard from the surround-sound speakers positioned around the entire club.

Diva D entered from stage left, wearing a red one-piece leotard, black six-gallon cowgirl hat, and six-inch red stilettos. She kept her eyes covered with her hat and did a floor routine first, making her way across the stage and assessing the crowd.

The crowd leaped to their feet. A man in the front row yelled, "Yeah!" while an older gentleman shouted, "Have my baby, Diva D!" from the back. Danielle got quickly distracted by whoever said that, yet she still reluctantly inched her way toward the pole, butterfly-danced her way around it, did a few side-to-side hip dips, then finally grabbed the pole with both hands, lifted herself up, and did an upside-down inverted V. The crowd whistled loudly and men from all over the club approached center stage, flooding it with dollar bills.

While upside down, Diva D did something unheard of . . .
She did the one thing she said she would never do while dancing . . . the one thing she said she would never do while up high
on the pole performing as Diva D . . . the one thing that separated her stage world from the real world—she looked down.

She looked down at all the dollar bills flooding the stage.

She looked out at the hungry men screamed for more, and
she looked out toward stage entrance left and saw her three
young fans watching her intently.

Suddenly she felt bad about what she was doing, flipped
right side up, landed on her feet, and announced, "I can't do
this," to the crowd, and ran off the main stage.

ONLINE DATE #6: THE PK

"So I saw on your profile that you're a PK." Shenita blew and
took a sip of her tomato soup, which preceded her steak dinner
at Chuck's Chop House Restaurant.

"Yeah. I'm extremely blessed to be a preacher's kid," Chris
said proudly.

Shenita admired the fact that not only was Chris extremely
handsome, he was also well put-together. He wore a navy blue
suit jacket and a blue-and-silver matching tie, and his navy blue
dress shoes looked like they had just been spit-shined. Shenita
could definitely appreciate a well-dressed man, and the confidence Chris exuded as he spoke led her to believe that he just
might be the one.

"So what was it like growing up a PK? I hear it can be pretty
challenging for some," Shenita said, curious.

"That's true," Chris said with a sip of his water, then set his
glass down.

He then took a deep breath and said, "Some PKs end up all messed up because they daddy didn't spend any time with them and spent more time in the church than with the family."

Shenita nodded in an attempt to show empathy.

He continued, "Some PKs grow up actually despising the church and even hating God because they feel God took they daddy away from them."

Shenita wondered where all this was coming from.

Chris continued, "They feel like the church is better than them and they just nothing but some seed that just gets in the way of they daddy's ability to advance the kingdom, so some PKs run away from home at the age of twelve and go stay with their alcoholic uncle, who gives them forties every night and introduces them to weed and has them strung out all night, skipping school and thinking the world is against them and just grow up hating everybody!"

Shenita's eyes widened as she asked carefully, "Would this, by chance, be you?" Chris suddenly threw his hands up, backed out of his seat, and said, "Man, forget the church, forget God! I want my daddy back!" he yelled and started wailing like a baby at the table.

Shenita looked around at everyone in the restaurant staring their way.

She scooted up in her seat, patted his hand, and said, "I'm sorry, Chris. I—I surely didn't mean to strike a nerve by bringing back any old memories." *Sheesh,* Shenita thought.

Chris wouldn't stop crying; eventually his nose ran. "Why, God, why? Why you take my daddy away?" he demanded.

"Here," Shenita said, handing him a napkin, "it's going to be okay."

"Really?" Chris asked, taking the napkin and blowing his nose.

"Really," Shenita assured him. "Hey, have you ever thought about going to see a therapist? They're here to help, you know."

Chris nodded, said, "Okay," and blew his nose again.

The suited waiter came by the table and asked, "Is everything okay over here?"

"Everything is just fine, right, Chris?" Shenita asked in a motherly tone, and Chris nodded again.

"You know what," she said to Chris, "I just remembered I have something I need to take care of. I've gotta run." She faced the waiter and asked, "May I have the check, please?"

Sparks burst inside Danielle's dressing room as she was taking off her heels. He swore at her something crazy while flailing his Montecristo at her.

"Sparks, get out of my face, I don't want to hear that right now," Danielle said, and gave him the hand.

Sparks smacked her hand down, grabbed it, and got in her face. "Woman, you listen to me," he said.

The three teenagers, who were near the stage entrance, were now standing outside Danielle's dressing room, trying to sneak up and hear what was going on.

"I made you, and I can break you," Sparks said with glaring eyes. "Now you take your little tail back out there on that stage and give the people what they want!" he yelled as he pointed to the stage.

Danielle attempted to keep a calm tone. "Sparks, first of all," she said, "I would suggest you get your stank breath out my face."

Sparks stood up and folded his arms, expecting her to comply with his command.

"And second of all," Danielle said, and got up, "to answer your suggestion, or shall I say your *demand,* I got news for you, Sparky, I'm the captain of this here ship," she said, pointing to herself, "and this ship is about to set sail. I'm outta here."

"Are you threatening to leave me again?" Sparks asked. He then motioned for his six-foot-seven bodyguard to stand near him, while the other bouncer remained at the dressing room door.

"Am I hearing you right?" Sparks asked, then cracked his knuckles.

Danielle looked at his knuckles like she wasn't fazed, then looked back in his face.

Though he may have thought he had some backup in the form of his bodyguards, Danielle knew she had all the backup she needed all around her in the form of a host of angels, and a God who said He would never leave her nor forsake her.

Danielle cracked her knuckles, too.

"Excuse me. Excuse me, I'm trying to get through," said a nasally voice near the dressing room door. The bouncer had stopped whoever it was at the dressing room entrance, yet he insisted on getting inside.

Danielle looked to see who it was, and she couldn't believe her eyes—it was Little Willy, trying to force his way inside her dressing room.

Danielle did a double take, and Sparks looked at the door, wondering who had the audacity to try and get inside one of his dancer's dressing rooms and why the bouncer couldn't seem to keep the little man away.

In the midst of the confusion, Danielle grabbed her bag, hid her face with her hand, and squeezed through the side dressing room door and headed toward the back exit when a tall, slender man in a gray trench coat and black fedora turned her around and stopped her.

"Where do you think you're going?" he asked in a gruff voice.

"Excuse me?" Danielle said.

"You're not going anywhere until you give me what you owe me," he said.

"Owe? Joker, I don't owe you anything," Danielle said, and he slapped her.

Stunned by the slap and its sting, Danielle held her cheek and just looked at him. She checked her hand to make sure she wasn't bleeding, and she wasn't.

She tried to run away, but the mystery man held her until Sparks was in front of her, and this time Little Willy was standing right next to him with a stupid grin on his face.

"Well, well," Sparks said, chewing on his same wet Montecristo.

"Looks like our little kitty cat tried to get away," he said. Danielle looked at Sparks, then looked at Little Willy and hoped this was just some nightmare she needed to be awakened from.

"Looks like I found one of your church members here, Mr. Willy Beckerson," Sparks said, patting Willy's shoulder. Sparks continued, "He said he thoroughly enjoyed your performance onstage tonight, even though he only got to see the abridged version."

Danielle gave Willy a look of desperation, but he only returned it with that same plastered grin of his.

"I told him I would have you go back onstage to earn honest pay for an honest day's wages, and you know what?" Sparks said.

Danielle looked at Sparks, confused, hardly able to stand up straight, as she was still being held hostage by the man in gray.

"Willy here said that's fine," Sparks continued, as if they were having a normal, mutual conversation. "He said he's willing to make up for your sudden stage fright by allowing you to accompany him in that back room there and take care of him," Sparks said, and eyed the VIP room. "If you know what I mean," he added. "And I'm sure you do." He added.

"Hex naw!" Danielle spouted.

"Your church brother Willy, here, said he'd be willing to give me this," Sparks said, and just then Willy pulled out a thick wad full of hundred-dollar bills from his pants pocket.

"No!" Danielle said, then tried again to get out of the man in the gray coat's grasp, but he wouldn't let her go.

Sparks continued, "He said he had some luck on the slot machine over there at the casino and that he hit the big one."

Little Willy closed his eyes and kept smiling.

Sparks then got in Danielle's face and whispered in her ear, "So I figure this, mama, you give the people what they want," he said and pointed to Willy. "And what he's dishing out will be enough to cover what you missed by not finishing your dance on that pole, and then some. I may even be able to peel you off some and give you a little more bonus money." He squeezed her waist, and Danielle shed a single tear.

Sparks then stood up straight and pronounced loudly, "Now go on in that VIP room and make it rain!"

"No, Sparks," Danielle said softly.

"No?" Sparks said, and looked around. "Did this trick just tell Sparks no?"

Everyone around him shrugged their shoulders.

"Now I'm sure you wouldn't want your little church members to find out about your nine-to-five here at Club Xtasy. Willy!" Sparks said, and Little Willy pulled his Android phone out of his left back pocket and played back video footage from when Danielle was on the pole tonight.

Danielle held her head low.

"Aw, what's wrong, kitty cat?" Sparks walked up to Danielle and lifted her chin to reveal her red-stained eyes. "Cat got your tongue?"

Danielle spat in his face.

Sparks didn't budge, but wiped it off and licked his fingers.

"Now how about this," he continued. "Since you want to act ornery tonight, you take care of Willy over there, and when he's through with you, you let Gray here get some of that, and when he's through with you then you can give me my own private dance, like we used to do back in the good old days. Except this time I want more than just a dance," Sparks said, and laughed. "How 'bout that, fellas?" He turned outward and laughed out loud. "Three for the price of one!" he said, and kept laughing.

"Hey, tonight," he added, "a round of drinks on me! I been waiting a long time for this! I waited over three years for a piece of this kitty cat. Lawd hammercy." He hungrily looked Danielle up and down. He walked up to her again and gave her a wet kiss on the cheek.

Danielle stared at the ground then looked dead in his face with regained strength and said, "I said *no!*" and kicked Sparks between his legs, turned around and karate-chopped Gray in his neck, then picked up a nearby bottle of wine and smashed it on his head.

Danielle next made a mad dash to the exit door.

Sparks arose slowly, reached in his coat pocket, pulled out a 9-millimeter, and next thing you know, three shots rang out.

Except the shots didn't come from Sparks.

Princess Dream, who witnessed the whole thing, fired three shots in the air with her .38, causing just enough chaos and confusion to allow Danielle to make it out of the building, run to her car, and whip out of the parking lot around the corner and down the street until she hit the Lodge Freeway going 100 miles per hour.

Danielle didn't look back until she'd made it to the privacy of her own apartment complex.

She ran inside, slammed her apartment door behind her, and collapsed on her black couch, exhausted and thanking God that she made it out of there before it was too late, and praying that no one had followed her home.

CHAPTER 45

"I'm through!" Shenita yelled inside her house after her last horrible date with the PK.

"I'm through! I'm through, I'm through, I'm throoouugh!" Shenita proclaimed. She was so tired of horrible date after horrible date after horrible date. If this last string of dates was any indication of where her love life was headed, then she figured she might as well just throw in the towel.

She was tired of being humiliated, tired of being embarrassed. Just tired. She was frustrated, more than anything else, that her little effort to "take matters into her own hands" was getting her absolutely nowhere.

She grabbed her Mac from the coffee table, logged on to equallyyokedup.com, and was about to cancel her account altogether and e-mail them later for a refund when she noticed a special alert blinking on her profile page.

It was an alert letting her know that she received a match from someone in which she and the other person were, according to their records, 100 percent compatible with each other. This was the first time Shenita had ever received such an alert; she figured she sure wasn't 100 percent compatible with those other jokers she had gone out with.

She clicked on the alert to see the profile it referenced, and what it revealed shocked her to no end.

Right in front of her face was a face shot of none other than her church buddy Terrell. She rubbed her eyes to see if his picture was still there and it was. Funny thing was, she had re-membered seeing that picture before, as it was the same profile picture he used for his Facebook page.

"You have got to be kidding me," Shenita said. She couldn't believe it.

Just when she was about to give up on love, give up on everything—here comes this familiar face whom she adores, reminding her now that love still might be out there and that it might not have given up on her after all.

Surely Terrell wouldn't agree to go out with me or ask me out, she thought suddenly. She checked on his page and saw that he hadn't viewed her page at all yet. Surely he received the 100 percent match alert just like she did.

She concluded it was too risky, and if Terrell wanted to ask her then he knew where to find her, and that this matching site was just one more way for him to get in touch with her, if he really wanted to.

Shenita was deleting the profile pages of her previous dates that turned sour or were just flat-out crazy when her cell rang.

She checked and saw it was RayShawn and answered.

"Hey, honey!" she said.

No one said anything on the other end.

"Hello?" Shenita said, "Ray Ray, is that you?"

"Yes," RayShawn answered, sounding as if he were crying.

"Are you okay?" Shenita asked.

After a brief pause RayShawn said, "No."

"I'm coming over there," Shenita said, then hung up the phone. She couldn't remember the last time her normally bubbly friend was upset, so she figured it must be pretty serious. She grabbed her bag, hopped in her Benz, and drove to the other side of town to check on her friend.

Shenita bammed on RayShawn's front door because she remembered his doorbell no longer worked. She peeked and saw his used red Corvette in the driveway, so she knew he was home. She wondered what was taking him so long to come to the door. She banged on it again.

Bam Bam Bam Bam Bam

RayShawn, in his black-and-white doo rag, looked through the peephole, and Shenita said, "Open up, Ray Ray, it's me, Shenita."

He unlocked the top bolt and door-handle lock on the main door, opening it to reveal the screen door, which he also had to unlock. He let Shenita in without saying a word. His eyes were red from crying.

Instead of inviting Shenita in or offering her something to drink, he plopped on his yellow couch. Shenita noticed he was wearing nothing but a white tee and light blue shorts. *Has he showered at all today?* she wondered.

Shenita walked inside, then headed over and sat right next to RayShawn.

She placed her hand on his knee and asked, "What's wrong, hon?"

He held his head down.

Shenita lifted his head and said, "C'mon, you can tell me."

After another pause RayShawn finally fessed up. "It's Dante."

"Dante?" Shenita asked. "What's wrong with Dante?"

"He's sick," RayShawn said, sniffling.

"Oh, I'm sorry to hear that. I'm sure he'll recover in no time," Shenita assured him.

"He went for a regular checkup the other day. They did some blood work, and he tested positive for HIV," RayShawn said and cried hysterically.

"Oh, no!" Shenita said. "I'm sorry, love." She grabbed his head and placed it on her shoulder.

He sobbed in her arms a few moments more, sat up and wiped his tears with his hands, and added, "But that's not even the worst part."

"What's the worse part?" Shenita asked, wondering what could be worse than testing positive for HIV.

"He left me!" RayShawn said, and cried again. "He moved out!" he said in between choking up.

Shenita grabbed RayShawn's head and held it again. "Shh-hhh," she said as she felt his tears on her bare shoulder. "It's all right; it's going to be okay."

RayShawn sat up again and said, "I told him it was okay. I told him together we could fight this thing. But he said he loved me too much for me to have to see him go through this. He said he loved me too much and didn't want me to get it. I haven't even been tested yet, and I told him I don't care if I get it; I don't care! I only want to be with him!"

RayShawn said, and cried harder and louder on Shenita's shoulder.

Shenita didn't know what to say at this point. She just held his head and let him get it all out. She hummed "Jesus Loves Me" in his ear and rocked him, hoping that would help make at least some of the pain go away.

CHAPTER 46

After Pippa grew tired of driving around the city of Detroit and surrounding suburbs for the last four hours on roads seemingly leading nowhere, she eventually made her way to her own driveway.

She slowly placed her car in Park, and before opening her car door she paused for a moment, then stared at her worn hands. She was so tired. Tired of driving around wasting gas going nowhere, but more important, she was tired of feeling like for the last thirty-two years she had done nothing but waste her life, and tired because for the last seven years she'd spent her life wanting a man who didn't even want her back, who wasn't even thinking about her, but was willing to take anything from her that she was willing to give, including the one thing she thought she would never allow anyone to ever take away: her dignity.

She looked at her left hand and eyed her still-empty ring finger. She chose not to wear any rings on her hands, because she figured the only ring that would ever matter or would ever be worth anything is the one that would symbolize lifelong love. But now, at thirty-two, she's still in the same boat as her friends. No husband.

She thought she had found a husband in Elijah; surely he was every man she wanted and could ever need, but what she thought was her knight in shining armor turned out to be a nightmare.

Pippa pulled down her car visor and looked intently at the reflection in the mirror. She looked at her slanted eyes, she looked at her big nose, and she looked at her mouth and tiny lips. She looked at her hair and how frizzy it was. She looked at her eyes again and thought, this time, that she had seen tea bags growing underneath.

For the first time in her entire life, as she looked in the mirror she didn't like what looked back at her.

She felt ugly.

She felt old.

She felt no one would ever want her, and that she must be ugly, otherwise Elijah would have chosen her over Lynette. She figured she must be ugly, otherwise she wouldn't have gone the last two years of her life without a date, and she wouldn't have spent seven years at a church where not one male ever approached her to even ask her out for a cup of coffee.

She thought about her friends.

She thought about Shenita and how now, suddenly, she had her pick of seemingly a new man every other day. Even though Pippa initially condemned Shenita for demonstrating a lack of faith by putting herself out there online, Pippa now admired Shenita for her courage. *It took a lot of courage to put your heart on the line for the sake of finding love, but then again,* Pippa thought, *maybe it's worth it.*

She thought about Danielle and how she was so carefree and

so pretty and how no matter where they went she always seemed to have men falling at her feet. She secretly admired Danielle for her outgoingness and charm, and wished that she had the same.

She thought about Jackie and how she was so smart and beautiful at the same time. She knew Jackie could have any man she wanted, too, if only she would learn to trust again. Then Pippa figured she knew where Jackie was coming from, because she thought she had found trust in Elijah, and look what he did to her.

Pippa slammed the car visor mirror shut and dragged herself to her front door.

As soon as she unlocked the front door and opened it, Teacup sprang off the couch, leaped into her arms, and licked her all over her face.

Pippa smiled for the first time all day.

In her misery while driving around aimlessly, Pippa neglected to care for or about the one soul who had always been by her side no matter what, and who was always happy to see her even on an empty stomach—Teacup.

"Hi, baby!" Pippa said, returning Teacup's kisses. "Mama missed you, yes she did," she said and proceeded to the kitchen cabinet to pull out her favorite can of gourmet dog food. Teacup ate like she hadn't eaten in three days, let alone seven hours. She was done with all of her food within minutes and looked up at Pippa, who watched over her while she ate, and begged for more. Pippa reached inside her cabinet once more and pulled out a doggy treat and threw it in the bowl. Teacup ate it in its entirety, then ran around the front room like she now wanted to play.

Pippa garnered enough strength to at least let Teacup outside in the backyard to handle her business. As soon as she was done Pippa pooper-scooped it up, then slowly walked back into the house. She called three times for Teacup, who ran in circles, indicating she wanted to stay outside in the dark and play, until she finally got the hint and rushed back inside.

Even though it was a nice, unusually warm night, Pippa wasn't up for going outside or doing anything that required exerting any type of energy. She was so depressed about what had happened earlier today that for a moment, while she was driving, she had felt like driving off a cliff.

"Come here, baby." She picked Teacup up and made it back inside. She led Teacup to the couch, sat down, and held Teacup in her arms like a baby. Pippa thought about Elijah again and cried. She looked at Teacup, who stared back at her with big pretty brown eyes, and said, "Teacup, you may very well be the only baby I ever have," then wept some more.

CHAPTER 47

"Hey," Shenita said, and gently lifted RayShawn's head off her shoulder. "I know what we can do; I know what we can do to help Dante," she said.

A disheveled RayShawn looked over at Shenita and asked, "What can we do?"

"Let's pray!" Shenita said.

"Aw, hex naw!" RayShawn said. "I ain't 'bout to pray, naw, that ain't gon' work."

"What do you mean, that ain't gon' work?" Shenita asked, "Prayer always works."

"I don't *think* so," RayShawn said. "It won't work when the God *you* serve is against me."

Shenita cocked her head and looked at him. "RayShawn!" she said, "Is that what you believe?"

"It's not what I believe, it's what you believe. It's what that church you go to believes and what all them other so-called pastors and preachers believe. Adam and Eve, not Adam and Steve, right? Naw, I ain't about to pray." He gave Shenita the hand, then scooted to the other end of the couch. "As a matter of fact, I'm good. You can go home now, Shenita."

"Wait a minute," Shenita said, shaking her head. "Oh no, you not about to get off that easy. How long have we known each other, now, eighteen years since high school?" Shenita asked. RayShawn added the years in his head, then nodded.

"You were the same kind, sweet RayShawn when you came to Emory High after you got transferred in from another school, and when have I ever, *ever* treated you any differently since I've known you?" Shenita asked.

RayShawn just stared at her.

"And even after I got saved right after high school graduation, not even since then have I treated you any less special than the friend you are and always have been to me," Shenita reminded him.

RayShawn looked downward.

"And for you to now sit there and say that I think the God I serve and love with my whole heart is *against* you, you who He created before the foundation of the world, you who He loves with an everlasting love, you who He thinks of every morning when you wake up and every night when you go to sleep, how could you say that, RayShawn?" Shenita asked, choking up.

RayShawn placed his hand on top of Shenita's hand. "I didn't mean it like that," he said. "It's just that, you will never understand, Shenita. You will never understand what it's like to go to a church and be hated and have everybody staring at you and your boyfriend and judging you just because you're gay. Everybody's not like you, Shenita, everybody doesn't look inside and see a person's heart—all they see is abomination, and Sodom and Gomorrah. It's like I'm a constant reminder, to some, of everything that God is against and everything that

God hates. But you know what, I've come to a point in my life where I've learned to accept that. I accept the fact that I may never live up to God's expectations, or anyone's expectations, but what I don't want to accept is how now Dante, the one person I truly loved who loved me back for me, is leaving me, and I didn't even do anything wrong. I didn't even do anything wrong, Shenita. All I did is love him, but why is he leaving me?"

"RayShawn," Shenita said, and looked straight into RayShawn's eyes. "That's the very same question that God is asking you."

RayShawn's eyes watered up again.

"God is saying all He ever did is love you, but why are you leaving Him? It's not about what people think, Ray Ray, it's about what you think about the God who loves you in spite of. He may not agree with all that you do, but He still loves you just the same. All He wants is for you to come back to Him. He never left you, RayShawn. When you were molested that night at the age of eight, He didn't leave you then, and He hasn't left you now."

RayShawn cried hysterically.

Shenita lifted her hands and worshipped God.

In all the years they had known each other, RayShawn had never told Shenita, or anyone for that matter, that he was molested by a distant male cousin at eight years old. Right then Shenita knew that God was using her to speak a Word of knowledge according to 1 Corinthians 12 to encourage her friend.

CHAPTER 48

While rubbing Teacup's belly Pippa suddenly thought about something. She thought about how more than four hundred people who were either her close friends, family, or acquaintances believed she was in a relationship according to her latest Facebook status. She grabbed her laptop and logged on to her Facebook account so she could change her relationship status to "single."

On second thought, she peeked at all the well wishes on the thread since she'd changed her relationship status to "in a relationship." She scrolled through all the "That's wonderful!" and "God is good" and "Go, Pippa" and "God is faithful" and she figured she didn't want to destroy anybody's faith by changing it back to "single" so soon . . . that, along with not wanting to admit to the whole world that she was just in a so-called relationship that didn't even last two weeks.

Instead of changing her status, Pippa perused her news feed instead. She scrolled through pictures of exotic meals folks had for dinner, pictures of puppies that made her smile, then she got to pictures of cute babies and family photos and couples hugged up celebrating their anniversaries and she was immediately saddened. She longed for the day she would be able to take pictures of her and her boo out on a night on the town, or pictures of her showing off her baby bump with her husband, whoever he was, kissing it. Pippa sighed as she concluded that it might never happen for her. She figured she was in her thirties now, which made it harder to conceive, and who would want her, since she didn't look like a top supermodel?

She next spotted a Facebook status that immediately caught her attention. It was a status update about something that happened recently to someone she knew. Within minutes, more updates flooded her news feed, requesting prayer for this person as a result of what went down at a Detroit club earlier today. She kept scrolling, and then spotted a video clip detailing what happened.

Pippa clutched her mouth with her hand and yelled, "Oh, my Lord, no!"

Danielle paced in her apartment, still nervous about what happened earlier at the club. She tried to pray, but her prayers turned to worry and her mind got off track and she would pace again.

She ran to her door, looked out of the peephole, opened it, looked up and down both sides of the hallway to make sure no one was coming, then closed it. She did this three times.

She paced the floor again. *Oh, my God. What am I going to do? Should I leave? What if he knows where I live? As a matter of fact,*

Sparks has a copy of my driver's license on file, what if he sends his boys to come and get me? I gotta get out of here, Danielle thought, then ran to the door and opened it.

"What a minute!" Danielle said, and shut the door. "Where am I gonna go? I don't want to put anyone else in danger; what if Willy tells him about all my friends, then he finds out where *they* live!"

Danielle plopped on her black couch, shaking, nervous. She bit her nails on both hands, grabbed Mr. Cuddles, looked to each side, and then turned on the TV to add some type of sound in the house to try to calm her nerves.

"The Internet!" Danielle remembered. "What if Willy put that video of me on the pole on the Internet? It's probably all over Facebook by now!"

Danielle grabbed her laptop and logged on to her account and immediately went on Willy's page. She didn't see any video of her posted by him. As a matter of fact, she noticed he hadn't posted anything since yesterday, and Willy normally posted stale jokes or quotes from classic cartoon characters five or six times a day.

Suddenly a post appeared in real time on Willy's wall right, before Danielle's eyes.

It read: *I'm so sorry to hear about what happened to you, Willy. I'm praying for you.*

What happened to Willy? Danielle thought.

Just then a breaking news story came on local television.

The female news anchor described the scene of a shoot-out that took place at a local Detroit club. One person was critically injured and had been transported to ICU at Open Door Hospital downtown. They said the club was raided by police and that the owner, Samuel "Sparks" Witherspoon, was arrested for serving alcohol without a liquor license and for employing minors. It also made mention of three teenage girls who were arrested for working while under seventeen. The report described them as a sixteen-year-old and two fourteen-year-olds, and the camera panned to a shot of the three girls, all with their faces blackened out because they were minors, but whose profiles were similar to Princess Dream's and her twin sisters, being handcuffed and escorted inside a police car.

The news reporter said the person shot had been identified as a Mr. Willy Beckerson and that there were no further details available at this time.

"Oh God, no!" Danielle proclaimed.

Shenita wiped the tears from RayShawn's eyes, grabbed his hands, and said, "Now can we pray for Dante?" and he nodded his head.

Shenita prayed, "Father God, in the name of Jesus, we give You all the praise, all the honor, and all the glory. We thank You that You are Jehovah Rapha, and we come to you on behalf of Dante, asking that You will heal his body, Lord. Touch his body, heal his mind, and give him peace. Heal him now, Lord, from the crown of his head to the sole of his feet. We bind HIV right now in the name of Jesus, and we bind any work of the enemy, for we know that he is under our feet and we have authority over him. Ministering angels, go forth, right now, to cause what we have prayed in agreement to come to pass right now in Jesus' name. Amen!"

"Amen," RayShawn said softly and smiled.

"Now there's that smile that I like," Shenita said, and smiled in return.

"I love you, Shenita," he said, then gave her a big hug.

"I love you too, Ray Ray," Shenita said.

CHAPTER 49

"So, Mrs. Ledbetter," Jackie stated in her office on Monday morning while thumbing through the pile of papers her new client, Mrs. Carla Ledbetter, had just presented her with. "It looks like you just provided me with enough information that I need in order to present a proposal to your ex-husband's attorney for an amount that I'm sure you will be most satisfied with," Jackie assured her. Thankfully, Mrs. Ledbetter had provided Jackie with enough documentation and evidence to prove, without a shadow of a doubt, her ex's verbal and physical abuse and other marital transgressions.

"Thank you so much, Jackie," Mrs. Ledbetter said while staring at her with glassy hazel eyes. Mrs. Ledbetter shifted her long light brown hair back and said, "If it weren't for you I have no idea where I would be or what I would do right now."

Jackie peeked from underneath her papers and through her eyeglasses, smiled, and said, "No problem, Mrs. Ledbetter. It's what I do."

"I appreciate you for it," Mrs. Ledbetter said, then lightly touched Jackie's right hand and gently rubbed it. "And please," she said softly, "call me Carla."

Jackie snatched off her glasses.

"Dining in today?" Mrs. Washington asked Shenita as she stopped at her office door.

Startled, Shenita jumped up in her seat after preparing a press release for a charity fund-raiser.

"Oh, I'm sorry, Mrs. Washington, you scared me," Shenita admitted.

Shenita sat up straight, straightened her navy blue pantsuit, then put on her patent-leather navy pumps that were underneath her desk, as she was initially barefoot until her boss decided to stop by and check on her.

"Don't let me startle you," Mrs. Washington said. "I was just wondering if you would like to have lunch with me today, that's all—on me." Mrs. Washington asked with a hopeful expression.

"I'm sorry, Mrs. Washington," Shenita said again. "It's Monday, and Jackie and I normally have lunch together on Mondays. Maybe another time?" she asked, still not sure about the idea of going to lunch with her boss, who not only signed her paychecks but was the mother of the son who'd decided to break their date at the last minute with no excuse given.

"That's fine, Shenita, suit yourself," Mrs. Washington said.

"Mrs. Washington, I'm sorry it didn't work out with Christian," Shenita said before she left.

"My son?" Mrs. Washington asked and perked up. "Did you two go out yet?"

"No," Shenita said. "We keep missing each other," she

claimed. "I guess we're both too busy. Now just isn't a good time for either of us, I guess."

"You kids these days," Mrs. Washington said. "You get so caught up in your own workloads and your own agendas that you forget about what's really important."

"I know—"

"Actually, you *don't* know," she corrected Shenita. "Hopefully one day you'll wake up, girl; hopefully you *will* know before it's too late."

Shenita looked at her and thought about what she said.

"Enjoy your lunch," Mrs. Washington said, "and tell your *girlfriend* I said hi."

Did she just try to insult me? Shenita wondered. Not quite sure, Shenita shook it off then straightened up her desk as she prepared to meet Jackie at their usual spot.

"She did what?" Shenita asked Jackie while eating chicken fingers. Jackie thoroughly enjoyed her Waldorf salad as she spoke in between forkfuls of greenery blended masterfully with red-skinned apples, celery, walnuts, raisins, grapes, and mayo.

"Girl, she rubbed my hand, and then looked at me like I was lunch,"

"For real?" Shenita asked. "So what'd you do?"

"I told her our session was done and I asked her to leave," Jackie said plainly.

"Wow, you're a good one," Shenita replied.

"Shenita, has it come to this?"

"What?" Shenita asked, chewing.

"Have I become so hard and bitter toward men that now

women have no problem hitting on me? Maybe she sees my pain. Maybe she can see through to my soul and sees my relationship issues with men. Maybe she's right."

"So you're thinking about becoming a lesbian now?" Shenita asked.

"No," Jackie assured her. "Girl, you know I will never swing that way. That is *not* for me."

"Just checking," Shenita said with a raised eyebrow.

Jackie sighed and continued, "My concern is, why would my client even feel comfortable with hitting on me like that? I must be giving off some 'I hate men everywhere' vibe or something."

"You hate men everywhere?" Shenita asked, confused. "When did I miss that memo? I didn't get that press release."

"No, I don't hate men," Jackie said, eyes lowered. "Just extremely disappointed, I guess."

Shenita stopped chewing a moment and eyed her friend. "Be encouraged, sis. Hey, whatever happened with Jermaine?" Shenita asked, trying to pick up from where they left off in their last convo yesterday morning after church.

"I don't want to talk about him right now," Jackie said.

"All I'm saying is," Shenita said, "you have a tendency, Jackie, to not really give these men a fighting chance."

"No, I don't," Jackie defended herself.

"Hold up now, hold up. Hear me out before you bite my head off. What I'm saying is, it's like with us, your girlfriends, you give us this long rope of grace. We all get on each other's nerves sometimes; actually, I would even venture to say most of the time, but with us it's like you eventually forgive and forget, or you even apologize, like you did with Danielle yesterday even though you felt you weren't even in the wrong. But for some reason, for *some* reason with men, instead of a long rope of grace, you give them a little piece of string . . . like a little bitty piece of yarn no longer than half an inch. And as soon as they cross that line and use up that little half a piece of string . . . you're done with them and they're out of here. Case closed. Why is that?" Shenita asked with her head cocked to the side.

"Interesting analogy," Jackie said. "Did you make that up yourself?"

"Nah, you not gon' get off that easily, Jacqueline Downing," Shenita said. "Your sarcasm is not going to throw me off this time. All I'm saying is, Selah. Think on that."

"All right, *Dr. Phil,*" Jackie said, and the two of them laughed. "Now that I have been psychoanalyzed, what's been going on in Shenita's world?"

"Well, if you must know," Shenita began, "Shenita's world has been full of ups and downs and round and rounds like a Ferris wheel. At this point I'm just trying to keep my two feet on the ground."

"English, please?" Jackie asked.

Shenita laughed. "I'm good. I'm just out here in the game, that's all. You gotta get in the game in order to play to win, right?"

"I don't know about that, it depends on what game you're playing and what quarter you're in," Jackie said.

"I guess you're right," Shenita said. "For some reason I feel like it's fourth quarter for me, and that I'm about to be shifted into overtime. But it's all good; Coach Jesus has my back. I'm about to be His MVP. I'm about to make my Coach proud."

"Well, you do just that," Jackie said, and took a sip of her club soda. "I'll be cheering you on from the stands."

"Aw, c'mon now, Jackie!" Shenita said.

"What?" Jackie asked sweetly.

Back inside her Benz on the way to the office, Shenita got an inner unction to call and check on her friend, Pippa. Initially ignoring it as Shenita figured Pippa might be busy with a client at the nursing home, the unction persisted and Shenita eventually followed through and gave her friend a ring.

"Call Pippa," Shenita told her car phone.

Doubting herself, after three rings Shenita wondered if it was a bad idea to call after all.

"Hello," a soft voice said.

Shenita checked her phone to make sure it had dialed the right number. Surely this wasn't her usually chipper friend Pippa sounding like this.

"Hello," Pippa said again.

"Pippa?" Shenita asked.

"Oh, hey, girl," Pippa said. "I gotta remember to put your car number in my phone. I forgot again and almost didn't answer. I'll do it when we hang up." Pippa grabbed her family-size bag of chips and crunched on a few while petting Teacup with her free hand.

"Did I call you at a bad time? Are you working right now?" Shenita asked, still trying to figure out what was wrong.

"No," Pippa said plainly, "I called off work today."

Shenita was really shocked now, as Pippa never called off work unless she was really sick. "Are you okay? Are you sick?" Shenita asked.

Pippa crunched in Shenita's ear then shifted on the couch as she hadn't showered all day and was still in her pink-and-white onesie.

"I'm not sick, Shenita, I guess."

"You guess?" Shenita asked. "Girl, what's wrong? You can tell me." Shenita wanted to get to the bottom of whatever was wrong with her friend.

"Well, if you must know, Shenita, I think I *am* sick."

"You are?" Shenita asked, confused.

"I'm sick of being single," Pippa clarified.

"Oh! I get it now. I thought you were going with ole boy from church? What's his name? Elijah."

"Elijah," Pippa said. "Funny you should mention his name. What's even funnier is while I was going with him, he wasn't going with me," Pippa said.

"I'm sorry, Pippa," Shenita said and wished she could be there to comfort her instead of having to go back to work to finish a press release that had to go out today. "Girl, you be encouraged. You're a beautiful, smart, intelligent woman of God with a servant's heart. Elijah didn't even deserve you; you're too good for him. You deserve someone who's going to love you unconditionally, someone who's going to cherish the ground you walk on, and someone who will treat you with the utmost respect."

"You think so?" Pippa asked, sniffed, and wiped her nose.

"Pippa, I've never told you this before, but I think you are a wonderful woman of God with a heart of pure gold. You love the Lord with all your heart and you love people with all your heart as well. If whoever you're with doesn't appreciate that, then obviously they weren't the one for you in the first place."

Pippa blew her nose into the phone.

Shenita pulled over into a neighborhood street and parked in front of someone's house.

"Pippa, do you mind if I pray for you?" Shenita asked.

"Now?" Pippa asked.

"Sure," Shenita said.

"Okay," Pippa agreed, then held the phone close to her ear as she lay down and closed her eyes.

"Father God, in the name of Jesus I pray for my friend and Your daughter right now, Lord. I pray that You strengthen her and bless her mind with peace and that she will look to the hills from whence cometh her help, knowing her help comes from You. I pray that You help her by showing her the beautiful, attractive, loving, virtuous woman she really is, and that You would grant her the desires of her heart in due season but, as for right now, that You comfort her and let her know that she is not alone and that You are forever with her, always leading, guiding, protecting, and keeping her.

"I pray that Pippa guards her heart and continues to have faith and trust in You, and that she will hold fast to her profession of faith, knowing that You are faithful Who hath promised and that right now You are all the man she will ever need, want, hope for, or desire.

"I pray that *You* be her husband according to Isaiah 54:5 and that *You* be her knight in shining armor right now and that *You* keep her in Your loving arms and warm embrace.

"Lord I pray that you impart in her the confidence she needs, the self-assurance she needs, and the hope that she needs, knowing that all of her confidence is in You.

"I thank you, Lord, for being that Good Shepherd to Your daughter Pippa, and that You will continue to lead, guide, and direct her on the path You have for her life, and that she will continue to look to You for strength, look to You for peace, and look to You knowing that in You she is already complete. I pray all these things in Jesus' mighty name. Amen."

"Amen," Pippa said on the other end.

Shenita worshipped God on the phone, and Pippa slowly but surely thanked God as well. They thanked Him for His goodness and His grace, and Pippa also thanked and praised God for her friend.

CHAPTER 50

After spending the whole morning having breakfast, thumbing through *Essence* magazine, and watching TV, Danielle turned the TV off and sat quietly in her front room.

She looked around the room and listened to the silence that represented the present reality of her whole world right now, as she still had yet to figure out what she was going to do.

Where will I work now that I've left Xtasy? Where will I live, and should I move? What if Sparks gets out of jail soon; what if one of his lawyer friends gets him off early? What about the girls, are they all right? Are they all in jail now, or are they in juvi? Danielle's head hurt just thinking about everything all at once.

She reached to the side of her couch and grabbed the one thing that might provide some answers. She picked up her big, burgundy Bible from the small coffee table, then cracked it open. Apart from reading the Bible along with other congregants at church on Sundays, Danielle hadn't read her Bible on her own at home in a few weeks.

She had no clue where to start and just opened to a random page in the Old Testament.

A certain passage of scripture she had highlighted seemingly leaped from the page.

It read, *For I know the thoughts that I think toward you, saith the Lord, thoughts of peace, and not of evil, to give you an expected end. Jeremiah 29:11*

Danielle sat and thought about that scripture.

She thought about what had happened to her in the last two weeks, with her finances, with her going back to Xtasy and all that happened as a result. She thought about those three girls and how they turned out to be only babies after all. She thought about what sort of role model she must have been for them. She thought about how, in going back to swing on that pole, she was only doing so to please herself, and how not once did she remember asking if her decision totally pleased God.

Yet and still, here is God talking to her now through this scripture, telling her that even though she might have done things in her past that He did not agree with, and even though she made some wrong decisions and got caught up in the wrong crowd, which might have ultimately cost her life, here He is still telling her that in spite of it all He doesn't think any less of her or harbor any thoughts of evil toward her but that He still has thoughts of peace about her to give her an expected end.

Danielle saw that above the word *expected* she had written the words *hope* and *expectation* in red, which were the original Hebrew definitions of the word *expected;* the pastor had pointed out the day she was directed to that scripture in church last year.

Danielle thought about how so much had happened in only a few years' time. A few years ago, when she gave her life over to the Lord, she remembered how she was so happy and so at peace with her soul.

In spite of Sparks telling her she wouldn't amount to anything when she first decided to quit working at Xtasy, and in spite of other dancers telling her she was making a big mistake, Danielle left anyway, and then received so much peace— the kind that passes all understanding—that though she left a couple thousand dollars a week behind, what she received in return, by choosing to follow God instead, to her, was priceless.

Danielle lovingly recalled her journey in Christ, how she used to be so on fire for Him—telling everyone she met all about Jesus and inviting everybody to her new church home.

She remembered auditioning for the choir and how the choir director, Brother Earl, loved her voice so much that he immediately made her an alternate praise team leader. Danielle was so honored and privileged every time she received the opportunity to usher in worship and praise and set the stage for the pastor to preach the Word of God. To her, there was no greater joy than to be used by God.

For those few years Danielle remained faithful to her pastor, faithful to the choir, faithful to her church, and faithful to her friends. Though her relationships with men were rocky, she was consistent in one thing—that she loved God more than she would ever love any man, which was why she decided, after her final one-night stand eleven months ago, that she would, from that day forward, remain celibate until marriage—just like her friend Shenita.

Danielle figured if Shenita could do it, then she could do it, too, and that they served the same God and that God was not a respecter of persons.

Danielle wished she had Shenita's boldness and tenacity when it came to the things of God. She considered Shenita a solid Christian who, no matter what, could not be moved.

It was Shenita who encouraged her that day, three years ago, to leave Xtasy with no turning back. It was Shenita who told her she was more valuable than that and to allow God to be her Sugar Daddy and total money supply. But even though Danielle physically left the club that day, a part of her still remained.

A part of her still wanted to dance in order to feel sexy and alive.

A part of her still loved how she commanded attention with her every move and loved to be the object of every man's desire as they spoiled her with dollar bills.

A part of her still loved to feel wanted and loved, even if it was only a fantasy.

Danielle held her head down in shame.

She felt not only had she let Shenita down by going back to work at Xtasy, she'd also let God down.

She read the scripture again, out loud this time, "For I know the thoughts that I think toward you, saith the Lord, thoughts of peace, and not of evil, to give you an expected end."

She was led to continue reading the next two verses, "Then shall ye call upon me, and ye shall go and pray to me, and I will hearken to you. And ye shall seek me, and find me, when ye shall search for me with all your heart."

Danielle couldn't even remember the last time she actually prayed to God, besides reciting grace over a meal. She viewed these additional two scriptures, which weren't highlighted in her Bible, as God's invitation for her to seek Him in prayer so she could truly find all the answers she needed.

"God, I need You," Danielle prayed with hands folded and head bowed.

"I need You, now," she admonished. "I need You to move on my behalf. I need You to tell me what I need to do." She paused and heard nothing, then continued praying. "I'm sorry, Lord;

I'm sorry for not treating my body like the temple You gave me. I'm sorry for being led by flesh by doing what I wanted to do and not totally trusting You to provide. I'm sorry for not living up to Your expectations and I pray that You help me be strong." Danielle still heard nothing, and kept praying. "I pray for those three girls, Lord. Lord, they're just babies. Please cover and keep them and protect them from all harm and get them off the streets. Please watch over them and lead them to Your love." Still silence. "God, I need you to tell me what to do!" Danielle yelled in frustration, yet still heard not a single thing.

Defeated, Danielle prayed in the Spirit for twenty minutes straight and then worshipped God in song and thanked Him for His grace and for loving her enough not to leave her even when she went her own way and did her own thing.

By the end of her time with the Lord, she had peace about her next step. She knew there was at least one thing she had to do right away tonight.

CHAPTER 51

Once Shenita left their lunch early to head back to finish her press release, Jackie remained at the restaurant to take an extended lunch.

Jackie thought about Jermaine. She noticed he didn't poke his head in her office door today like usual and figured maybe he'd decided to give up on her. *Maybe he got tired of trying, and maybe he got tired of having to sort through all my baggage,* she thought. *Why should I care anyway?*

No matter how much she tried to get over this man and get him out of her head, she never seemed to get over his boyish grin and kid-in-a-candy-store-like ways. It didn't take much to please him, and though he had his master's degree and was a top contender to make partner at another firm, he still took time to smell the roses and focus on what was really important in life—and Jackie secretly admired that about him.

She thought about what Shenita had said earlier, about how she seemed to have extended grace for her girlfriends but not when it came to men. She knew Shenita was referring to Jermaine.

In spite of him getting on my nerves a few times, did he really do anything wrong? Jackie thought. *Like Shenita said before, it's not like he plopped a ring on my finger, why was I acting so territorial?*

Jackie pulled out her cell and did the unthinkable. She dialed fast, in case she changed her mind, and gave Jermaine a call.

"Hello?" Jermaine answered on the first ring.

Jackie didn't immediately respond.

"Jackie?" Jermaine asked.

"Hi," Jackie said in a normal tone.

"Hi . . . what's up?" he asked.

"I hadn't seen you at the office today and decided to check on you before I called the feds."

Jermaine laughed on the other end. "Very funny," he said. "I actually took off today. Personal matter. How've you been?"

"I've been great, and you?"

"A lot better . . . now." Jermaine said.

"Jackie . . . do you have plans this evening? I'd like to take you somewhere, if you don't mind."

Jackie thought a moment and said, "Nah, I'm not really feeling a restaurant tonight. I'm working on this case and—"

"All work and no play makes Jackie a—"

"Employed attorney," Jackie finished his sentence.

She suddenly wondered why she called him anyway. *Did he forget all about what happened on our last date?* Jackie wondered.

"Actually, I wasn't thinking dinner," Jermaine clarified. "I was thinking somewhere else. I think you'd like it. It's not a date either, really. I mainly just want to talk to you."

"We can talk now," Jackie said, knowing good and well she wasn't in the mood for any deep conversation while heading back to the office.

"For what I have to say to you, in person would be a lot better," he said. "Besides, it'll help me."

"Help you?" Jackie asked.

"C'mon, Jackie, enough with all the questions. Can I pick you up or not?" Jermaine asked impatiently.

For a brief second Jackie admired Jermaine's new "take charge" attitude.

She thought a moment, then decided on a compromise. "Can I meet you there?"

"Okay, fine." Jermaine gave in and gave her the directions.

CHAPTER 52

Though she was fifteen minutes late, Danielle mustered up enough courage and discreetly stepped inside the back choir room during choir rehearsal.

"Danielle!" Brother Earl said, delighted as he spotted her walk in while everyone else held hands in a large circle. Danielle found it odd that they were all in a circle now—they normally took prayer requests after prayer rehearsal was done.

"Glad to see you here, Sister Danielle!" Brother Earl said. "You came at just the right time."

"I did?" Danielle asked while observing all eyes were on her.

"You sure did, come on over here with the rest of us; don't be shy!" He motioned for her to join the group.

Danielle entered the circle next to Pippa and held her hand, and she gave her a warm smile.

Brother Earl then announced, "It has been brought to our attention that one of our own has had something horrible happen to him. Our very own Willy Beckerson, whom most of us here know as Brother Willy, was shot and is now in critical condition at Open Door Hospital."

Danielle was shocked about what she'd just walked into.

"Sister Danielle," Brother Earl said, facing her, "it would be our pleasure if you would do the honors and pray for Brother Willy, for his total healing in this situation."

Danielle replied, "Oh, no, I'm sorry, Brother Earl. I can't pray for Willy. I'm not feeling well, emotionally, right now. I think it'd be best if you got someone else to pray for him."

Danielle couldn't believe the choir director had called on her to pray for the man who was about to rape her in the VIP room at Xtasy. She could still see that stupid grin on Willy's face as his shrimpy self stood there beside Sparks, flashing his gambling proceeds like he was "the man."

Danielle could never see herself praying for someone like that. She figured someone like that needed more than prayer; he needed a good old-fashioned butt-whooping.

"I hear you, Sister Danielle, but sometimes the best way to heal yourself emotionally is to pray for someone else. Even the Word talks about how Job's personal situation changed when he prayed for his friends," Brother Earl persisted.

Willy is not my friend, thought Danielle.

Danielle looked at Brother Earl and everyone else in the circle, then back at the choir director.

"I can't," she told him.

"I'll pray for him," Pippa volunteered, and prayed, "Father God in the name of Jesus, we pray right now for our brother and Your son, Willy Beckerson. We pray that You heal his body right now, Lord, and that You cover him with Your grace and Your love. We stand in agreement that he is healed from the crown of his head to the sole of his feet, and we decree that he is coming out of ICU and that he shall live and not die and declare the works of the Lord! In Jesus' name, amen. Hallelujah!"

"Hallelujah!" everyone repeated.

"Thank you, Sister Pippa, for that wonderful prayer," Brother Earl said.

After that the circle broke and Brother Earl asked that everyone get in their respective sections, as choir rehearsal was about to begin.

Before being seated, Danielle approached Brother Earl and asked to speak to him for a moment.

"Sure, what is it, Danielle?" he asked.

"Brother Earl, I want to thank you for all your faith in me in having me as one of your praise team leaders here at the church."

"Oh, well, you're welcome, and it's my pleasure," he said.

"Lately I've got a lot going on in my personal life, and I'm led to let things go so I can focus more on God and my relationship with Him."

"I understand that, Sister Danielle. Sometimes we try and do too much and we lose sight of what's really important, which is maintaining that one-on-one fellowship and intimacy time with Him," he said.

"That's so true, and with that said, the reason I came to rehearsal today was to say . . . that I thinks it's best that I step down from the choir and the praise team."

Brother Earl didn't understand.

"I'm sorry it has to be this way. I'm not sure how long it's going to be but it's something I have to do, I'm led to do, right now, for myself," Danielle explained.

Brother Earl sighed and said, "Well, we're going to miss your angelic voice, Sister Danielle, but I understand. Thanks so much for stopping by and letting me know."

"You're welcome," Danielle said, and turned around and headed out.

Pippa spotted her leaving and popped up and followed after her.

"Hey, Danielle," she said, out of breath as she caught up with her by the exit door. "You leaving already?"

"Yeah," Danielle said.

"What's wrong? I know earlier in there you said you were sick. Are you okay?" She walked with Danielle out into the parking lot.

"I'm fine, Pippa. Thanks for asking," Danielle said as she stopped at her car door.

"You sure?" Pippa probed.

"Hey," Danielle said, and resumed her normal boisterous tone, "I'm good. What about you, Miss Thang? Let me get a good look at that ring," she said to change the subject, reaching toward Pippa's left hand.

Pippa faced the ground and said, "It's not there."

"Really?" Danielle said. "That joker! Where he at? I'ma get him!"

Pippa smiled sheepishly. "Thanks, Danielle, but you guys were right, and I was wrong. Elijah just took advantage of my kindness, I guess," she said softly. "In the end, the ring I thought was mine went somewhere else."

"Where?" Danielle asked.

"To Lynette."

"Lynette?" Danielle said in shock.

"Yeah."

"Lynette is married! What, she's about to get married twice? She's a polygamist now?" Danielle asked, upset.

"Married?" Pippa said, louder than she had ever gotten.

"Yes. Married," Danielle said. "She was my boss—the one who fired me. She was messing around with a man at the office when I was there, so it actually doesn't surprise me that she's trying to get Elijah all tangled up in her spiderweb. Oh, what a tangled web we weave—the nerve of her!"

"Are you serious?" Pippa asked.

"Yup."

"Then I gotta warn Elijah!" Pippa said and grabbed her cell phone. "I gotta tell him; I gotta warn him!"

"Pippa, no," Danielle said.

"I gotta let him know! It's my duty as his sister in Christ to warn him about this Jezebel who's about to break his heart. I gotta tell him, I gotta warn him!" Pippa said, and dialed his number.

"Pippa, no!" Danielle said, and snatched her phone out of her hand then hung up the call.

Pippa looked at Danielle in utter shock.

Her eyes grew glassy. "But I gotta tell him, I gotta warn him. She's about to hurt him!"

"Pippa," Danielle said, and placed her arm on Pippa's shoulder. "Elijah wasn't concerned about breaking your heart when he did what he did." Pippa's eyes watered.

Danielle continued, "He's a big boy; he'll find out about Lynette on his own soon enough. All we can do is pray for him. He doesn't need you in his life to save him anymore, Pippa."

"But I gotta tell him; I gotta warn him!" Pippa said desperately, then broke down in tears in the parking lot. Danielle grabbed her friend's head and held her as she cried.

CHAPTER 53

Jackie parked her car and looked around at the brown, orange, and yellows leaves left dangling on the trees and the freshly cut yet still moist green grass, wet from last night's rain.

She texted Jermaine to see where he was only to have him pull up right behind her and park right next to her.

He got out of his car and stood beside her car door and opened it for her once she unlocked it.

He helped her out of the car and said, "Hi, Jackie. Glad you could make it. You look great." Jackie accepted his chivalrous gesture and thanked him for his compliment. She still had on her work clothes—brown pantsuit and thick-heeled brown pumps, and wondered if she was overdressed for this outdoor excursion.

Without saying much, she followed Jermaine as he led her through the grass in the park and up a hill. She wondered if they were going hiking, if so she definitely missed that memo and wished she had known so she could have brought DEET and hiking boots.

After walking seemingly for a long time, as Jackie's calf muscles now hurt, she thanked God once they made it to the top of the mountain and then stopped as Jermaine looked over at the gorgeous outdoor view, taking in the mountains and the small cabins below.

Jermaine inhaled the fresh northern Michigan air, then exhaled with an "Ahhhh."

Jackie looked at him and eyed the scenery, still wondering why he'd brought her out here.

"Don't you just love that fresh air?" he asked.

"Mmm-hmm."

"Kinda makes you want to go camping or on a nice hiking trip or something."

"Not in this suit," Jackie said, revealing her thoughts.

Jermaine looked over at her and laughed. "Oh yeah, I forgot, I didn't quite tell you where we were going exactly."

"No, you didn't."

"That's okay though, you know I love surprising you."

"Mmmm," Jackie said, thinking, *If this man doesn't tell me why he had me come way out here on top of some mountain then I will roll my butt back down, get in my car, and go back home.*

"Shhh, you hear that?" Jermaine asked.

"What?" Jackie wondered.

"Total silence," he said. "Total peace."

You've got to be kidding me, Jackie thought, and wondered if she could make it home in time to catch the next episode of *Law & Order.*

"You know, I used to come here a lot to just think, meditate, and pray," he said.

"Nice," Jackie said, looked around, and stuffed her hands in her pockets as it grew chilly.

"Doreen said it's good to have a place to get away from everything and just reflect."

"Doreen?" Jackie said. *Is he bringing up his ex again? She has a name now? Great,* she thought.

"Dr. Doreen Smith, my therapist," he clarified.

Jackie wondered where this conversation was headed.

He continued, "I actually met with her earlier today, which was why I didn't make it into the office."

Jackie remained silent. For some reason, she felt now would be a good time to listen.

"She's a Christian therapist, and she suggested I come here and let it all out," he said.

Jackie raised her eyebrows.

"I told you I was divorced before," Jermaine said.

"Yeah," Jackie said.

"It kinda tore me up inside, ya know. I thought she was the one. I thought I was everything she ever wanted in a husband, but after I was married it turned out that I wasn't and that she preferred my old college roommate instead."

"She cheated on you?" Jackie asked.

"Yeah," Jermaine admitted. "They reconnected through Facebook, and I guess she confided in him about me and they met up privately for lunch. I found this out after I hired a private investigator."

"Really?" Jackie asked, impressed by his efforts to provide a burden of proof.

"Sad thing is," Jermaine continued, "I know that the breakdown of our marriage took place way before she cheated. Cheating was just her way of escape, I guess. In the end, she didn't really want me. I don't even think she ever really wanted to get married."

"Jermaine, I'm sorry to hear that," Jackie said. She'd never heard of a man being so willing to open up and express his true feelings; she could hear the hurt and the pain in his voice.

She didn't know what else to say. She had no idea he had gone through so much. She commended him for maintaining his composure and tact while still making a nice life for himself.

"We came here for our first date," he said.

"Here?" Jackie asked.

"Yeah. She was into the outdoors as much as I was; we'd come here pretty often, actually."

"Oh," Jackie said, and wondered why he'd brought her to such a place that was obviously shared sacredly between him and his wife.

"Part of me hasn't really let her go," Jermaine continued. Jackie wondered if she was just there to replace his therapist and continue his session with her after-hours. She wasn't quite sure how much more of this she could take.

"Part of me wishes we were still together," he said.

"Jermaine," Jackie said, and looked back, "I think I better head back—"

"No, wait," Jermaine said, and continued looking outward.

"Dr. Smith said I should come here one last time, and say my peace to my ex, Diane, one last time."

"That sounds wonderful, Jermaine, and I commend you for what you're doing, but I just don't think I—"

"Hold on," he said. "Dr. Smith suggested I do this with someone I consider very special in my life; she suggested I not do this alone."

Jackie folded her arms and decided to stay.

Jermaine then reached into his beige trench coat pocket, pulled out a wilted white rose, and sat it on the grass in front of him.

"Goodbye, Diane," he said to the flower. "Dr. Smith said sometimes you have to do something tangible to say, 'goodbye' to your past, so that you can move on, or let go and let God so you can say 'hello' to your future," Jermaine said, and with that Jackie inched closer to him and wrapped her arm around his.

"Hello, Jackie," he said to her, and smiled.

"Hello, Jermaine," she said, and rested her head on his shoulder.

CHAPTER 54

"I'm so sorry," Pippa said, and rose from Danielle's shoulder while they stood by Danielle's car inside the church parking lot. "I didn't mean to ruin your top with my foolish tears."

"Oh, girl, you're fine. That's what friends are for, right?" Danielle said.

"Right. I'm glad you're my friend," Pippa said.

"Aw, girl, it's all good. God puts people together as friends for a reason, right? We need each other."

"Yes, we do," Pippa agreed. "Speaking of which, I'm glad we were all able to pray for our friend Willy today. It's sad what happened to him. My question though, is, why on earth was he at a strip club?"

"It's a not a strip club," Danielle corrected her, "it's a pole-dancing club. They're not naked and they don't take off all their clothes."

"Well, it's the same thing if you ask me. It's still the devil's den. What was he doing there? Then again, I guess we all have skeletons in our own closets. Goodness," Pippa said.

Danielle felt compelled to confess to her friend. "Pippa, can I ask for your prayers for me, too?" she said.

"Sure, what's wrong?" Pippa asked.

"Well, the reason I know all about Club Xtasy is because I used to work there."

Pippa gasped. "You what?!"

"I used to work there. Not strip! I was a pole dancer."

"Oh, Danielle, I didn't know," she said with a pitying look on her face.

"That's okay, and I know you didn't know. I worked there before I got saved and went back to work there again, but I just left again, and I'm not going back this time."

"Praise God! God is good. I'm so glad you got out of that place! Hallelujah!"

"Yeah, well, unfortunately it still may haunt me."

Pippa didn't quite understand.

"I was there the night the shoot-out took place." Pippa held her mouth and gasped again. "Except," Danielle continued, "I was able to escape."

"Oh, Danielle," Pippa said and hugged her neck. "I'm so glad you made it out! I'm so glad the blood of Jesus covered and kept you, my sister. Praise the Lord!"

Danielle returned the gesture and looked up and thanked God once again for getting her out of there.

Danielle broke from Pippa's grasp and completed her prayer request. "Yeah, well, I made it out safe, but obviously Willy didn't, and these three young girls who were minors were arrested and didn't make it out either. What's going to happen to them once they get out of juvenile hall, *if* they get out? I don't even know who their parents are, or if any of their relatives even know they've been arrested," Danielle continued, choked up. "I'm afraid that when all is said and done they'll have no-where to turn but the streets."

Pippa grabbed Danielle's hand.

Danielle continued, "And the oldest girl, she reminds me so much of myself when I was her age. I just thought I was so grown and thought I knew it all. No one could tell me nothing. All I wanted to be was a positive example for her, and she ended up saving my life. Now I have no way of get-ting in touch with them and making sure they're okay." Tears like rivers rolled down Danielle's face. "Instead of being a role model, I feel like all I've done in their lives was be a hindrance, an example of what *not* to do and what *not* to become. I don't know what's going to become of them and I'm scared for their lives. Please pray for them and for me."

Pippa paused a moment and then moaned.

"Oh, the burden, the burden!" Pippa said as she watched her friend wail. Pippa continued, "The burden you have for those three girls. And not just those girls, but many young ladies like them you have yourself the burden for, for in them you see yourself."

Danielle kept crying.

Pippa suddenly spoke in an authoritative voice and said, "Don't weep, My child; don't cry for them. I have given you the power and all you need to do is claim the victory. The victory is in you. The burden you have for those three was ac-tually given you by Me, so *you* go and find those girls. *You* go and search them out. They will be freed through *your* hands, and just like you have remained faithful in following Me, they will be faithful and follow you as you follow Me, saith the Lord of Grace."

Danielle then lifted her hands and she and Pippa got their shout on in the parking lot until it grew dark. She thanked God for speaking a prophetic Word to her through Pippa. She was so excited because now she knew exactly what to do.

Shenita stood up with the rest of the baseball fans in the stands at Comerica Park as the Tigers scored a home run that surged them ahead of the visiting team.

"Yay!" Shenita yelled. She stood up and looked around to see if there was anybody there who was single and looked good to her before she sat back down. She had forgotten all about the single Tigers ticket she purchased a while ago for this Monday-night game.

They say a good place to meet men is at sporting events, however this game didn't prove so fruitful, as most of the men in her surrounding area were all booed up with their girlfriends and wives dolled up in Tigers face paint and base-ball caps. The one group of men she did see who appeared to be single were surrounded by enough beer to host a keg party and wildly yelled at the players like they were drunk.

Oh, well, Shenita thought as she munched on her loaded nachos. Though she wasn't much of a sports fan, she figured she might as well suffer through the rest of the game to at least get her money's worth.

Just then her cell rang. It was Jackie.

"Hello," Shenita answered.

"Hey, girl!" Jackie said.

Shenita looked at her phone again to make sure it was Jackie calling her and not Pippa or Danielle.

"Hey, Jackie, you sound happy. What's up?"

"That's because I *am* happy. God is good!" Jackie proclaimed.

"All right now, all the time," Shenita said.

"Where are you?" Jackie asked. "What's all that noise in the background? You at a party?"

Shenita spoke louder into the phone. "No, I'm at a Tigers game."

"Really? With who?"

"Myself. Can't I just enjoy a nice evening out at the ball game alone? Must we always have to go somewhere in groups? That may be one of our problems as singles. You know what I'm saying?" Shenita asked, itching for an "amen."

"Well, that may be *your* problem," Jackie replied, "but it's not mine, because I'm not single anymore."

"What?" Shenita asked. "What'd I miss?"

"A lot, girl, a lot. Jermaine and I are dating!"

"Really? Wow! Awesome! Touchdown!" Shenita said and then said, "Oh, I mean home run! Out the park! I *am* at a base-ball game."

Jackie laughed on the other end. "Yeah, I'll fill you in on the details later, but the main reason I called was to remind you of your party this Friday."

"My party? What party?" Shenita asked. Her neighbor gave her a menacing look, as if she'd spoken too loudly near her ear.

"What party?" Shenita said more softly this time.

"Your white party! Remember? The one I said I'd throw for you celebrating your being abstinent till marriage for eleven years straight? The celibacy party! You forgot already?" Jackie asked.

"Oh, yeah, *that* party. Girl, I'm sorry. I did forget. With so much going on lately, I think I would forget to put my head on straight if it wasn't already glued to my neck."

"Yeah, *that* party. I'm having my yacht cleaned today, since it's so beautiful out. There may even be a jazz concert at Chene Park that we can go over to and view from the water. Wouldn't that be nice?" Jackie asked.

"Real nice. So, yeah, definitely count me in. I gotta go before this lady throws her pretzel at me," Shenita said.

"What?" Jackie asked.

"I'll tell you later; we'll chat."

"Okay, we'll chat. Bye."

Once home, Danielle made a mad dash to her computer for some intense searching. Not quite sure where to start, she googled the only name, or somewhat-name she had—Princess Dream. While no individuals were listed, not even in Google Images, Danielle decided to search Facebook to see if Princess Dream had ever used her stage name inside the social media world.

Sure enough, a name search for Princess Dream Detroit brought up a thread in which someone jokingly used her stage name in conversation. Danielle clicked on the page that brought up Princess Dream's Facebook page and saw that her real name was Priscilla Princeton.

After a few clicks and more searching Danielle found all of her contact information, including her e-mail address, more social media handles, and two phone numbers.

"Bingo," Danielle said, and dialed the first number.

The first number rang and went to Priscilla's voice mail. It sounded like it was her cell, so Danielle figured if she was in jail, or juvie, more than likely, she wouldn't have access to a phone. She prayed the second number listed would lead her somewhere. She called it and an older lady immediately answered the phone.

Once home, Shenita fixed a dinner of steak, mashed potatoes, and broccoli, and eventually decided to go ahead and check equallyyokedup.com one more time to see if anyone, Terrell in particular, had tried to reach out to her. She figured if he hadn't, then she would just cancel her account and demand a refund for real this time from the so-called divine matchmaking website that obviously wasn't working for her.

She logged on and saw she had a new message in her in-box. Sure enough, it was from Terrell: *What's up, Love! How's my favorite church shawty? Wanna hang out Friday night?*

Shenita squealed, then looked up and thanked God.

She was relieved and figured maybe all those crazy dates with Mr. Wrongs were necessary to lead her up to her future Mr. Right.

Shenita replied and told Terrell she'd love to go out with him on Friday night. Before she sent the e-mail, though, she remembered that Friday was the same day as the white party.

Shoot, Shenita thought. She didn't want their first date to be around a bunch of people, mainly people from church they both already knew. She wanted more one-on-one time alone with Terrell because she knew at that white party he'd be mingling all over the place.

I know, we can go on our date, first, and then maybe go to the white party together afterward, Shenita thought and hit Reply to send the e-mail. She decided not to tell him about the white party just yet, because she wanted to focus on their special night together, as she was about to partake of a night on the town with the man of her dreams—the man she'd been waiting for all this time.

CHAPTER 55

"So why'd you find me?" asked Priscilla Princeton, aka Princess Dream. She sat back in her chair in a gray jogging suit, with folded arms and a tilted head, as Danielle visited her inside the local juvenile hall detention center.

"Because I was worried about you," Danielle admitted. "And I wanted to make sure you and your sisters were okay."

Priscilla gave her a suspicious glance. "For real?" she asked.

"For real," Danielle said.

"You know," Danielle said, and shifted in her seat, "sometimes, when I look at you, especially when I looked at you when we were over at Xtasy, it was like I was looking at a reflection of myself in the mirror. You remind me a lot of myself when I was your age."

"Really?" Priscilla asked.

"Really," Danielle said. Priscilla twiddled her fingers.

"Why'd you save me?" Danielle asked in reference to Priscilla's airborne gunshots that distracted Sparks and led to her escape.

Priscilla shrugged her shoulders and looked downward.

"You're not going to tell me?" Danielle asked.

"I guess. In a way, I kinda liked you. I guess I looked up to you."

Danielle lowered her eyes.

"I had never seen anybody stand up to Sparks the way you did, and I didn't want them to hurt you, the way I've been hurt," Priscilla confessed.

Danielle wiped a tear from her eye.

"I'm sorry, Priscilla," she said. "I'm sorry I let you down."

Priscilla looked at her, confused. "What do you mean?"

"I was supposed to be a positive role model for you, an example, and I ended up being everything but and getting you put in here."

"No, you didn't. I don't mind being here. It's safe."

"Right," Danielle said softly, and looked around at the other rooms and the other young glum faces and passersby. It looked more like the county jail than a detention center for minors.

"Diva D," Priscilla said.

"Please, call me Danielle."

"Danielle," Priscilla said, "before you came here tonight, I asked God if He were really real to send me a sign. I was cold. I was scared. I was alone. I needed to know that somebody, at least one person on the other side, really cared about me. I was here with my sisters and didn't know what to do with them. I prayed just yesterday, and then you showed up today to check on me."

Danielle forced a smile.

"Now I know God is really real," Priscilla said, then sniffed and wiped her nose.

Danielle took off her cross necklace and handed it to Priscilla. "Here," she said. "Keep this with you. Wear it at all times. It represents the cross and all Jesus did for you. If you were the only person on this earth, God still would have sent Jesus to die for you, because He loves you that much."

"Really?" Priscilla asked.

"Really," Danielle said.

"Hey," Danielle continued, "there's someone else here who wants to talk to you."

Priscilla's grandmother entered and Priscilla's face lit up like a Christmas tree. Her grandmother had been like a mother to her since her own mother died due to a drug overdose when she was four and her sisters were two, never thought she would see Priscilla again, and she also didn't know if her granddaughter, whom she hadn't seen in four months, was alive or dead.

They gave each other a big hug, and instead of scolding or questioning her as to why she ran away with her two younger sisters, Priscilla's grandmother thanked heaven above for sending her grandbaby back into her arms once again.

Her grandmother turned to Danielle with tired eyes now filled with hope and said, "Thank you."

Danielle replied, "No, thank *you*. You have one special lady there. Your granddaughter saved my life."

CHAPTER 56

Shenita sat in a quaint deli café for lunch on Friday afternoon and listened intently to Danielle as she told her everything that happened with the club and with Willy, Sparks, Priscilla, and the twins. Shenita almost couldn't believe all that had happened to her friend in such a short amount of time. She was truly thankful that God saw fit for her friend to make it out of that ordeal alive, and now wondered what Danielle's next move would be.

"Girl, you are truly blessed," Shenita said, taking a bite of her chicken breast sub as she soaked in all that her friend had just told her. She was extra careful not to spill any mustard or mayo on her tangerine three-piece pantsuit. "God's grace is definitely more than sufficient for you," Shenita said. "What happened to you could've gone in so many different directions; but God!"

"Amen; but God for real," Danielle agreed as she bit into her corned beef sandwich. Danielle, who was more casual considering she no longer had a typical 9-to-5 or late-night gig to clock into today, wore fitted navy blue jeans and a black V-neck top.

"And to think, He spared your life, He even spared your reputation; that video could've gone viral in seconds," Shenita said.

"You're right. That's why I said I'm not going back there ever again, and that's the main reason I stepped down from the choir. I gotta take some time to work on myself and rebuild my fellowship with God and pray more about my purpose. Before I can be a light and an example for someone else, I need to make sure my own light doesn't burn out in the process."

"I hear ya, girlie, and I understand," Shenita said. "You take all the time you need. God will show you the way."

"He sure will; He has before and I know He'll do it again."

Shenita laughed. "You preaching, Evangelist Peterson."

"Aw, girl, don't go wishing that on me!"

"I'm just saying!"

The two of them laughed.

"Seriously, do you know where you're going to work now that you totally gave up the club?" Shenita asked.

Danielle paused for a moment and said, "I have an idea."

"Really, what is it?"

"Well, I've been praying and I'm really led to open up my own dance studio for girls."

"Oh, yeah?" Shenita said. "I believe you mentioned that to me before. Is there going to be a pole-dancing class?"

Danielle laughed. "There might be," she admitted. "But it'll mainly be for married women looking to add some extra spice in their marriages or something."

"All right now!" Shenita said and gave her a high five.

"I've been wanting to open the studio for years," Danielle continued. "Along with aerial fitness for adults, I'll offer ballet, African, and jazz dance classes for Detroit youths at a reduced rate. Maybe I can see about getting a grant to help fund it so that some of the kids who may not be able to afford can win scholarships to take the classes for free. Or maybe I can get enough money so they all can attend for free. Who knows? I haven't looked that much into it yet, but that's the plan . . . eventually."

"Danielle, that would be awesome!" Shenita said. "When I get married I can get my pole dance on for my boo!"

"Girl, you are so crazy," Danielle said.

"What made you decide to do it?" Shenita asked.

"I just think back as I was growing up; all I wanted to do was dance. Dancing is such an outlet. When you dance you feel so free, so alive; it's one way to take all the pain away, especially when you're dealing with not-so-ideal circumstances. It'll be a way some of these kids can reduce all the stress on their lives. They deal with so much these days, with pressure from their peers at school, their environment; stuff that I wasn't even thinking about. It'd be great if I could hire Priscilla and her sisters on as interns. It'll give them an alternative to the streets, and something to look forward to."

"Not only them," Shenita added, "it would give tons of kids something to look forward to. It would be a perfect outlet for so many youths, an outlet for their own artistic expression. Girl, who knows, you may rear up the next Debbie Allen in your dance studio."

"I guess I never thought of it like that. Amen. I receive it. God will make it happen . . . one day."

"Girl, forget one day, do you have a building picked out for it yet?" Shenita asked.

"No, I've had my eye on a couple places, but I'm trying to figure out how I can fund it. When I was having financial problems my credit went straight to the toilet, so financing a building may be out of the question. At least right now."

"Well, who needs a loan"—Shenita pulled her checkbook out of her black Coach bag and wrote out a check—"when you already have funding?" She ripped it out and handed Danielle the check for $5,000.

"That should at least cover some of the down payment," Shenita said.

Danielle grabbed the check and her eyes widened and her mouth fell open when she read the amount. "Oh, Shenita, girl, you don't have to do this!" Danielle said.

"I know I don't have to, I *want* to. It's your dream, and I know it'll help so many young girls."

"Oh, Shenita!" Danielle said, then rose and gave her friend a huge hug.

"Thank you so much!" she said, and sat back down and fanned her watering eyes.

Danielle couldn't believe it. She thanked heaven above while Shenita checked her phone.

"Oh, and I just got a text back from Jackie," Shenita said.

"Jackie?" Danielle asked.

"Yeah, I just texted her about what you're doing, and she texted back that she wants to add another ten thousand dollars on top of what I just gave you. She said she'll give it to you after church on Sunday."

"Are you serious?" Danielle said with tears streaming down her face.

Shenita nodded with a huge grin.

"Are you serious?" Danielle repeated.

"Yes, girl, God is GOOD!"

Danielle was speechless. Her mascara was completely ruined

at this point. Danielle screeched and she and Shenita hopped up and did a bunny-hop victory dance by their seats in the small restaurant.

Danielle was so thankful that she had friends who loved her enough to sow into her dream and the lives of so many young girls, and she was so thankful that she served a God Who loves her so much in spite of, Who holds her entire future in His hands and Who, every day, shows out on His love for her and promises to give her an expected end.

CHAPTER 57

After changing inside the restroom after work into a black off-the-shoulder sweater, cream-colored skinny jeans, and gold boots, Shenita headed downtown, reached her destination, and parked in the Detroit Institute of Arts parking lot, as she and Terrell had decided to drive separate cars and meet up at the infamous art museum for their first date.

She stepped out, straightened her orange-and-red tweed coat, and walked inside, wondering if he was there yet, as she didn't see his black Crown Victoria in the parking lot and didn't see him inside.

She was about to text him from the lobby area when she felt warm breath against her neck.

"Hey," Terrell said.

Shenita turned around and gave him a huge Kool-Aid grin. "Hey, Terrell," she said.

"Excuse me, but, uh, you think a brother can holla at you a minute? You looking good, girl." he said.

"You are so silly," Shenita said and patted him on the shoulder of his wool charcoal jacket. She could feel his muscles through the jacket and thought to herself, *Lawd hammercy. Help!*

"No, seriously, it's funny I'd meet you here," Terrell said.

Shenita wondered where he was going with this.

He continued, "I just checked this certain Christian dating website and a girl who looks just like you appeared on my profile page and it said we were, like, a hundred percent match or something; I could swear the two of you could be twins!"

"Terrell!" Shenita said and cracked up. "That *is* me, silly goose, now let's go farther inside; it's chilly standing here in this lobby."

Shenita had a wonderful time eyeing each work of art as she and Terrell gave their honest opinions about every one. She was surprised Terrell had such an artistic eye. She thought he was more into sports than the arts, but now, after perusing the Asian and African art collections in different rooms Shenita could tell that he was well versed in both. He seemed so engrossed while examining each artifact, pointing out intricate details and even reading the history of every piece out loud. Even surrounding couples and students paused to hear his personal commentary.

Shenita's favorite collection within the DIA was the General Motors Center for African American Art, which included artwork from the 1900s, with a strong emphasis on graphic art.

For a short period of time, Shenita and Terrell took off in separate directions to view the art on different ends but by the time they finished the final piece they met back in the middle toward where they first started. Shenita didn't mind the split at all, she actually looked forward to grabbing a bite to eat and getting briefed on his thoughts on his finds.

Once Shenita turned the corner, exiting the collection, she spotted Terrell in the hallway playing with his cell.

"Hey you," Shenita said from behind him, mirroring his earlier greeting.

"Hey," Terrell said, slightly startled.

"My stomach's growling, you hear that?" Shenita said and laughed. "Let's grab a bite to eat in the cafeteria."

"Sounds like a plan to me!" Terrell said, then put his cell away.

"There's a lot of people here tonight," she commented and took a bite of her turkey panini.

"Yeah," Terrell said, taking a bite of his as well. "I read somewhere that a law passed to allow all Detroit residents to have free entry here."

"Really, wow!" Shenita said.

"Yup, even for school bus tours. Pretty awesome," Terrell said.

"Awesome, indeed," Shenita said, then leaned forward. "So I guess that makes me a real cheap date tonight, huh?"

Terrell laughed.

Shenita laughed as well but was partly serious, as she noticed Terrell didn't offer to pay for her sandwich when they were at the cashier's counter.

"Ah, you got me!" Terrell said, then laughed again. "Girl, you know a brother gotta save up," he joked.

"For what?" Shenita probed, wondering if he was about to purchase a new ride or something.

"For little TJ! My future son! I'm already getting ready for his future, all I need is the missus. I've already saved up enough money for her engagement ring, now all we gotta do is make this thing happen, you know what I mean?"

Shenita laughed nervously, then cocked her head to the side.

"Oh yeah, and Shenita, I'm glad you accepted my invitation to hang out with me tonight. I got some great news!"

"Really, what?" Shenita asked. *This date is getting more exciting by the minute,* she thought.

"You know the dating website we connected on?" Terrell asked.

"Yeah, of course," she said.

"Well, I've been on a lot of dates from that thing, and I tell you, girl, some of them women were straight-up scary. Gold-diggers, princesses, undercover freaks—you name it. They need to screen who they allow on *that* site," Terrell said, and Shenita nodded her head, looking downward as she pondered some of the nightmarish dates she had been on as a result of that website.

"But you know what?" Terrell said then scooted in his seat, "Last night I went out with this girl, I mean woman of God, and she was banging!"

Shenita looked up.

"Not only was she fine as all get-out, she's as sweet as pie, plus she's a member of our sister church on the east side." He referenced Abundant Life Tabernacle Saving Grace Church pastored by Pastor Solomon's brother, Pastor Robert. Though their church name was slightly different, both churches were founded and still overseen by Pastor Solomon.

"For real?" Shenita asked.

"Yeah, she serves in, like, three auxiliaries: prayer center, singles' ministry, and children's church on Sunday mornings for both services, and you know how much I love the kids."

Shenita couldn't believe his childlike excitement, and the fact that he would spring this on her in the middle of their date, or maybe it wasn't even a date at all . . .

Terrell continued, "I always wanted to be with someone who loves the kids as much as I do, and she, I mean, Cheryl, does."

Cheryl? Shenita thought, *Oh, no, now she has a name, too?*

After a brief pause Terrell looked Shenita in the eye and said, "Shenita, I think she could be 'the one.'"

Shenita's heart was crushed, however she dared not let Terrell know.

She wanted to be sincerely happy for her brother in Christ; she tried deep within herself to find something, *anything* that spelled "joy" for her brother but she couldn't, so in the meantime she decided to just fake her way through.

"Really?" Shenita said. "You mean you think she's your wife? Already?"

"Well, I'm not saying she's definitely wifey, but she's definitely in the running. I mean, the way she made me feel yesterday on our first date, it made me want to be with her, like, every day. Oh, and our conversation went on for hours! As I was dropping her off at home we ended up talking in my car for six hours straight, until the sun came out the next day, and she was so cool with it! Can't you see these dark circles under my eyes?" He stretched his left eye with his index finger. "That's why I'm so tired."

Shenita chuckled and said, "Wow, Terrell, I really don't know what to say." Terrell looked as if he expected her to say more. Noticing his eagerness, Shenita suddenly squealed and said, "Oh, Terrell, I'm so happy for you!" then rose and gave Terrell a big church hug. He hugged her back, lifted her up, then placed her feet back on solid ground.

Deep inside, Shenita wished that hug came after his professed adoration for her and not his proclamation of a new love interest.

Terrell sat back down in his seat and continued, "Amen, God is good. And to think she goes right to our sister church, so that means she believes like we believe, Shenita. Hallelujah!"

"Hallelujah indeed," Shenita said halfheartedly, then took a sip of her water.

Following lunch, Shenita and Terrell walked out together and Terrell opened her car door for her. Shenita smiled and thanked him for a nice time and repeated how she was sincerely happy for him and that she hoped his next date with Cheryl continued to confirm what he was feeling for her on the inside.

Shenita drove away, waving to Terrell, and once he was out of sight she pulled over to the side of the road and cried profusely.

She grabbed tissues out of her glove box and blew her nose like she had a cold. She couldn't believe what had just happened to her and felt like the "love gods" were laughing at her.

Look at you, you made a fool of yourself, said a voice in her head. *And to think you thought he was it. I don't think so!*

Shenita shook her head to make the voice go away.

She felt like kicking herself for ever agreeing to go out with Terrell in the first place; she felt she should have known that all of his flirtatious banter at church only masked how he really felt about her, and that an invitation to "hang out" wasn't really a date at all.

She was mad at herself for ever thinking she even had a chance with Terrell. Though it seemed like they would be perfect for each other, for some reason he couldn't see it. And it was that "for some reason" part that she might never understand and it ate her up inside.

What's wrong with me? Shenita thought. She was tired of being single and couldn't understand where she kept going wrong with men. *You're never going to get married,* the voice in her head returned. "Shut up!" She yelled.

Shenita had never felt so rejected and hopeless in her entire life, and decided it was time for her to call on someone for answers.

"Call RayShawn," she told her car, and RayShawn answered on the first ring.

"Hey, Queen," he said and Shenita didn't immediately respond.

"Hey," Shenita said dryly.

"What's wrong, Love?" RayShawn asked.

"I just left my date with Terrell from church."

"Ooh goodie, how'd it go?"

"Actually, it didn't go. It went. As a matter of fact, let him tell it, it wasn't a date at all; it was like him babysitting his little sister."

"Excuse me?" RayShawn asked, baffled.

"He rejected me, RayShawn."

"He rejected you?"

"He basically told me I wasn't the one in so many words; he met somebody else." Shenita's eyes welled up again.

"Girl, bring your little tail over to my place right now."

CHAPTER 58

"Now what is this nonsense foolishness you are talking about, Miss Love?" RayShawn asked after he prepared Shenita a cup of green tea and placed two oatmeal cookies beside it on a tray table in front of her while she sat on his yellow couch holding tissues.

"RayShawn, Terrell and I were a perfect match, according to equallyyokedup.com. He asked me out only to tell me he met some other chick on there and went out with her yesterday and now he's 'in love.' He basically dumped me before our relationship ever had a chance to even begin. I should have known this was coming, though. I mean, I am supposed to be his sister in Christ, first, before anything else, right? In this case, though, I don't think there'll ever be anything else."

"Sister in Christ? And you sitting here looking like you looking? Girl, if I was a single man looking for a wife I would've snatched you up a long time ago. I don't know what's wrong with him. He must be blind or something. I may need to lay hands on him to help recover his sight."

Shenita smiled and said, "RayShawn, you always know the right thing to say."

"It's my pleasure, Shenita Bita Fofita," he said and rubbed her neck.

Shenita closed her eyes. "It's like, I just feel like I want to be married so bad. I want to have kids! I feel like I'm a decent person. I've never cheated on any boyfriend in my entire life. I don't think I'm ugly and I try to be sweet, for the most part, but all I end up with are crazy people who end up in love with me, and the ones who are really saved that I really like don't ever like me back or just don't say anything. I don't get it, RayShawn. I just don't understand."

"Love," RayShawn said as he continued massaging her neck, "like you tell me, you are just going to have to put it in the Lord's hands. What does that song say—after you've done all to stand? You've done all you can do, boo. Now all you can do is rest on His promises and stand on His Word."

Shenita opened her eyes and looked at him strangely.

"What?" RayShawn asked.

"Aren't you the same one who told me to 'go get yo' man, girl' and 'forget about waiting on the Lord, it's time for you to go get him' and 'forget he that findeth, it's time for some *she* that findeth?"

"Who, me?" RayShawn asked innocently.

"Yes, you," Shenita said.

"Aw, girl, obviously that ain't working for you, so I'ma need you to sit your little fast tail down right now before you cause any more ruckus up in here. I'm looking out for your heart now, boo boo. You gotta keep it guarded; gotta keep it guarded. Woosah," he said and massaged her shoulders even harder.

"RayShawn." Shenita laughed, then said seriously, "I don't know what I would do without you."

"I don't know what I'd do without you either, Shenita Love," he said, then the two of them lovingly looked into each other's eyes and Shenita leaned over to kiss him.

Startled at first, RayShawn closed his eyes and leaned in to meet her the rest of the way when the front door suddenly flew open and Dante's large frame stood in the doorway with two suitcases and a heated look on his face.

"What the?" he said gruffly when he spotted his man about to kiss some strange female on the couch.

"What's going on here?" he growled loudly.

RayShawn shot up like a rocket, fixed his white tee, and said, "Dante! You're home! I'm so glad you came back!" Ray-Shawn ran over to give him a hug, but Dante shoved him away.

"I *thought* I was coming back home," Dante said. "I call myself coming home to take you back, but who is that?" he asked, pointing to Shenita, who sat there embarrassed.

"Oh, her, that's just my friend from high school. We were just catching up on old times, that's all. She had something in her eye and I was about to blow it out for her. I promise that's all it was," RayShawn said in desperation. "I don't want her. You know I would never step out on you, honey. I'm so glad you're back." RayShawn approached Dante once again and held on to his bulging arm. "As a matter of fact, she was just leaving, right, Shenita?" RayShawn asked then, while Dante wasn't looking, he motioned to Shenita that he'd call her soon enough after everything blew over with Dante.

Shenita looked at Dante's angry glare, then back at Ray-Shawn's desperate glance, then again at Dante, whom she next saw gently brush RayShawn's arm, which held on to him like his life depended on it.

It was then that Shenita knew where RayShawn's heart really was and that she had definitely overstayed her welcome.

She arose, grabbed her purse, and quietly walked out.

CHAPTER 59

After utter humiliation at RayShawn's, I sat on the floor in front of the couch, stared into space in the dimly lit front room, and took a swig of this nasty, fruity-tasting wine cooler I purchased from the corner liquor store on my way home.

Prior to tonight, I had never been much of a drinker.

I hadn't had an ounce of liquor in over fifteen years, but for some reason, tonight I felt I needed something tangible to help me forget some of the pain I felt inside and ease my mind a little bit.

I took another swig and gagged.

I forgot how disgusting alcohol, no matter what flavor and no matter what percentage, really was. I squeezed my temples as my head throbbed.

Lord knows I knew I wasn't supposed to drink, but I was tired of being the good girl. Besides, where has all this "good girl" crap gotten me so far? Nowhere. I'm thirty-five, I'm still single, and I feel more alone now than I've ever felt in my entire life.

I held my head back and drank half the bottle.

I grabbed my trusty old black book from the coffee table

and opened it to where I had written my old set of rules, which were now all crossed out except for *Rule #1 Never Chase*.

I grabbed a pen from the table and crossed that rule off, too, knowing good and well that in my recent quest to find love I was the main one doing all the chasing. The only thing I wondered, though, was where all this chasing had gotten me, exactly. My search for love had landed me right back where I first started, even worse, because now I felt more alone now than ever before.

I set my black book back down, then eyed the big blue-and-silver book next to it—the book that at one point in my life was my lifeline, my joy, my everything. The one book that I used to count on for all the answers to life's tough questions, and the one book I would always rely on to take the pain away—my Bible.

"I believed in You," I told it.

"I believed in You!" I yelled. "I believed Your Word was true, I believed You when You said You would bless me with all the desires of my heart. Well, then, where they at, Lord, huh? Where they at?" I demanded.

"Here I am, thirty-five, no husband, no baby. I just knew I was going to be married by twenty-five, and not only that, nobody even want me! Not none of my exes," I clumsily counted on my fingers, "not Terrell; I can't even make RayShawn want me!" I said, knocking the wine cooler bottle over, giving my white plush carpet a big pink stain.

I got up and paced the floor, rubbing my forehead.

"Why are You torturing me?" I asked, gripping my Bible as if it were supposed to speak back. "What did I ever do to You? All I ever did was follow the Bible, go to church, pay my tithes, stay celibate, sing, jump up and down, thank God for my breakthrough coming through—and I can't even get a husband out of the deal?" I said.

"I did everything You told me to do, God. Everything! And You lied to me! You lied!" I cried.

"I've been faithful to You, Lord," I said ruefully. I sat on the couch, wiping the endless flow of tears from my face while finishing off the rest of the bottle. "I've tried my best to stay true to You. I never set out to sin on purpose. I repent every time I do."

I bit my nails. "I've given you over a decade of my life, Jesus; all I've done was live to please You. It's always been all about You, Lord; I'm your slave till the end, right, but what about me? When is it my turn, Lord? What about what *I* want? What about what *I* desire?" I wondered wholeheartedly.

"When am I going to be able to love someone unconditionally?" I asked softly. "When am I going to have a chance to matter to somebody? Anybody? I mean, what did I do, Lord?" I asked. "Whatever it is, I'm sorry. I'm sorry, Lord. Please, please don't make me have to live this way."

I curled myself into a ball on my long white couch and tried to go to sleep, but I couldn't.

I began to hear thoughts torment my mind, saying, *You're nobody. You're nothing. You're alone. You're not responsible for anyone, so who cares if you live or die? God doesn't really love you. If He did He would have blessed you by now. You know why He hasn't blessed you yet? Because you don't deserve it. If you died tonight, no one would care anyway. Nobody calls you their wife. Nobody calls you their mom. Nobody even calls you their girlfriend. You don't have anybody to wake up to. Nobody's happy to see you. Even your parents moved to Florida so they could get away from you. You want to know why? Because you're nobody, you're nothing. Nobody cares if you live or die.*

"No!" I screamed to get rid of the voice in my head. "Shut up!" I yelled, but it only grew louder.

I tossed and turned back and forth on the couch but kept hearing the same phrases over and over.

For the next ten minutes the voice persisted. I felt hopeless, helpless, like God had totally forsaken me for complaining to Him and had now totally given me over to the devil. The voice persisted, and I ran to the bathroom and splashed some cold water on my face.

Then the doorbell rang.

Who in the world could that be this late at night?

I halfheartedly dried my face with a towel, then answered the door.

"Who is it?" I asked.

"It's me," a female voice said. It sounded like Jackie, but I wasn't sure.

"And me," a chipper voice said.

I looked through the peephole and saw Jackie and Pippa, both dressed all in white, staring at the door.

Oh, shoot! The white party! I had forgotten all about it.

"Hey, y'all," I said with a forced smile as I opened the door.

"'Hey, y'all'?" Jackie said, and helped herself inside with her hands on her hips. "Shouldn't you be somewhere, Miss Thing? Look at you—you're not even dressed! As a matter of fact, you look a hot mess!"

She must have noticed my hair all over the place, like Frankenstein's bride, and my red-stained eyes mixed with running mascara. I was more ready for a masquerade ball than for any white party.

"Gee, thanks," I said. "On the other hand, you two look stunning," I said, barely able to stand up straight. The not-so-Mad Dog 20/20 must have been kicking in.

"I've never seen you this dolled up before, Jackie," I said in reference to her short silk white strapless dress with silver stilettos and long silver earrings. Jackie's short red hair was brighter, and spiky instead of curly, and her makeup looked fabulous.

"I got a makeover done at the mall earlier today," Jackie admitted.

"Mmm-hmm," I said. *Her man must be there tonight.*

"Shenita!" Pippa belted while stooped down holding her long white dress at her knees as she noticed the pink carpet stain and the knocked-over bottle in the front room. "Have you been drinking devil juice?"

Oh, shoot, the jig is up.

"Huh?" I asked, as if I didn't know what she was talking about. "Devil juice? Nah, not me. Now, a little wine cooler punch? Maybe."

I leaned over, then held on to the edge of the marble kitchen counter, and Pippa asked me, "Are you drunk?"

Jackie examined me, then stared at the spilled wine cooler bottle. "Be honest, now, Shenita," she said. "I remember you told me the last time you drank anything you were in college and got tipsy off a sip of wine cooler. And now you drank the whole bottle? Oh no, you gotta come with me," she said, and then grabbed me and led me over to the couch.

Why are they making such a fuss over me? Why don't they just leave well enough alone?

"C'mon, Shenita, c'mon," Jackie said as she positioned me upright on the couch and sat next to me.

"Shenita, you're scaring us," Jackie said, shaking. "Tell us what's going on with you tonight."

"But I thought . . ." I said, pointing to the door. "What happened to the party? Aren't y'all supposed to be at the party?" I asked, scratching my head.

"The party, my dear, was for you, remember?" Jackie said. "We wondered why you weren't there and been trying to call you for the longest time, but your phone must be off or something, so we came over to check on you."

"But what about the party?" I asked.

"It's fine; Jermaine's there holding it down for the guests till we get back," Jackie said.

I knew it.

"They'll be all right," Jackie continued. "The real question is, what's going on with you? Why are you here drinking when you should be partying with us?"

"I'm not in the mood for a party," I responded solemnly. "You still with Jermaine?" I asked, and replied, "That's good," before she had a chance to respond. "At least somebody wants you," I said and noticed Jackie and Pippa exchange strange looks.

"Nobody wants me," I elaborated. "Nobody even cares if I live or die."

There. I admitted it.

"What?" Jackie belted.

"At least that's what I keep hearing in my head," I clarified. "Nobody even cares if I live or die."

"The devil is a liar!" Pippa shot up. "Ah, naw, we can't have the enemy take our friend out like this. You done messed with the wrong one now, Devil. Stand her up we about to pray!" Pippa said, and threw her pearl earrings on the floor.

Pippa laid hands on my head, and Jackie followed suit as Pippa declared, "Satan, I bind you in the name of Jesus! The blood of Jesus is against you! I command you to loose your hold of my friend's mind right now in the name of Jesus! God,

You said whatsoever we bind on earth shall be bound in heaven, and whatsoever we loose on earth shall be loosed in heaven, so, Satan, I bind you up right now, in Jesus' name! Get out of her mind, stop tormenting her mind, You have no place here, Devil, so quit harassing and oppressing my friend!"

Jackie prayed in the Spirit in agreement with Pippa as I lifted my hands, surrendered all, and cried.

"Comfort now, Jesus," Jackie prayed. "Comfort now. Encourage now, Jesus. Encourage now. Keep her now, Jesus, keep her now. Keep her mind, keep her spirit, keep her soul. Encourage her soul in the name of Jesus! Soul, why are you cast down? Hope, thou, in God!"

"When the enemy comes in like a flood," Pippa added, "the Spirit of the Lord shall raise up a standard against Him!"

I forced myself to shout in between the tears. I forced myself to shout in spite of the pain. "Hallelujah! Hallelujah!" I said.

Jackie and Pippa kept praying over me until the Spirit of victory broke loose.

We shouted and praised God with our whole hearts and laughed and cried and hugged one another.

In the midst of our praise, the doorbell rang.

Pippa got the door while Jackie hugged me tightly, not letting me go.

"Who is it?" Pippa sang. She looked out the peephole and saw Danielle looking at her in a sharp white pantsuit.

"It's me, Dani," Danielle said.

Pippa opened the door, hugged her, and said, "Hi, Danielle."

"Hey," Danielle said. "Sorry I'm late. The Lord was dealing with me about Willy, so I just left visiting and praying for him at the hospital. He's going to be all right."

"Really? Wow—the Spirit of the Lord is really moving on

people's hearts tonight! So glad to hear he's going to be fine."

"Yeah," Danielle said. "I thought y'all would be at the white party by now, but when I got there they told me you all came over here. Why are y'all still here?" Danielle asked, and looked over and saw Jackie embracing me in tears.

"What happened; did somebody die?" Danielle asked.

"No," Pippa said as she let Danielle inside. "God is good, that's all. We're just over here encouraging each other."

"Really? What's wrong?" Danielle asked as she made her way inside and approached Jackie and me as we kept hugging one another like no one else was in the room.

I overheard Pippa whisper loudly to Danielle, "The enemy was telling Shenita that she didn't matter to anybody and had her feeling like no one cared if she lived or died."

"What?" Danielle exclaimed.

"It's all good now, though," Pippa said in a regular tone. "Jackie and I prayed for her, so she's going to be okay."

Danielle interrupted Jackie's and my embrace and asked me, "What's this I hear you talking about nobody cares about you?"

I wiped my tears and said, "I'm sorry, Danielle, I didn't mean to bring you in on all this. I know you have a lot on your plate right now."

"Oh, no, no, no, no, no!" Danielle said and grabbed my arm, then sat me down on the couch with Pippa and Jackie joining us.

"Nothing, I mean nothing, that I have going on will ever stand in the way of my being here for you," Danielle said. "You're my friend, and I love you. I'm here for you. We're here for each other." Danielle, Pippa, and Jackie all looked at one another and nodded.

"Shenita, whenever I was in trouble, whenever I needed someone to talk to, laugh with, talk about some of these crazy men with . . ." I laughed with a sniff. Danielle continued, "You were there. You have been a solid rock and a great example for me in my Christian walk, and even when I first told you about my former life you didn't judge me; instead you loved me and helped me get out of there. Even though my hardheaded self went back, you still supported me while I was going through everything and encouraged me along the way. And what you and Jackie did for me in sowing seed to my dream was priceless." Danielle looked at Jackie, then back at Shenita, and wiped a tear from her own eye. "You're a gem, Shenita—a real diamond, and I love you."

Pippa spoke up. "Yeah, and when I told you about Elijah, you didn't tease me or tell me how crazy you thought I was. You encouraged me." Everyone agreed. "And when I told you how it all blew up in my face you still encouraged me and prayed for me and gave me the strength I needed to go on, and I will always love you for that, Shenita. I really do care about you." Pippa gave me a huge hug.

Jackie fought back tears by fanning her eyes. She touched my thigh and eventually shared some words. "Shenita, you . . . you helped me to see myself even when I didn't want to see myself. You helped me get over myself and taught me how to forgive and give love another try even when I wanted to give up and no longer believed in it. You showed me how to love myself and to have confidence and faith and trust in men again when I thought there was no hope." Jackie cried, and Pippa gave her a tissue.

Jackie continued, "And to even fathom that the enemy had your mind so warped as to think you didn't matter to anybody? The thought of me not having you in my life, Shenita . . . I wouldn't know what to do." Jackie choked up even more, and Pippa rubbed her back.

"We love you, chica," Danielle said.

"I love y'all, too." I said and we gave one another a group hug on the couch.

"It's, like, you touch so many lives," Danielle added. "You love on everybody you meet. Look at Krissy, your coworker, somebody you barely know personally—you invited her to church and next thing you know she got saved! That's love. And your friend from high school, RayShawn, what would he think if he knew you were over here going crazy like this?"

"He would kill me," I said, and we all laughed.

"Patience," Pippa said as she solemnly stared at the coffee table. "The Spirit of the Lord says patience."

Jackie, Danielle, and I bowed and prayed in the Spirit to see what else the Lord, through Pippa, had to say:

"Oh that my precious daughters might see how beautiful and wonderful you are to Me. If you would simply trust and believe, you will see I am all the man you will ever need. Sure, I grant the desires of your heart, but as you wait on Me our love will never part. I love you more than anything in the world, you see. Oh that you may just have faith and believe in Me. For patience is key to your victory. Love and embrace her, for she'll never leave thee. Be steadfast, unmovable in your faith in Me. Don't be weary in well doing, for all you do I see. Don't believe the lies of the enemy; you're never alone; you wake up every morning to Me. So sing and dance and shout some more, for though you sow in tears ye shall reap in joy."

The four of us shouted and praised God at the top of our lungs.

I laughed, Danielle and Jackie shouted, and Pippa worshipped God in song in the Spirit. We thanked God for that on-time Word that we all needed to hear, and we were grateful that God took the time to show up in the midst of us.

We hugged and told one another "I love you," and laughed and cried some more.

As all of this took place I didn't even hear my cell ringing from the kitchen counter until I noticed Danielle sneaking toward it.

Danielle regained her composure, cleared her throat, and answered my phone.

"Hello."

"Uh-huh."

"I see," she said.

What in the world? Is she answering my phone posing as me?

"I understand."

"Sure."

"Till then," she added.

"Bye." And Danielle ended the call.

"Now what was that all about?" I asked.

"Nothing much, girl," Danielle said and moseyed herself back to the couch and sat down as if she didn't just answer my phone and conduct a conversation like she was me. Everyone else joined her on the couch. Pippa blew her nose.

"By the way," Danielle said to me, "some guy named Christian apologized a million times for not being able to take you out last week."

Christian?

Danielle continued, "Something about he's a pediatrician not only here in the states but that he also volunteers in Africa? He said he thought he was free last weekend but his pastor called him at the last minute with an emergency and he had to go to Africa to save a child's life—something like that."

"What?" I asked, perplexed.

"Anyway, he asked me if I wanted to go out next Friday

night, me meaning you, that is, and I said 'sure.' By the way, he's picking you up at eight, capish?"

I sat there dumbfounded.

Jackie gave Danielle a high five and said, "Good job!"

"A doctor who loves Jesus?" Pippa said. "You go, girl!" and hit my leg.

"I guess," I said. "But, Danielle, you didn't even know—"

"Aw, girl, be quiet. The man's picture came up on your caller ID and he was fine, so I answered the phone. I figured you'd give him twenty questions if you were talking to him, so I decided to help *you* out. If it work out it work out, if it don't it don't, meantime life is good, God is good, and you now have a date next Friday night. Now, are y'all ready to go to this white party?" Danielle asked, wiping her eyes with tissue. "Y'all already ruined my makeup with all this crying, I can't stand to waste a good outfit, too."

We cracked up.

"Alrighty, then," I said, "I'll go get dressed; give me about forty minutes, or I can meet you all there."

"That's okay, we'll wait," Danielle said, and the three of them agreed. "It'll give us all a chance to chat some more and catch up on each other's lives."

"Besides, waiting is actually a good thing," Jackie said with a wink. "There's always a blessing in the wait."